Praise for Colette Caddle

'A fine escapist read' *Irish Independent*

'If you like Marian Keyes, you'll love
Colette Caddle' *Company*

'Will have readers laughing and crying
every step of the way' *Irish Times*

'An engaging, warm slice of life
with which all women will be able to identify.
Highly recommended' *Publishing News*

'A warm, irresistible Irish author for all ages.
Heaven knows how they do it, but they
have that special magic' *Bookseller*

'Caddle seems to know instinctively what
women readers want' *Ireland on Sunday*

'Skilfully written, by an accomplished
Irish author, the characters are intriguing
and the story is deftly paced . . . you will
enjoy this one!' *Irish Independent*

Colette Caddle

Always on my Mind

**SIMON &
SCHUSTER**

London · New York · Sydney · Toronto

A CBS COMPANY

First published in Great Britain by Simon & Schuster UK Ltd, 2010
This paperback edition first published by Simon & Schuster UK Ltd, 2011
A CBS COMPANY

Copyright © Colette Caddle, 2010

The right of Colette Caddle to be identified
as author of this work has been asserted in accordance with sections
77 and 78 of the Copyright, Designs and Patents Act, 1988.

1 3 5 7 9 10 8 6 4 2

Simon & Schuster UK Ltd
1st Floor
222 Gray's Inn Road
London WC1X 8HB

www.simonandschuster.co.uk

Simon & Schuster Australia
Sydney

A CIP catalogue record for this book
is available from the British Library

ISBN 978-1-47112-706-9

This book is a work of fiction. Names, characters, places
and incidents are either a product of the author's imagination
or are used fictitiously. Any resemblance to actual people, living
or dead, events or locales, is entirely coincidental.

Typeset by M Rules
Printed and bound by CPI Group (UK) Ltd, Croydon, CR0 4YY

In loving memory of my bright, beautiful and brave cousin Denise Prizeman-Healy

Always on my Mind

Chapter One

'That's so sad, isn't it?' Molly was crouched over the steering wheel, gazing absently at the lines of traffic in front of her.

Declan chewed on a nail and continued to stare out the passenger window. 'What?'

'Michael Jackson, he's dead, haven't you been listening?'

'No, I've been too busy wondering if I'm going to make my flight. I told you not to come this way, there's always a tailback.'

Molly was unperturbed by his grumpiness; Declan always got worked up when he was travelling. She put a placating hand on his thigh. 'I'll get you there.' Her thoughts returned to the deceased singer. 'You know, I'll never forget the first time I saw the *Thriller* video. It was at Clodagh Reilly's eighth birthday party, and I cried so much her dad had to take me home.'

Declan checked his watch. 'Don't bother looking for parking, just drop me at the entrance.'

'But I want to come in—'

'There's no point, Moll, I'll be going straight through. It takes forever to get through security these days and it will be even worse at this hour of the morning.'

'I'll go into the car park, and if I can't find a spot on the departures level, I'll drop you; fair enough?' He gave a reluctant nod.

The lights changed and the traffic moved off slowly. Molly suppressed a grin as Declan sat forward as if willing the cars in front to move faster. 'Do you have your phone?'

He patted the pocket of his new grey suit. 'Yes.'

'Driver's licence?'

He shook his head. 'I brought my passport, just in case.'

This time Molly couldn't prevent herself from smiling. It had been years since a passport was necessary when travelling between Ireland and the UK, but Declan still couldn't bear to travel without it. 'What about credit cards, sterling and have you got a copy of your CV?'

'Check, check and check.' He sighed.

She patted his leg. 'Stop worrying, they'll love you.'

He grasped her hand tightly in his and gave a reluctant smile. 'You're biased.'

'True, but I'm also right. Anyway, it wouldn't be the end of the world if you didn't get this job with Enco; you're doing okay in Kelleher's.'

'Kelleher's is struggling,' he reminded her. 'They could go under tomorrow, for all we know.'

'As could Enco.'

He shook his head. 'Well, thanks for those encouraging words, Moll.'

'Sorry.' She grinned and drove through an orange light and turned left into Dublin airport.

'Don't forget you have to go and pay those bills.'

'I have them in my bag; I'll go to the bank in the airport after you've gone through.' Molly pulled into the short-term car park and drove up to the departures level, slamming on the brakes when she saw a large BMW reverse out of a parking spot. 'Excellent!'

Declan was out of the car before she'd even turned off the engine and she hurried after him. 'Boarding pass?'

He opened his jacket and checked his inside pocket. 'Yeah.'

'And you're on the six o'clock flight home?'

He nodded.

'I'll be waiting,' she promised, almost trotting now to keep up with his long, purposeful stride. 'Then we could go for a bite to eat.'

'I don't know, Molly, I'll probably be exhausted.'

'We'll play it by ear. If you're too tired, we can always pick up a takeaway instead.'

They reached the gate and Declan pecked her on the cheek, then turned to go.

'Remember, Declan,' she called after him, 'they'd be damn lucky to get you.'

He stopped and turned around slowly. 'Did you really cry at *Thriller*?' he asked, his eyes softening.

She held out her hands. 'Hey, I was only eight!'

He came back and pulled her into his arms. 'I don't deserve you,' he murmured against her ear.

'True.' She smiled and breathed in the fresh scent of shampoo, mingled with cologne.

'Sorry I've been so moody, it's just I really want this job—'

'I know, and I hope you get it.'

He kissed her slowly and then smiled. 'See you tonight.'

Molly watched until he'd disappeared from view and then, still smiling and savouring his kiss, made her way to the escalator down to the arrivals area. It was packed as usual, and it took her a good five minutes to fight her way down to the bank. There were three people queuing and, with a resigned sigh, she got in line. A loud laugh made her turn around and she smiled as a group of young men in blazers tossed a rugby ball around between them. They looked to be in their mid-twenties and seemed vibrant, fit and carefree, and very easy on the eye. As she watched, they were joined by a slightly older man who clapped his hands for their attention and spoke to them in rapid, fluent French. As they tucked the ball away and started to gather their belongings, their minder looked around to check the departures board above Molly's head and their eyes met. Molly froze.

'Next, please.'

Molly turned to see the clerk gesturing impatiently and she hurried to the counter, handed over her card and forms, and as the girl studied them, she turned back to look for him, but he had disappeared into the crowd.

'Could you enter your pin number, please?' the clerk said.

'Oh, yes, sorry.' Quickly, Molly finished her business and walked back through the arrivals hall, scanning the crowds around her, but he was nowhere in sight. Not knowing whether to feel relieved or disappointed, Molly left the airport, got into her car and drove home in a daze.

Luke Fortune. She hadn't seen him in almost twelve years. It was hard to believe it was that long. For the two years preceding that, he and Ruth had been her life, and then they were gone, leaving a gaping hole that Molly didn't think she'd ever be able to fill. But, as her mother had said, time heals. Except that was crap. Time didn't heal. You just discovered reasons to go on, found ways to cope, crawled your way through each minute, waded through each day, dragged yourself through one week and then the next and then the next. Molly had thrown herself into her studies and that had got her through the first few years – she had abandoned the plan to train as a doctor and instead switched to psychology. And now she had her work and she had Declan and life was normal again. Time didn't heal. It just made you realize that you were not in control; that you had to accept that some-times, things happen.

Ignoring the post on the hall table, the laundry basket waiting by the washing machine and the cereal bowls in the sink, Molly made herself a coffee and sat staring out at her bland matchbox garden and drifted back in time; sweet and bitter memories intermingled. Luke was more solid now than he had been as a teenager. His dark hair was cut shorter and he seemed more reserved, but then that was hardly surprising. But his eyes were as blue and clear as ever and she smiled as she thought of the slightly crooked nose and how he'd broken it playing in the under-eighteens' final, refusing point-blank to go off. He'd scored the winning try and been carried off the pitch on the shoulders of his team-mates. Molly had been so proud of him that day. Proud of his skill, his courage and so proud that she, Molly Jackson, was his girlfriend.

Luke probably would never have even noticed her if she hadn't been his twin sister's best friend. Of course Molly had a crush on Luke Fortune from the moment she'd set eyes on him, but then so had most of the other girls in their school. Not only was he a skilled sportsman and very attractive, he was surprisingly modest, even shy. It had never occurred to Molly that he would reciprocate her feelings. He was always friendly and nice, but she'd thought that was for Ruth's sake. It was a shock when he came over to her at the school disco on the night of her sixteenth birthday and asked her to dance. And that was that. For the first time in her life, Molly had a boyfriend.

Molly chuckled as she remembered how awe-struck she'd been that first night as they lurched around the dance floor. Even now, she wasn't too sure what he'd seen in her. She'd had a mane of unruly hair, mud-coloured eyes and her chest, sadly, wasn't developing at the rate Ruth's was. But Luke didn't seem to mind. In fact, he was always telling her she was gorgeous.

They started dating, which, at that age, basically involved meeting after school and walking home together, usually with Ruth and whoever she was seeing at the time – there was usually some lovestruck boy in tow. Molly's mum and dad loved the effervescent Ruth and welcomed her brother into the Jackson home with the same enthusiasm. And Molly's little brother, Rory, an avid rugby fan, had treated Luke like some kind of deity. It was the happiest Molly had ever been. But only two years later—

The phone rang, making her jump. She reached across to pick it up. 'Hello?'

'Molly? Where are you, what are you doing?'

Molly sighed at the cross tone of her older sister. 'At home having a coffee, why?'

'You're supposed to be here, remember? Orla's waiting.'

'Oh, shit! I'm so sorry, I completely forgot.'

'Just get a move on. Orla has another appointment at eleven.'

'I will, please tell her I'm sorry. I'll be as quick as I can.' Molly hung up, grabbed her bag and ran back out to Declan's car. She didn't usually drive, preferring to cycle the twenty-minute journey to her sister's home in the leafy suburbs of Clontarf, but she didn't have that luxury today. Laura reminded Molly at every opportunity that she was very lucky that Orla Keane, one of Dublin's top dressmakers, had deigned to make Molly's wedding and bridesmaids' dresses. It had been Laura's idea to ask Orla to make the dresses and Molly, appalled at the meringue-style gowns she'd seen so far, had happily agreed. She had felt a little intimidated initially, as Laura talked of this woman in almost reverential tones, but Orla turned out to be a lovely person and seemed to understand immediately what Molly wanted. From that moment, Laura had practically taken over all the wedding arrangements.

'Don't you mind?' Molly's best friend Ellen had murmured one evening when Laura had taken the table plan from Molly and started to rearrange it.

Molly had shrugged. 'She enjoys it and she's a lot better at it than I am.' And so when Laura had told her about a wonderful baker who made the most amazing wedding cakes and the photographer who was a true artist and the only one worth using and took her to the exclusive manor house thirty miles outside of Dublin, Molly found herself going along with all of her sister's suggestions. Declan was simply relieved that he wasn't expected to get involved. Other than the cars and the suits, he didn't have a thing to do and, even then, Laura had furnished him with a list of suitable companies to contact.

It took only ten minutes for Molly to get from her minuscule garden flat in Sandymount to Laura and Robert's spacious, detached home in the leafy cul-de-sac in Clontarf. The electric gates were already open and Molly could imagine her sister pacing her chic, immaculate living room and watching the driveway, whilst apologizing to Orla for her sister's absent-mindedness. Molly parked between Orla's van and Ellen's Mini, and hurried past Laura's shiny black 4×4. 'Sorry,' she said as Laura opened the door.

'It's okay, we started without you,' Laura replied, a martyred look on her face. 'Ellen's having her fitting first, though how Orla can work around that bump is beyond me.'

Molly followed her into the living room and smiled at the sight of her hugely pregnant friend draped in aubergine silk. Orla was sitting on her heels, glasses on her nose and with a mouthful of pins. 'I'm so sorry, Orla, I lost track of time. Hi, Ellen.'

Orla waved and continued pinning while Ellen winked at her. 'We may need more material,' she joked, patting her bump.

'By the wedding day you'll be a tiny little thing again,' Molly said and gratefully accepted the mug of coffee her sister handed her.

'If I'm not, you must find someone else. It would be a shame to waste this dress.'

Molly shook her head and smiled. 'You're the only one I want and I don't care what you wear.'

Orla stood up and took the pins from her mouth. 'Don't worry, it will be fine. The empire line will hide a multitude, and I've left plenty of material around the bust line. Just get the best bra you can; you should get measured up about two weeks before you're due.'

'Are you going to breastfeed, Ellen?' Laura swivelled questioning eyes on her. 'Because if you are, you must wear breast pads. You don't want to leak at the altar.'

Ellen groaned. 'Oh, God, I hadn't even thought about that.'

Molly shot her sister a reproachful look. 'It's only a dress. Your little baby is a lot more important, Ellen.'

'Quite right, and there are ways of dealing with these things,' Orla grinned. 'I've had plenty of brides with leaky boobs.' She carefully lifted the dress over Ellen's head and laid it across the sofa. 'Okay, Laura, your turn.'

Laura took the dress and went into the next room to change.

'Excuse me a sec, I just need to make a call,' Orla said, and went into the hall.

'So what kept you?' Ellen asked when they were alone. 'Were you delayed at the airport?'

'No. Well, sort of . . .' Molly trailed off as she thought about Luke. Was he thinking about her too, she wondered, or had he not given her a second thought? Perhaps he hadn't recognized her. She'd changed a bit since the last time he'd seen her. No more teenage acne, no braces, and her brown hair was a shorter, shinier bob and her boobs had grown—

'Molly?'

'Sorry?' She looked up to find Ellen watching her curiously.

'You were miles away. Is there something wrong?'

'No, not really, it's just—'

Laura breezed in and did a twirl. 'Well, what do you think?'

'You look lovely.' Molly smiled. She and her sister had the

same colouring, but Laura was slightly taller and curvier and carried herself with more confidence.

'Stunning,' Ellen agreed. 'It's such a wonderful colour, Molly. It goes with Laura's dark complexion and my fair one, it was a great choice. If you ever fancy earning an extra few bob, you could turn your hand to fashion.'

'Please!' Molly burst out laughing.

'Don't waste your breath, Ellen. My sister has an aversion to getting rich.'

'Money isn't everything, you know,' Molly said, hating the defensive note in her voice. 'I love working for *Teenage Kix.*'

'You're a trained psychologist, working as an agony aunt for a crappy magazine.' Laura gave a frustrated shrug. 'You could have your own practice by now. I don't know why you bothered with all that studying if you were going to settle for a dead-end job.'

Molly was just opening her mouth to reply when Orla arrived back. 'Sorry about that. Oh, Laura, you look lovely! I just need to adjust that neckline . . .'

'What's up?'

Laura had told Molly to take her wilting friend out to the cool conservatory and get her some iced water. Ellen had been telling her some of her ideas for the nursery, but Molly hadn't heard a word.

'Sorry, Ellen, it must be the weather; I can't seem to concentrate on anything today.'

Ellen watched her through narrowed eyes. 'What's happened?'

'Nothing.'

'Don't give me that. You know I can see right through you. Have you had a row with Declan?'

Molly met her friend's piercing gaze and shook her head. 'No, nothing like that. I just saw someone I haven't seen in years.'

'A man?'

Molly sighed. 'My first boyfriend.'

'Oh, wow, that's amazing.' Ellen perked up, her weariness forgotten. 'What's he like? Has he changed? What did he say?'

'We didn't talk, I just saw him in the distance.'

'Oh.' Ellen was disappointed. 'Did he see you?'

'Yes, though he may not have recognized me without the braces and acne,' Molly grinned.

'You should have gone over and said hello. Or was he with someone, is that it?'

'He was with a group of guys and I was queuing for the bank. By the time I'd finished, he was gone.'

'Oh, that's so sad!'

'Molly, your turn,' Laura called from the other room.

'He's probably married with a gang of kids,' Molly said, standing up.

'True.'

Molly hesitated. 'Don't mention it to Laura, will you?'

Ellen frowned. 'Okay, but why?'

Molly shrugged awkwardly. 'Oh, you know, she'll just go on and on about it and I'm not in the mood.'

Ellen nodded in sympathy. 'No problem. My lips are sealed.'

Chapter Two

Molly smiled across the table at Declan as he talked. 'They're such a proactive company, Moll. They're not panicking about the recession, they're looking for opportunities and, believe me, there are plenty out there. They've hired ten people in the last two months – ten! Everyone else seems to be letting people go. And they really seem to get where I'm coming from.'

'Was everything okay for you?' A waiter stood over them, gesturing at their empty plates.

'Terrible, take it back,' Declan said, as he did every time they came here, which wasn't quite as often as it used to be.

'It was lovely,' Molly smiled.

The waiter smiled back. 'Good. Can I tempt you with dessert? We have a wonderful chocolate cheesecake as our special tonight.'

Declan sat back in his chair and patted his stomach. 'Not right away, thanks.'

'That's fine.' The waiter poured the last of the wine into Declan's glass. 'Just call me when you're ready.'

'I'm so glad it went well, Declan,' Molly said when they were alone again.

'It really did. I don't have the job yet,' he grinned, 'but it's only a matter of time. And then, my darling, we'll be eating out a lot more and we can buy a big house in Clontarf next to your sister's.'

'I don't want to be that near to her.'

He laughed. 'Thank God for that.'

'I don't even want a big house,' she added, 'not while it's just the two of us anyway. But a garden would be nice.'

'And a den with a huge flat-screen TV and a pool table—'

'You can have a pool table, or me, but not both,' Molly retorted.

Declan frowned. 'I'll have to think about that.'

'Don't take too long,' she warned and then yawned.

'What were you up to today that has you tired at nine o'clock?'

Immediately, Molly thought of Luke, but she quickly pushed him to the back of her mind. 'I had a dress fitting at Laura's this morning. Then I went to the supermarket. Then Dad called to tell me he's taking up salsa-dancing—'

'You're kidding!'

Molly shook her head, laughing. 'Nope. He's trying to persuade Mum to go with him, but she says she'll have much more fun at home without him.'

'Sometimes I wonder why your parents have stayed together, they seem to lead totally separate lives and they're always arguing.'

Molly looked at him in surprise. 'They don't argue, they banter and enjoy every minute of it. Anyway, you and Gareth are always talking about the rows your folks used to have.'

'They were more like battles than rows,' he admitted.

'But you need to have some kind of spark in a marriage,' Molly argued, 'or you'd die of boredom. I mean, look at Laura and Robert. I've never heard them argue; in fact, they barely seem to communicate, and have you noticed they've started to call each other Mum and Dad?'

Declan nodded. 'And Laura talks at him, rather than to him. It's a bit sad at their age.'

Molly searched his face, suddenly worried. 'We won't end up like that, will we?'

'Course we won't. When I start to get bored with you, I'll just find myself a new woman.'

'Would it kill you to say something nice?' she complained.

'I'm just joking.'

'You're hilarious. You know, a girl wrote in to me one time to say that her dad was always making fun of her mother, or playing practical jokes on her.'

'Let me guess, she topped herself?'

'Nope. She put arsenic in his mashed potato.' Molly flashed him an evil grin. 'So, dessert?'

'Er, no,' Declan gulped and put a hand to his throat. 'I don't fancy it any more for some reason.'

Molly laughed. 'Let's go home.'

'Dying to get me into bed and ravish me, eh?'

Molly frowned. 'No, I have a worried teenager I want to check on.'

'What's she worried about? Her face, figure or boyfriend?'

'Don't poke fun at what I do.' she snapped.

'Hey, don't be so touchy, Moll,' Declan protested, frowning. 'I was just kidding.'

'I'm sorry. It's just Laura was taking a pop at me this morning for not having a real job.'

'She can talk,' he snorted. 'She's *never* had a job.'

'She does have two children,' Molly said, feeling obliged to defend her sister.

'Yeah, two kids *and* a cleaner,' he pointed out.

Molly shrugged. 'I suppose we'd all do the same if we had the money.'

'Anyway, tell me about your troubled teenager.'

Molly sighed. 'She's fourteen. She seems quite shy and is in love with her maths teacher.'

Declan smiled. 'Well, it's the right age for a crush, I suppose.'

'As long as that's all it is, but there was something about the tone of her message I didn't like.'

'Have you replied?'

She nodded. 'Yes, I made light of it, said she shouldn't beat herself up, that it's perfectly normal. However, I advised against sharing her feelings with her teacher as it could make things awkward between them and make the class uncomfortable for her. I told her that it was unlikely he felt the same way and that, even if he did, he wouldn't act on it, as it would be illegal for him to get involved with a minor.' She sighed. 'I also said that if he has flirted with her in any way – and I'm terribly afraid he might have – she should tell her parents or the principal.'

'Do you think she'll take your advice?' Declan asked.

'Probably not.' Molly looked at her watch.

'Come on, let's go. I'm shattered anyway, to be honest.'

She studied him, taking in the redness of his eyes and the line that seemed to be permanently etched between them. 'You've had quite a day, and you've been stressed out for weeks.'

His smile was grim. 'You noticed.'

'Yeah, amazing, isn't it? And you usually hide it so well! Please tell me the new job would be less stressful than the current one. I hate seeing you worried all the time.'

'Who isn't worried at the moment?' He raised a hand to attract the waiter's attention. 'But I would be a lot better off, I'm sure of it. Enco are going places. They're not fire-fighters, they're trailblazers. This could be a really big step up the ladder for me, Moll. For us.'

'You know that I'm the last person to care about ladders, I just want you to be happy.'

'But it would be nice not to have to worry about money,' he argued.

'Yes,' she admitted. 'But at least we don't have to pay for the wedding and we're saving for the deposit for a house.'

'True,' he admitted. 'But I don't want to even think about house-hunting until I know if I've got this job or not, Molly.'

'That's fine. I've enough on my plate at the moment. Laura has me running around like a mad woman. Between bands, table plans, shoes and favours—'

He turned his head, frowning. 'Favours?'

She waved a hand. 'Trust me, you don't want to know.'

'Don't let her take over, love. This is *your* wedding.'

'Is it?' Molly laughed. 'I'm not so sure.'

He stopped and turned to her. 'We could always hop on a plane to Vegas and just have a big bash for everyone when we come back.'

'If we hopped on a plane to Las Vegas, I wouldn't be able to come home again,' she assured him. 'My family would never forgive me.'

'That's crap. Your mother is the coolest woman I know. Your dad could still throw us a party, so he'd be happy, and Rory wouldn't care as long as there *was* a party. Laura is the only one who'd mind, and I can't say I'd lose sleep over upsetting her.'

'That's no way to talk about your future sister-in-law. How would you feel if I talked like that about Gareth?'

'I can't even imagine it,' he said with a wry smile. 'You get on better with my brother than I do.'

Molly grinned. It was true. Declan's little brother was a sweetheart, and they'd liked each other on sight. But though Gareth and Declan looked a lot alike, there the similarities ended. Gareth was as laidback and carefree as Declan was serious and intense. Molly sometimes thought, if you could mix the two of them together, you would have the perfect man.

At home, Declan flopped in front of a sci-fi movie with a beer, while Molly made a mug of tea, sat at the kitchen table, and opened her laptop. It took a couple of minutes to get online.

Molly didn't want to even wonder why, and what some people got up to at night on the Internet. She logged onto *Teenage Kix* and quickly keyed in her user ID and password. Her sister didn't realize, but there was a lot more to her job than answering a couple of letters in a weekly magazine. Molly and her two assistants answered mail and email for three teenage publications and their associated websites. It was also their job to police the forums. For the most part, there weren't any problems, but occasionally Molly would withdraw a post because it was cruel, bitchy or completely inaccurate. It never ceased to amaze her how spiteful teenagers could be. She didn't remember any of her friends ever behaving like that, but then, when she was that age, bitching was confined to gossiping on the phone or in corners. Technology today was brilliant, but it also allowed nasty people to be nasty on a much greater scale.

Molly's assistants, Tess and Carl, were straight out of school, which had its advantages. They were close enough in age to the kids to understand their issues and were au fait with the slang and abbreviations that sometimes left Molly completely at a loss and feeling ancient.

She scrolled down through the new messages. There were thirteen in all, but nothing new from BettyBlu – the girl with a crush on her teacher. But then that wasn't such a surprise. In this business you had to get used to the fact that you rarely learned the outcome of a problem. Molly hoped her fears were misplaced and that BettyBlu's teacher was completely ignorant of his student's feelings.

She took a sip of her tea and scanned the new messages on the open forum. One was from SallyK about diet, and already there had been three replies from other kids offering their, off-the-wall and possibly dangerous, advice. Grimacing, Molly tried to decide whether to withdraw these answers, or just add a post giving more sensible tips on healthy diet and exercise. She decided on the latter, although she knew that trying to stop people following silly, faddy diets was like trying to stop the tide from turning. She quickly put her own past together and ended it with the web addresses of official organizations that could help with any weight issues. As she pressed enter, she felt depressed and helpless. Perhaps SallyK would heed her advice, but it was unlikely.

'You mustn't let it get to you,' her editor, Sue, had advised her once before when she'd expressed her frustrations. 'All you can do is advise them and suppress messages advocating any dodgy practices. Kids want to gossip and swap ideas and be silly and irresponsible and that's all part of growing up. If we don't facilitate them, they'll go elsewhere and there are plenty of teenage forums that have little or no supervision. Isn't it better that they use *Teenage Kix*, a site monitored by a trained psychologist?'

And that's what clinched it for Molly. She knew that Sue was right. She'd trawled through other, similar, websites and been horrified at the apparent lack of supervision. At least *Teenage Kix* controlled content and provided helpful information.

Molly quickly read through the other new posts. There were the usual mix of worries about boyfriends, best friends and difficulties at school. Molly replied immediately to a troubled young boy – YUGI – who seemed to be suffering some minor bullying, and passed on contact numbers and information on useful websites, in case he felt he needed further help. Her main message to him – as it was to all bullying victims – was not to keep it to himself. She published her reply and was just opening the final message when Declan walked in. He bent to kiss her neck. 'Crap film. Come to bed.'

'I'm nearly finished. I'll follow you.'

'Don't be long,' he warned, and with another kiss went through to their bedroom. Molly turned back to her screen.

> I'm 14 and I'm writing about my friend – I'm really worried about her. She used to tell me everything, but in the last few weeks she's become very secretive. We've always been close, but she doesn't want to be around me at all any more. And she doesn't seem to care about the stuff that used to really matter to her. Maybe you think I'm making a big deal out of nothing but, trust me, this is completely out of character. I'm really worried about her. Please tell me what to do.

It was signed 'Smithy'. Molly didn't hesitate. Alarm bells were ringing; this sounded like a girl in trouble. She started to key in her answer, her fingers almost moving faster than her thoughts.

> You are a GREAT friend, Smithy. Trust your instinct, you know your friend. You think something is wrong, and it probably is. She may be depressed and need some help to get better. I think your first course of action is to tell her your concerns and try to persuade her to talk to an adult – a parent, a trusted teacher or doctor. If she won't agree to do that then I think you should do it on her behalf. She may be angry with you, but you can't worry about that right now. Your priority must be to get her help.

Molly added the usual contact information, then logged out and switched off her machine.

In the bedroom, Declan was already snoring softly and when she slipped into bed and leaned over to kiss him, he didn't budge. Molly reached across him to switch off the lamp and then pulled the covers up to her nose. Though she was tired, she no longer felt sleepy. She wondered what was happening with BettyBlu and if Smithy had read her reply yet. But most of all, she wondered where Luke was right now. Feeling disloyal, she turned on her side, away from Declan. Not that she had any reason to feel guilty, she was just indulging in some harmless reminiscing about an ex. Yet she wondered: if Luke had approached her, if he'd suggested they meet up, what would she have said? Probably yes. Not that she expected or wanted anything to happen between them – she'd just like to know if he was happy. Still, perhaps it was just as well they hadn't gotten a chance to talk. There was nothing to be gained from dragging up the past. They couldn't change it, and it would be painful for them both. Anyway, if he'd felt the inclination, he'd have come over, wouldn't he? But he hadn't. Despite what she'd told Ellen, Molly knew he'd recognized her, and so must have made a conscious decision not to approach her. Molly was surprised by how much that hurt. Of course, that was probably just ego. In her imagination, he would have rushed over, told her that she looked more beautiful than ever – which would be true as she was now clear-skinned and had a decent hair style – and then he'd kiss her. And how would that feel? Molly touched her lips. He'd last kissed her as a boy, but he was very much a man now. Resolutely closing her eyes, Molly turned over and slipped an arm around her fiancé's waist. Luke Fortune was her past, but Declan was most definitely her future.

Chapter Three

It was a tradition in the Jackson family to have brunch in the family home every Sunday, not that it was a formal affair. It had been Belle's idea. After Laura got married at the tender age of twenty, she had a dread of the family growing apart and decided it would be a good way for them all to catch up and to keep a protective eye on her elder daughter.

Laura had got pregnant at nineteen, and though Belle and Oliver had promised her support in any way they could, Laura had decided to marry in haste and lie about her dates. She had felt embarrassed to be caught out and was relieved that Robert and his parents felt 'he should do the right thing'. It was a difficult time, probably not helped by Rory holding up an imaginary shotgun and shooting it every time his sister came into a room.

Once the reality of married life and coping with two babies hit home, Laura and Robert were only too happy to come to brunch every week. The twins were born just five months after the wedding day, and home cooking was a luxury rather than a priority.

They would arrive promptly each Sunday, Robert licking his lips and Laura hastily handing over the babies to her family. Belle would cook up a feast and Rory would be sent out to fetch the morning papers. And while Oliver scrambled eggs, Molly would be charged with watching over her niece and nephew to give her sister a much-needed break. Laura would sit at the kitchen table asking Belle's advice about colic and nappy rash and feeding problems, while Robert retreated to the other room to slump in a chair and catch up on some sleep.

As the years went by and all their lives changed, the arrangement became looser and, of course, not all the family were in attendance at all times. When Rory left school, he decided to take a year to tour Australia before he started college and stayed on for five. He left a huge gap. Belle and Oliver, especially, missed him and, when he returned, he moved back into the family home, started his law degree and carried on as if he'd never left. Laura was disgusted that at twenty-eight her brother was still living off their parents but, as Oliver gently reminded her, he had promised to support all his children until they'd finished their education. 'And I'd have done the same for you, had you wanted it.'

When Molly started to date Declan four years ago, he too joined the Sunday gathering and now, although he often went to the gym on Sunday mornings, he usually made it in time for brunch and then retreated to the living room to watch the football with the rest of the men.

This Sunday, however, Declan was working overtime, and Robert had taken the twins swimming and would arrive later. Laura had offered to scramble the eggs and Oliver sat with Molly at the table making a half-hearted stab at the crossword. While Belle monitored the rest of the food, she quizzed her younger daughter about her wedding plans.

'Ask Laura,' Molly said with a grin. 'She knows more about what's going on than I do.'

'Weddings don't organize themselves,' her sister retorted with an irritable glance over her shoulder. 'If it was left to you, we'd be lucky to get a mug of tea and a cheese sandwich after the ceremony.'

'She's right,' Belle said. 'You should be grateful you have such a capable, organized sister.'

'I am, although we all know that she enjoys planning this wedding as much as I hate it. You should go into business, Laura. Everyone uses wedding planners these days.'

Laura looked around to check if her sister was making fun of her.

'I'm serious,' Molly said.

Belle nodded. 'She's right. You'd make a superb wedding planner.'

'I'd love it,' Laura admitted, 'only I doubt I'd be in much demand in the current economic climate.'

'That depends on how you sell yourself,' her father said, tapping his pen against the folded newspaper. 'You could specialize in how to get married on a budget, for instance.'

'Great idea, Dad,' Molly said, impressed. 'Everyone wants their day to be special but they don't know how to achieve it without spending a fortune. They just don't have the imagination to come up with something that's innovative but cheap.'

'You should think about it, Laura,' Belle said. 'You were saying that you fancied getting out of the house more.'

Laura kept stirring the eggs. 'I was thinking of taking up golf.'

'Golf's good too. I could teach you, if you like.'

Laura rolled her eyes. 'Dad, you can't play golf.'

'I can, but I choose not to,' he corrected her. 'It's so time-consuming and life's too short. But if I had my lovely daughter to accompany me, well, that would be different. Or you could always come salsa-dancing with me,' he added. 'Your mother won't.'

'That's because you can't dance,' Belle said mildly. 'I have deformed toes to prove it.'

'Isabelle Jackson, wash your mouth out, I'm a great dancer!' Oliver grinned. 'It's just that I'm better at freestyle.'

'Aren't you worried about him going alone?' Laura asked her mother. 'Classes like that are full of desperate single women.'

Belle threw back her head and laughed. 'They're welcome to him.'

Oliver gave a resigned shrug and stood up. 'The woman doesn't appreciate me. I'll go and pull Rory out of bed.'

'Seriously, Mum,' Laura said when he'd left the room. 'You shouldn't let him out on his own, he's not that bad a catch.'

Belle raised her eyebrows. 'I'm sure he'd be flattered you think so.'

'She's got a point,' Molly smiled. Her dad might be bald and very slightly eccentric, but he had chocolate-brown eyes that were always full of laughter and he positively oozed charisma. 'There are lots of women who'd snap him up.'

'Yes, you shouldn't be too smug,' Laura added.

'I'm not smug, Laura, I just happen to trust him. I know that's an old-fashioned concept, but it works for us.'

'You're right, Mum, sorry. I'm sure he'd never look at another woman.'

'He's a man, for God's sake,' Laura muttered.

Belle looked up as her husband returned. 'Is Rory awake?'

'He grunted and sat up, so I'd say that's a yes.'

Laura scowled. 'He drinks too much and doesn't study enough. I'll be amazed if he ever qualifies.'

'It *is* the weekend,' Oliver said mildly.

'And you're not here all week,' Molly added, jumping to her brother's defence, 'how do you know if or when he studies?'

'Oh, please, you know as well as I do that he's a lazy shit.'

'Language,' Belle said.

'I wonder who she could be talking about.' Rory shuffled into the room, yawning widely. Though only a year younger than Molly, he looked about twenty, and even unshaven and dishevelled, still managed to look handsome.

'I wonder who?' Laura shot him a dirty look as he took a pint glass from the cupboard and went to the tap to fill it.

'No fighting, children,' Belle warned. It was the only rule

about the Sunday ritual; you could come or not come, you could stay all afternoon or just drop in, but she would not tolerate any arguments. 'Now, Molly, what would you like?' she asked, a warmed plate in her hand.

'One sausage and lots of egg, please.' Molly put four slices of bread in the toaster.

'Make the tea, Oliver, would you?' Belle asked, putting Molly's plate on the table. 'Rory?'

He filled his glass again. 'Do you have to ask?'

'The works.' She smiled and loaded her son's plate, before holding it out for Laura to add some egg. 'Oliver?'

'Just bacon and egg, please.'

While Laura carried two plates of egg for her and her mother to the table, Belle put the rest of the food into the oven to keep warm. 'Is Declan coming over?' she asked Molly as she took her seat.

'No, he had to work.'

'Again?' Belle's brow creased in concern.

'Again.'

'They work him hard in that place, don't they?' Rory observed.

'Tell me about it.'

'You look tired yourself, Molly,' her mother remarked.

'I haven't been sleeping great,' Molly admitted. When she wasn't lying in the darkness thinking of Luke and Ruth, she was experiencing the most awful nightmares at the moment.

'Well, it can't be the stress of the job,' Laura murmured, earning dirty looks from all of her family. 'What? I'm just saying, it's not exactly rocket science.'

'It carries enormous responsibility,' Oliver said, 'and knowing Molly, I'm sure she spends a lot of time thinking and worrying about those kids.'

Molly flashed her dad a grateful smile. 'I do have a case at the moment that I'm concerned about. It's a young girl who's worried that her friend is depressed and might do something stupid.'

Belle laid down her knife and fork and looked at her in dismay. 'It's no wonder you're not sleeping.'

'So what did you tell her?' Laura asked.

Molly heard the edge in her sister's voice. Already she was being judged and found wanting, and Laura didn't even know the facts yet. 'I told her to try and persuade her friend to talk to a trusted adult and if she couldn't, then she should tell an adult of her suspicions.'

'And what happened?' her father asked.

Molly pushed egg round her plate. 'I don't know. I may never know.'

'It must be hard.' Belle patted her hand.

'I think it's irresponsible of magazines to dole out advice to vulnerable children; they probably cause more problems than they solve.'

Rory looked at her in disgust. 'Don't be so fucking stupid—'

'Rory!' his mother exclaimed.

'Sometimes it's easier to ask advice from an anonymous stranger,' Molly said quietly.

'It's a pity kids don't feel they can talk to their parents,' Oliver said sadly.

'No teenager talks to a parent,' Belle reminded him, earning a nod of approval from her son.

'So they talk to other kids, who give them all sorts of misinformation, and that's where forums like ours come in.'

'But what about all the dodgy forums that are out there?' Rory asked. 'It's almost impossible to control what kids are exposed to these days.'

Molly shrugged. 'All parents can really do is educate their kids, talk to them and monitor what they do online.'

'This is very depressing,' Belle said. 'I think it's time to change the subject.'

Molly followed her mother's gaze and saw the stricken look on Laura's face. 'You don't have to worry about Ash or Adam, Laura, they're great kids.'

Laura shot her a small, grateful smile.

'Yes, at fourteen they are both very mature,' Oliver agreed. 'Do they use these chat rooms?'

'God knows what they do, but when they use the laptop, we make sure they stay in the same room as us so we can keep an eye on them.'

Belle reached for the coffee pot and topped up her cup. 'That seems sensible. Speaking of the twins, what time are you expecting them?'

'About two.'

'Want me to make them some fresh scrambled egg?' Oliver popped his last piece of toast into his mouth and dusted off his hands.

'No thanks, Dad. I'll warm some baked beans and they can have them with the sausages. Robert prefers his egg fried anyway.'

Molly stood to carry her plate to the sink. 'Could I use your computer, Mum? I just want to check something.'

'Of course.'

Molly took her mug through the archway into the makeshift study area. It had been their playroom when they were children, but now her parents used it to house their papers and books. There was a desk, two squishy armchairs and an enormous old bookcase that Oliver had inherited from his dad. The walls were painted a warm honey, the floor was golden oak and family photos covered every surface. Molly loved this room. It oozed both her parents' personalities and its warmth was what made a house a home. She'd like to create such a room when she and Declan bought a house. Their flat was bland and characterless, like a hotel, only a very cheap one. Molly had tried to liven it up with cushions and pictures, but her heart wasn't in it. She didn't like the cold, north-facing rooms and positively hated the thin carpet that ran through them that was the colour of porridge, although porridge looked nicer.

She sat down at the desk and pulled the keyboard and mouse towards her. It was open on a gardening page. Molly left it, opened a new window and signed on to *Teenage Kix*. There were a few new messages on minor issues that she was happy to let Carl and Tess deal with, but there was nothing from either BettyBlu or Smithy. It had been over a week now, and it was unlikely they'd make contact again. Molly just hoped they'd both followed her advice. In the kitchen, Rory's mobile started to ring and he ducked into the garden to take the call; must be a girl, Molly surmised. Her dad had gone into the living room and she could hear Laura telling their mother about the bridesmaids' dresses as they stacked the dishwasher and tidied the kitchen. She should really go in and help, but Laura was being particularly annoying today and Molly wasn't in the mood. She was worried about Declan. He was in terrible form at the moment because he hadn't heard back about the job he'd applied for. It hadn't helped that his boss had just announced that they were putting together a redundancy package in an effort to control company costs. Declan was almost sick with worry, and looked positively grey in the face. Molly was sympathetic, but she couldn't really understand his concern; so what if he lost his job? They didn't have kids or a mortgage to worry about; they would manage. He was clever, and if he was made redundant it would be because of the recession and no reflection on his personal ability. He would easily get another job and, if he didn't, they could always go abroad for a couple of years. Backpack around the world picking up odd jobs as they went; it would be fun. Molly felt quite excited at the thought. But she knew that Declan would be horrified. He would never be comfortable living his life from day to day. He always liked to have a plan. In fact, he even liked to plan his holidays down to the smallest detail.

Luke had been completely different. He'd loved life and

embraced every day as if it was his last. Everything was an adventure with him, and his enthusiasm had been hard to resist. If it was a cold, wet day, he'd drag her down to the beach for a walk. He was first up to volunteer for any charity stunt, the more hare-brained the better. And he'd always dreamed of travelling the world.

Idly, she keyed his name into the Google page and pressed search. It came back with a huge number of results, but it turned out they were about some scientist and his research into UFOs. Molly changed the words to Luke Fortune + Dublin and pressed search. Nothing.

She tried Luke Fortune + rugby and bingo! But before she got a chance to check the results, a voice in her ear made her jump.

'What are you up to?' Rory asked as he leaned across her and read what was on the screen.

'Nothing,' she mumbled, elbowing him out of the way and making a grab for the mouse, but he got there before her. 'Please, Rory.'

'Luke Fortune!' He turned startled eyes on her.

'What about Luke Fortune?' Laura said, coming to join them.

Molly glared at her brother and he mouthed 'sorry' at her.

'I was just messing.' She moved the mouse and closed down the search, but not before Laura had seen what was on the screen.

'Why on earth were you looking up Luke?'

Molly sighed. 'I saw him at the airport last week, and I was just wondering what he was doing in Dublin.'

Laura's eyes widened. 'Did you talk?'

'No, I only saw him for a second.' Molly stood and stretched, then looked at her watch. 'I'd better get going, I have a load of shopping to do.'

'I wonder what he's up to these days,' Laura mused. 'Does he still play rugby?' she asked Rory, who was a fountain of knowledge when it came to the sport.

'No, he retired a couple of years ago,' Rory said, although he was still watching Molly.

'Laura,' Belle called from the archway. 'You'd better get Robert's egg on; they'll be here any minute.'

Laura reluctantly went back out to the kitchen and Rory touched her hand. 'You okay?'

'Sure.' Molly gave him a reassuring smile, carried her empty mug back into the kitchen and gathered up her things. 'Need anything at the shops, Mum?'

'Oh yes, actually, could you get me some bread?' She followed her daughter out into the hall. 'And some of those chocolate biscuits we like too,' she murmured, looking round for her purse. 'When you get back we can have a cuppa and a chat.'

Molly refused to take the money, smiling. 'Why do you want to have a chat?'

Belle raised an eyebrow. 'I need a reason?'

Chapter Four

Molly wandered around the half-empty supermarket in no hurry to rush back to her parents' house. She didn't want her sister picking up where she'd left off, and she wasn't even sure she wanted to have a 'chat' with her mother. Molly decided to drop the shopping off at the flat before returning to her parents' home in Blackrock. Surely by then her sister would have left, her brother gone out with his latest squeeze, and her dad would be at a neighbour's house for the weekly poker game. Perhaps Declan would be home, although he'd warned her it would be 'a late one'. No surprise there; she hardly saw him these days. The job and workload had been getting him down, but at least there had been light at the end of the tunnel in the form of this new job prospect. Sadly, that light was dimming fast and she seemed to spend all her time walking on eggshells. 'Would it be too much to ask to have a clean shirt in the morning?' he'd growled on Friday as he rooted through the brimming laundry basket looking for a half-presentable shirt. And then this morning when she'd asked him what time he'd be home at, he'd muttered something about working overtime to pay for the phone bill. This was completely unfair, because Molly hardly ever used the landline, much preferring her mobile. She wished Enco would call and tell him the outcome of the interview, one way or the other, because if he didn't snap out of this mood soon, she'd give him a punch. It had been almost a relief when he'd said he had to work today and wouldn't be joining the Jackson clan for brunch.

It was usually an occasion Declan looked forward to. He got on with all her family, bar Laura, and it meant, he joked, that he got at least one decent meal a week. It was true Molly didn't take after either parent when it came to culinary skills. Thankfully, Declan was quite handy in the kitchen, but with the hours he was working lately, he didn't have the time or energy to cook, so at the moment they were living on ready meals, pot noodles, take-out or Molly's only speciality, chicken curry made with sauce from a jar and boil-in-the-bag rice. It didn't matter how many times her mother showed her how to get rice fluffy and dry, Molly couldn't master the art, and didn't lose sleep over the fact. There were too many good books to be read, she reasoned, and too few hours in the day to waste time worrying about food. That's why God had invented takeaways.

Declan was not home when she got back. The brooding, bleak silence of the flat when Molly opened the door, told her she was alone. She dragged the bags into their tiny kitchen, noticing that Declan's cereal bowl was still on the draining board and the table covered with spilt sugar and toast crumbs. Molly resolved to give the flat a quick clean once she'd put away the groceries. It might, just might, cheer her grumpy fiancé up. It was almost six by the time she was ready to return to her mother's, leaving the flat relatively clean and a cheery note on the table, promising to be home by eight, armed with pizza.

*

'Bread and biscuits.' Molly handed her mother the bag.

'Lovely.' Belle smiled and led the way through to the kitchen. 'You've missed everyone, I'm all alone.'

'What a pity.' Molly grinned and plonked herself down in a chair.

Belle poured coffee for them both, opened the biscuits and sat down. 'So. Luke Fortune.'

Molly sighed. 'Gee, Mum, don't beat around the bush, will you?' She added two sugars to her coffee and stirred.

Belle nibbled on a biscuit and waited, her eyes concerned.

'I saw him at the airport when I dropped Declan off last week.'

'Oh, my goodness,' Belle gasped, instinctively covering her daughter's hand with her own. 'That must have been quite a shock. Is that the first time you've seen him since . . .'

Molly nodded, swallowing back the tears. 'Yes.'

'My poor darling. It must have brought back so many memories. Poor Ruth.'

Molly nodded, pulling out a tissue and blowing her nose.

'How is he?'

'We didn't talk; he was there and then gone again in a matter of seconds.' She sighed. 'It just made me wonder about him, how he's getting on, how life has been for him. That's why I was looking him up on the Internet. I thought that if he was still involved in rugby, there might be something about him on a website.'

'And did you find him?' Belle asked quietly.

Molly shook her head. 'I had only just keyed in his name when Rory opened his big mouth and Laura came running. I should have waited until I got home to play Clouseau.'

'Poor darling. And that's when you suddenly remembered you had to go shopping.'

Molly smiled.

'You know it's okay to talk about him and about Ruth? We all loved them, there's no need to keep it all locked up inside.'

'I don't,' Molly protested. 'It was all a long time ago, Mum. It was just seeing him again.'

Belle studied her, brows knitted in concern. 'I'm worried about you, Molly. For someone who's getting married in a few weeks, you don't seem too excited.'

Molly frowned, thrown by the sudden change of subject. 'Of course I am, I just don't understand what all the fuss is about. Declan and I would be just as happy getting married under a tree.'

Belle shot her an exasperated look. 'Then why didn't you say so? It's your day, Molly.'

'I don't care much either way about the wedding, Mum. It's the marriage that's important.'

'You're quite right. But . . .' Belle trailed off.

'Yes?'

'You're not having second thoughts, are you?'

Molly looked at her in astonishment. 'No! Of course not.'

'It's just that when you start wondering about ex-boyfriends—'

'It wasn't just any boyfriend, it was Luke! Don't you think it would be a lot weirder if I'd just shrugged it off?'

'You're right, darling.' Belle gave her hand a reassuring pat. 'So, how does he look?'

Molly smiled. 'The same, really. Still gorgeous.'

Belle chuckled. 'Was he alone?'

'No, he seemed to be in charge of a group of French guys.'

'And did he see you?'

'Yes, although I'm not sure he recognized me. Now, can we please change the subject?'

Belle searched her face. 'If you're sure you're okay.'

'I'm sure.'

'And you promise, if you do want to talk about him or Ruth—'

'I'll tell you.'

Belle nodded, satisfied. 'So, how's Declan? Is he at least excited about the wedding?'

Molly sighed. 'He's too worried to be excited.'

'Work?'

Molly nodded.

'And he hasn't heard anything about the job he interviewed for?'

'No.'

'I thought you said he was sure he had it?'

'He was. That's why he's so miserable.'

'Things will work out; he's a clever lad.'

'Try telling him that. He's convinced it's only a matter of time before he's made redundant.'

'At least *you've* got a job.'

Molly pulled a face. 'I'm not exactly earning a fortune, as Laura constantly points out.'

'But you know that you could, if you needed to,' Belle said gently.

Molly looked at her. 'Are you disappointed that I didn't become a GP in a nice, posh private clinic, Mum?'

Belle smiled. 'You know that I've always understood and supported your reasons for changing direction. I told you back then that I didn't mind *what* you did, as long as you felt fulfilled and happy. I think at *Teenage Kix*, you're both.'

Molly shot her a grateful smile. 'What about Dad?'

'What about him?'

'Does he feel I've let him down?'

Belle looked at her, bewildered.' How can you even ask that? You know your father's very proud of you. It wouldn't matter what you did, he'd be proud of you. You're a good person, you're clever and you're kind – what's not to be proud of?'

Molly adopted a coy look and fanned her face. 'Stop, you're making me blush. Tell me, is Laura adopted?' Belle almost choked on her coffee and Molly hurriedly passed her some kitchen roll. 'Sorry.'

'Why on earth would you say that?' Belle wiped her eyes.

'It's just, you and Dad aren't remotely materialistic. Rory

couldn't give a monkey's about money and neither could I, but it seems to be everything to Laura.'

Belle's expression sobered. 'That's not true.'

'Oh, come on, Mum. She never misses an opportunity to brag about her designer shoes and handbags, the posh restaurants she eats in and the five-star holidays she takes. She thinks she's better than the rest of us.'

'She doesn't.' Belle said with an emphatic shake of her head. 'If anything, she feels inferior, and is a little jealous of you, and of Rory too.'

Molly gave an incredulous laugh. 'Laura? I don't think so.'

Belle looked mildly amused.

'What?' Molly demanded.

'For someone who's an expert on the human mind, you haven't a clue what's going on inside your sister's, have you?'

Molly frowned. 'Are you serious, Mum? Is there something wrong? Has Laura got problems?'

Belle shook her head. 'All I'm saying, is that I always thought that bragging about one's position in life was a sign of insecurity.'

'It often is.' Molly agreed, straight-faced, 'Or it could simply mean that one's an obnoxious show-off.'

'Molly Jackson!'

'I'm kidding, Mum.' She laughed, but stopped when she saw that her mother wasn't amused. 'You're not seriously worried about Laura, are you?'

'No, I just wish you would make more of an effort to get on with her.' Molly opened her mouth to protest, but closed it again when Belle held up a finger.

'You're very different, I realize that, but she's your sister and I expect you to be more tolerant and a lot more appreciative of what she's doing for you. Is that asking too much?'

'No, but—'

'Good.' Belle stood up and went to the fridge. 'Now, would you like to stay for dinner? We're having salmon.'

'No thanks. I promised Declan I'd pick up pizza on the way home.'

'You really shouldn't eat so much rubbish, it's bad for your skin.'

Molly put a self-conscious hand to her cheek. 'What's wrong with my skin?'

Belle smiled. 'Nothing, now, but you need to look after it, especially for the big day.'

With a groan, Molly stood up to go. 'Okay, now I believe you; she's not adopted.'

As she cycled home, Molly considered her mother's comments about Laura, but she still found them hard to credit; it was probably just Belle's maternal, protective instinct at play. And Laura did need protecting, she supposed, for she seemed to bring out the worst in people and she could brag for Ireland. Molly had an ongoing bet with Rory as to how many names Laura would drop of a Sunday afternoon. As she turned up the road to her flat, a car slowed down next to her and she smiled when she saw it was Declan.

'Hello, gorgeous, can I give you a lift somewhere?'

Molly laughed, relieved that he was obviously in better form. 'My mammy told me never get into a car with a strange man. I'll race you instead.' And she took off at speed, and was hopping off her bike before he pulled up outside the house.

'That doesn't count,' he protested, 'you went through a red light!'

'Did not, you imagined it.' She reached up to kiss him. 'You seem happier.'

'I am.' His eyes twinkled. 'I got a call from Ed Dawson.'

'Who?'

'He's the HR manager for Enco Ireland.'

Molly looked at him. 'And? What did he say?'

'Nothing. I had the mobile switched off, but he left a message. He wants me to call first thing.'

'Oh.' Molly said, deflated, and led the way up to the door. 'Still, that's got to be good news, hasn't it?' She opened the door and then turned to search his face. 'How did he sound?'

Declan shrugged, but he was smiling. 'Okay.'

'Declan, stop teasing me. What do you think?'

'Really?' he asked as he lifted her bike into the hallway.

She nodded.

He grinned. 'I think I've got the job.'

'Oh my God, I'm so proud of you!' Molly threw her arms round his neck and hugged him. 'I knew you'd get it; they'd be nuts not to take you on.'

He smiled down into her face, tenderly tucking her hair back behind her ears. 'You've been great, Moll. Thanks for putting up with me.'

'It hasn't been easy,' she said, only half-joking. Their relationship had been more strained in the last six weeks than it had been in the whole time they had been together.

'I'll make it up to you,' he promised, squeezing her to him. 'Let's go out for a slap-up meal on Saturday, and we could go clubbing afterwards.'

'Listen to you!' Molly teased, but she was thrilled to see him so happy. She just hoped it wasn't premature. 'Let's not make any plans until you've talked to this man though.'

'Okay, but I'm sure I've got it. He'd never have called if it was bad news, he'd have written or emailed. A phone call usually means an offer.'

'What if it's not enough?' She didn't want to rain on Declan's parade, but she couldn't bear it if he built his hopes up and was then brought down to earth with a bang.

'They know what my current salary is, Moll. Even if they only offered the same, I still get a car, healthcare and expenses on top of that; we would be more than comfortable, believe me. We could even afford to move.'

'I thought you didn't want to think about moving yet?'

'I don't want to *do* anything about it yet,' he corrected her, 'but I don't see any harm in us thinking about it, do you?'

'No harm at all,' she grinned, hugging him again and crossing her fingers behind his neck.

Chapter Five

9.10 p.m., Saturday, 11th July

'Are you sure we can afford this?' Molly hissed as she looked at the menu, horrified at the exorbitant prices.

'Not every week, but I think on this occasion we're entitled to push the boat out. I told you I'd make it up to you,' Declan reminded her with a tender smile. 'Have I told you how gorgeous you look tonight?'

'You mentioned it.' Molly smiled. 'But it's fine if you feel you need to say it again.' Ellen had done her hair and it hung in gentle glossy curls around her face and she'd found a little black dress in TK Maxx for thirty-five euro that, though quite demure, clung in all the right places. With expensive stockings, her highest pair of heels and glossy red lips, she knew she was looking her best. Molly was relishing Declan's attention and his general good mood since Enco had offered him the job. It was like a weight had been lifted from his shoulders since he'd got the call confirming the job offer. He was walking tall, head up, and his eyes shone with a new confidence. Tonight, in a black shirt under his grey suit, he looked self-assured, poised and good enough to eat. And in a couple of months, he'd be her husband.

*

Molly reminded him of the fact later that night, when they were smooching on the crowded dance floor at 80's night in Club Nassau. 'Do you realize that, in exactly eight weeks, we'll be having our first dance together as a married couple?'

'Mmm.' His smile faltered and he pulled her closer so her face was buried against his neck.

Molly pulled back, frowning. 'Declan?'

'Shush, let's dance.'

Her eyes narrowed. 'Declan?'

He sighed and led her back to their table. 'I didn't want to tell you tonight.'

Molly stiffened. 'Tell me what?'

He shot her a wary look, and twisted his glass between his hands. 'It's about the wedding—'

'You want to call it off?' She grinned.

He sighed. 'I don't want to call it off, Moll, but I'm afraid we have to postpone it.'

'Excuse me?' She blinked. It was really loud in here, perhaps she hadn't heard him correctly.

'We have to postpone the wedding,' he shouted, just as the song ended and heads turned to look their way.

'What the hell are you talking about?' Molly said, ignoring the smirks, snorts and looks of pity from the neighbouring tables.

Declan stood up. 'Let's go; we can't talk here.'

Feeling slightly sick, Molly snatched up her bag and stormed out ahead of him. They hopped into a waiting taxi and Declan opened his mouth to speak, but Molly held up her hand. 'Save it till we get home,' she told him and turned to stare out the window. She was angry and upset, but she wasn't going to make a show of herself in front of the taxi driver; she'd already been humiliated once tonight.

*

Once inside the flat, Declan went straight to the fridge for a beer. So he needed Dutch courage, Molly thought sourly. She sat down at the small kitchen table, folded her hands in her lap and waited. He continued to stand, drinking straight from the bottle and shooting her nervous looks. 'It's the job,' he said finally and, turning a chair round, sat astride it and leaned on the back. 'I need to go to Japan.'

'When?'

He chewed on his bottom lip for a moment before answering. 'Monday week.'

'What? But you haven't finished up at Kelleher's, you have to work a month's notice—'

'I talked to them and they agreed to let me finish up next Wednesday.'

Molly struggled to get her head around all this new information. Declan had only handed in his notice last Tuesday and they were letting him leave just a week later. 'Well, if you're going that soon, you'll be back in time for the wedding, won't you? How long do you have to go for? A week?' She frowned when he didn't answer. 'Two?'

He took another swig of beer and swallowed. 'It's ten weeks, Moll.'

'Ten!' She stared at him in disbelief. 'But that's ridiculous.'

He shrugged. 'Apparently it's standard procedure; all European management staff must go to Japan for a ten-week induction course before taking up their post.'

'Couldn't they send you after the wedding?'

'They've been trying to fill this position for months, Moll. They need me as soon as possible.'

'You didn't ask,' she murmured, hearing the hurt in her voice and wondering if he did too. 'Did you even tell them you were getting married?'

His eyes didn't quite meet hers. 'They know I'm engaged.'

'You didn't tell them that the wedding is in eight weeks?'

'Moll, I was afraid I'd lose the job offer,' he protested. 'And we really can't afford for that to happen, don't you see that? This is a huge opportunity. Jobs like this don't come along every day. Let me get settled in, then we can get married.'

She leaned on the table and rested her head in her hands.

'There's nothing I can do, Molly.' Declan looked at her, his expression a mixture of annoyance and frustration. 'Anyway, what's more important, one single day or a job that's going to affect our entire future?'

When she spoke, it was a struggle to keep her voice calm and steady when she just wanted to scream at him, and possibly even throw something. 'You could have explained the situation. If it was a problem, they would have said so. But you didn't think it was worth mentioning.' She stood up and went to the door. 'Maybe this is for the best. Maybe we should just forget the whole thing.'

'Oh for God's sake, don't be so bloody stupid.' He stood too, angry now.

'Stupid?' Her eyes filled with tears. 'Yes, I think I have been.' And, going into the bedroom, she banged the door closed and locked it. She didn't give a damn where he slept tonight, but it certainly wasn't going to be with her. But Declan made no attempt to follow her. After a few minutes, she heard the front door bang and, peeking through the curtains, she saw him striding down the road without a backward glance. Feeling utterly miserable, Molly got ready for bed, turned off the light and lay wondering where he'd gone. How could such a wonderful evening turn into such a miserable one?

She tossed and turned all night, sleeping fitfully. Finally, she dragged herself out of bed, made some strong coffee and immersed herself in other people's problems. It was almost noon when he let himself into the apartment. He came into the kitchen and his eyes met hers. 'Hi.'

She sighed, noting his conciliatory tone and the dark circles under his eyes. 'Where did you get to?'

'I spent the night in Gareth's. I thought you'd want some space.'

'You thought right.'

He sat down across from her. 'I'm sorry, Moll, I really am. But you have to understand that the reason I didn't tell Enco about the wedding is because you've said all along that it was just one day; that it was the marriage that was important. I knew that you'd be disappointed, but I really believed that if I asked you, you'd have agreed.'

'It would have been nice to have been asked,' Molly mumbled.

He watched her steadily. 'And what would you have said?'

'I'd have told you to level with them,' she retorted. 'You're joining Enco as a senior member of their management team, Declan. Don't you think you should act like one?'

His eyes narrowed. 'What's that supposed to mean?'

'You need to stand up for yourself.'

'I do stand up for myself,' he said, clenching his fists. 'But I made a conscious decision not to tell them about the wedding. I want them to see me as a team-player, not someone who wants time off before I've even started.'

'Oh for God's sake, you're getting married. No company would be that unreasonable.'

He sighed. 'Maybe you're right, but I didn't want to take that chance. I've got to get out of Kelleher's or I'll go mad, Moll. I'm not kidding.'

She saw the almost desperate look in his eyes and nodded slowly. 'Okay.' She closed down her laptop and stood up.

'Where are you going?'

'To shower. Mum's expecting us.'

'Do we have to go?' he groaned.

'Yes,' she snapped. 'They need to know what's happening, and I don't see why I should have to tell them alone.'

'Okay, okay,' he held up his hands and turned away.

Molly was tempted to go and put her arms around him, but something stopped her. She felt angry and hurt, and she wanted him to hurt too. And *he* could be the one to break the news to her sister. For the first time that day, Molly smiled. Standing up to Enco would have been a doddle compared to standing up to Laura.

Oliver threw open the door, smiling, his hand outstretched to Declan. 'Congratulations, lad, I'm delighted for you.'

'Thanks, Oliver,' Declan said, looking embarrassed.

Belle hurried out to greet them too and went up on her toes so that she could kiss Declan's cheek. 'Wonderful news, Declan, I'm so happy for you.' She led the way into the kitchen.

Wiping his mouth on a napkin, Robert immediately stood to shake Declan's hand. 'Good man, well done.'

'Congratulations, Declan.' Laura gave him a little wave from the other side of the table before turning to her children. 'Ashling, Adam, what do you say?'

'Congratulations,' the twins chimed obediently.

Declan grinned at them. 'Thanks, kids.'

Rory thumped down the stairs and, coming into the kitchen, slapped Declan on the back. 'My man!'

'Hey, Rory.'

'So you're going to be loaded now, are ye?' Rory flopped into a chair and grinned up at his future brother-in-law.

'I wouldn't go that far,' Declan said. 'Although I'll definitely be in a better position than I was in Kelleher's.'

'Wouldn't count on it,' Robert muttered, 'no one's safe these days.'

'Oh, Robert,' Belle protested. 'Let him enjoy his moment.'

'Sorry.' Robert smiled and returned his attention to his food.

'If you two have finished, go inside and let Molly and Declan sit down,' Laura told the children.

'Can we watch telly?' Adam asked.

'Of course,' Oliver said.

Molly smiled at the children as they shuffled past and then sat down next to her dad, leaving Declan to take the seat next to Laura.

'A little bit of everything for you, Declan?' Belle asked.

'Grand, thanks.'

Belle smiled. 'And you, Molly?'

'Just some scrambled egg, Mum, thanks.'

'So, when do you start?' Oliver looked expectantly at Declan.

'The week after next.' Declan nodded his thanks as Belle set a plateful of food in front of him.

Robert raised an eyebrow. 'Aren't Kelleher's objecting?'

'No, they're being quite good about it, but then, I suppose it's a relief that I left before they had to give me a redundancy package.'

'You should have taken some holiday leave and you could have helped me with the arrangements,' Laura teased.

Molly gave Declan a sharp nudge and he put down his knife and fork and turned to face Laura. 'About the wedding . . .'

'Yes?'

'I'm afraid we have to postpone it.'

Laura laughed, but stopped as she looked past him and saw her sister's face. 'Tell me you're joking.'

Molly bent her head over her eggs and left Declan to answer. She didn't see any reason to help him through this, no reason at all.

'I'm sorry, Laura, it's true,' Declan said. 'I have to go to Japan on a training course and I'll be away for ten weeks. I leave on the 20th.'

'But you can't!'

'Laura,' Oliver held up his hand. 'I'm sure Declan wouldn't be going if he didn't have to.'

'Unless he's getting cold feet,' Rory said, and received a kick under the table from his mother. 'Ow!'

'I'm not getting cold feet,' Declan said firmly, looking at each member of the Jackson family in turn. 'And I realize how much hassle this will cause.' He gave a helpless shrug. 'All I can say is, I'm sorry.'

'Well, I suppose if you have to go, you have to go.' Laura snapped, her fingers tightening around her mug. 'So what's the new wedding date?'

Molly and Declan exchanged a look of surprise. 'We haven't got one yet,' she admitted.

'Do you still want to marry him?' Rory asked. 'Or will I take him outside and break his legs?'

'Tempting, and last night I might have taken you up on your offer.' Molly smiled at her brother.

'You need to decide on a new date,' Laura insisted.

'What do you think?' Molly asked Declan.

'Well, I'll be back in Dublin on the 18th of September and I'll need time to settle into the job. How about November?'

'November?' Laura screeched.

'You're kidding?' Molly stared at him.

Declan looked taken aback at their reaction. 'Er, no. Why, what's wrong with November?'

Laura looked incredulous. 'For a start, we're wearing summer dresses; we'd freeze in them in December.'

'Couldn't you just wear coats over them?' Robert volunteered, earning a withering glance from his wife.

'Molly?' Belle looked at her daughter. 'What do you want?'

Molly felt more than a little shell-shocked. 'I'm not sure.'

Belle shot her husband a meaningful look and stood up. 'I think we should leave Molly and Declan to talk. Everyone's finished, right?'

Rory grabbed some toast and then obediently followed the others out of the kitchen.

*

'I don't know what to say, Moll.' Declan rubbed a weary hand across his eyes. 'Nothing I say is going to be right. If it's a big deal having the wedding in winter, then maybe we should wait until next year.'

Molly blinked, not quite sure how to respond to that.

'Moll?'

She looked up to find him watching her; he looked positively defeated. She forced a smile. 'Why don't you go and watch the footy? I'll talk to Mum and Laura and see what they think.'

Relief flooded his face and he reached over to give her a quick hug before standing up.

Molly was stacking the dishwasher when her sister and mother returned.

'Well?' Laura demanded.

Molly didn't even look up. 'We haven't decided anything, but I was thinking that maybe we should leave the wedding until next year.' She looked up and caught her mother watching her anxiously. 'I think it would be for the best.'

Laura emptied the dregs of the coffee into the sink and set about making a fresh pot. 'We probably won't lose any of our deposits if we can specify a new date.'

Molly closed the door of the dishwasher. 'I need to think about it, Laura.'

'Quite right,' Belle agreed, taking down three clean mugs. 'There's no rush.'

'But there is, Mum,' Laura started, receiving a glare from her mother.

Molly bit her lip. 'Sorry.'

'It's not your fault,' Laura muttered.

'No, of course it isn't, nor Declan's,' Belle said firmly.

Laura raised an eyebrow. 'How do you make that out?'

Molly couldn't bring herself to defend Declan. 'We'll reimburse you if you lose any deposits, Mum.'

'Don't be silly, I'm not worried about the money.'

'That's not the point,' Laura said stubbornly, 'you shouldn't suffer because of this.'

'No, you shouldn't,' Molly agreed. 'Honestly, Mum, we'll figure something out. Declan keeps telling me how rich he's going to be. He can absorb any extra costs, it's only fair.'

'You really need to decide on a new date,' Laura said again. 'I won't be able to negotiate any deals until you do.'

'Okay. Just give me some time though.' Molly stood up.

Her mother caught her hand as she walked towards the door. 'It will all be fine. It's much more important that Declan finds his feet and is happy.'

Molly felt a pang of guilt. 'I know.' She bent to kiss her mother. 'See ya.'

She was silent on the drive home and, as soon as they got there, she changed into her cycling gear and took out her bike.

'Where are you off to?' Declan asked, giving her a wary look.

'I thought I'd drop over to see Ellen and fill her in.'

He nodded. 'Want me to do anything while you're out?'

Molly shrugged. Declan offering to do housework meant he must be feeling guilty.

'Tell you what, I'll nip down to the supermarket and get in something nice for dinner, how about that?'

'Sure, great.' And with a swift peck on his cheek, Molly cycled off, just relieved to be on her own for a while to gather her thoughts. She would go and see Ellen, but first she needed a bit of space. She turned left onto the seafront road, in the opposite direction to her parents' house and, putting her head down into the wind, she picked up her pace, concentrating all her thoughts on her breathing. For some people it was yoga or meditation that calmed them, for Molly it was cycling. She loved being outdoors, she adored the speed she could work up, and as she pushed herself harder and harder, she loved how it crystallized her thinking. She had resolved many issues on this bike, both professional and personal. She hoped that she could solve this one too, only she didn't think it would be that simple.

'Hey, this is a surprise,' Ellen smiled when she opened the door. 'Want a towel?'

Molly put a hand to her wet face and laughed. 'Yes, please,' she said breathlessly.

'How far have you cycled to get you into that state?' Ellen said, returning with a towel and handing it to her.

'Just to Howth.'

Ellen's eyes widened. 'Crikey. That must be ten miles.'

'About that, and diverting to your house, it's about a twenty-five-mile round trip.'

Ellen filled a glass with water from the tap and handed it to her with a shrewd look. 'You must have been pretty stressed.'

Molly grinned. 'A little.'

Ellen nodded and waited.

'The wedding's postponed.'

Ellen's eyes widened. 'Oh, Molly, why?'

'Declan has to go to Japan for a ten-week induction course. He leaves Monday week.'

'Oh, you poor thing.'

'It does mean that you have a little more time to get your figure back,' Molly joked.

Ellen grinned. 'And I appreciate that, but I hope he isn't going to Japan on my account.'

'No, he's definitely going for himself.' Molly could hear the bitterness in her own voice.

'You're annoyed.' Ellen looked at her, her eyes full of sympathy.

'Of course I bloody am. Declan didn't even try to get the time off for the wedding; in fact, he didn't even tell Enco that we *were* getting married!'

'You said yourself that he wanted this job more than anything, Molly; maybe he was afraid to tell them. There were probably tons of other candidates for the job.'

'But he could have explained the situation,' Molly insisted. 'Then, if they said no, fair enough. He didn't even try. He didn't think or care about the consequence of his actions. Laura's got to cancel all the arrangements and it could cost my folks a fortune.'

Ellen frowned. 'Surely not, when you're only changing the date.'

Molly looked away and said nothing.

Realization dawned on Ellen. 'Are you having second thoughts about marrying Declan?'

'No, but I'm wondering if he is. Perhaps this is just an excuse, Ellen. Living with me is one thing, but signing a marriage contract is something else.'

'No way, you're wrong.' Ellen was adamant. 'Declan is happy with you.'

'I know that, but it's not quite the same thing, is it?'

'Don't do or say anything rash, Molly,' Ellen advised, caressing her bump.

'I won't,' Molly promised, but she couldn't look her friend in the eye.

Chapter Six

12.35 p.m., Monday, 13th July

Laura should have been furious over the wedding being postponed, but in a way she was relieved. Once Molly and Declan decided on a new date, she would be very busy trying to charm people out of penalizing them for changing the date at such short notice, and trying to make the arrangements fit the new date. And when she was busy, she didn't have time to think. When she was busy, there was more chance of her sleeping. While she was immersing herself in her sister's life, there was less time for her to wonder what had happened to her own. While her brain worried about photographers and flowers, the church and the organist, she had less time to dwell on how immeasurably sad she felt. She sometimes tried to figure out when she had started to feel this way. Had it been when the twins started in secondary school? She had found that difficult. It seemed to signal the start of adulthood, of secrets, of independence, and she had mourned the loss of her babies. Also, with them out of the house for such a large portion of the day, she'd felt lonely and useless. She regretted now that she hadn't spent more time with them when they were young. But she had been so young herself, too young to be stuck with two noisy, demanding babies all day long. When the twins started primary school, Robert had wanted to try for another child, but she'd been horrified at the thought. She was only just getting her life back, had only just squeezed back into a size ten and the idea of going through pregnancy again, followed by sleepless nights, was completely abhorrent. But if she'd listened to Robert, she would have a nine-year-old now, who would still want to spend time with her and wouldn't shrink from her hugs.

Laura threw the dregs of her coffee down the sink and carried an armful of laundry upstairs. With a cursory knock, she went into Ashling's room. Her daughter was sprawled on the bed, still in her pyjamas, headphones in and texting. Wrinkling her nose in disgust, Laura went to the window and threw it open. 'This place stinks. I've told you before about eating crisps up here.'

'Don't you ever knock?' Ashling scowled, pulling her earpieces out.

'I did, you just couldn't hear with all that rubbish frying your brain.'

'There's nothing rubbish about The Script, they'll be bigger than U2 one day.'

'I'm delighted for them. Now, will you get dressed and clean this place up, please? It's almost lunchtime. Dad was right, I should have sent you to summer camp for a few weeks; you wouldn't get away with lounging around all day there. Look how lovely it is outside.' She waved at the sun streaming in the window. 'You should be out there, enjoying this amazing weather.'

'Whatever,' Ashling mumbled as her mother left the room.

Laura swung around and studied her with narrowed eyes. 'Excuse me, did you say something?'

'No.'

'Good. I'll expect you downstairs in ten minutes; call your brother.' Laura went into her own room to make the bed, vowing to talk to Robert again about increasing Magda's hours. The cleaner only came in twice a week, but with the kids at home all day during the holidays, Laura needed a lot more help than that. She was about to go back downstairs, when the sound of the twins' voices on the landing stopped her. The only way she found out anything these days was by eavesdropping.

'You've to get dressed,' Ashling was saying, 'and you'd better clean your room or you're in for it.'

'Is she in another one of her moods?' came Adam's reply, making Laura wince.

'When is she not in a mood? Although, as you're the apple of her eye, you won't suffer.'

'Shut up.'

'Shut up yourself,' Ashling retorted before going back into her room. Laura waited until she heard the bathroom door close on Adam before hurrying downstairs, tears pricking her eyes. Her granny had always said you should never 'earwig' on other people's conversations; you only heard bad things about yourself. But it wasn't the words Ashling had used that Laura minded – she'd said worse about Belle in the past – it was her tone that hurt. It was so scathing, so dismissive. Robert would say she was attaching too much significance to standard teenage lingo, but Laura didn't think so. She didn't imagine the glazed look that came over her children's faces when she tried to talk to them. They weren't like that with their grandparents; Ashling would gossip away to Belle for hours if she could, while Adam liked nothing better than to argue the merits and flaws of soccer players and teams with Oliver.

As for Robert, well, her daughter became a different person once he put his key in the door. That might have something to do with the facts that he was always good for the 'loan' of a fiver and that Ashling could wrap him around her little finger. Her daughter might ask her permission to go to a sleepover at a friend's house and Laura would say no, not on a school night. Within an hour of coming home, Ashling would have curled up on the sofa beside Robert, begging him to intervene. Then, over dinner, Robert would casually say, Is it such a big deal for Ash to spend the night studying with her friend? Studying silly magazines like Molly's, Laura would fume. But then Ashling would use her trump card.

She was top of her class. No one could accuse her of slacking. And so, Laura would have to give in and Ashling wouldn't be able to resist shooting her mother a triumphant look. It was almost as if she were another woman, competing for Robert's attention, which, her sister would no doubt say, was exactly what she was.

Adam was easier, though no more communicative. But his silences, slovenly behaviour and occasional moodiness weren't personal, he just didn't think much beyond his own little world. And if he felt like sharing, then it was his twin he turned to. Laura hoped her daughter did likewise, but she doubted it. Ashling was a strong-minded girl who rarely invited guidance or advice. She was almost exactly like Laura had been at the same age, and look what had happened to her.

'I thought you said lunch was ready?' The lady in question stood, arms crossed, in the kitchen doorway.

'By the time you've laid the table, it will be,' Laura retorted, putting the grill on and taking out bread and cheese.

'Why do I need to lay the table? Can't we eat it on our laps and watch TV?'

'No. Set the table.' Laura slammed thick slices of cheddar onto bread and shoved it under the grill.

'Ah, Mum, please?' Adam loped in and went straight to the fridge for the milk carton. '*The Simpsons* are on in a minute.'

'*The Simpsons* are on almost every station at some point in the day,' Laura pointed out but felt too tired to argue. 'Go ahead, watch your silly programme if you want to. Why on earth would you want to sit and have lunch with your mother?'

With a grin, Adam patted her head and turned to give his sister a thumbs-up. 'Result!'

While the two of them sprawled in front of the TV munching cheese toasties, Laura sat in the kitchen with her black coffee and

Ryvita, staring blindly out into their landscaped garden. Was this it, she wondered, miserably. Was this the sum of her life at only thirty-three years old? It wasn't how she'd seen things at eighteen. Then she was sure, just as Ash was now, that her life was going to be one great big adventure. Oliver had always told them that if they worked hard they could do and be anything. And she had listened and worked hard. Sadly, she hadn't listened as closely to her mother's gentle pep talks about boys and so had ended up pregnant with twins at just nineteen.

Robert had swept her off her feet. Looking at him now, it was hard to believe he was capable of that, but Laura had been more easily impressed back then. Robert was from a posh family and, though he was only a college student, he had his own car and a seemingly bottomless wallet. While her girlfriends were sharing pizza with their dates, Robert was taking her to proper restaurants. When he'd taken her away for the weekend, it had been to a hotel – no camping site for him. And then, on her nineteenth birthday, he'd presented her with a gold locket and she knew that this was love.

The phone rang, making her start. When the twins made no move to get it, she went out to the extension in the hall. In a couple of years, when they started dating, she'd probably be killed in the rush to answer the phone. Although, in this era of mobiles and texting, landlines with no privacy were probably redundant. Still, for all she knew, Ash and Adam might already be involved. They might be dating already – the thought made her feel sick. 'Hello?' she answered, distracted.

'Hi, darling, it's me.'

Well of course it's you, Laura thought irritably. Why did he feel he had to say that every time? Didn't he think she'd recognize his voice after fifteen years together? 'Hi.'

'How are you? Any news?'

'No news.'

'Are the kids there?'

'In front of the TV.'

He chuckled. 'Where else! Could you drop my navy suit to the dry-cleaners, Laura?'

'Sure.'

'Great, thanks. I should be home around the usual time. See you later.'

'Bye.' Laura hung up. And this was the man who'd swept her off her feet. Robert seemed so boring, so sedentary and so middle-aged now. On a good day, he irritated Laura. On a bad day, she could barely stand the thought of being in the same room as him, let alone share his bed. She went back into the kitchen and then cursed when the phone rang again. Robert had obviously remembered some other menial task he needed her to do.

'What?' she barked into the phone.

'Laura?'

She closed her eyes briefly. 'Oh, hi, Mum.'

'Is everything okay, darling?'

'Yes, of course. Sorry for being so short, I'm just in the middle of something.'

'I won't keep you,' Belle promised. 'It's just that Dad and I are going out to Greystones for a walk as it's such a nice day and we wondered if the twins would like to come along and give you a little break.'

'Oh, thanks, Mum, you're so good but I think they have an aversion to sunlight. They're currently in front of the TV with the curtains closed. Hang on though, I'll ask.' She held the phone to her chest. 'Kids, it's Nana. She wants to know if you'd like to go to Greystones.'

'Yeah, cool.' Ash was beside her in seconds, smiling broadly.

Laura stared at her, wondering why she couldn't elicit that sort of reaction from her daughter. If she'd been the one to suggest a walk, Ash would have refused point-blank. She swallowed hard. 'What about you, Adam?' she called.

'Yeah, okay.'

'They'd love to go, Mum.'

'Wonderful. See you in about thirty minutes.'

After waving them all off, Laura debated what to do. Have a relaxing soak in the bath and watch some of the rubbishy soaps that she daren't switch on when the kids were around? Or perhaps she'd phone the beautician and see if they could fit her in for a facial and manicure. Or she could always go into town and have a browse round the shops, shopping usually cheered her up. Although she didn't think it would today; for some reason her mood was very dark. Perhaps she'd phone Penny. They weren't exactly friends; Penny's only son was at school with the twins and they'd served on a couple of committees together, but she was always saying they should meet up for coffee or something a little stronger, so why not today?

'Oh sorry, darling, I'm up to my elbows in pastry! I have a dinner party tonight and, in a moment of sheer lunacy, decided to make dessert from scratch!'

Laura laughed. 'I'm sure it will be gorgeous. Call me next week and we'll arrange something.'

'Lovely, can't wait. Bye, darling.'

Laura put down the phone feeling envious of Penny's guests. She wouldn't mind getting dressed up and having a night out and a laugh; it would be even better if she didn't have to take Robert with her.

Finding the house too quiet, Laura eventually decided to go into town and within a couple of hours had bought some silky new lingerie and a soft brown leather bag with a price label that would make Robert's head spin. She was hesitating over a stunning choker that was horrendously expensive, when her mobile rang. She looked at the display and saw it was her mother. Frowning, she answered it. 'Hi, Mum, is everything okay?'

'Oh yes, Laura. I was just wondering if it would be okay if we took the children to the cinema and then out to tea.'

'Of course, if you want, although I think you'll find it hard to agree on a movie.'

Belle laughed. 'We already have; we're all dying to see the new Bond film.'

'Oh, I see. Well, I'm in town, perhaps I could meet you—'

'Sorry, darling, we're actually going to Dundrum town centre.'

'Oh, okay. Well, have fun.' Laura hung up and handed the choker to the sales assistant. 'I'll take this.' She walked smartly out of the shop, heels tapping, and decided to go for a coffee. She was looking around, trying to decide where to go, when her eyes rested on the Westbury hotel. Minutes later, she was nestled in a plush sofa in a corner of the elegant lounge and looking at a menu.

A pretty young girl came over, smiling. 'Good afternoon, madam. What can I get you?'

'Good afternoon. I'll have . . . a gin and tonic, please.'

The girl nodded. 'Certainly, madam.'

As she waited for her drink, Laura smiled to herself, feeling deliciously naughty and quite decadent. She'd occasionally had an afternoon drink with girlfriends, but she'd never ever done it alone. 'Silly me,' she murmured, marvelling at how her mood had lightened.

This was lovely, much nicer than sitting in a smelly, noisy cinema. She had never understood the attraction, and taking the children along to Disney movies when they were younger had been a trial. And yet, thinking of her parents and children huddled together in the darkness and scoffing popcorn made her feel a pang of jealousy. How had her parents managed to maintain a relationship with her sullen children when she couldn't?

The waitress returned with her drink and a dish of nuts and she took a grateful sip. She felt like throwing it back, but then she'd look like some sad lush when, in fact, she was just a woman enjoying some quiet time in very pleasant surroundings.

'Not a bad way to spend the afternoon, is it?'

Laura turned her head to see a man sitting nearby. She hadn't noticed him before, but then he was half-hidden by a potted plant. 'It is, although I feel a bit naughty,' she replied with a giggle.

'We could be naughty together,' he held up his glass, his eyes crinkling at the corners. 'Can I tempt you to another?'

Laura hesitated for only a moment and then smiled slowly. 'Why not?'

Chapter Seven

7.20 p.m., Thursday, 16th July

Molly sat in front of the TV with her laptop on her knee. Technically, she had finished work for the day, but she couldn't help scanning the message boards in the hope of finding BettyBlu or Smithy. She found a bitchy exchange going on between some girls who seemed to be just looking for a row. One girl, Jess, was down because she'd been dumped and another girl had told her to cop on, get a life and stop being such a loser, that it was no wonder her boyfriend dumped her. Molly couldn't help grinning, but still Tess, who was on duty, shouldn't really have allowed this exchange. She emailed a mild rebuke to her assistant, asking her to keep an eye out for more posts on this thread, and had just switched off her machine when she heard Declan's key in the door. She froze, dreading what she had to do. Ellen had tried to talk her out of it, but Molly was adamant. If there was one thing her training had taught her, it was to trust her gut.

'Hi, love.' Declan came into the room, flicking through the post. He'd met some colleagues for a last lunch before his departure and then gone shopping for new socks, shirts and an enormous holdall.

'Hi. How did it go?'

He shrugged. 'Yeah, okay. Still working?'

'Just finished, but I haven't had a chance to make any dinner.'

'Thank God for that.' He bent to kiss her, grinning. 'Don't worry, I'll go out and get something and then we'd better agree a date or your sister will murder us.'

'Don't worry about Laura. It's what we want that matters.'

He kissed her again, then straightened. 'I'll go take a shower and then I'll go and get dinner. Oh, by the way, Gareth said he might drop over.' He hesitated. 'Or do you want me to put him off?'

'No, of course not.' Molly looked away, afraid to meet Declan's eyes. When he'd gone into the bathroom, she put her laptop on charge and went to make some tea. She didn't really want it, but it gave her something to do with her hands and perhaps it would calm her. She had just set the pot and two mugs on the table when Declan returned, looking gorgeous in faded denims and a black T-shirt. She had a moment of doubt, but dismissed it; she was doing the right thing.

'So, what do you want to eat?' he asked.

'I'm not hungry yet. Sit down, I want to talk to you.'

'Sounds serious.' He lowered himself into the chair opposite. Molly said nothing, just poured the tea.

'You're scaring me now, Moll. What is it?'

'It's about the wedding.'

'I've told you, pick a date and I'll do everything I can to fit in with it.'

She added milk before replying. 'I don't want to, Declan.'

'I know you don't want to postpone it, Moll, but there's nothing I can do now.'

'No, that's not what I meant.'

'What then?' He frowned, confused.

Molly stared into her tea for a moment, then raised her eyes to meet his. 'I don't want to pick a new date, Declan. I don't want to get married.'

'What?' He stared at her.

'I'm not convinced any more that you want to marry me—'

'That's ridiculous.'

'And I'd prefer to leave it just for now,' she continued. 'We can discuss it again once you've settled into your new job but, for now, I think we should forget all about it. And honestly, Declan, I'm not angry.'

'But?' he prompted, his expression guarded now.

'Your decision not to tell Enco about the wedding was a bit of a blow and it has made me re-think taking such a big step.'

He looked totally baffled. 'So you don't want to split up?'

'No, I'm just suggesting that we shelve the marriage idea for a few months.'

'If that's what you want.'

His expression was closed and she couldn't figure out if he was hurt or relieved. 'Be honest, Declan. Isn't it what you want too?'

'Of course it isn't, but as this is all my fault, then I suppose I have to accept it.'

The doorbell rang and she sent up a silent prayer for Gareth's wonderful sense of timing.

With one last look that was reproachful and something else Molly couldn't pinpoint, Declan went to answer the door. Molly stayed at the table, allowing them a moment alone. Would Declan blurt out everything or wait until he was in the pub with a couple of beers inside him?

The answer was clear when Gareth bounced into the kitchen moments later, a broad smile on his face. 'Well, how's the bride-to-be?'

She shot Declan a quick glance. 'Grand, thanks. Come to drag your brother to the pub?'

'Are you coming?'

'No, I think I'll have a bath and an early night.'

Declan frowned. 'What about food?'

'Why don't you grab something at the pub? I'll make a sandwich.'

'Sure?'

She smiled. 'Yeah, sure.'

He slipped into his jacket and gave her a brief peck on the cheek. 'Okay then, see you later.'

'Have fun,' she said with forced cheeriness.

Alone, Molly's composure deserted her and, resting her head on her arms, she allowed the tears to come. What had she done? Why couldn't she have just turned the other cheek and agreed a new date for the wedding? Was she just making a point, sulking because Declan had put his job before her? The doorbell rang and she groaned, quickly wiping her eyes on her sleeve. Perhaps she wouldn't answer it, it was probably someone selling something. The bell went again and again and again. For God's sake! Molly got to her feet and stormed out to the door, ready to give who-ever it was a good telling off. 'What the hell do you think you're doing?' she demanded as she flung it open.

Laura blinked at the attack. 'I just dropped in to say hello. Is it a bad time?'

Molly stood back to let her sister in. 'Sorry,' she mumbled and, blowing her nose, led the way into the kitchen.

'Are you okay?'

'Fine.'

'You don't look it.'

Molly made a face. 'Hay fever.'

'Ah.'

'Where's Declan?'

'Gone to the pub with Gareth. I was just going to have a long bath and an early night.' Molly knew she was being rude, but she didn't trust herself not to break down, and the last person she wanted to cry in front of was her sister.

'Oh, right. Well, I just wondered if you'd come to a decision.' Molly frowned.

Laura looked at her in exasperation. 'On a new date for the wedding?'

Molly turned to the sink and began to wash up. 'We've decided to postpone making a decision until Declan comes back.'

'But you can't do that! Our only hope of hanging on to the deposits is if we can give them a new date.'

'If you give them a new date, there's a good chance we'd have to change it again,' Molly pointed out, not looking at her. 'They wouldn't be happy with that either, would they?'

'But what's the problem? Why can't you just pick a date and have done with it?'

'It's not going to happen, Laura. Just leave it,' Molly said, with more force than she'd intended.

'Have you and Declan had a fight?' Laura persisted. 'Has this something to do with Luke Fortune?'

'What? No, of course not!' Molly shook her head in astonishment. 'Why would you say that?'

Laura shrugged. 'You haven't been yourself since you saw him.'

'How can you say that? You've only seen me a couple of times since.'

'And you haven't been the same.'

Molly's mouth settled into a sullen line. 'I'd really like to take my bath now.'

With a shrug, Laura turned to leave, but paused in the doorway, her face thoughtful. 'Perhaps you're right. Maybe you should take stock before taking the plunge.'

Molly looked at her in surprise. 'Really?'

'Yeah. I'll take care of the cancellations first thing. I'll let you know how I get on.'

'Thanks, Laura,' Molly said, suddenly feeling guilty for the way she'd talked to her sister. 'I'm sorry for messing you about.'

Laura shrugged. 'Don't worry about it, you did what you had to do.'

Molly thought of her sister's words when she was lying in the bath, the water barely covering her body – if they ever did move, the size of the hot water tank would be one of the first things she'd check. Had Laura hit on something that she hadn't? Would it have occurred to her to cancel her wedding plans if she hadn't seen Luke that day? It was true he'd been on her mind a lot. She found her thoughts returning frequently to the past and she'd had difficulties concentrating on her work. What stunned her was that Laura had spotted her preoccupation. Giving up on her tepid bath, Molly stepped out, towelled herself dry and, wrapped in her terry robe, went out to fetch her laptop. Curled up on the sofa, she once again typed in Luke's name and the word 'rugby' and pressed the 'search' button. The usual results came back, results she'd studied a number of times already. It had to be him. She sat staring at the screen and then, on impulse, picked up the phone.

'Are you in bed?'

Ellen laughed. 'You're kidding, I'm just in from work. Thursday is late night at the salon, remember?'

'I forgot, sorry. So you probably just want to fall into bed.'

'No, I want to sit down, soak my feet and have a nice cup of tea.'

'Could I come over?'

'As if you need to ask. I'll put the kettle on.'

Throwing on a tracksuit, Molly took out her bike, pulled on her helmet and set out for Marino. Unlike her flat, Ellen's house was most definitely a home, full of warmth, welcoming and pretty. It was small, with only two bedrooms, but Ellen had knocked down walls to create a wonderful dual-aspect open-plan kitchen and living area that was airy and bright. The garden was tiny, but Ellen had filled it with flowers and it was a wonderful place to relax on a sunny afternoon.

As Molly pushed open the gate and took the helmet off her still damp hair, Ellen was already in the doorway, looking anxious. Molly grinned. 'It's okay, there's nothing wrong, I just fancied a chat.'

'Suits me.' Ellen smiled and, leaving her bike in the porch, Molly followed her inside. 'Tea? Green, peppermint, ginger—'

Molly wrinkled her nose. 'Ginger?'

Ellen rubbed her tummy. 'Wonderful for indigestion, which I seem to get a lot of these days. I think Buster has reduced my stomach to the size of a golf ball.'

Molly laughed. 'Builder's tea for me, please.'

'Coming up.'

'I don't care what you say about Buster,' Molly said, studying her friend, 'pregnancy really suits you; you look wonderful.' And it was true, Ellen's long blonde hair had a healthy shine and her blue eyes were bright and clear.

Ellen raised her eyebrows. 'It must be the lack of food and sleepless nights.'

'You'd never know,' Molly assured her, 'and your skin looks amazing.'

'My skin _is_ good,' Ellen admitted, putting a hand to her cheek. 'Probably because I can't ever stand the smell of chocolate at the minute and I'm living on water and herbal teas.'

'I can't believe you only have four weeks to go.'

'Four weeks and two days. Oh, lord, I hope I don't go over my time.'

'If you do, I'll feed you hot curry morning, noon and night,' Molly promised. 'Buster will come out like a bullet!'

Ellen grinned. 'My mother says she has lots of tricks to induce labour up her sleeve.'

'Is she excited?'

'Is she what? First grandchild, she's over the moon! Pity I can't say the same for Dad.'

'Is he still upset?'

Ellen poured the boiling water into two mugs and handed Molly one. 'He just doesn't understand why I want to do this alone. As if having Andrew around would enhance any child's life.' She gave a humourless laugh. 'More like, teach Buster how to roll a joint, snort a line of coke and get a fifty out of Mum's wallet without getting caught.'

Molly shot her a sympathetic look. She was so preoccupied with her own problems and Ellen was always so cheerful, that sometimes she forgot that Ellen was about to become a single mother. 'You're better off on your own. Not that you are on your own,' Molly added hurriedly, realizing how awful that sounded. 'You've got me and Declan and your folks, of course, we'll all look after you and Buster.'

'You still on for being my number two?' Ellen asked with a tremulous smile.

'Course!' In the very unlikely event that Ellen's mother wouldn't be around when she went into labour, Molly had promised to be in the delivery ward with her friend. 'My wellies are cleaned and shiny and in a permanent state of readiness by the front door and I've even bought the *Dummies' Guide to Delivering A Baby* and I study it every night.'

'Eejit,' Ellen said with an affectionate smile.

'I could move in with you if you want,' Molly offered. 'Then you wouldn't have to worry about him popping out when you're on your own.'

Ellen pulled a face. 'Firstly, babies don't usually just "pop out", Moll.'

'You know what I mean. The offer's there if you want it.'

'Thanks.' Ellen's eyes were thoughtful as she sipped her tea.

'When are you giving up work? It can't be easy being on your feet all day.'

'The end of the month and no, it's not, but Ruby has been great.'

'Why wouldn't she be? You're her best hairdresser, she's probably terrified you won't come back.'

'I can't afford not to,' Ellen said. 'Anyway, you didn't come over at this hour of night to talk about maternity leave. What's up? Have you set a new date?'

'No.'

Ellen looked at her. 'Molly?'

'I'm not going to, Ellen.'

'What?'

'I've decided it's better to wait.'

Ellen's eyes narrowed. 'Is this Declan's idea?'

'No, honestly, it's mine.'

'I don't get it, I thought you couldn't wait to get him up that aisle.'

'Exactly.' Molly cringed. 'I've been the one driving everything and I'm wondering now, if I hadn't, well . . .'

'That's guys for you, Moll, don't read too much into it. Declan loves you.'

Molly nodded. 'I think so too, but maybe it's time I let him take the driving seat for once. I've told him we'll talk about a new date when he gets back from Japan, but I'm not going to push it.'

Ellen looked doubtful. 'What does he think about this?'

'He doesn't seem impressed, but I'm sure he's secretly relieved.'

'Where is he now?'

'Gareth's taken him out for a pint.'

'Are you sure you're doing this for the right reasons?'

Molly groaned. 'Now you sound like Laura.'

'You told Laura?' Ellen looked surprised and a bit put out.

'She dropped in and caught me at a weak moment. She thinks I'm acting like this because I saw Luke.'

Ellen's eyes widened. 'Is she right?'

'Maybe,' Molly admitted.

'Oh, Moll.'

'Don't say it like that.'

'What is it about this guy? Okay, he was your first love, but you were just kids. Why are you even thinking about him?'

'I'm not sure I ever actually stopped,' Molly admitted, tears in her eyes.

Chapter Eight

'When I met Andrew, I knew immediately that it was different; that he was someone special,' Ellen said, putting her feet up on the footstool and resting her hands on her bump.

Molly looked at her in surprise. Ellen hadn't mentioned her ex in ages; it usually upset her and she was trying hard to be positive, convinced her mood would affect the baby.

'Before him, you went through guys like hot dinners,' Molly teased. It had been when they worked together in a beauty salon in the centre of Dublin. Molly had been a poor university student, washing hair and sweeping floors to earn some spending money. Ellen, two years older, had been training as a hair stylist.

Though very different, they had hit it off straight away. Ellen was the one who forced Molly to abandon her books every so often and go dancing. But while Ellen was always dating, Molly shied away from men.

'You're not a lesbo, are you?' Ellen had asked one night after Molly had knocked back a particularly gorgeous guy.

'Don't think so.' Molly had grinned. 'Wanna check?'

'Seriously though, why don't you date, Moll?'

'I do date.'

'Not for long. As soon as a guy gets the teeniest bit serious, you give him his marching orders.'

'Once bitten . . .' Molly had said.

'It was Luke, wasn't it?' Ellen said now, her eyes widening as the realization dawned upon her. 'He was the reason you didn't want to date anyone, you were pining for Luke.'

Molly rolled her eyes. 'I was not pining. And, if you remember, between university, the salon and studying, I didn't exactly have time for dating.'

'I couldn't understand it at all,' Ellen smiled. 'My folks were so strict when I was at school that I couldn't wait to find myself a fella.'

'You found a lot more than one!'

'I was man mad,' Ellen agreed, unabashed.

'And then you met Andrew and fell madly in love.' Molly wasn't surprised Ellen had fallen for the boy from Donegal; he was a catch with his curly brown hair, blue-green eyes and that oh-so-sexy accent.

'He was gorgeous,' Ellen murmured, patting her tummy. 'Let's hope the good genes and not the self-destructive ones are passed onto Buster.'

'This baby is going to be fine,' Molly was firm. 'Nurture is as important as nature and you're going to be an amazing mum.'

'I think Andrew would have been a great dad too, if he could only have straightened himself out,' Ellen said, tears in her eyes. 'I know it's wrong, but I can't help blaming his family; they must have seen the signs and did nothing to stop him. Still, I was guilty of that myself for a while, wasn't I?'

'It's human nature to give people you love the benefit of the doubt, to convince yourself that there isn't really a problem.'

But the more Molly learned about the workings of the human mind, the problems people faced and the signs to watch out for when things started to go wrong, the more she'd realized that Andrew was in trouble. She'd noticed the mood swings, the sudden temper, and she'd agonized over whether she should say something to Ellen. She kept hoping that he would sort himself out and she wouldn't have to, but instead, Andrew got worse. Molly couldn't help herself being watchful around him and, of course, Ellen had finally noticed.

Declan said she should just tell Ellen, but Molly knew that her friend wouldn't want to hear the truth. Finally, one night after a party at Ellen and Andrew's flat, when everyone else had gone home, Andrew had gone to bed and Declan was snoring on the sofa, it came to a head. Ellen had confronted Molly and demanded to know why she didn't like Andrew. Molly had tried to avoid answering, had told Ellen she was imagining things, that she'd had too much to drink and was talking rubbish, but Ellen wouldn't let her off the hook. And so, finally, backed into a corner with no obvious way out, Molly had told her. 'He's an addict, Ellen,' she'd said, hating the fact that she had to be the one to break her friend's heart.

But Ellen hadn't believed her, had accused her of being jealous, of not wanting her to be happy, oh, of all sorts of things. And then she'd told Molly to get out and never come back.

It was over a year before Molly had heard from her again. She could still remember that night so vividly. Declan had opened the door and then made himself scarce while Molly drew her friend into their small sitting room.

'I knew he dabbled in drugs.' Ellen had sat on the edge of the sofa, pale and thin, a ghost of her former self. Molly particularly remembered her nails; the nails she had spent so much time manicuring were now chipped and neglected. 'I thought he had it under control. Except, of course, he hadn't. And I pretended, just like his friends and his mum and dad, that it wasn't really happening.' And she'd looked at Molly, her eyes empty and hopeless. 'But I came to tell you that I've stopped pretending now.'

'I nearly lost you because of him,' Ellen said now. 'But even then, I couldn't walk away. How many times, Molly? How many chances did I give him?'

Molly shifted over on the sofa and squeezed her hand. 'You did everything you possibly could, Ellen, and you were right to try. But I'm afraid that you can't help anyone with an addiction unless they want to be helped.'

'It was only when I found out that I was pregnant that I knew I had to leave,' Ellen said now, her hands caressing her bump.

To make sure that he didn't pester her or turn up on her doorstep when she was obviously pregnant, Ellen had left the prestigious salon in the city, taken a job in a tiny hairdresser's in the suburbs and bought her little house in Marino. She'd got it quite cheap as it was in a sorry state of repair, but renovating it gave her some much-needed distraction. She'd scrubbed, scraped, painted and papered. She'd dug the garden, had the bathroom suite replaced and then, with love, planned the nursery.

'Have you heard how he's doing?' Molly asked.

Ellen shook her head. 'I promised Barbara, his sister, that I'd keep in touch, but I haven't. I'd like to know if he's okay,' she explained, 'but I'm not sure I could handle it if she told me he was worse, or even on the streets.'

Molly hugged her. 'This is a small town and bad news travels fast; you'd have heard if he was in real trouble.'

Ellen smiled. 'You're right.'

'And you leaving was probably just the wake-up call he needed, he might even be in rehab right now.'

'I hope so.'

'Will you tell Barbara about Buster?'

'I don't think so, at least not yet.' Ellen's brow creased with worry. 'She'd be sure to tell Andrew, and then he'd want to see the baby and I don't think I could allow that, Molly. He'd have to be clean for quite some time before I could trust him near Buster.'

'Of course, Buster must come first, you're quite right. Anyway, you don't have to worry about it right now, just concentrate on your baby and think of all the happy times ahead.'

'I'm trying to, but sometimes I can't help feeling guilty. Andrew's going to be a father and he has a right to know that.'

'He has no rights until he gets help. You're not trying to hurt him, Ellen, you are simply protecting your child.' Molly sighed. 'Is that what's keeping you awake at night?'

'No, I think that's more to do with getting kicks in the ribs and having to wee every five minutes,' Ellen said, pulling out a tissue and blowing her nose. 'Anyway, enough about Andrew, we're supposed to be talking about you and Luke. And Declan – let's not forget your fiancé.'

'I haven't forgotten him,' Molly protested.

'But?'

'It's just that Luke and I have history.'

Ellen looked at her curiously. 'Go on.'

'Do you remember me telling you about my friend, Ruth?' Molly asked.

'The girl that died?'

Molly nodded. 'Luke was her twin brother.'

'Oh my gosh!'

'After Ruth died, their mother fell apart. Their dad worked as an IT consultant for a large multinational and he put in for a transfer. They moved to Bordeaux a month later.'

'And you never saw Luke again?'

Molly shook her head. 'Not until that day at the airport.'

It was time for Ellen to give the hug. 'You poor thing. How come you didn't tell me about this before?'

'It was too hard, I suppose. I think I was in shock for a long time and then, once I started university, I escaped into my books. It was how I coped.' Molly looked up and smiled. 'Until a certain nutty hairstylist insisted on dragging me out clubbing – that helped too.'

'I'm glad.' Ellen searched her face. 'It must have been quite a shock seeing him again.'

'It was,' Molly said, 'but you know, perhaps it was meant to be.'

'How do you mean?'

'Don't you think it's strange that Luke turns up out of the blue, just as Declan's about to leave? It seems like fate.'

Ellen looked alarmed. 'I'm not sure what you're saying, Molly, but I have a feeling I'm not going to like it.'

Molly chuckled. 'Don't worry, I'm not planning on hopping on a plane to Bordeaux.'

'Thank God for that,' Ellen muttered.

'I don't have to.' Molly's smile was triumphant. 'Because Luke's coming here.'

Chapter Nine

Molly had tried to be grown up about the situation, but she was finding it hard. As a counsellor, she could understand and even excuse Declan's actions. But as a girlfriend, as a prospective wife, she found she couldn't. The long and the short of it was that she'd come last on his list and that not only hurt, but it shook her confidence in what they had together. How could she trust him now? How did she know if or when he would put someone or something before her and their marriage? And when they had children, would they always have to take a back seat to his career too? Still, she made a real effort to hide her feelings and pretend that everything was okay. She tried to be understanding and supportive, but she had been finding it more and more difficult, as once Declan had apologized for letting her down, he'd thrown himself into preparations for his trip and seemed to be really looking forward to it. Pig.

And now they were here, back at the airport, and he was his usual jittery, hyper self and she could see that, in his head, he'd already left. She wondered why she'd bothered coming with him. He glanced at his watch – the third time in as many minutes – and she stood up abruptly. 'Look, I'm going to go.' She forced a smile. 'You'll be happier down at the gate.' Even if the plane wasn't due to take off for another couple of hours.

He stood too, looking relieved. 'Yeah, no point in you hanging around this place.'

Molly nodded. 'Right, well, good luck. I hope it goes well.' Dear God, she'd be shaking his hand in a minute and saying 'cheerio'!

'I'll phone as soon I get there,' he promised.

'Do. Safe journey.'

He took her in his arms and though she tried to respond, she remained stiff as a board in his embrace. He kissed her gently and looked into her eyes. 'I'm sorry, Moll. Wait for me?'

Molly gave a nervous laugh. 'Of course. Go on, get out of here.'

He smiled, hugged her one more time, and slinging his bag over his shoulder, strode purposefully away, pausing briefly at the door to wave.

Molly kept her smile in place as she raised her hand, and then he was gone. For a mad moment she thought of running after him and telling him that she loved him, that of course he was right to go, that he had her blessing and she was sorry for being unreasonable, but her feet refused to move and, after only a moment's hesitation, she turned on her heel and walked towards the escalator. In Arrivals, she made her way towards the bank, looking around her all the time. Stupid! She shook her head. What did she think? That he'd be standing in the exact same place as last time, waiting for her? Her mobile rang and she fished it out of her pocket, checking the display before putting it to her ear. 'Hi, Ellen.'

'Is he gone?'

'Yeah.'

'Come over.'

Molly continued walking aimlessly around the arrivals hall, looking around her. 'I dunno, I've got stuff to do.'

'Don't give me that. Come over right now, we've got to talk.'

Molly sighed. 'Okay. I'm on my way.'

It had been a mistake to tell Ellen what she was thinking of doing, Molly realized as she drove to Santry, turned down through Coolock and then right onto the Malahide road. She had expected her friend to be much more receptive to the idea; she had always been the daredevil, and Molly had expected her to see this as a great adventure. But Ellen had been very dubious, and begged her to reconsider. Molly couldn't understand her concerns. Surely it was a very sensible thing to do, and the perfect time to do it. In fact, the more Molly thought about it, the more she convinced herself that it really was fate. Still, Ellen didn't know the whole story, although Molly had a feeling that if she did, she'd be even more worried.

As she turned into the narrow street where Ellen lived, Molly was surprised to see a large 4×4 parked outside the house, and positively confused when she realized it was Laura's; what on earth was she doing here? But by the time she'd parked Declan's car and climbed out, Molly had figured it out and her blood began to boil. Ellen opened the door before she could ring the bell and gave her a guilty, apologetic smile. 'Hi.'

'How could you?' Molly hissed, and barged past her into the kitchen where Laura was sipping coffee and leafing through one of Ellen's maternity magazines. 'There's no point in trying to talk me out of it, I've made up my mind.'

Laura looked up, her face blank.

'I hadn't told her,' Ellen mumbled from behind.

Molly closed her eyes and sighed.

Laura watched them both, eyebrows raised. 'I can't wait.'

Molly threw Ellen a murderous look and sank into a chair.

'I'm sorry, Molly, but I was worried about you.' Ellen hastily poured her friend a coffee.

'What on earth is there to worry about?'

'Sorry. Maybe it's my hormones.'

'You blame everything on your hormones,' Molly retorted.

'Is either of you going to tell me what's going on?' Laura asked mildly, 'or shall I just pretend I'm not here?'

Molly looked from her sister to Ellen and then back again. 'Fine, I'll tell you, but I don't want any lectures—'

Laura tossed the magazine on the table. 'Oh, for crying out loud, Molly, you're worse than the twins, just spit it out.'

'Right, I will.' Molly swallowed hard and then met her sister's curious gaze. 'I've decided that I'm going to try and find Luke.'

Laura blinked. 'Luke Fortune?'

'Do you know any other Luke?'

'Don't be smart,' Laura retorted automatically, in the same voice she used with her children. 'But where will you start? It's a bit like looking for a needle in a haystack, isn't it?'

'No, I've already found him – sort of.'

'Through the rugby?'

Molly nodded.

'Hello?' Ellen looked at Laura, her eyes round in disbelief. 'Why are you asking her how she's going to do it, the question surely is *why* she's even thinking of doing it?'

Laura nodded and looked at her sister. 'So, why are you thinking of doing it?'

Molly smiled. This wasn't the reaction she'd been expecting. 'He's been on my mind a lot since I saw him in the airport. I'd like to see him properly just one more time.'

'I say it's a bad idea. She's only doing it because she's mad at Declan.'

'That's not true—'

'It is.' Ellen was adamant. 'If he wasn't on his way to Japan, you wouldn't have given Luke a second thought. Come on, Moll, you're the psychologist, I shouldn't have to tell *you* this.'

Molly experienced a moment of doubt. Was Ellen right? Was her proposed search less about Luke and more about Declan? She looked back at her sister, who was remaining uncharacteristically silent. 'What do you think?'

'I think you should do it.'

Molly blinked, but Laura seemed serious. 'You do?'

'What!' Ellen spluttered out a mouthful of ginger tea.

Laura shrugged. 'I'm sorry, Ellen. I realize you brought me here to dissuade her, but I happen to think it's a good idea. Luke was special and he left so suddenly that I'm sure Molly must have questions she'd like to ask him. And with Declan off in Japan, this is the perfect, perhaps her only, opportunity.'

'That's it, exactly.' Molly shot Ellen a triumphant look, although she couldn't remember the last time she and Laura had agreed on anything, which was slightly worrying.

'I don't like it,' Ellen repeated. 'What do you hope to achieve? You haven't seen this guy in how many years?'

'Twelve, nearly thirteen.'

'Well then. You're both completely different people now. He's probably married with a gang of kids.'

'It won't make any difference. Molly and Luke were very close for two years,' Laura said quietly. 'I'm sure he'd want to see her as much as she wants to see him, even if it's only to catch up.'

'I didn't realize you'd dated for so long.' Ellen looked at Molly in surprise. 'Is he the only guy you went out with apart from Declan?'

Molly hesitated and then nodded.

'Luke was the kicker for his school's rugby team and he was gorgeous,' Laura told Ellen. 'All the girls were mad about him, but he only ever had eyes for Molly.'

Molly flushed. 'He was shy, most people didn't realize that. When he was on the rugby field he was fearless and confident, but off it, he was just your average teenager.'

'That's so sweet.' Ellen's face softened, caught up in the romance of it all.

'He practically lived in our house,' Laura continued. 'Mum and Dad loved him and Rory followed him around like an adoring puppy.'

'And then Ruth died and he moved to France. But why didn't you keep in touch?'

Laura fell silent and looked at Molly.

'I'm not sure,' Molly admitted. 'I suppose it just wasn't the same with Ruth gone.'

'Oh well, in that case, I suppose it's not such a bad idea,' said Ellen, reluctantly.

'So what next?' Laura asked. 'Are you going to go to Bordeaux?'

'No need. Luke runs a company that arranges for French rugby teams to come to Ireland for a mixture of training and *craic*. I thought I could accidentally bump into him in their hotel.'

'Good idea.' Laura nodded in approval. 'You don't want him to think you've turned into a stalker.'

'So, is he here right now?' Ellen asked, her eyes lighting up with excitement.

'No, but he's coming over in a couple of weeks,' Molly pulled a face, 'there's just one problem.'

'Oh?' Laura raised an eyebrow.

'He's not coming to Dublin, he's flying into Shannon.'

'Well you can't go down there to see him, that wouldn't exactly be bumping into him,' Ellen pointed out. 'If I wasn't as big as a house, I could have gone with you and we could pretend we were having a little holiday.'

'I thought I'd just take the train down and spend the day there.'

'But you can't go alone,' Ellen protested. 'And a few hours may not be enough.'

'Ellen's right,' Laura agreed, 'but I have a solution.'

'You do?' Molly looked at her.

'I'll come with you.'

'There's really no need,' Molly protested, horrified at the thought.

'But why would you be down in Limerick alone?' Ellen protested, ignoring the desperation in her friend's eyes.

Molly shrugged. 'Any number of reasons. I could be visiting friends or family or on business; he won't know I'm only there to see him.'

'No, I insist.' Laura looked positively animated now. 'And that way, if anything goes wrong, I'll be there to bail you out.'

'But what about the twins and Robert?' Molly asked, grasping at straws.

A brief shadow crossed Laura's face. 'They'll hardly notice I'm gone.'

Molly had another stab at dissuading her. 'I don't want to drag you all the way to Limerick on a wild goose chase.'

'You're not dragging me, I'd like to come. It'll be fun.'

Molly blinked. The words 'Laura' and 'fun' didn't go together, at least, not in her experience. 'Okay then. But,' she held up a finger, 'you can't tell anyone why we're going, not even Robert.'

Laura shrugged. 'Fine.'

'I mean it,' she looked from Laura to Ellen, 'this stays just between the three of us.'

'Of course.' Ellen gave a solemn nod. 'So what's the plan?' she asked, sipping her tea and looking expectantly at Molly.

'I just told you the plan.'

Ellen sighed. 'You go to Limerick. You walk into the lounge of this hotel. You see Luke, you smile, you go over,' she spread out her hands, 'what happens next?'

'Oh.' Molly frowned. 'I haven't really thought that far ahead.'

'Oh, for goodness sake.' Laura rolled her eyes in exasperation and stood up. 'I'm going to the loo.'

Molly waited until Laura had gone upstairs and the door had closed behind her before she spoke. 'I just want to see if I feel anything, Ellen. Do you know what I mean?'

Ellen sighed. 'Yes, but I'm not sure a brief meeting will give you your answer.'

'I have to try, but I really wish *she* wasn't coming.' Molly raised her eyes to the ceiling.

'Sorry, but I think it would be a mistake to go alone. Anyway, she seems very cool about the whole thing. I thought she would blow a gasket.'

'It is odd. Still, she probably isn't too bothered who I end up with, as long as she's got a wedding to arrange.'

'Don't be so hard on her,' Ellen hissed as Laura clattered down the wooden staircase. 'I think she's just trying to be nice.'

'You really must carpet those stairs and the landing and bedrooms,' Laura said as she sat back down at the table.

Ellen stared at her in dismay. 'But it took me ages to varnish those floorboards.'

Molly hid a smile behind her hand. This must be another example of Laura trying to be nice.

'It's not very practical when you have a baby in the house.'

'But the experts link carpets to all sorts of breathing problems,' Ellen told her.

Laura waved a dismissive hand. 'Trust me, when they're babies, having a quiet house is a lot more important than a bit of dust. When you've spent hours trying to get them to sleep and you've crept away to make some tea or have a shower and then you drop something on your nice, shiny, *loud* floorboards, that's when you'll understand the value of carpet.'

'Don't mind her,' Molly said, kicking Laura under the table.

'Don't kick me, Molly. There's no point in pretending that motherhood is all fun and games. It's not, it's bloody hard work, it will break your heart and you'll get precious little thanks for it.'

'Laura, shut up,' Molly said, shooting her sister a furious look.

'She needs to know,' Laura insisted. 'I wish someone had told me what to expect.'

'Well thanks, Laura,' Ellen said calmly. 'I know you mean well. Oh, is that the time? I have a check-up in an hour.'

'You never mentioned you had an appointment,' Laura said suspiciously.

Ellen laughed. 'Hormones. Ask Moll. I'm forgetting everything these days.'

'She is,' Molly agreed, deadpan.

'I'll drive you, if you like,' Laura offered.

'That's okay, Mum's picking me up. Do you want to come with us, Molly, and get the lay of the land?'

'I'm her number two in case her mother isn't around,' Molly explained as Laura looked at them in confusion.

'*You*?' Laura shot Ellen a worried look. 'You must be mad, Ellen. Molly doesn't know the first thing about babies.'

'She doesn't need to know anything about babies,' Ellen said staunchly, 'she just needs to hold my hand.'

Molly gave her an affectionate smile. 'I can do that.'

Laura took her bag and stood up. 'Right, well, I'll leave you to it. I'll be in touch, Molly, to discuss tactics. We need to come up with a story about Limerick.'

'Sorry?'

'We have to explain to everyone why we're going there,' Laura said with exaggerated patience.

'Oh right, okay.'

'But don't worry, I'm sure I'll think of something.'

'Great.' As Laura walked out into the hall, Molly looked at Ellen and rolled her eyes.

Ellen giggled and hurried after Laura. 'Thanks so much for coming.'

'No problem,' Molly heard her sister reply, 'and you heed my advice about that floor.'

'She's unbelievable,' Molly said when Ellen had closed the door and returned to the kitchen.

'I don't think she even realizes she's doing it,' Ellen said as she tried to find a comfortable position on the wooden chair.

'I could throttle you for encouraging her to come to Limerick, she's going to drive me crazy.'

Ellen grinned. 'It will be fine. You never know, you might even enjoy yourself.'

'She'll spend the journey down telling me how and what I should say to Luke, and the journey back telling me what I got wrong,' Molly assured her.

'Just concentrate on the reason you're going,' Ellen advised. 'Concentrate on Luke and what you're going to say to him and forget about Laura.'

Molly sighed. 'I'll try, but if I stab her with one of her Jimmy Choos, on your head be it.'

Chapter Ten

2.45 p.m., Wednesday, 29th July

Laura sat on her sunny patio, sipping mineral water and absently flicking through a fashion magazine. The children had gone rollerblading with their friends – at least that's what they'd told her – and the house was strangely silent. But she wasn't able to concentrate on any of the articles as she was preoccupied, trying to think of a good reason why she and Molly would suddenly take off for Limerick together. It would be easier to come up with a reason for Molly to go alone, but Laura wasn't about to let that happen – she needed to get away. She'd offered to accompany her sister on impulse, but the more she thought about it, the more she realized it was exactly what she needed. It would be nicer to go alone, but there was no good excuse for her to do that, so this was the next best thing.

And though it made sense that Molly, upset over the wedding and missing Declan, needed to get away for a few days, the family would be stunned that Molly had asked her sister to accompany her; if Ellen couldn't go, Belle would naturally be Molly's next choice.

Tossing her magazine aside, Laura got up, went inside and crossed the kitchen to the study. This was where they kept all their important papers and household bills. She opened a side drawer of the polished oak desk and pulled out the file she was looking for. In it were various brochures that she received on a regular basis from the numerous hotels she and Robert had stayed in over the years. She took it back outside and started to look through the contents. As she did, she found several special offers; one, a free entry to a draw for a weekend away when you spent more than two hundred euros. Laura put down the brochure and smiled. Problem solved.

When Robert opened the front door, he sensed immediately that something was different. He frowned as he set down his brief-case and stood for a moment, trying to figure out what it was. His son walked out of the kitchen, a bottle of water in one hand and PSP in the other.

Adam grinned at his father's puzzled expression. 'She's cook-ing dinner,' he said with a 'don't ask me' shrug before disappearing upstairs.

And that was it, Robert realized. The unmistakable scent of roasting beef, his mouth watered. Were they having guests and he'd forgotten? Laura never cooked real food as a rule. It was all salads and risottos or, her latest passion, Moroccan cuisine; Robert thought he would puke if he had to eat another bowl of tasteless grey couscous. He took off his jacket, hung it carefully on the coat rack and, loosening his tie, followed his nose. 'Something smells good.'

Laura turned from where she was stirring gravy at the cooker and smiled. 'Hello, darling, did you have a good day?'

Robert studied her for a moment, had he walked into the wrong house? Usually he was lucky to get a hello, never mind a smile. 'Not bad. Are we expecting company?'

'No, I just thought it would be nice if we all sat down to dinner together for a change and everyone likes roast beef. Although,'

Laura rolled her eyes, 'Ashling is making noises about becoming a vegetarian.'

Robert chuckled. 'Where is she?'

'Sulking because I made her clean the windows. Honestly, she just wants to sit around all day doing nothing.'

I wonder where she gets that from, Robert mused, suppressing a smile. 'What about Adam? Did he do anything?'

'He cleaned my car, he did quite a good job too. Dinner will be about an hour. I've opened a bottle of wine. Why don't you take a glass into the garden, it's a lovely evening.'

Robert stared at her as he rolled up his tie and left it on the counter. 'Good idea. Will I pour you some?'

'Beat you to it!' Laura admitted with a guilty giggle, nodding towards the glass on the table.

'Good for you.' He gave her an affectionate smile. Just occasionally, he caught a glimpse of the girl he'd married; it made him realize how much she'd changed. Taking his wine and his newspaper, Robert went out to the garden and sat down in one of the comfortable loungers on the patio. He took a sip of his drink and settled down with a sigh of pleasure to do the Sudoku puzzle, but it wasn't long before he felt his eyes grow heavy.

'Dad?'

He opened his eyes to see Ashling standing over him looking miserable. It never ceased to amaze him how grown-up and childish she looked, all at the same time. The full lips, long lashes and high cheekbones were those of a beautiful young woman. The sullen expression and long, skinny legs covered in bruises were those of a child.

'Hello, sweetie, how are you?' He took her hand and kissed the fingers covered in biro.

Ashling threw herself into the chair beside him. 'Fed up. Mum's picking on me again. There's always something, I just can't seem to please her.'

Robert knew that feeling. 'All you have to do is pull your weight around the house, Ashling, and she'll be happy.'

'But that's not fair; she doesn't expect Adam to do a thing.' Ashling's large green eyes filled at the unjustness of it all.

'I thought he cleaned the car.'

Ashling's snort was disdainful. 'He spent about ten minutes hoovering it out and she gave him a tenner.'

Robert's eyes widened, that did seem a bit excessive, but then Laura had always had a soft spot for her son. He'd teased her about it when the twins were babies, saying that Adam was the apple of her eye. Mistakenly, he'd told this to the children recently, resulting in Ash nicknaming her brother Granny Smith. She teased her brother with a smile, but Robert sensed his daughter was hurt and he was sorry he'd said anything. 'I'll have a word later,' he promised her now. 'Why don't you help me with this Sudoku puzzle? I can't seem to get my head in gear at all today.' Smiling, Ashling pulled her chair closer and, leaning her head on his arm, studied the newspaper. He breathed in the lemony smell of her shampoo and marvelled at the different shades of gold running through her auburn mane. How had he and Laura managed to produce such striking children?

It had been the shock of all shocks, and he'd thought his life was over when Laura had told him she was pregnant. But from the moment he'd held his children in his arms, he'd known with certainty that they were worth any heartache that came with being a young parent. And there had been a lot of that. His parents had been furious when he finally plucked up the courage to tell them the news. Robert had said he'd give up college and get a job but, despite their anger, his parents would have none of it. He and Laura must marry and they would support them while he continued his education. By comparison, Belle and Oliver had taken the news quite well. They were more concerned that their daughter was being press-ganged into marriage and even offered to help raise the child, suggesting that the enormous decision of marriage be left until a later date. Robert had been relieved by their understanding and good sense, but Laura wouldn't hear of it. She wanted a ring on her finger and fast. Not that Robert had minded; he was crazy about her, but he did think that his parents were being ridiculously old-fashioned and simply worried about appearances. And Laura, despite her broad-minded parents, felt the same. She was mortified that she'd been caught out and positively trembled with horror at the idea of being labelled an unmarried mother. And so the wedding was arranged in Rome for the following month. Laura was a bundle of nerves, but Robert had put his reservations and fears firmly to one side. He was doing the right, the honourable thing. Laura and the baby were his responsibility. He loved her, and he was confident he would love their child. Marrying at just twenty-three didn't bother him greatly either. He had never been a wild child, teenager or young man. His grandfather maintained he'd been born middle-aged; perhaps he was right. Robert had never had any longing to travel, to sow wild oats, to live a little before settling down. The idea of having a little family of his own gave him a warm, fuzzy feeling that happily outweighed his fears.

He was just getting used to the idea and was quite excited when they went for that first scan, and were hit with a second shock; they weren't expecting one baby, but two. Laura had cried all the way home and had wailed even louder when her father had hugged her and said that they were doubly blessed. Robert, though he tried to hide it, had also been overwhelmed by the responsibility he would have to shoulder. He was just twenty-three and a student. He'd never earned a proper wage, still lived at home and received a monthly allowance from his father. How on earth could he look after a wife, never mind a wife and two children? And yet, when he'd seen the ultrasound image, he'd got a lump in his throat. And the more Laura cried, the more he was determined to look after her and them. And he had. He had worked hard and, in between lectures and studying, he had done more than his fair share of feeding, changing and pacing the floor.

Adam had been an easy baby from day one, content to sleep and eat. But Ashling suffered from colic and her plaintive cries seemed to ring through the house morning, noon and night. Those first eight weeks had been tough and Laura had, he knew, begun to resent the unfairness of being weighed down with such responsibility at only twenty. He also knew that she was beginning to realize that leaving home had been a mistake and that life would have been much easier if she'd stayed put and allowed Belle and Oliver to share the burden. When she got tearful and angry, Robert sometimes suggested that she move back to her parents' house for a while, but Laura would just accuse him of wanting to be rid of them so he could resume his wild life as a student. As if he had ever led a wild life.

'Dad, did you hear me? Eight there and four here.' Ashling was leaning across him and stabbing the page with her finger.

'I told you I wasn't thinking straight,' he chuckled and filled in the numbers. 'What did you do today?'

She shrugged against him. 'Nothing much.'

'Did you see your friends?'

She shook her head. 'Maria's gone to Cork, Ev is in the Maldives and Sarah flew to Marbella this morning. I wish we were going somewhere.'

'We had three wonderful weeks in the South of France in June,' he reminded her.

'That was boring, there was nothing to do.'

She was right. Laura had booked them into a five-star hotel near Cannes that had a golf course, a sumptuous health spa and a

Michelin-starred restaurant, but there was little entertainment for kids. Adam spent his time either whacking balls at the driving range or slouched in one of the fashionable lounges, playing computer games. Ashling, while she humoured her mother and had a couple of facials, spent the rest of her holiday sprawled by the pool reading paperbacks. A camping holiday with plenty of activities and droves of other kids would have been a much better and healthier option, all round. Robert patted his thickening waist. If he was kind, he would say Laura had made a mistake in picking such an adult environment. If he was honest, he would say his wife had been totally selfish in booking it. 'I'll take you to the cinema at the weekend,' he said now. 'Will that cheer you up?'

Ashling raised an eyebrow. 'Do I get to choose the movie?'

He sighed. She would pick a romantic drama, whereas Adam would want to see something loud and violent. 'No, I think I should.' A comedy usually kept both of them happy.

'Ashling, come and set the table,' Laura called from the kitchen.

'Why can't Adam do it?' Ashling shouted back, glowering.

'Because I'm asking you.' Laura's voice was tight with annoyance.

'Go on, sweetie.' Robert gave her a gentle push. 'I'll make sure Adam stacks the dishwasher.'

Happy with that, Ashling went inside and Robert sipped his wine and stared into space. He could hear his wife and daughter in the kitchen, Laura barking orders and Ashling muttering replies. Was every family like this, he wondered. As the children got older, there always seemed to be some animosity bubbling beneath the surface. Yet when the twins were alone together, they appeared to get on remarkably well, it was just around their parents that tempers flared. He was to blame as much as Laura, he had to admit. When she was hard on Ashling, he was hard on Adam. And when she was on the warpath, he was inclined to retreat to the study under the pretence of paying bills and leave his family to fight it out between them.

'Dinner!' Laura called cheerily from the doorway. Robert frowned as he went inside. She must have maxed-out her credit card again. Still, at least he'd get a decent meal out of it.

When the children had retreated to the TV room, Laura produced some Stilton and poured him a glass of his favourite port. Robert cut himself a slice of the luscious cheese and bit into it, savouring it as it melted on his tongue and the sharp flavour filled his mouth.

'I have some news,' Laura said, looking at him, her eyes sparkling.

Robert swallowed the cheese with a gulp. It couldn't be good news or she wouldn't have needed to soften him up. At the same time, she didn't look exactly guilty or penitent. Crikey, maybe she was pregnant! No, he remembered grimly, it certainly couldn't be that.

'Robert?' Laura was looking at him.

'Yes, sorry, news, you say?'

'I got a call today. It seems I've won a competition.'

He looked at her in happy relief. 'Well, that's marvellous, darling. What have you won?'

She gave a small, girlish laugh. 'I'm not entirely sure, to be honest. It's a short break in a hotel in Limerick, but I don't know any of the details. Apparently they're going to send me a voucher.'

'Excellent.' He frowned. 'I'll need to check the diary; it's out of the question before September, I'm afraid—' He broke off as he saw her smile falter and a flicker of guilt in her eyes. 'What?'

'Well, I was wondering if you'd mind if I took Molly. It's just that this whole business with Declan and the wedding, well, it's really knocked her for six. I thought a little holiday would be exactly what she needs.' Laura shrugged her slim shoulders. 'It might take her mind off things. Would you mind, Robert?'

He shook his head and smiled, genuinely touched by her thoughtfulness. She and Molly weren't particularly close, yet she was willing to do this; it was nice to know that she still had a soft centre, even though he didn't see it often. When she'd mentioned the prize, he'd thought maybe this was the perfect opportunity for them to recover some of their intimacy; he couldn't remember the last time they'd made love. But perhaps some time apart would prove as effective. He'd take some leave and do things with the kids and she would return more relaxed and calmer than she had been of late.

'Robert?' she was looking at him, her eyes anxious.

'I think it's a wonderful idea, Laura, and very sweet of you.'

'Well, it's not as if I'm paying.' She seemed embarrassed by his praise.

'You're a good sister,' he insisted. 'I'm sure she'd love to go.'

Laura hopped to her feet. 'I'll go and call her right away.'

'Good idea.' But Robert was already alone with his cheese and port as Laura disappeared into the study and closed the door behind her.

Molly was dozing in front of the telly, the remains of her tasteless microwave dinner congealing on the sofa beside her, when her sister phoned.

'It's all organized,' her sister said without preamble.

'Laura?'

'I've figured out a reason for us to go to Limerick.'

Clenching the phone between her ear and shoulder, Molly carried her plate back out to the kitchen, scraped the food into the bin and dropped the plate in the sink.

'Did you hear me?'

Molly roused herself to answer her sister. 'Limerick, great, yeah.'

'Well, don't you want to know what it is?' Laura asked, sounding annoyed.

'Tell me.' Molly stifled a yawn.

Laura quickly filled her in on her ingenious plan, sounding positively exuberant. 'So, all I need to know is when you want to go and how long for,' she finished.

Molly went into the sitting room in search of her trusty notebook and flicked through the pages until she found the necessary information. 'The next tour is the 5th to the 9th of August, but I'm not sure which hotel they're staying in.'

'I can easily find out,' Laura said, unfazed. 'I'll get onto it first thing tomorrow.'

When Molly put down the phone, she was bemused by her sister's enthusiasm. She knew that Laura and Declan weren't exactly buddies and that she'd been quite fond of Luke, but was she seriously thinking that Molly would get back with her old boyfriend? It was a ludicrous idea, laughable almost. It wasn't why Molly wanted to see him; she had no aspirations in that direction at all. She simply needed to see him again, to talk to him. Then, she felt sure, she'd be able to put the past behind her and concentrate on her future with Declan.

Chapter Eleven

12.15 p.m., Sunday, 2nd August

'You're kidding!' Rory shot his mother an incredulous look. For once he was up, showered and dressed rather smartly in beige combats and a blue shirt that complimented his blond hair and blue eyes.

Belle, who was laying strips of bacon and sausages on the grill pan, smiled. 'Is it so bizarre that your sisters would want to go on a little holiday together?'

'Duh! Yeah! When have they ever *chosen* to go anywhere together?'

Belle's brows knitted together as she considered this. 'They went on a scouting trip to Wexford,' she said triumphantly.

'Doesn't count.' Rory grinned. 'You made Laura go because Molly wanted to, and you said she was too little to go alone; Laura wouldn't talk to you for days.'

Belle sighed. 'Well, they're adults now. Molly's been through a tough time. I think it's wonderful of Laura to offer to take her away. It just goes to show that blood is thicker than water.'

'Or that Laura is desperate to get away from Robert and the kids,' Rory muttered darkly.

'What was that?' Belle frowned, unable to hear him over the sizzling bacon.

'Never mind. Is everyone coming today?' He licked his lips and glanced anxiously at his watch.

Belle looked at him in amusement. 'Everyone. What time will Natalie be here?'

'Around half twelve.' He attempted a nonchalant shrug, but he knew that his mother could see right through him. God, he hated introducing a girl to his family, and bringing her to a Jackson brunch was madness. Between Laura's caustic comments, his father's wacky wit and Molly's intensive scrutiny, it was enough to send anyone heading for the hills. At least he could rely on his mother to behave. 'Look, Mum, don't let them scare her off, will you?'

'I'll make them behave,' Belle promised. 'You really like this girl, don't you?'

'She's great,' he admitted. 'No idea what she sees in me.'

Belle gave him a hug. 'She sees what we all see: a handsome, funny, intelligent young man.'

He grinned. 'You're very slightly prejudiced.'

'I was actually holding back,' she nodded to the dozen eggs on the counter.

'Now, break them into that bowl and start whisking.'

'That's Dad's job,' he said, though he did as he was told. 'Where is he anyway?'

'At Mass.'

'Mass?' Rory stopped to look at her. 'But he's Presbyterian.'

'Well, he hasn't really been anything for years,' Belle reminded him, 'but he's decided he wants to explore his spirituality and experiment with different religions.'

Rory absorbed this. 'Well, I suppose as midlife crises go, it beats buying a Harley or getting a tattoo.'

Belle laughed.

'Are Boring Bob and the terrible twins going swimming?' he asked as he beat the eggs.

'Not today, and the twins aren't terrible.'

He grinned. 'Ah! So you agree Bob's boring.'

'I do not. I find Robert quite restful and calming; the sort of person you'd want on your side in a crisis. I don't know what he must make of my mad family. Sometimes I think he must wonder what he married into.'

'Sometimes I think he must wonder what he married. Laura was lucky to find such a decent, tolerant man. I don't know how he puts up with her.'

'Why must you always be so cruel to your sister? Remember, if you get smart with Laura, she may take it out on Natalie.'

Rory had already thought of that. 'I am going to be on my best behaviour,' he promised. 'Anyway, I'll be too busy eating to talk; I want to get Natalie out of here as quickly as possible.'

'So why put yourself through it?'

'She wanted to meet you all,' he admitted, keeping his head bent over the eggs.

'I see. So it really is serious.'

He looked up and gave a small shrug. 'I do really like her.'

Her eyes widened. 'I see. How long have you been dating?'

'Three weeks. I know that's not long,' he added hurriedly when he saw his mother's lips twitch, 'but we really click, Mum.'

'It happens that way sometimes; when it's right, it's right.'

'Did you know you loved Dad straight away?'

'Lord, no! I thought he was a conceited, egotistical flirt and when he asked me out, I told him it was never going to happen.'

Rory turned to look at her, smiling. 'But he didn't give up.'

She shook her head. 'Not at all; it just seemed to encourage him. We went to all same dances and, as soon as the music started, he'd come straight over and ask me to dance.'

'And you refused.'

'Every time,' she laughed. 'And he'd dance one dance with each and every other girl in the room, but always stood at the bar during the slow sets.'

'Ah, so you were watching him.' Rory grinned.

'Yes,' she admitted. 'And then, one evening he wasn't there, and I found myself looking around for him and watching the door, waiting for him to walk in.'

'Did he come?'

She shook her head. 'No, and I didn't dance with anyone all night. I suddenly realized that he was the only one I was interested in. I left early and, as I walked out into the street, he came towards me on crutches. He'd broken his ankle in a football match earlier that day and had to go to the hospital. As soon as he got home though, he'd begged his dad to help him get washed and changed and drive him to the dance.'

Rory smiled at the dreamy look on her face. 'So you were finally going to dance with him and he couldn't.'

'I was and we did, although it was more of a three-legged hop than a dance. And that was that. We've been together ever since.'

Rory opened his mouth to say something, when the doorbell rang. He looked at his watch.

'I wonder who that is. It can't be Natalie, she wouldn't come so early.'

'Why don't you answer the door and find out?' Belle suggested.

Rory hurried out, wiping his hands on the seat of his jeans. He immediately recognized Molly's outline. 'Where's your key?' he asked impatiently as he opened the door.

'And hello to you too,' she muttered, stepping into the hall.

Immediately, he regretted snapping at her. She looked pale and glum and there were dark circles under her eyes. 'You look like shit.'

'Cheers. Have you thought of joining the diplomatic corps?' She dropped her bag and threw her denim jacket over the banister.

He leaned against the wall, watching her. 'I hear you're going away with Laura. Sounds like fun, I'm so jealous.'

'Look, she offered, it's free, and I could do with a break, okay?'

she said, sounding defensive. 'Surely even you can understand that.'

'Hey, I'm just messing,' he reached out awkwardly and tousled her hair.

Molly pushed his hand away. 'Yeah, well, I'm not in the mood.'

Belle smiled warmly as Molly came to hug her. 'Hello, darling, how are you doing?'

Molly smiled briefly. 'Fine. Who's coming today?'

'Everyone, including,' Belle lowered her voice although Rory was still in the hall, 'the new girlfriend.'

'Really?' Molly was momentarily distracted from her own misery. 'What's her name?'

'Natalie. He seems to really like this one, so be nice.'

'You're talking to the wrong daughter,' Molly told her. 'Want me to do anything?'

Belle looked around. 'No, I think everything's ready, but you could go on toast duty.'

Molly gave a half-hearted salute and sat down in the chair next to the toaster. She was rarely asked to do anything other than make toast or tea as she always managed to burn something.

'Have you heard from Declan?' Belle asked as she transferred the bacon into a dish and slid it into the oven to keep warm.

'Yeah, he phones either late at night or first thing in the morning because of the time difference,' Molly explained, 'but we only talk for a couple of minutes; he's always afraid it will cost a fortune.'

Her mother's eyes were full of sympathy as she sat down. 'I know it's hard, darling, but he'll be back before you know it and you can start to make plans again.'

Molly just nodded, not ready to confide in her mother that she was having doubts about making plans at all. 'Where's Dad?'

'At Mass.' Belle held up a hand and shook her head. 'Don't ask.'

Molly grinned for what felt like the first time in days. 'Mass, salsa, you have to hand it to him, his interests are diverse.'

'He gets crazier every year. Now, tell me, how's Ellen holding up?'

'She's enormous and tired and fed up. I feel a bit guilty about going away and leaving her, but she insists she'll be fine.'

'You're only going to Limerick – aren't you?'

'I think so.' Laura had warned Molly to remain vague until she was sure of where Luke would be staying.

'Then it wouldn't take long to get back. Anyway, I can assure you that her mum will be sticking to her like glue over the next few weeks. And it's very unusual for a first baby to come early.'

'That's what Laura said.'

'She's right.'

'Isn't she always,' Molly murmured.

Belle shot her a reproachful look. 'It's very good of her to take you away like this. She and Robert could have enjoyed a nice romantic break together.'

'It is nice of her,' Molly agreed, although she wasn't convinced Laura's motives were entirely altruistic; she seemed more enthusiastic about the trip than Molly was.

The doorbell rang and there were voices in the hall. Belle stood up, and put a hand up to tidy her already perfect hair. 'This must be Natalie,' she whispered. 'Now please, Molly, behave, for Rory's sake.'

'Of course I will,' Molly said, hurt that her mother felt she had to ask. 'You know I'd be thrilled if he finally found someone special.' Rory's luck with women had been sadly absent so far. The girls he fell for were either bitches, completely wrong for him, or already involved. The last one, Jenna, had been a fitness coach who'd turned out to be both possessive and controlling, and had positively stalked him when he'd finally had the courage to dump her. Molly prayed Natalie would be different.

The door opened and her dad walked in. 'Oh, it's just you.'

'Thanks very much,' he retorted.

'Sorry.' She smiled, standing up to hug him. 'We thought you were the new girlfriend.'

'She's here too,' he said. 'They're just having a private moment in the porch.'

'What's she like?' Belle asked.

'No strange body piercings or visible tattoos and she doesn't seem to be armed, so quite normal for Rory.'

Molly giggled. You could always rely on Dad to lighten the mood. 'How was Mass?'

He pulled a face. 'A bit disappointing. The priest was about ninety and spoke in a low monotone throughout. I think I nodded off at one stage.'

'You should go to one of these new evangelical services,' she suggested. 'Lots of singing, swaying and clapping – much more your sort of thing.'

His eyes lit up. 'Yes, I like the sound of that. I'll go online later and see what I can find.'

'Why the sudden interest in religion, Dad?'

'I'm getting older, my darling, and it's harder to be an atheist when you have one foot in the grave.'

Belle rolled her eyes. 'You're only sixty-three and as healthy as a horse.'

He splayed his hands, eyes wide. 'How do you know? How do any of us know? Patrick McNulty jogged every day, never ate red meat, smoked or drank, and he keeled over at fifty-two.'

Belle winked at her daughter. 'He died of boredom.'

'You can scoff,' her husband said with mock severity, 'but you won't find it so funny when those pearly gates are closed in your face.'

'I was planning on going in the other direction anyway,' Belle said airily. 'You know how I hate the cold.'

'Such blasphemy—' Oliver broke off as the kitchen door swung open and Rory stood there, a tiny, dark-haired girl at his side.

'Everyone, this is Natalie,' he said shyly. 'Natalie, my folks, Oliver and Belle, and this is my sister Molly.'

'Welcome, Natalie. Come along in, my dear,' Oliver smiled.

Belle crossed the room to kiss her cheek. 'Hello, Natalie, welcome.'

'Thank you.' The girl took the chair next to Molly. 'Hi.'

'Hi.' Molly gave her a warm smile. At least this one looked normal enough.

'You've just walked in on a religious debate,' Oliver informed her. 'My family are teasing me because I believe in God.'

Natalie stared at him. 'That's a joke, right?'

Oliver frowned. 'No, I actually think I do.'

Natalie looked around, eyes wide. 'And the rest of you don't?'

'Sure we do,' Rory said hurriedly, with a nervous laugh. 'Don't mind them, Nat.'

'So what do you do, Natalie?' Oliver asked, sitting down next to her.

'I'm in my second year of university.'

'Excellent. And what is it you're studying?'

'Christian Theology.'

Oliver leaned forward, resting his chin in his hands, delighted. 'But that's fascinating, and very timely. I'm currently re-evaluating my own spirituality.'

Natalie's eyes lit up. 'How wonderful!'

Molly looked from the girl to her mesmerized father, her mystified mother and a red-faced Rory. The doorbell rang and she jumped to her feet. 'I'll get it.'

Molly hurried to the door and smiled at Ashling and Adam. 'Hi, guys.' She looked past them and nodded at her brother-in-law. 'Hi, Robert, how's life?'

'Fine, and you?'

She shrugged. 'You know.'

He coloured. 'Sorry, that was a silly question.'

'No, really, I'm fine,' she assured him, touching his arm. 'And thanks for letting me take your place on this holiday.'

'Happy to do it.' He patted her hand clumsily.

'You seem in good form,' Laura remarked.

'Dad's decided he's a born-again Christian and Rory's new girlfriend is here and she's a theology student.' Molly smiled. 'Let's say, I think it's going to be an interesting lunch.'

Laura sighed. 'She's not another headcase, is she?'

Molly put her head on one side. 'Too early to say, but Dad's thrilled to have some stimulating conversation for a change.'

Adam groaned. 'We don't have to stay long, do we, Dad?'

'Don't be rude.' Robert glared at him. 'You'll go in there and be polite or you won't get any pocket money for a month.'

Molly's smile faltered. 'Sorry, Robert, I shouldn't be leading your children astray.'

'Believe me, they don't need much encouragement.'

'Aren't you lot hungry?' Belle said from the kitchen door and opened her arms as Ashling ran to her. 'Hello, darling, hello, Adam. My, you get taller every time I see you. Come and meet Rory's lovely friend.'

After the introductions were made and Belle and Laura had served the food, Oliver brought his elder daughter and her family up to date on the conversation so far. 'We've been talking about religion; very apt on the Sabbath, eh?' He chuckled. 'Perhaps you'd like to say Grace, Natalie.'

Natalie obediently joined her hands together and bent her head. 'Thank you, Lord, for the food we eat, and bless and protect this wonderful family, Amen.'

'Amen,' they all chorused rather self-consciously, Adam and Ash nudging each other and smirking.

'Natalie is studying theology,' Oliver explained as they started to eat, 'isn't that interesting?'

Laura paused, her fork halfway to her mouth. 'It's certainly different. What do you hope to do when you qualify, Natalie?'

'Become a nun,' Adam mumbled, making his sister snort and earning a dig from his uncle.

Laura glared at her children and offered Natalie an apologetic smile. 'Teenagers.'

'It's fine,' Natalie said with a gracious nod. 'Ideally, I'd like to be involved in some sort of counselling role, preferably within the Catholic Church.'

Molly opened her mouth to comment, but shut it again when she saw the look of pure panic on her brother's face.

'Very commendable.' Belle beamed. 'More toast, Natalie? Or some more coffee?'

'No thank you, Mrs Jackson.' She looked at Belle with curious eyes. 'Rory tells me you're a Catholic.'

'I was raised a Catholic,' Belle corrected her.

'But you didn't raise your children as Catholics.'

Molly bristled at the accusatory tone, but her mother was wearing a calm, tolerant smile.

'No. Oliver was raised as a Protestant, but we both considered ourselves agnostics, so we agreed to raise our children to be good human beings and let them make up their own minds about their faith when they were old enough.'

Natalie looked from Belle to Laura, and then Molly. 'And have you?'

Molly gave a non-committal shrug. 'Still considering my options,' she said, realizing her brother would throttle her if she upset his girlfriend.

Laura had no such reservations. 'I don't feel the need to get involved in organized religion,' she said curtly.

'But what about the children?' Natalie pressed. 'Don't you think in these troubled times that the Commandments would help them to follow a safe path through life?'

'Robert and I are quite capable of steering our children safely through life,' Laura snapped.

'And they're doing a great job,' Oliver said staunchly.

'Oh, I don't know,' Molly teased the children, in an effort to lighten the mood. 'They can be right terrors when they want to be.'

Natalie looked at Rory in admiration. 'But you've found your faith, despite everything.'

'He has?' Oliver turned startled eyes on his son.

Natalie beamed at him. 'Like father, like son.'

Rory looked like a rabbit caught in headlights and the twins started to titter. Belle hurried to save her son. 'Molly was speaking to Declan,' she announced to no one in particular, before shooting her daughter a beseeching look. 'Weren't you, Molly?'

Molly quickly swallowed a mouthful of bacon. 'Yes, that's right.'

'How's he getting on?' Robert asked.

'Well, I think, although he could only talk for a few minutes and there was an echo on the line.'

'Molly's fiancé is working in Japan at the moment,' Rory explained to his girlfriend.

'What does he do?' she asked.

'He's an engineer.'

'It must be hard being apart.' Natalie looked at her with eyes full of sympathy.

Molly smiled. 'He's only been gone a couple of weeks and he'll be back at the end of next month.'

'And then we have a wedding to plan,' Oliver said, beaming.

'Molly's a counsellor,' Ashling said, a propos of nothing, and they all turned to look at her. 'What? She is.'

Natalie looked from Ash to Molly, her eyes lighting up with interest. 'I didn't know that.'

'Actually, she's a psychologist,' Laura corrected her daughter.

'Still, I'm sure you two would have a lot in common,' Oliver remarked.

Molly looked at her father in dismay. 'My counselling is more to do with acne than theology,' she joked, afraid that Natalie would pin her in a corner for the afternoon to discuss the meaning of life. She had planned to hang around for a while as she was at a loose end with Declan away, but now she was having second thoughts.

'You deal with a lot more serious problems than that.' Her brother shot her a look that was half-reproachful, half-pleading.

Molly sighed. She did feel sorry for him, but where did he find these women? Natalie had only known them five minutes and she'd jumped straight in and started to quiz them on their religious beliefs – seriously odd. She offered Natalie a polite smile. 'Sadly, I do. I'll fill you in some other time. Unfortunately, I have to rush off today. I'm going to see a close friend. She's in her last few weeks of pregnancy and quite nervous.'

Natalie's face lit up and she looked quite pretty. 'How wonderful, a new life! She and her husband must be so excited.'

'There is no husband,' Laura said baldly.

With a pained expression, Belle made a dive for the grill. 'More bacon, anyone?'

Chapter Twelve

Molly had little time to reflect on her own problems over the next couple of days; work was all-consuming and she was worried about three particular cases, children – for that's all they were – who were crying out for help. Tess and Carl would be here in a minute for their monthly meeting, and Molly was determined that these kids didn't fall through the cracks like Rebecca had. Molly sighed at the memory. Rebecca had been a twelve-year-old who'd contacted *Teenage Kix* because she was worried about her mother's moods. Molly's then boss, Ally, had asked some questions and established that the woman must be suffering from depression. As she was on tablets and seeing a doctor on a regular basis, she had simply advised Rebecca to be understanding and supportive and to try not to worry too much; she was a young girl and she should enjoy life and trust her mother was getting the best possible care. But it turned out that Rebecca's concerns had been well founded. Her mother hadn't been taking her medication and had also been drinking and, one night when Rebecca's little brother was teething and inconsolable, the mother took her baby, walked up to the local railway bridge and jumped off. They rarely got to find out how things turned out for the children that turned to *Teenage Kix* for advice, but this case had been on the news and plastered all over the papers for days. Rebecca was now with a foster family.

Ally had needed counselling after that episode and retired a few months later. It had shaken Molly, and caused her to question what she was doing. Was it irresponsible to give out advice in a magazine and over the Internet when you knew nothing about the person's situation other than the information they gave you? Molly didn't really believe so. So she had sat down with the magazine's publisher and editor and presented them with more stringent guidelines to avoid such a tragedy ever happening again. She had come up with a template for the most common problems, but the basic advice to all children was to turn to a trusted adult for help. And if Tess or Carl had any doubts or concerns about any particular cases, they were to immediately refer them to Molly.

Though they were young, Molly felt her two assistants took their jobs seriously and had matured enormously in the last year. She had taught them to read between the lines; to look beyond the obvious for the underlying problems. A girl desperately unhappy because she is overweight, could well be the victim of bullying. A child who sends in a number of questions on different issues may be lying simply to feel they are the centre of attention, which in itself suggests there might be a lot more going on than immediately apparent.

'We need to see ourselves almost as a post office,' Molly had explained to both her superiors and assistants. 'We sort through the letters and we redirect them to their correct destination. Ultimately, we want children with serious problems to talk to a trusted adult who can help them. We must try not to get too involved, or the children will spend all their time online, lapping up sympathy rather than actively looking for help.' Thankfully, there had been no serious incidents since Rebecca – at least, Molly thought with a resigned sigh, none that they knew of. But between Declan and Luke, she was distracted at the moment and she wanted to take Carl and Tess through emails and posts she was concerned about so that they could keep an eye out for any problems she may have missed.

The doorbell rang and Molly went to answer it. Her flat was the handiest place for such meetings. The *Teenage Kix* offices were based in a business park off the M50 and not easily accessible without a car. But her flat was near a DART station and was an easy commute for Tess travelling from Kilbarrack and Carl from Bray. They were chatting happily on the doorstep when she opened the door. 'Hey, you two. How are things?'

'She's in lurvvvv,' Carl crowed and received a dig from Tess.

'You're just jealous. He's always fancied me,' she confided in Molly.

'In your dreams!'

Molly laughed. 'Are you really in love?'

Tess smiled. 'It's early days, but he's a fine thing. I'm not saying any more, though. I don't want to jinx it!'

Molly led the way into the kitchen and put on the kettle. 'Tea, coffee, Coke or water – fizzy and straight?'

'Ooh, tea for me, I'm gasping.' Tess sat down at the table and kicked off her sandals.

'Fizzy water and a peg please.' Carl pinched his nostrils together.

'My feet do not smell.' Tess protested with a toss of her purple-streaked hair, then she grinned at Molly. 'Not long now to the big day. I am so looking forward to it. I've never been to a wedding before, well, not the full thing.'

'Ah.' Molly pulled a face as she took a bottle of water from the fridge and tossed it to Carl.

'Ah?' Tess frowned. 'What does that mean?'

'I'm afraid the wedding is off, for the moment anyway.'

'No way!' Tess gasped.

'Way.'

'How come?' Carl straightened to his full five-six and stuck out his chest. 'Did he dump ya? Do you want me to go round with me mates and sort him out?'

'How did you ever get a job as an agony uncle?' Tess asked, shaking her head in despair.

Molly laughed. 'Declan's got a new job working for a Japanese company. They've sent him out to Osaka on a ten-week induction course; he won't be back until late September.'

'Oh, poor you, that's rotten. So what's the new date?'

'There is none yet.' Molly concentrated her attention on making the tea. 'We'll let him settle into his new position before we decide.' She handed Tess a mug and Carl a packet of biscuits and led them into the small sitting room. 'Right, let's go inside and get started.'

'Will I go first?' Tess asked, sitting cross-legged on one end of the sofa.

'Go ahead.' Molly sat at the other end with her pad and pen, her laptop on the arm of her chair beside her. She took a sip of her tea and gave Tess her full attention.

'Okay, first I have a situation with a thread on sex.'

'There's a surprise,' Carl drawled, sprawling in the armchair and putting his feet up on Molly's coffee table.

'She's fourteen, madly in love and wants to go on the pill, but is afraid to tell her mother. She's asking for advice. I suggested she talk to her mother, older sister or maybe an understanding aunt. I also pointed out that she would be breaking the law. That she shouldn't feel pressured into having sex. That being on the pill still wasn't 100% successful and that it wouldn't protect her against STDs.'

'It sounds like you covered all the bases.' Molly nodded her approval.

'The problem is that there are three other girls on the forum who are adding their pennyworth. It's not bad enough for me to pull it, I did consider that, but it's definitely not helpful. One reply said she probably would be safe enough to have sex without protection at least once; that at her age she was unlikely to get pregnant. I left it but posted a strong rebuttal.'

'Jeez, do these kids get any sex education?' Carl groaned running a hand through his unruly dark locks.

'You were right not to remove it, Tess,' Molly said thoughtfully. 'I'm guilty of pulling a lot of posts like that, but perhaps leaving them there and then pointing out that they are completely inaccurate, may be more effective.'

Carl nodded. 'Yeah, I think we are being a little conservative; we remove too many posts.'

Molly looked at him. 'You never mentioned it before.'

He reddened and shifted in his chair. 'Yeah, well, I'm only a novice. You're the expert.'

Molly looked from him to Tess. 'You know I value both of your opinions. I don't always have all the answers.'

Tess grinned. 'No kidding.'

'Don't push it,' Molly growled. 'Okay then, from now on, let's be a bit more relaxed on the negative posts, but follow them up immediately with a correction. And we continue to remove any posts that are aggressive or insulting.'

'Agreed.' Tess nodded vehemently.

'I'm not sure I do,' Carl said, frowning. 'We could use posts like that to illustrate bullying behaviour.'

'Okay, give me some time to think about it,' Molly said at last. She could see Carl's point, but she wasn't going to rush into a decision.

Tess nodded and made a note. 'Fine. Now, I have a letter.' She pulled a piece of pink notepaper from her file.

'A *letter*?' Carl stared at it in astonishment.

Tess smiled. 'I know, it's the first in ages. Most of the correspondence is through email or texts, but I suppose this girl is a little old-fashioned.'

'Or she doesn't have access to the technology, or,' Molly frowned, 'she's afraid she wouldn't be able to use a computer in total privacy.'

'I never thought of that,' Tess said. 'You could be right; listen to this.'

Please help.
My friend is really not well. I've tried to talk to her, told her I think she needs help, but she just won't listen. I'm so afraid she might do something silly.

'I had something very similar a few weeks back,' Molly murmured. 'Is it signed Smithy?'

Tess checked and nodded. 'Yes, it is.'

Molly leaned forward, frowning. 'Go on.'

Her behaviour is getting stranger every day. We used to spend a lot of our school holidays together, but now she makes excuses to get away from me. I don't see her hanging around with any of our usual friends – I'm not sure where she is half the time, I can't talk to any of her family – I can't explain why. It's complicated, but I just can't. Please, please print a reply to me on next week's page.
Thanks, Smithy

Molly bit her lip worriedly as she reached for her laptop. 'It doesn't sound good, does it? But I wonder what happened to stop Smithy using the message board.'

'She may have to share the machine with the rest of the family,' Carl suggested.

'Then why not text?' Tess asked.

'Perhaps she was afraid of someone seeing an automatic acknowledgement,' Molly mused.

Tess nodded. 'Of course, I forgot all about that. So, will I put together a reply, or do you want to answer this one?'

Molly sighed. 'I already have, but for some reason Smithy won't or can't follow my advice. Or perhaps she wasn't able to sign on.'

'She did ask you to print your reply in the magazine.'

'Yes,' Molly nodded. 'Leave it with me, I'll put something together.'

'Aren't you going away?' Carl asked.

'Yeah, tomorrow, but I'm taking my laptop; no rest for the wicked, eh?' She smiled and turned back to Tess. 'Anything else?'

'No, that's it.'

'Great. Now, Carl, what have you got?'

They spent another thirty minutes discussing Carl's cases, and then Molly's, before calling it a day. 'Remember, you can get hold of me any time,' Molly told them as they got ready to leave. 'I'll be checking my email regularly and obviously I'll have my phone on at all times.'

'Not *all* the time,' Carl said with a grin, 'you're supposed to be going on holiday.'

'It's just a short break,' Molly said, shifting uncomfortably.

'You deserve it.' Tess gave her a warm hug. 'Go and have fun, we'll take care of everything.'

Molly waved them off and then went back inside. She went into her bedroom – how quickly she'd started thinking of it as hers – and started to pull clothes out of the wardrobe.

Laura had been over last night to warn her that the hotel they were going to was extremely upmarket.

'I do have good clothes,' Molly said, indignant.

'Yes, but you don't wear them,' Laura had pointed out. 'You're always in jeans or those dreadful lycra things.'

Molly had given a defensive shrug. 'They're practical, especially when I'm on the bike.'

'Well, now you're going on holiday, so dress up.'

'It's not really a holiday,' Molly had pointed out.

'Uh, no, you're going to meet your ex; why on earth would you look well?'

Molly had to laugh, sometimes her sister could be quite funny. And when they were settled on Molly's sofa with coffees, they'd shared a giggle about Rory's new girlfriend.

'What a nut,' Laura exclaimed. 'Where on earth did he find her?'

Molly felt compelled to defend Natalie. 'She's actually quite pretty when she smiles.'

'Not that she does that often.'

Molly had looked at her sister and thought of pots and kettles. 'Dad's crazy about her.'

'There you go then; she's definitely weird.'

'I'm just struggling to see what they have in common, what they talk about.'

'God knows.'

'Ha! God knows, very good!' Molly giggled.

'I can't believe she questioned me about the way I was raising the children, the nerve of her.' Laura shook her head in disbelief.

'I thought you were going to pull her hair out.' Molly grinned.

'You can talk,' Laura retorted. 'You almost ran out of there when Ash told her you were a counsellor.'

'I was terrified I was going to be stuck with her for the afternoon.'

'Well, at least you have something in common,' Laura pointed out.

Molly shook her head in exasperation. 'My job is helping people cope in this world, not preparing them for the next.'

'Oh, well, we'll probably never see her again. Rory will soon tire of her.'

'I wouldn't count on it. The fact that he brought her to brunch means it must be serious.'

'Then God help us all,' Laura said with a groan. 'So, how are you feeling about our big adventure?'

'Nervous,' Molly admitted.

'Do you still fancy him, Moll, or do you just want to see him so you can talk about Ruth?'

Molly looked at her in surprise; Laura was more perceptive than she gave her credit for. 'A bit of both. We never had much time alone together after the accident, so we never got to really talk about what happened. I'd like to know how he coped and how he's doing now.'

'So you're not planning on dumping Declan and running off to France with Luke?' Laura probed.

Molly laughed. 'What makes you think he'd even want me? He's probably married. At the very least, he'll have a girlfriend.'

'And will you tell him you're engaged?'

'Laura,' Molly groaned.

'Oh, come on, don't tell me you'd be doing this if he'd turned into Mr Blobby.'

Molly had to laugh at that. 'Well, no, maybe not.'

'So you do still fancy him.'

'Maybe I do,' she admitted, 'but I love Declan.'

'But he chose Japan over you,' Laura said bluntly.

Molly stared at her. 'So you do think it was wrong of him to go?'

Laura shrugged. 'I think you're right to think long and hard before marrying him.'

Molly had got rid of Laura very soon after that, she had got too close to the bone, tactless as ever, it had left Molly feeling depressed. It had also helped her make up her mind on her wardrobe; she had no intention of dressing up like a dog's dinner. She would wear her combats and a pretty lace top for travelling. She had a denim shirt-dress to change into for dinner tomorrow evening, a pair of black linen cut-offs with a matching top for the day after, and her jeans and white shirt for travelling home. Laura would be very unimpressed but tough, she wasn't going to change for her, or Luke, or anyone else for that matter. After packing her small bag, Molly took a short, shallow bath – at least in a hotel she had some hope of having a long, hot one – went to bed and read her book. Her eyelids were beginning to droop when the phone rang.

She reached out a hand to grab it, smiling when she heard his voice. 'Hey you.'

'*Ohayo*, or should I say *oyasuminasai*?'

'Doesn't really matter, I haven't a clue what you're on about anyway.'

'*Ohayo* means good morning and *oyasuminasai* means good-night. It's amazing how quickly I'm picking the language up, Moll. I suppose it's because I'm listening to it all day, although they all speak excellent English. So, how are you?'

Molly pushed herself up on to her elbows. 'Fine, you?'

'I'm enjoying the whole experience, but of course I miss you.'

'Yeah, sure,' Molly teased.

'I am.' He sounded slightly miffed.

'Just kidding,'

'How's work?'

'Fine.'

'And Ellen?'

'Tired, nervous, excited – you know.'

'No, haven't a clue,' he chuckled, 'but I can imagine. Tell her I was asking for her.'

He fell silent and Molly racked her brains for something else to tell him, realizing there were often awkward silences in their brief phone conversations these days. In the past, they used to prattle on for hours about little or nothing, but since he'd gone to Osaka, each conversation seemed to grow more stilted. 'I'm going away for a few days with Laura tomorrow,' she said finally.

'Sorry? What was that? I think we have a crossed line.'

She grinned. 'I know, I must be mad. She won some competition and the prize was a three-day break for two in this fancy hotel in Limerick.'

'Very nice, but how come she's not taking Robert?'

'Er, I don't think he could get away and Mum said she should take me, that it might cheer me up.'

There was another pause and then he asked, 'Do you need cheering up?'

'I do a bit,' she admitted.

'I'm sorry, Molly. I'll make it up to you, I promise.'

'I know, don't worry about it. Listen, it's late, I can hardly keep my eyes open and Laura's picking me up at the crack of dawn.'

'Okay, darling, have a wonderful time, but don't go falling in love with a Limerick man.'

Molly closed her eyes, consumed with guilt. 'I won't.'

'Goodnight, Moll, I love you.'

'Goodnight, Declan, take care.'

Though earlier she had been sleepy, now Molly was wide awake. She stared at the ceiling, feeling guilty for deceiving Declan, but it wasn't like she'd been unfaithful or was planning to either. She couldn't imagine ever doing anything like that, although she'd never been tempted, she realized. If Luke threw his arms around her and told her he'd never loved another woman the way he'd loved her, what would she do? Despite mulling over it long into the night, Molly wasn't sure of the answer.

Chapter Thirteen

10.05 a.m., 5th August

'This traffic is dreadful.' Laura drummed red fingernails against the wheel. 'If you'd been ready at nine, like we'd agreed, we'd have been out of the city by now.'

'The roadworks would still have been there,' Molly retorted. 'Anyway, what's the hurry?'

'It's a good hotel and I plan to make the most of the facilities while we're there.'

'Just remember that you didn't actually win a competition. What are you going to say to Robert when the bill rolls in?'

'I'll use my own credit card; Robert hardly ever checks my statements.'

'Great,' Molly murmured, wondering what it must be like to have someone else pay for everything you needed and wanted. She didn't think she'd like it. Was Luke a rich man, she wondered?

With that, the traffic started to move and within minutes they were on the N7 and heading west. Laura had the classical music channel on low, although Molly was pretty sure her sister had never been into that kind of stuff; she had been a big fan of REM and Bryan Adams in the early nineties. Had marriage and the kids changed her? Molly doubted it. It was much more to do with this new persona Laura had assumed when Robert bought the house in Clontarf. From day one, Laura seemed hell-bent on convincing anyone that cared that she belonged there. She started to talk differently, dress differently and, to use a Rory phrase, 'act posh'. He thought it was hilarious. 'She's turned into a Stepford Wife!' But so what, if it made her happy? Only, underneath the expensive clothes, jewellery and perfect make-up, Molly got the feeling that Laura was discontented; especially after what Belle had said. Not that Laura would ever admit it. She would be furious if Molly so much as hinted that her life was anything other than perfect. And that was fair enough too, Molly knew. People had different ways of getting through the day, who was she to criticize?

'Have you heard from Declan?' Laura asked, breaking in on her thoughts.

Molly nodded. 'He phoned last night.'

'Did you tell him we were going away?'

Molly looked at her. 'Of course.'

'But not why.'

Molly bristled. 'Well, obviously not.'

Laura seemed not to notice her sharp tone, or if she did, she wasn't bothered by it. 'He's really made it, hasn't he? This a top job.'

'I don't know, maybe.'

'You don't fly someone all the way to Japan unless you have big plans for them. You should do some house-hunting while he's away. I could come with you.' Laura's face lit up at the thought.

'I wouldn't buy a house without Declan.'

'No, but you could come up with a short-list.'

Molly gave a non-committal shrug and turned to look out at the passing scenery.

'By the way, you won't lose your deposit if you have the wedding reception before the end of next year.'

'Great.'

'And I've sent a note to all the guests telling them we had to reschedule.'

'You did?' Molly turned and looked at her sister in surprise. She had completely forgotten that the invitations had gone out last month and that people would need to be informed of the change of plan.

'Somebody had to,' Laura replied with a sanctimonious shrug.

'Thank you,' Molly said, realizing that her mother was right and she did sometimes take Laura for granted.

'No problem. At least the presents hadn't started arriving, it would have been a nightmare returning everything.'

'I'd have let Declan do it,' Molly retorted. 'He got us into this mess.'

'Then it would never get done,' Laura pointed out, 'unless he got his mother to do it.'

'If he could find her, that woman changes men and countries at such a rate it's hard to keep up.'

Laura chuckled. 'Our parents seem more normal than most, don't they? Robert's mum and dad are terribly stiff and formal. Fifteen years on, I still have to call them Mr and Mrs Dillon.'

'Funny, Declan was only saying he couldn't understand why Mum and Dad stay together given how much they argue.'

Laura looked at her in surprise. 'They don't argue.'

Molly laughed. 'That's exactly what I said, but I suppose to someone from outside the family it seems that way sometimes. After all, they're so different and have such diverse interests.'

'I still think she's mad to let him out on his own so much, there are too many middle-aged man-eaters out there.'

'He wouldn't look at another woman.'

Laura said nothing.

Molly looked at her. 'Do you know something that I don't?'

Laura kept her eyes on the road. 'I'm just saying, Mum should be more careful.'

Molly turned in her seat. 'You *do* know something, tell me.'

'Okay! I think Dad had an affair.'

'No!' Molly stared at her, shocked. Oliver was the last person she would ever have suspected of adultery. 'When? How do you know? No, I'm sure you're wrong; he wouldn't.'

Laura gave an irritable shrug. 'Fine, it never happened.'

'Sorry.' Molly sighed. 'Tell me.'

'It was when I found out I was pregnant—'

'That's fifteen years ago.' Molly did a quick calculation in her head. 'He would have been forty-eight or forty-nine?'

Laura nodded. 'And he still had hair. I'd gone to his office to talk to him, I thought it would be easier if I told Dad first, Mum and I were always arguing at the time.'

Molly nodded, remembering the rows and slamming of doors.

'I was sitting, waiting for him, and the receptionist was phoning around looking for him, but couldn't find him. And then some-one said he'd gone on a late lunch and was probably in Kelly's, the pub on the corner. So I went down and there he was, sitting at a table in the back with this other woman from the office.'

'Well, that doesn't mean anything,' Molly scoffed, she should have known Laura would have got things out of proportion. 'Colleagues are allowed to have lunch together.'

Laura threw her a scornful look. 'They were holding hands.'

'Oh!' Molly felt deflated. 'Still, perhaps she was upset about something and he was consoling her, Dad's so easy to talk to.'

'But you didn't see his face when he saw me. He looked so guilty, so shocked.'

'Well he would,' Molly reasoned. 'His daughter had just seen him holding hands with another woman.'

'Believe what you like, I know what I saw.' Laura turned up the volume and tapped along as the six speakers belted out the Toreador song from *Carmen*.

Molly stared out at the passing countryside, not sure what to make of the conversation. She found it hard to believe that her father would have had an affair, Belle was an attractive woman and, back then, she had been positively beautiful. Laura had just jumped to the wrong conclusion. And even if this woman was more than a colleague, it might have been a one-off. Something might have been about to happen and Laura's timely interruption had stopped it in its tracks.

Molly reached across to the radio and turned the volume back down. 'What happened next?'

Laura sighed. 'He jumped up and asked what was wrong. I told him I needed to talk to him in private. She excused herself and left, she couldn't get out of there fast enough.'

'Do you know her name? What did she look like?'

'Forget it, Molly, it was years ago.'

'Then why even bring it up?' Molly retorted, annoyed. How could Laura just drop a bombshell like that and then expect her to forget it? Her sister didn't bother replying, just turned up the volume on the radio again.

Molly rested her head against the window and stared out. There was no point in trying to drag information out of Laura, not now, but Molly was determined to revisit the subject over the next couple of days. She wondered if her father had been involved with the woman, really involved. And if he was, had her mother noticed he was different? It was frightening to think that this could happen in a marriage as strong as theirs. Or that a man like Oliver could be capable of such behaviour. And if he was, then what hope was there for the rest of them?

She had dozed off and was dreaming about something to do with her schooldays when Laura woke her.

'Molly, we're nearly there. Tidy yourself up, for goodness sake, you could run into Luke in reception.'

Molly felt her stomach do a flip at the thought that she might see him so soon. She pulled down the sun visor and checked her appearance in the mirror. Her cheeks were flushed from sleep and her hair was a bit dishevelled. With trembling fingers, she tugged a brush through it and had just applied some lip gloss when Laura pulled into the hotel car park.

'Wow, this is nice.'

Laura, who'd stayed in most of the best hotels in the country and was less easily impressed, gave a dismissive shrug. 'It's fine.'

As Laura searched for a parking spot, Molly twisted around to get a better look at the modern glass building that seemed to shine in the sunlight peering through the clouds. The Shannon ran along the other side of the road, and though it was a busy city location, Molly could still hear the water gurgle past. 'As it's a rugby holiday, I'd imagined a more rural location,' she remarked.

'Thomond Park, the main stadium and base of Shannon RFC is only down the road and this is a very central location for sight-seeing and socializing.'

Molly smirked. 'You're not into rugby, how do you know where the grounds are?'

'It would be a bit silly to come all this way to search for a rugby team and not do some research first, don't you think?' Laura said with exaggerated patience.

'I suppose so,' Molly agreed, feeling foolish. Apart from estab-lishing the name of Luke's company, she had left the rest to her sister. Perhaps that meant that she didn't really want to find Luke after all.

'Come on, let's check in and take a look around.'

The reception was bright and airy, with soft leather sofas scat-tered with bright cushions. A girl smiled broadly at them as they approached the desk.

Laura gave her name and soon they were being whisked up to the third floor in a silent lift, and then led down a corridor to their room. As Laura tipped the porter, Molly crossed the room to look out of the floor-to-ceiling window, and then back at the very comfortable-looking beds dressed in sumptuous satins of plum and lime green. 'This room is bigger than my whole flat,' she said as Laura started to unpack her overnight bag.

'It is a tiny flat,' Laura agreed. 'You definitely need to start house-hunting.'

Molly flopped into the chair by the window. 'Leave it, Laura,' she said, feeling weary.

'Fine,' Laura snapped and picked up the phone. 'According to Luke's itinerary, they should be out all afternoon, but we'll probably catch up with them in the bar or restaurant this evening. So, I'm going to book myself in for a facial and a massage, what about you?'

'I think I'll just go for a walk.'

'Don't you want to look your best?'

'I'd prefer a walk,' Molly said, although she knew she sounded like a stubborn child.

'Suit yourself. I'll book a table for dinner. Is seven-thirty okay?'

'It's a little early, isn't it?'

'I'd have thought you'd want to make the most of your time.'

'Fine.' Molly stood up and headed for the door.

'Aren't you going to unpack?' Laura looked at her in exasperation. 'All your clothes will be creased.'

'I'll do it later. Enjoy your pampering.'

As she wandered along the banks of the Shannon, Molly found herself thinking not of Declan or Luke, but of her father and Laura's shocking revelation. In her years of study, Molly had learned that the experts had numerous theories as to why people cheated. Many believed that adulterers simply wished to avoid intimacy and close attachments with their partner, but that wasn't Oliver. As both a husband and father, he was hugely demonstrative and open, much more so than most men. Molly dug her hands into her pockets and trudged on. Perhaps there really was an innocent explanation for his behaviour. Oliver was the sort of person who invited confidences, confessions and hard-luck stories. He was always sympathetic and ever patient, and it would be typical of him not to explain himself; if it was innocent, he would feel no need to.

Molly immediately felt better, although why a possible infidelity so long ago should trouble her, she wasn't entirely sure. It was probably because she simply couldn't see Oliver as being the unfaithful sort. Laura had to be wrong, and that was something that Molly found much easier to believe.

Chapter Fourteen

As Molly made her way towards the city, she pulled out her phone and called Ellen.

'You're there?' her friend said excitedly. 'Have you seen him yet?'

'No. Laura says we'll probably bump into them tonight.'

'How do you feel about that?'

'Do you know, Ellen, I'm not sure what I feel about anything at the moment,' Molly said honestly. 'Now I'm here, I feel a bit silly.'

'That's a good sign.'

'It is?'

'Yes, it means you're really in love with Declan and Luke just happened along when you were feeling low.'

Molly had to smile at Ellen's simplistic explanation.

'And when you do meet Luke, just remember how happy you are with Declan. Remember what you have together. Remember how you felt when you got engaged.'

Molly's smile faded. 'I was thrilled, Ellen, but I think he would have been just as happy if we'd continued on as we were.'

'But you wouldn't have been?'

'No.' Molly admitted. 'I needed him to show his commitment

to the relationship, I needed reassurance that we were both in this for the long term.'

'And he did.'

'Yes, but did he only do it to keep me happy?' Molly asked.

'If keeping you happy was that important to him, then I don't think you have anything to worry about, do you?' Ellen paused. 'Are you looking for reasons to doubt him, Molly?'

'I don't know, Ellen, maybe I am.'

'You have to remember the good things about your relationship,' Ellen urged.

Molly felt tears prick her eyes. 'I'm not sure I can at the moment.'

'Then I'll help you. Every day, I'm going to remind you of something good about Declan.'

Molly smiled. 'Are you going to make it up?'

'No, I am not! Mind you, with the way my memory is at the moment, it won't be easy. I'm going to hang up right now and start figuring out tomorrow's thought for the day.'

Molly laughed. 'Don't you have anything better to do?'

Ellen's sigh was audible. 'Not really. I'm tempted to go back to work, although I'd probably cut someone's ear off. I can't seem to concentrate on anything these days. I'm just waiting and I'm so fed up with it.'

'It won't be long now,' Molly soothed. 'And remember what Laura said, enjoy the rest while you can; you'll be getting precious little once Buster comes along.'

Ellen groaned. 'And on that cheerful note, she said goodbye.'

Feeling marginally better, Molly switched off her phone, picked up her pace and headed into town. At first, she just wandered the streets, looking absently into shop windows. Then she saw an elephant nightlight and, smiling, she hurried inside. Something for the nursery might cheer Ellen up. Though she normally hated shopping, Molly found herself wandering around the store, charmed by the miniature clothes and pretty soft toys. She couldn't really afford to spend that much, but still . . .

'Where on earth have you been?' Laura snapped when Molly finally let herself into their room, laden down with bags. 'It's almost six-thirty.'

Molly dropped her load and laughed. 'I walked into town, did some shopping and then just had to stop for a rest and a cuppa before I started back.'

'Haven't you heard of taxis?' Laura asked sarcastically. 'And why didn't you tell me you were going shopping? I'd have liked to come along.'

'Sorry, it was a spur of the moment thing. I saw this gorgeous baby shop, so I decided to pick up a few things for Ellen.'

'*You* went into a baby shop?' Laura eyed her with disbelief. 'You never bought me anything when I was pregnant.'

'I was fifteen!' Molly looked at her sister with exasperation.

'Even so.' Laura was sulky. 'You never paid any attention to me.'

'You were the centre of attention in our house for more than a year,' Molly retorted. 'And what about all the babysitting I did for you?'

'Only because I paid you,' Laura shot back.

'Oh, please. I cannot believe that we are arguing about stuff that happened when we were teenagers.' Molly shook her head tiredly and headed for the bathroom. 'I'm going to take a bath.'

'You don't have time.'

'Fine! I'll take a shower.'

'What about your clothes? What are you going to wear? You still haven't unpacked.'

Molly closed the door on her and turned the key, not even bothering to answer. Laura stared at the closed bathroom door and turned away in frustration. Molly's bags were where she'd dropped them and Laura automatically started to tidy them into a corner. A cuddly multi-coloured hippo fell out and she picked it up and stroked the soft, velvety toy. There had been no such show of celebration when she was expecting Adam and Ash. Both families had been reeling from the shock that she was pregnant and when they found out it was going to be twins, Robert's mother had looked positively appalled. Oliver and Belle had been a lot more understanding, but even they had been more concerned than happy. Laura didn't remember feeling any of the excited anticipation that Ellen was brimming with, despite the fact that she was going to be a single parent. Her overriding feelings had been embarrassment and humiliation. At a time when all of her friends were starting careers or going into their second year of college, she was preparing for motherhood. Robert had been little or no help. He was in his final year of college and studying hard and, when he was around, Laura sometimes caught him looking at her enormous bump with a mixture of shock and horror.

Things hadn't improved when the children were born. Those first weeks had passed in a blur of swollen breasts, sleepless nights and continuous crying. Oliver and Belle had tried to help, but Laura had been determined to show them that she could cope just fine without them. She had made a mistake getting pregnant, and a bigger one rushing into marriage, but she was damned if she was going to admit it.

As Laura sat cuddling the hippo and staring out at the Shannon, tears filled her eyes. She had been so lonely and miserable and, though she would never have admitted it, she had resented her babies, particularly Ash. It was completely irrational, but she had taken it personally that her daughter didn't want her milk and would not be comforted by her. Insult was added to injury that Ash quieted immediately, the moment her hesitant and mostly absent father took her in his arms. Laura now realized that she was probably suffering post-natal depression, but she was too young to realize it then. All she knew was that she didn't want to be pitied. She assured her girlfriends that it was bliss not having to work or study and that setting up home with Robert and her babies was all she could have dreamed of.

It had been more like a bloody nightmare, she thought now, dabbing at her wet cheeks. It had got easier once the twins were in a routine and Robert got a job, but he worked long hours and Laura often felt lonely and isolated. Thankfully, he earned good money from the start, and she could afford to pay her sister to baby-sit for a few hours once a week, allowing her to go shopping, meet friends for coffee, and just feel like a normal person again. If it hadn't been for that, she thought she might have gone completely mad.

The sound of Molly warbling in the shower pulled her back to the present. It was nearly seven o'clock, and she hadn't even taken out something to wear; how could she be so blasé, given she was about to meet her old flame? The shower was still running, so Laura gave into temptation and took a peak in Molly's small bag – how could it possibly hold enough for their three-day stay? Laura had only spied some denim and a rather cheap-looking top when the shower stopped. She hurriedly zipped up the bag again and returned to her place by the window.

The denim turned out to be a simple but pretty dress that, miraculously, was not full of creases. Molly's hair, which she had towelled dry and then simply brushed back from her face, hung in soft waves around her heart-shaped face and made her look sweet and innocent. She looked barely twenty, never mind approaching thirty, Laura thought sourly, draining her glass of gin and tonic. Having spent all afternoon in the beauty salon and an hour on her make-up, she knew she didn't look remotely as pretty as her sister.

'It's a bit quiet, isn't it?' Molly murmured, taking a sip of her drink and looking around at the almost deserted lounge.

'Perhaps they've already gone in to dinner.' Laura signalled the barman for another drink.

'Shouldn't we go in? I thought you'd booked a table for seven-thirty.'

'It doesn't look like that will be a problem, does it?' Laura pointed out.

'Perhaps I should ask reception if he's here.'

'Don't be silly.' Laura looked at her in exasperation; sometimes her clever little sister could be terribly thick. 'If you do that, then how can you pretend that us being here is a total coincidence?'

Molly grinned. 'Good point, I didn't think of that.'

'We need to agree a signal,' Laura mused.

'What do you mean?'

'If Luke is here and he comes over, you need to let me know if you want me to leave you alone together.'

Molly looked amused. 'You missed your vocation, you should have been a private eye.'

'Lucky for you,' Laura retorted, as the waiter set down her drink. 'So, what do you think?'

Molly shrugged. 'How about if I take off my ring and move it to a different finger?'

'You meet your ex and you start messing around with your engagement ring.' Laura shot her sister an incredulous look. 'You might as well tell him that you're his for the taking.'

'Okay then, I'll take off my watch and change the time.'

'Fine. If you do that, I'll say I'm going up to the room to call Robert and the children.'

'Then what?'

Laura shrugged. 'That depends on you. If you want some time alone with him, text me and I'll keep out of the way. Otherwise, I'll come back after thirty minutes.' Molly gave a reluctant nod and Laura eyed her impatiently. 'I really don't understand you, Molly. You wanted to see him and now that we're here, you look like a lamb on its way to be slaughtered.'

'This isn't easy for me, Laura.' Her sister glared at her.

Laura took in Molly's worried face and her irritation ebbed away. 'You're here now, Moll,' she said softly, 'you may as well go through with it.'

'You're right,' Molly agreed with a weak smile.

Laura picked up her bag and stood up. 'Ready?'

'Ready.'

After all the build-up, her heart hammering in her chest, Molly felt disappointed. 'It's like being at a funeral,' she whispered, looking around the dining room in horror. There were only three other parties in the restaurant and, for the most part, they were eating in silence.

'It will liven up once the boys arrive,' Laura said, although she too looked doubtful. 'Is it always so quiet?' she asked the waiter after he'd taken their order.

He laughed. 'Not at all, you should have been here last night, we had a crowd of French rugby players in and the place was buzzing.'

Molly exchanged a look of pure relief with her sister. 'Will they be around later?'

'Sorry, girls, but you've missed the boat; they left this morning.' He winked at them and left.

'They've gone! But they should have only just got here.'

'They must have changed their itinerary.' Molly couldn't

believe that after travelling this far, she'd missed Luke. 'He's probably back in France by now.'

'Oh, this is just typical of you,' Laura raged. 'I organized everything and the only thing you had to check, you got wrong.'

'I did not get it wrong.'

'You must have.'

Molly stood up and threw down her napkin.

'Where are you going?'

'To get my laptop so you can see the itinerary yourself,' Molly said and stalked out of the restaurant. What the hell had happened? she fumed as she took the lift up to the room. Had she got the dates mixed up? No, she was sure she hadn't.

Back in the restaurant, she handed the laptop to her sister with a flourish. 'It wasn't my fault, see for yourself.'

Laura scanned the website while Molly looked around her, and wondered what she would do with herself for the next two days.

'You idiot!' Laura shook her head in disgust.

'What?'

'The dates you looked at were for a schoolboy tour,' Laura explained with exaggerated slowness, 'the adult tour started on the 2nd.'

'I'm sorry.' Molly flushed, she felt very stupid. 'So we've missed them.'

'Maybe not,' Laura said thoughtfully.

'What do you mean?'

'They haven't gone home, they've moved on to Galway. They'll be there for three days.'

Laura read down through the details on the screen and then looked up and smiled. 'Then they go to Dublin and they fly home on the 9th.'

'So I could still see him,' Molly murmured, her spirits rising.

'Yes, I just need to check where they're staying in Galway.'

Molly frowned. 'No, I mean I could see him in Dublin; we're not going to Galway.'

'Why not?' Laura asked. 'There's not much point in staying here.'

Molly was about to answer, when the waiter returned with their food. 'Now, ladies, can I get you anything else?'

'No, we're fine, thanks,' Molly smiled. When he was gone, she looked back at her sister. 'You've paid for three nights, Laura. We can't just leave. And I'm sure they're staying somewhere equally luxurious and expensive in Galway.'

Laura shrugged. 'That's not a problem.'

Molly shook her head.

'What?' Laura demanded.

'I'm just wondering how you'll cope if Robert is ever out of work.'

'Robert's an accountant; he'll never be out of work.'

'Even so, it's not fair to charge him with two hotels when he doesn't even realize he's paying for one,' Molly said, appalled at Laura's lack of scruples.

Ignoring her, Laura set aside her plate and pulled the laptop closer. After a few minutes, she closed it with a snap and stood up.

'Where are you going?' Molly asked, mystified.

'Stay here, I'll be back in a minute.'

Molly watched her march out of the room and sighed. She looked up and caught the waiter's questioning gaze and gave him a reassuring nod and ate some food although she didn't feel remotely hungry.

Within minutes, Laura was back. She sat down and spread her napkin carefully across her lap, a smug smile on her lips. 'All taken care of.'

'What do you mean?'

'Luke is using a sister hotel in Galway,' Laura explained. 'I've arranged for them to transfer our booking there and it won't cost a penny.'

'Are you sure?' Molly looked at her suspiciously; this was all a little too convenient.

'Absolutely.'

'But how do we explain to everyone that we came to Limerick and ended up in Galway?'

'That's easy, we'll just say we weren't happy with the hotel and demanded to be moved.'

'As if they'll swallow that,' Molly protested. 'How could we possibly complain about a freebie?'

Laura frowned in confusion. 'But I would always complain if a hotel wasn't up to scratch, free or not.'

And Molly realized that she would and, what's more, Robert would know that.

'So, in the morning, we're off to Galway.' Laura smiled.

'You're enjoying this,' Molly accused.

'Well, it is quite exciting, and I won't be exactly sorry to leave this lively bunch, will you? It would be fun to meet up with Luke's Frenchmen and, lord knows, I could do with some fun.'

Molly watched her sister closely and heard the touch of sadness in her voice. 'What does that mean?'

Laura concentrated her attention on removing the bones from her fish. 'It doesn't mean anything, don't analyse me.'

'Stop being so defensive,' Molly retorted. 'It was a simple question.'

Laura put a delicate morsel in her mouth and took a sip of her drink before replying, 'After so many years of marriage, there isn't a lot to get excited about, that's all,' she said finally.

'Well, there's a cheerful thought. Thanks for that.'

Laura smirked. 'You asked.'

'You couldn't wait to get married.'

'What did I know?' Laura's tone was dismissive.

'And if you could switch the clock back?'

'What do you mean?'

Molly studied her sister, but Laura wouldn't meet her eyes. 'Would you still marry Robert?'

'Probably. Who'd choose to be an unmarried mother?'

'Are you saying that you didn't love him?' Molly asked.

'I suppose I did, but if I hadn't been pregnant, I certainly wouldn't have got married at twenty.'

Molly didn't reply. She ate some food, but though it was beautifully presented and cooked, it seemed tasteless. Laura, she noticed, was tucking in with gusto and seemed unaffected by the conversation. It made Molly feel both depressed and disillusioned. Was this what her mother had been hinting at? Had she known that Laura was unhappy with Robert? But then, hadn't they all? Molly remembered from the start that she and Rory couldn't understand what Laura saw in Robert. He wasn't a bad person, just not a very interesting one and, even at twenty-two, he'd seemed stuffy and self-important.

'Is there something wrong with your food?' She looked up to see Laura frowning at her. 'Do you want to send it back?' She was already looking around for a waiter.

'No, Laura, it's absolutely fine. I think it's just nerves, I'm not very hungry.'

'Well, you can relax for tonight, you're not about to run into Luke. I tell you what, why don't we go into town after dinner?'

Molly looked startled. It hadn't occurred to her that Laura would want to go out. 'I really should get some work done.'

'That's fine, but I think I might go out for a while,' Laura said, with forced casualness.

'On your own?'

Laura shrugged. 'I'm not tired, and there's no point in me sitting here watching you work.'

'Okay then,' Molly said, realizing she didn't much fancy that either, 'but take a taxi, it's too dark to walk into town alone.'

Laura raised an eyebrow. 'I didn't know you cared.'

Molly smiled. 'Just make sure you come back; tomorrow we're going to Galway.'

Laura laughed. 'It's a pity that they're not touring the country, we could be their groupies!'

Molly laughed too, thinking that no one looked less like a groupie than her perfectly coiffed sister although, thanks to three G&Ts and two glasses of wine, Laura was considerably more relaxed. It occurred to Molly that perhaps this was why Laura had wanted to come with her; she simply needed a break from Robert and the children. Feeling slightly more tolerant towards her sister, Molly thought it would be nice if they both found the answers they were looking for and returned to Dublin with a clearer picture of what they wanted and needed in life.

Chapter Fifteen

9.20 p.m., Wednesday, 5th August

Laura found her way to Dolan's pub and bought a drink. She would normally have sat at a table, but tonight she'd thrown caution to the wind and sat at a corner of the bar. She swayed and tapped her foot in time to the traditional musicians who were playing a lively jig that had the crowd hopping. It wasn't really her kind of scene, but this was where the taxi driver had suggested, saying it was the spot to come to for a good bit of *craic* and, she had to admit, there was a wonderful atmosphere. Her eyes wandered around the crowd and she was pleased to see a mix of all ages and types. While there were plenty of couples and groups of girls, she was gratified to see that there were as many men. As she turned back to the bar to take a sip of her drink, her eyes locked with a man at the other end of the bar. That was the third time she'd caught him watching her. This time, he didn't look away, but smiled. He was with a group of men though, and she wasn't entirely sure if he was smiling at her or at something one of his colleagues had said. He looked to be late thirties, slightly thick around the middle, but tall, with a shock of silver hair and, from what she could see, he had good teeth. Laura had a thing about teeth. She was constantly nagging Robert to go and get something done about his, they were yellow and crooked, and not at all attractive, but Robert wasn't very image-conscious and only visited a dentist if he was in dire pain.

Laura took out her mobile phone and checked for messages. She'd called Robert from the taxi on the way over, but he'd been out with the children and said he'd call her back later. That was over an hour ago, and Laura was torn between annoyance and misery; her family seemed to be managing just fine without her.

'They're good, aren't they?'

She looked up to see that the silver-haired charmer was now at her side. Up close, she realized he was probably the wrong side of forty, but he had gorgeous blue eyes and a very sexy smile. 'Not bad,' she said with a brief smile and turned back to watch the group.

'On your own?'

She made a show of looking around her. 'It looks that way.'

'Shame. You should come and join me and my colleagues.'

'I'm fine right here, thanks.'

He grabbed a nearby stool and sat down next to her. 'You're right, it is much better here. Can I get you a drink?'

Laura looked down at her wine glass and then up into his face, pretending to think about it.

'You'd be doing me a great favour,' he confided. 'I'm bored out of my mind over there. We've been in meetings all day and they're still talking business.'

Laura looked at the group and noticed that the other men were a lot older and quite a grey-looking bunch. 'Then I suppose it would be cruel of me to refuse.' She smiled at him.

He held out his hand. 'Matthew Carroll.'

Laura put her hand in his, hesitating for only a moment. 'Molly Jackson.'

His eyes crinkled. 'You don't look like a Molly.'

'Don't I?'

'No, more a Penelope or Isabel.'

'How strange, Isabel is my mother's name.'

He smiled and then nodded at her glass. 'Another one of those, or would you prefer something stronger?'

'Wine is fine, thank you.'

He ordered her drink and a pint of Guinness for himself, and Laura warmed to him even more. Robert only ever ordered a glass of shandy these days, a drink she thought of as slightly effeminate; Guinness was a real man's drink. 'So, what do you do?' she asked.

'I'm in marketing.'

'And what do you market?'

He pulled a face. 'Pharmaceuticals, terribly boring, which is why I've had enough of that lot,' he nodded his head towards his group.

She smiled. 'Are you based in Limerick?'

'No, Cork, but I'm responsible for the Munster area, so I'm up here quite often. How about you? Do I detect a Dublin accent?'

She nodded.

'So, what brings you to Limerick, Molly?'

'I'm on business too. I work in the fashion industry and I'm travelling around visiting designers.'

He raised an eyebrow. 'Very impressive, and a lot more interesting than pharmaceuticals. So, will you be in Limerick for long?'

She shook her head and gave him a sad smile. 'I'm heading to Galway in the morning.'

'In that case,' he said, moving closer and bending to whisper in her ear, 'we must make the most of our evening.'

Laura shivered as she felt his lips brush her skin. 'I suppose we must.'

Molly had done a good evening's work. As Luke wasn't here, and wasn't likely to walk around the corner, she'd felt more relaxed and, having settled herself in the corner of the lounge with a pot of tea and her laptop, proceeded to read every message posted over the last forty-eight hours – no mean feat. And, halfway through, she'd felt rewarded for her work when she came across a message from BettyBlu raving about a boy in her class that she was just mad about and looking for advice about how or should she approach him. Molly heaved a sigh of relief. It looked as if the maths teacher had been kicked into touch. It was nice to have a happy ending for a change. There were a couple of fairly sensible replies to BettyBlu's question, so she didn't get involved.

She finished her tea, closed down her laptop and was about to retire to the room when her phone rang. A glance at the display confirmed that it was Declan.

'Morning,' she said.

'Evening,' he replied. 'So, how's Limerick?'

Molly glanced around her. 'Quiet.'

'What are you doing?'

'I just did some work, now I'm heading to bed.'

'You're supposed to be down there for a break, Moll,' he reminded her, his voice faint.

'I know, but I like to keep in touch. Anyway, I got some good news. Remember the girl I told you about that I was afraid was involved with her teacher?'

'Yes?'

'She's got a crush on someone her own age.'

'Well that is good news.'

Molly smiled. 'Yeah.'

'So, how are you and Laura getting along?'

'Not bad. Although every time I think that maybe she's not so bad, she comes out with something I just can't believe. Do you know what she told me on the way down?'

'What?'

'That she thinks Dad had an affair.'

'Oliver?' Declan gave a hoot of laughter. 'That's ridiculous.'

Molly smiled, that was exactly the reaction she'd been hoping for. 'That's what I thought, but she says she saw him holding hands with another woman.'

'There'll be a simple explanation. Listen, sorry, Moll, got to go; I have a breakfast meeting. I'll call you tomorrow, okay?'

'Okay. Night, Declan,'

'Night, Moll, love you.'

It was eleven o'clock when Molly climbed into bed and she wondered whether she should phone her sister and check if she was okay. But she was a grown woman and well capable of looking after herself. Snuggling down, Molly drifted off to sleep, a smile on her lips as she imagined BettyBlu dreaming of her new, fourteen-year-old love.

She was woken by the door closing, a crash as something fell to the floor and then a giggle. 'Laura?' Molly sat up, rubbing her eyes.

'Were you expecting someone else?' Laura giggled again.

Molly reached out to turn on the lamp, but then realized that's what Laura had knocked over. She righted it, turned it on and watched, mesmerized, as her sister kicked off her shoes and stumbled towards the bathroom. 'Are you drunk?'

'Course not,' Laura slurred as she put her hand out to grasp the handle of the door, missed and slid to the floor.

'You are!' Molly grinned, wide awake now and sorely tempted to grab her mobile phone, take a photo of her pie-eyed sister and send it to Rory. 'Where have you been?'

'Some pub.' Laura dragged herself back onto her feet and leaned against the wall.

'On your own?'

'Well, I started out on my own, but that didn't last long.' Laura gave a lewd wink that looked comical given the smudged mascara around her eyes.

Molly's eyes widened; this was getting better and better. 'You met someone?'

'Matthew. At least, that's what he said his name was.'

Molly looked at her in confusion. 'Why would he lie?'

'The same reason I did; it's safer when you're married. I told him I was Molly Jackson.'

'What?' Molly spluttered. 'Why on earth did you do that?'

'What difference does it make? We're going to Galway tomorrow; you're never going to meet him.'

Molly shook her head in disbelief. 'So, exactly what did you and Matthew get up to?'

'We talked.'

'I think you did a bit more than that.' Molly's eyes dropped to the top three undone buttons of her sister's blouse.

Laura looked down, and then smirked at her sister. 'Oh, don't be such an old woman, it was just a bit of fun.'

Molly's eyes widened. 'You didn't . . .'

'We had a kiss and a cuddle, that's all. Where's the harm in that?'

'I think I must still be dreaming,' Molly muttered, shaking her head.

'Oh, come on, I'm sure you and Ellen get up to all sorts when you go out.'

Molly shook her head. 'No.'

Laura stared at her. 'Seriously?'

'Seriously.'

'Well, that will all change once you get married, believe me.'

'Are you saying that you make a habit of picking up strange men?'

'For goodness sake, it's just a bit of harmless flirting.'

'But what about Robert? Don't you love him?'

'It's nothing to do with Robert or love,' Laura said irritably, 'you don't understand at all.'

'But Laura . . .' Molly started, but her sister had already stumbled into the bathroom and closed the door. Molly turned off the light and slid back down under the covers feeling slightly shocked by her sister's behaviour. She'd always labelled Laura a bit of a prude, and here she was, rolling in drunk after cavorting around with a total stranger. Apart from seeming out of character, it was downright dangerous. It seemed Belle was right about Laura – something was definitely troubling her sister, but what?

Chapter Sixteen

9.40 a.m., Thursday, 6th August

Molly was beginning to think she'd imagined the whole thing. Laura sat across the breakfast table looking as immaculate and poised as ever, albeit a little pale. She had made no reference at all to her behaviour the night before, and instead chatted about the day ahead, filling Molly in on the rugby club's likely movements.

'They're playing a match this afternoon.'

'Against who?'

'Galwegians.'

Molly's face lit up. 'That was the club Eric Elwood used to play for. I'd like to go to that.'

'Don't be ridiculous, of course you can't go,' Laura said irritably. 'How could you possibly explain your presence?'

Molly sighed. 'So, what's the plan?'

'We'll go straight to the hotel and see them there later.'

'Are you sure they're going to be there this time?'

Laura gave her a scathing look. 'It wasn't my fault they weren't here last night, remember?'

'No, sorry. I wasn't having a go, it's just that after a match they'll probably go out for the night.'

Laura shook her head. 'They'll be having lunch in the club-house, but they should be back in the hotel for dinner.'

Molly had her doubts. 'These guys are on holiday, and if they win the match, they'll probably stay at the club drinking and then go on to a club.'

'I don't think so. They're heading to Dublin in the morning and they have a training session as soon as they get there. They won't be able to drink too much. And even if they do, remember Luke is the tour organizer so he would probably come back to the hotel on his own anyway.'

'And eat in his room, watching telly,' Molly pointed out, suddenly feeling very depressed. What on earth was she doing here? Perhaps they should forget Galway and just drive home.

Laura seemed to read her mind. 'We're here now and our room is paid for. If it works, it works, if not, you can catch up with Luke in Dublin,' she shrugged. 'Or not.'

Molly nodded. 'Okay.'

Laura dabbed her mouth with her napkin and stood up. 'Right, I'll go up and brush my teeth. Don't be long.'

'I won't,' Molly promised, taking a sip of her tea. Checking her watch, she decided to make the most of Laura's absence and phone Ellen.

'Molly, hi! So? What happened?'

'Nothing, he's not here.'

'How come?'

'I got the dates wrong and his group had already left for Galway.'

'Oh no, what are you going to do?'

'We're following them; we leave straight after breakfast.'

'It sounds so exciting.' Ellen sounded wistful. 'I wish I was there.'

'Trust me, you're missing nothing, although my sister did go on a bender last night.'

'I don't believe it!' Ellen gasped.

Molly immediately regretted her indiscretion. 'You're right, I was just kidding. So, have you any news?'

Ellen gave a tired sigh. 'None, but I do have your thought for today.'

Molly smiled and settled back in her chair. 'Go on then.'

'Okay. Do you remember a couple of years ago when you offered to do the night shift on that helpline because it was Valentine's day and they were short staffed?'

Molly laughed softly. 'I remember. Declan was disgusted because he'd planned a romantic evening in an expensive restaurant. It was his own fault, though, because he rarely remembered to send me a card, never mind take me out. How was I to know he'd suddenly discovered his romantic gene?'

'Ah, but do you remember what happened next?'

Molly nodded, even though Ellen couldn't see her. 'Yes. He came down to the centre with a picnic and a candle and flowers and sat with me all through the night.'

'Have a good day, Moll.'

'Bye, Ellen, and thanks.'

She was still smiling as she went upstairs to the room.

'What?' Laura, who was at the mirror refreshing her lipstick, shot her sister a curious look.

'I was just thinking about Declan and how sweet he can be sometimes.'

Laura groaned. 'So you want to go home.'

'No.' Molly flopped onto the bed and smiled at her sister's reflection.

Laura closed her bag and turned around. 'Good. Let's go before you change your mind.'

'Are you sure you're okay to drive?' Molly picked nervously at a nail.

'Sorry?' Laura frowned.

'You could be still over the limit,' Molly pointed out.

Colour flooded Laura's cheeks and she looked away. 'I didn't have that much to drink.'

'Excuse me? You couldn't walk!'

'That's a total exaggeration; if I couldn't walk, how did I get back here?'

'I was wondering the same thing.'

'We took a taxi.'

'You got into a taxi with a strange guy?' Molly shook her head in disbelief. 'Are you completely mad? You could have ended up anywhere.'

'Well, I didn't.' Laura opened the door and led the way into the corridor.

Molly hurried after her. 'So, are you going to see him again?'

'Don't be ridiculous.' Laura stabbed the button for the lift. 'Now, can you please drop it?'

Molly's lips twitched. 'Sure, as long as you don't come rolling home drunk again tonight.'

Laura scowled as she stepped into the lift. 'Lord, are you always such a nag? No wonder Declan left.'

'That's not a very nice thing to say,' Molly said, her smile disappearing.

'Well, you're not being particularly nice to me,' Laura retorted.

'Okay, let's call a truce. I don't want to fight.'

'Good, because my head is like a bag of hammers,' Laura admitted with a glimmer of a smile.

They stopped for petrol just outside the city and Laura came back with two bottles of water. Molly suppressed a grin as Laura downed two painkillers. She decided against teasing her delicate sister. This fallible, rebellious Laura was a lot more likeable than her prudish, judgemental alter ego, although Molly was concerned about her sister's uncharacteristic behaviour. She took a surreptitious look at Laura as her sister donned dark glasses and pulled onto the Galway road. She looked fragile, her mouth was a thin, discontented line and the eyes she'd just hidden were bloodshot and weary. Laura might be living it up, but she didn't seem to be enjoying herself too much, although for those few drunken moments last night, Molly had seen a spark that wasn't normally there. She sighed and stared out at the fields rolling past. Everyone had problems, it seemed, and most people didn't talk about them, but muddled through somehow. Molly thought of Smithy, and of Ellen, and then of Luke. Was he free of his demons now, she wondered? He'd looked well, and confident and happy, but perhaps he was just putting on a brave face like the rest of them.

'Would you like me to drive and you can have a snooze?' Molly offered as Laura yawned widely.

'No, it's okay, thanks.'

Molly shrugged. 'About the hotel bill, Laura. I'd like to go halves.' She'd looked over her sister's shoulder as she was settling the account and nearly fainted. Molly couldn't afford it, but she couldn't let Laura, or rather Robert, shoulder the full cost either.

'Don't be silly. Robert can afford it, you and Declan can't.'

Molly bristled at her tactlessness; it seemed nasty Laura was back and nice Laura had disappeared. 'We're not destitute,' she said.

'Fine, if you want to contribute, you can give me a cheque when we get back to Dublin.'

'Fine,' Molly said and wondered how much two nights in Galway would cost. 'You know,' she said, 'there's no reason for us to stay two nights; Luke will only be there for one. We may as well go home a day early.'

'But we can't,' Laura said quickly.

'Why not?'

'It would look odd and, anyway, I've booked for two nights.'

'I'm sure they wouldn't charge us if we tell them when we're checking in. Didn't you say you're a good customer of this hotel chain?'

'Yes, but still—'

'We can ask,' Molly said, reasonably. 'They can only say no.'

Laura gave a curt nod. 'Leave it with me, I'll see what I can do.'

Molly saw the grim look on her sister's face and wondered if Laura was annoyed at missing out on another day of beauty treatments or another night on the tiles. Well, that was tough. Molly had come to find Luke, not to waste time and money flouncing around the countryside with her unpredictable sister. But she could imagine Ellen's reproach, almost hear her saying how she was too hard on her sister; that Laura had only come to Limerick for Molly's sake and that she should be more gracious. But now Molly knew different, and she wasn't comfortable with watching on while Laura did her damnedest to be unfaithful. They lapsed into silence and it was only when they neared the city that Laura spoke, her voice full of nostalgia. 'I've always loved Galway,' she said. 'It's such a cosmopolitan city and it has the best shops and restaurants.'

'I love it too, and it's so full of character and history,' Molly agreed. 'The Spanish Arch, Salmon Weir Bridge, and then there's the cathedral. If Luke's going to be tied up all day, I may just indulge myself and play the tourist.'

'How exciting,' Laura muttered.

Molly looked at her in exasperation. 'What's wrong now? I don't expect you to come with me, you can spend the day in the spa. I'll be quite happy pottering around town on my own.'

'You're always so damn superior, aren't you?'

'Excuse me?'

'You take every opportunity to flaunt your fancy education. Well, I may be just a mother, but I'm not stupid.'

Molly stared at her, not sure whether she wanted to strangle or hug her. 'Laura, you are not *just* a mother, and I don't think you're stupid.'

'But you do think I'm frivolous and shallow.'

'This is ridiculous—'

'There you go again. My feelings are ridiculous. You're all the same,' Laura muttered under her breath.

'Who?' Molly asked, completely baffled by this attack.

'Forget it.'

'No. Please tell me.'

'Just leave it, I have a headache.'

'I suppose that's my fault too.'

Laura didn't bother answering, and Molly lapsed into an angry silence. All her concerns for her sister disappeared and she wished she'd left her in Dublin. She certainly wouldn't be beholden to her; she would be writing that cheque as soon as they got home. Molly decided that she would spend the day alone and Laura could do what she liked. She might even have dinner in town and then take her laptop into the hotel lounge in the hope of bumping into Luke. As for Laura, she could spend the evening working her way through every member of Luke's group for all she cared.

The rest of the journey passed in a tense and angry silence, and when Laura pulled up outside the hotel, she grabbed her bag and stalked inside without a word. Feeling miserable, Molly traipsed after her. This was going from bad to worse. Logic told her that she should patch things up with Laura straight away, or the remainder of their stay would be unbearable. And if they returned to Dublin not talking, Belle would be furious.

Molly sat in the stylish lounge and waited while Laura checked in. She could tell simply from her sister's body language that she was still fuming; God help the poor receptionist if she got anything wrong. The thought had no sooner entered Molly's head than she saw her sister gesticulating and the girl nod politely, a pained look on her face. 'Great,' Molly groaned and sank back in the chair.

'Ready?' Laura stood over her, eyebrows raised.

'I was ready ten minutes ago, is there a problem?'

'She had allocated us a room on the ground floor when I had specifically requested a room with a view of the water.'

'Does it matter? We're only here for one night.'

'Two, they wouldn't allow me to change the booking,' Laura said, not looking at her. 'And of course it matters. It's that attitude that encourages sloppy, second-rate service.'

'So, did you get what you wanted?'

'Of course.'

Molly couldn't help smiling.

'What?' Laura's eyes were suspicious.

Molly shrugged. 'You're a force to be reckoned with.'

'Are you trying to be clever?'

Molly stood up. 'Oh, Laura, can we please just stop bickering, I'm sick of it.'

'I have no problem with that,' Laura said, although her tone was as stiff and expressionless as her face.

'I don't know why you came,' Molly said as they made their way to their room. 'It certainly wasn't because you enjoy my company.'

'You are so ungrateful.' Laura threw open the door.

'I am not ungrateful.' Molly followed her in and was momentarily speechless. Yet again, their room was palatial and, yet again, Laura seemed oblivious. 'Look, I'm sorry if I have been smart or annoying or in anyway offensive,' she added with studied patience. 'Now, I'm going to go out for a while and let you relax. I think we could probably both use some time apart.'

'Okay then, but this time can you at least get back in time to have a bath and do something with your hair?'

Molly opened her mouth to retort, but thinking better of it, she slung her bag over her shoulder and left.

Her pace didn't slow until she was in the hustle and bustle of Eyre Square and she let out a long sigh as the buzz of the vibrant city reached out to her and she was able to take some long, slow breaths and put Laura out of her mind. She wandered around aimlessly for a while, then went into the Corrib shopping centre, out the other side and down St Vincent's Avenue, towards the cathedral. It was years since she'd last been here and she was surprised that she still remembered the way. When the building came into sight, she was stopped in her tracks, as she had been in the past, by the beauty of the building. Its sheer size and the way the sun glinted off the grey stone and bronze dome was enough to take her breath away. It had been built in the sixties and Molly knew there had been some controversy about the venture at the time, many feeling that the money would be better spent on the poor. But Molly doubted anyone would say now that it had been a bad investment. It was a striking piece of architecture and an undoubted boon to the beautiful city. She crossed the bridge – the cathedral was perched on an island in the centre of the River Corrib – and went inside, pausing to marvel at the octagonal dome, admire the organ, and then stroll on around the church to study the statues and artwork that made the cathedral a museum as much as it was a place of worship. She would have happily spent all afternoon there, but her stomach rumbling reminded her that it had been several hours since her continental breakfast. Reluctantly, she headed back into town and as it was such a nice day, she bought a sandwich and a bottle of water and took it into the park at the centre of

Eyre Square. There were bodies littered everywhere and there was an almost carnival atmosphere as people enjoyed the sunshine; you didn't get much of it in Ireland and so learned to enjoy it when it made an appearance.

Molly finally found some space and, even though it was quite near the road, she sank gratefully down onto the springy grass, kicked off her sandals and opened up her sandwich. When she'd finished eating, she stretched out on her stomach and watched the world go by. She pondered what to do next, more sightseeing or return to the hotel and enjoy the long, hot bath she'd been dreaming of? She quickly dismissed the latter; Laura might be there and she'd be stuck with her for the rest of the day. She could go for a swim, the hotel had a spectacular pool, or so Laura said, but she didn't have a costume with her so that was out. So it would be more sightseeing. But there was no rush. The sun was making Laura feel sleepy, and rolling over onto her back, she closed her eyes and enjoyed the feeling of the sun's rays on her face. Perhaps she'd just stay here for a little while longer . . .

It was a child crying, quite close by, that woke her with a start and she sat up rubbing her eyes. Glancing at her watch, she realized that she'd only been asleep for about twenty minutes, but she felt hot and disorientated and, slipping on her sandals, she headed for the cool of the shopping centre. She was standing, studying the floor plan, when she heard her name being called. She turned slowly, frowning, who could possibly be calling her? It must be some other Molly.

'Molly?'

This time the voice was louder, closer, and she whirled around. 'Luke?' She didn't have to pretend surprise; he was supposed to be in the Galwegians club house, not here, so close that if she put out her hand she could touch him.

'What are you doing here?' He came even closer and smiled down at her.

Molly gulped. 'I could ask the same question!'

He put a hand on her arm and bent to kiss her cheek. 'It's so good to see you again.'

Molly closed her eyes at the feel of his lips on her skin and inhaled his smell. When she stepped back, he was looking at her in wonder. 'I can't believe it, first the airport and now here, what an amazing coincidence. How are you?'

'Good.' She nodded and grinned like an idiot. She'd tracked him across the country and now that he was standing in front of her, she was completely lost for words.

'It's lovely to see you,' he said. 'You look wonderful; your hair's different.'

She tried for a casual shrug. 'It's been a long time.'

He checked his watch. 'I don't suppose you have time for a coffee?'

She made a show of examining the time too, and managed a small smile, despite the fact that her stomach was churning. 'Why not?'

Chapter Seventeen

3.15 p.m., Thursday, 6th August

Molly studied Luke as he made his way to the counter. He was still in good shape, but he had lost the gangly, boyish look. She noticed how the waitress flirted with him, and how completely oblivious he was to the fact; he hadn't changed much then. She frantically combed her fingers through her tangled hair and wished she hadn't gone to sleep in the sun; she could feel her cheeks were hot and could only imagine what a sight she must be.

He turned around and, with a tray held high, carefully weaved his way through the tables towards her.

'I got you a doughnut,' he said with a grin. 'Do you still love them?'

'I do. Thanks,' she said, doubting she'd be able to swallow a crumb.

'So, Molly.' His eyes searched her face. 'How are you?'

'I'm fine, you?'

He nodded. 'Pretty good.'

'How is everyone?'

'Dad's retired now and Sandra is married.'

'Little Sandra!'

Luke grinned. 'Little Sandra is twenty-four.'

'And your mum?' Molly asked anxiously.

'She's doing okay,' he said briefly. 'And the Jackson gang?'

'Mum and Dad are great. Laura too – the twins are fourteen now, would you believe?'

'Wow.'

She smiled. 'And Rory is as mad as ever. He still lives at home. He went off to Oz for a few years and then decided to come home and study law.'

Luke pulled a face. 'It's hard to imagine Rory in such a serious profession. What about you, Moll, what do you do?'

'I work as a counsellor for a teenage magazine,' she said over the rim of her cup.

'So you're a psychiatrist?'

'A psychologist.'

'I thought you had your heart set on becoming a GP?'

'After I'd experienced counselling myself, I realized that I might be better suited to psychology,' she explained, 'and the thought of helping young people appealed to me.'

His eyes softened. 'Why does that not surprise me? I wasn't quite as noble.'

'You made rugby your career?'

'Yes, I did go to college and trained as a P.E. teacher, although I've never actually taught. I played for Bordeaux until I was twenty-seven, but I was plagued with injuries and eventually had to retire.'

'I'm so sorry.' Knowing how much he'd always loved the sport, Molly realized how hard that must have been for him.

He gave an almost Gallic shrug. 'I was never going to play for France or Ireland, for that matter, but I was pretty cut up about it at the time. I worked as a coach at my club for a couple of years and then I met this English guy who ran rugby tours to the UK. They were a combination of training and sightseeing tours, with a visit to a senior game. He suggested I could do the same in Ireland and I thought, why not?'

'Great idea,' Molly nodded enthusiastically, feeling a terrible fraud. She knew this already; what would he think if she admitted that?

'Yeah, it's proven quite popular, and I do enjoy it. I get to come back to Ireland a few times a year and I'm still working in the sport I love. I can't complain.'

She smiled. He was older, he was more mature, more reflective perhaps, but he was still the guy she'd fallen in love with. Her eyes roamed over his face, the crooked nose, the hard, square jaw, the dimple in his chin and those eyes – as she met them she realized he'd been studying her in the same way. 'Well?' she raised an eyebrow. 'What's the verdict?'

He threw back his head and laughed. 'You've changed, you're all grown up.'

'I've aged, you mean.'

'You're more beautiful than ever.'

Flushing under the intensity of his gaze, Molly didn't know quite what to say. She should probably tell him about Declan, but found she didn't want to.

Luke took the decision out of her hands by glancing worriedly at his watch. 'I'm sorry, I have to go. I'd love to catch up properly, but I'm going to be tied up for the rest of the day, and tomorrow we're off to Dublin first thing. Are you staying in Galway for long?'

'Two nights; we go home on Saturday morning.'

'We?' he asked.

'I'm here with Laura.'

'Oh, right.' He smiled, actually looking relieved, or was that just wishful thinking on her part? 'We have a match on Saturday afternoon, but I could meet you after that.' He stopped suddenly. 'Sorry, you probably don't want to—'

'No, I'd like that,' Molly said quickly. 'It would be nice to talk.'

He closed his eyes briefly. 'I really would like that.'

'Great. Okay.' She was smiling like an idiot again.

'Well, if you give me your number, I could phone you on Saturday and we could arrange when and where.'

'Yes, right, of course.' And as Molly read out her number, he keyed it into his phone. They finished their coffees and stood up to go.

'Where are you staying?' he asked.

'The Radisson.'

His eyes widened in surprise. 'What a coincidence, so are we. Maybe I'll bump into you later.'

'Then you'll get to meet Laura again.'

He pulled a face. 'Is she as scary as she used to be?'

'More so,' Molly assured him, laughing.

They stood looking at each other and, though there was so much Molly wanted to say, to ask, she realized that just standing there, looking at him for a while longer, would be good too.

'Are you heading back to the hotel now?' she asked, finally realizing that one of them should break the spell.

'No, I have to go out to Galwegians and check in with my group. They won their match this morning and I've a feeling they'll be celebrating hard. It's my job to make sure they get back to the hotel in one piece.'

'Well, good luck with that. It was lovely to see you again, Luke.'

'And you. If I don't see you later, I'll call on Saturday.'

'Great.'

He hesitated for a moment, and then kissed her very gently on the lips. 'Bye, Molly.'

'Bye, Luke,' she said and walked away, resisting the urge to put her fingers to her mouth, just in case he was still watching. He wanted to see her again, she couldn't believe it. But then, why wouldn't he? It didn't mean he still loved her, just that he had as many questions as she did. They'd never had a chance to discuss what had happened. At first they were too shell-shocked and then, just when Molly felt she was ready, his father had whisked him off to Bordeaux. The thought of finally having that conversation on Saturday was a terrifying prospect; it would be painful for them both.

As she made her way back to the hotel, Molly laughed out loud. Laura would be disgusted with her. She'd found out exactly nothing about Luke. She didn't know if he had a partner, if he had kids – nothing. But she had been content just to sit there with him; she hadn't even thought to ask. Or, maybe, she just hadn't wanted to know. He hadn't asked those questions either, she realized. Was that because he didn't care, because he was afraid of the answer or because Ruth was their only remaining link? But the expression in those wonderful eyes had been so affectionate and tender, his kiss soft and sweet . . .

Molly was still thinking about it as she let herself into the room. Laura was prone on her bed, a cloth across her eyes, so she tiptoed across the room, picked up her laptop, and made to leave.

'Where are you off to?'

Molly turned to see her sister leaning on one arm, watching her through narrowed eyes. 'I thought you were asleep, so I was going down to the lounge to catch up on some work.'

'You can stay here if you want. I've a massage in ten minutes and then I plan to use the sauna and take a swim.'

'I think I'll go downstairs anyway.'

Laura looked bewildered. 'Why don't you come with me? Aren't you at all interested in looking your best for Luke?'

'Too late for that, I'm afraid,' Molly admitted. 'I've just left him.'

Laura swung her legs around and sat up. 'You've seen Luke?'

'Yes, I bumped into him in town. We had coffee together.'

'And?' Laura prompted.

'We might be meeting up in Dublin on Saturday.'

'But what's wrong with tonight?'

'He said he'll be tied up with the group all evening.'

Laura looked at her in dismay. 'Well, that's a bit of an anticlimax.'

'Sorry. Do you want to go home?'

'No.' Laura looked alarmed. 'The room is paid for and I've booked some more treatments tomorrow.'

'Fine, then we'll stay.'

Laura visibly relaxed. 'So, is he married?'

Molly sighed. 'I didn't ask.'

'Kids?'

Molly shrugged. 'I don't know what came over me, but my mind just went blank. Stupid, isn't it? I come all this way to see him and then I can't make normal conversation.'

Laura's eyes grew thoughtful. 'Interesting.'

Molly flopped down on her bed with a sigh. 'What does that mean?'

'If you didn't care about him, you wouldn't have reacted that way, would you?'

'I think it's probably more to do with the fact that I've spent so much time anticipating a conversation with him, that when he was actually sitting there right in front of me, I just couldn't find the words.'

'It's understandable, Moll.' Laura shot her a sympathetic look. 'Did you talk about Ruth?'

Molly shook her head. 'Never mentioned her.'

'Don't worry about it. You weren't expecting to meet him. You'll be better prepared on Saturday.'

'True.' Molly smiled gratefully, nice Laura was back.

'How was he with you?'

'Really nice, and he seemed genuinely happy to see me.'

'Obviously, or he wouldn't have asked to see you again. As my children would say, "Result!"'

As lavender-scented oil was massaged into Laura's back, she closed her eyes and considered this latest development. Not only was Molly on the brink of marriage to a successful and attractive man, she had Luke waiting in the wings to add a zing of excitement to her life. Laura couldn't help it; she was consumed with envy. Here she was, trapped in a dreary marriage with a man she could barely look at, a man whose touch filled her with loathing, while her sister had two attractive, interesting men after her. And as if that wasn't bad enough, Laura was to be deprived of any time with Luke's group of Frenchmen; there was simply no justice in the world. All she'd wanted was a little bit of fun, a short break away from her family, an opportunity to feel like an attractive woman and not just a mother, was that so wrong? Molly would probably be happier to go home tomorrow, but tough. At the very least, Laura was determined to enjoy Galway and any attention she might attract. If Molly wanted to hole up in their room with her damned laptop, that was up to her, but Laura was going to make the most of her time.

It wasn't as if her family would miss her. She'd called home again earlier, and Ash wouldn't even come to the phone. Robert had tried to make excuses for her, but Laura had clearly heard her in the background saying she didn't want to talk to her mother and that she'd only asked for her because her 'little apple' was out. It was like a knife through her heart, and the reason Laura had felt so reckless when Matthew Carroll had approached and started to chat her up.

The more the man had talked, the less Laura had liked him. He was a bit too loud for her taste, and his humour a touch bawdy, but he had clearly fancied her and that was flattering. In the cold light of day though, it made Laura feel quite pathetic. Would she throw herself at any man that looked her way, was that how desperate she'd become? Tonight, she resolved, she'd be more picky. She might not be as pretty as her sister, but she knew that she was still an attractive woman. Perhaps her more classic style would appeal to a Frenchman, she mused, although it didn't look likely now that she would find out. If Luke had said he wouldn't see Molly tonight, then they were obviously going out, but where? It couldn't be that difficult to find out. She resolved to have a chat with one of the porters later, although not when her sister was within earshot. Just because she wasn't going to have any male company, didn't mean Laura couldn't enjoy a little joie de vivre.

Molly sat in the lounge, a glass of water on the table in front of her and her computer on her lap. She hadn't done much work though, just kept re-living her brief time with Luke. He'd looked wonderful, vibrant, healthy and confident; a different person from the one that left Ireland twelve years ago. She wondered if he was as nervous as she was, about re-living the past, but he hadn't run for the hills when he'd met her, but bought her a coffee and suggested they meet again. Still, that was two days away, and perhaps he'd have a change of heart between now and then and not phone after all. Molly wondered how she'd feel if he didn't; she was terribly afraid she'd be distraught. And where did that leave Declan? It was hard to feel close to him when he was so far away and they couldn't talk properly. Perhaps she should start emailing him, although she knew he could only access his mail at work and wasn't comfortable being seen to use it for personal business. Molly was beginning to wonder if, in moving to Enco, Declan had jumped out of the frying pan and into the fire. They seemed terribly regimented, almost feudal in their rules and regulations.

She took another sip of water and signed on to *Teenage Kix*. She was glad she'd got so much done the night before, because today she knew she'd find it impossible to concentrate. It worried her that, feeling this distracted, she might not be as diligent as usual and, to that end, she sent emails to Carl and Tess asking them to be more vigilant than usual because the Internet access in the hotel was unreliable. This was a complete lie, of course, it was excellent, but she could hardly tell them that their boss didn't trust herself to do her job properly. Anyway, officially, she was on holiday. Even so, she decided to put together a reply to Smithy's last post. She was in the process of doing that when her phone rang. Picking it up, she glanced at the display and answered smiling. 'Hi, Ellen. This better not be a call to say you're in labour!'

'If only,' Ellen said with feeling.

'How are you?'

'Tired, but fine. No sign of action.'

'Well, you do still have nine days to go.'

'I know, but it doesn't stop me wishing and hoping. I can barely sleep, I'm so excited, Molly. I just can't wait to meet my baby.'

Molly's eyes filled at the emotion in her friend's voice. 'It won't be long. You need a project to keep you busy.'

'Like what? I've cleaned, painted and papered every surface, I've enough nappies to last the child for the first six months and I've even bought three different types of formula in case breast-feeding doesn't work out.'

'What about a name?' Molly asked. 'You can't call it Buster for-ever. Well, you can, but your folks won't talk to you again if you do.'

'It might be worth threatening that, just to see the look on Dad's face.' Ellen giggled. 'But I deliberately didn't pick names because I didn't want to tempt fate.'

'I know that, but I think it would be safe enough to decide on a short-list now, don't you?'

'I suppose so,' Ellen agreed, sounding a lot happier. 'I've always loved the name Ingrid.'

The name conjured up the image of a blonde, blue-eyed au pair or a strict, masculine matron type. Molly decided to keep her thoughts to herself. 'Ingrid Brennan sounds too much like Ingrid Bergman.'

'And I also like Marina,' Ellen said enthusiastically. 'And what about Ike?'

'Er, not great for a girl.'

'Ha ha.'

'I'm not sure your son would survive living on the north side of Dublin with a name like Ike,' Molly said honestly.

'Um, perhaps you're right. How about Marc with a "C"?'

'What's wrong with Mark with a "K"?'

'It's a bit ordinary. Greg?'

'Not bad. Jeremy?'

Ellen groaned. 'As in Kyle and Clarkson?'

'As in Irons and Paxman.'

'No, sorry, I don't think so.'

'I'll give it some more thought,' Molly promised.

'Do, but in the meantime, it's time for your thought for the day.'

Molly laughed. 'Go on then.'

'Do you remember last year, when we ran the mini marathon?'

Molly closed her eyes, groaning. 'How could I forget?' She'd done no training and, apart from her cycling, she'd never been the most athletic of women. But ten kilometres hadn't seemed far, and it *was* in aid of breast cancer. It would have been fine if she'd just walked most of the way like many of the women but, no, that would have been too easy. The fact that she'd bought new trainers for the big day was the final nail in the coffin. By the time she'd crawled across the finish line, her heels were blistered and bloody and she was close to tears. Declan had taken one look at her, scooped her into his arms and carried her to the car, which was parked a good ten minutes away. At home, he'd found a basin so that she could sit in front of the telly with her feet soaking in warm water and then gone out and fetched fish and chips, chocolate ice cream and a soppy video to watch while they ate. 'Thanks, Ellen,' she whispered now.

'Take care, sweetie.'

'Oh! Ellen, wait!' But her friend had already rung off before Molly could tell her about Luke. Still, there wasn't much to tell, it could wait. Her phone chirruped as a text message came in. It was from Ellen.

Damn hormones. Forgot to ask, any news on Luke?

Molly smiled and typed in her answer.

Nothing much. Talk tomorrow. x

Chapter Eighteen

9.20 p.m., Thursday, 6th August

'I suppose you're going straight up to bed now,' Laura remarked as they drank their after-dinner coffees.

'No, I think I'd better stay up tonight and keep an eye on you,' Molly retorted, but smiling so Laura wouldn't take offence.

'Very funny. Well, if you want to act as my chaperone, you'll need a jacket. I'm not hanging around here all night.'

'But it's lovely.'

Laura shrugged. 'Perhaps, but we're in the centre of Galway city; it would be a shame to sit in the hotel all evening.'

Molly put her head on one side and then nodded. 'You know, you're right, let's go.'

'You don't have to come—'

'No, honestly, I'd like to. It'll be fun.' She could just imagine Declan and Ellen's face if they heard her now.

'Okay then, let's go,' Laura said, looking less than enthusiastic. 'But don't nag about what or how much I drink. Or about anything else, for that matter.'

'Wouldn't dream of it, sis.' Molly grinned and led the way out of the restaurant. 'Where shall we go?' she asked when they were outside.

'Let's head towards the square and see if there's any music anywhere.'

'I never knew you were so into music.'

'There's a lot you don't know about me.'

'I'm beginning to realize that,' Molly murmured, stopping outside a brightly lit pub. 'Let's try here.'

'No, I don't like the look of it.' Laura walked on.

'What's wrong with it?' Molly hurried after her.

'Too busy. Let's check down here.'

'But most of the pubs are straight on,' Molly argued.

'I seem to remember there was a nice place this way,' Laura insisted, quickening her step.

'Fine.' Molly sighed. She didn't really mind too much where they ended up. She was too preoccupied thinking about Luke and being riddled with guilt because she wasn't thinking about Declan.

Laura pushed a door open and Molly's eyes widened at the throng of people. 'I thought you didn't like noisy pubs?' she said, but Laura ignored her and weaved her way through the crowd. As they reached the bar, a couple vacated two stools and Laura pounced on them with a triumphant look at her sister. Molly smiled. She could actually get to like nice Laura. 'What would you like to drink?' she asked, pulling out her purse.

'G&T, please.' Laura hoisted herself onto the high stool and looked around.

Molly attracted the attention of a smiling barman and ordered their drinks. 'Do they have music here?' she asked Laura.

'No idea.'

Molly followed her sister's gaze to a group of guys standing at the other side of the bar and sighed.

'What?' Laura's eyes were defiant.

'Nothing.' Molly didn't want a row. It was up to Laura if she wanted to mess around with other men, although Molly was determined she wasn't going off on her own with anyone. Getting into taxis with total strangers was madness in this day and age, and Molly had no intention of letting Laura out of her sight. Perhaps she was overreacting, but she thought there was something rather sad about Laura's behaviour. Molly could understand that sometimes people fell in and out of love, but surely it wasn't normal for Laura to be actively looking for a man. And it was clear from her behaviour last night, that it wasn't love or a new relationship she was after but fun and, possibly, sex.

'Can I get you a drink, ladies?'

Molly looked up to see a rather scruffy-looking character leering at them. 'We've already got one, thanks,' she said, turning her back on him. 'Don't give out to me for getting rid of him,' she warned Laura, 'he was disgusting.'

'No argument,' Laura agreed, but looking past her sister, she began to smile. 'But things are looking up.'

'Can I turn round?'

'No. A group of guys have just come in. Tall, dark and very dishy, and they're heading this way.'

'Well, of course they're heading this way, we are sitting at the bar.'

Laura arched an eyebrow. 'We'll see.'

'Why are you on the hunt for a man, Laura? Aren't you happy?'

'Who's happy?' Laura avoided her eyes and took a long drink.

'If you want to talk—' Molly stopped at her sister's withering look. 'I'm just saying—'

'Excellent,' Laura murmured.

'Sorry?'

'Pardon, mademoiselle?'

Molly turned to see a man holding her bag.

'Is this yours?'

'Yes, thank you.' Molly took it and tucked it beneath her.

'How kind,' Laura gushed. 'That doesn't sound like an Irish accent.'

'No,' the man agreed. 'I'm from France.' He waved a hand to the other men. 'We are here on a rugby trip.'

Molly almost choked on her drink.

'Really? How interesting. And are you having a good time?'

Molly watched her sister carefully. Laura wasn't in the least surprised to see Luke's gang; this was a set-up.

'Very good,' he said, moving closer. 'The weather has been great, the rugby better and the Irish hospitality,' his smile encompassed Molly too, 'superb.'

Molly rolled her eyes.

Laura ignored her and smiled at the man. 'Why don't you join us?'

Molly shot her a look of alarm. What was she playing at? If Luke came in . . . She looked around. Where was he, anyway?

'Luke! *Ici*!'

Molly shrank down on her seat and shot Laura a look of desperation. She heard him talk in rapid French close behind her and closed her eyes. This looked terrible, as if she'd come looking for him. She was sorely tempted to leave before he saw her but, even if she did, when he saw Laura, he'd know she'd been here. Although perhaps he wouldn't remember Laura – it had been a long time.

'Laura?'

Molly watched as Laura looked just above her head and smiled. 'Hello, Luke, how wonderful to see you again.'

He moved closer, his jacket rubbing against Molly's bare arm. She clutched her stool and smiled weakly. 'Hi, Luke, this is a surprise.'

The Frenchman was looking at the three of them. 'You know each other?'

'*Oui*.'

'So, introduce me!'

Molly risked a sidelong look at Luke and noted that, though he wore a smile, it looked slightly strained.

'Ladies, this is Gerard. Gerard, this is Molly and Laura.'

Gerard's eyes twinkled as he took Laura's hand and kissed it.

Molly groaned softly and Luke chuckled.

'Behave yourself, Gerard,' he warned, 'Laura's a married woman.'

A flash of annoyance crossed Laura's face. 'He's just being gentlemanly; Irishmen could learn a thing or two from the French.'

Gerard smiled delightedly and gestured to their glasses. 'Let me get you some drinks.'

'G&T, please.'

'Just water, thanks.' Molly smiled.

'Luke?'

'Water's fine.'

The Frenchman held out his hands to Laura. 'They are sticks in the mud, I think.'

'Not everyone needs alcohol to have fun,' Laura retorted.

Molly looked at her in grateful surprise, but Laura only had eyes for the Frenchman.

She turned back to Luke. 'Can we trust him?' she inclined her head towards Gerard.

Luke shrugged. 'I only met him on Sunday, but he's behaved himself so far. Is she divorced and looking for a new man?'

Molly shook her head. 'Just bored and, after a couple of drinks, she likes to flirt. She's harmless really.' She looked up into his face, slightly unnerved by his proximity. She could smell his cologne and feel his breath on her face. His navy-blue eyes were intent on her, making it hard for her to think straight. 'I thought you were tied up tonight.'

His smile was rueful. 'There was a traditional night planned at a hotel in Salthill, but two of the band came down with Swine flu so it was called off.'

'That's a shame,' she said politely.

His smile was warm and intimate. 'Oh, I don't know, I think it's worked out rather well.'

Molly flushed and was grateful when Gerard interrupted them with their drinks. He shook his head in dismay. 'You are well suited, both drinking your water.'

'Someone has to stay sober and get you all back to the hotel in one piece, eh, *mon ami*?' Luke remarked.

'And we are grateful.' Gerard bowed slightly, then turned back to talk to Laura.

Molly noticed her sister's hem had ridden up slightly and she was touching Gerard at every opportunity. She hoped Luke wouldn't notice, but when she looked back at him, he was looking at her, not Laura. 'You have to stop staring at me.'

'I'm sorry, I just can't believe you're really here beside me.' He looked down at her glass of water. 'Do you ever drink?' he asked.

She flushed, shaking her head. 'It wasn't really a conscious decision, I just couldn't bring myself to do it. You?'

'I used to have a glass of wine or a pint occasionally, but it terrified my mother so much, I stopped. It just wasn't worth it.' He looked at her.

They were both silent for a moment and then she looked at him. 'Have you ever told anyone?'

'About the accident?' he asked.

She nodded.

He shrugged. 'No, unless you count the counsellor my parents dragged me to when we got to France.'

'My folks did the same. She was a lovely woman. I could talk to her in a way I couldn't talk to Mum and Dad.'

'Is she the reason you became a counsellor?'

'Partly.' She left it at that and he didn't press her. 'How are your parents? Have they gotten over it? Sorry, silly question.' She shook her head at her own stupidity. 'Are they coping?'

'Better. Obviously, at the beginning it was hard, especially for Mum. Dad had his new job to occupy him, but Sandra and I were at school so she was just rattling around the house with nothing else to think about. She became very reclusive and depressed.

Finally, they put her on anti-depressants. She has the occasional relapse, but she's much better than she used to be.'

'It must be hard, though, having no one at home now.' She shook her head. 'Sorry, I'm assuming you don't live with them.'

His expression became more guarded. 'You're right, I don't.'

She forced a bright smile. 'Let me guess, you're an old married man with six kids.'

He shook his head. 'No kids.'

She gulped. 'So you're married?'

He nodded.

'That's great, I'm happy for you. Is she French?'

'Yes.'

'And doesn't she mind you nipping across the Channel with gangs of unruly rugby players?' Molly teased, congratulating herself on her composure.

'She does a fair amount of travelling herself, she's a flight attendant.'

'Oh, right.' Molly imagined a long-legged, younger and sexier version of Juliette Binoche.

His eyes searched her face. 'How about you? Are you married?'

'No, engaged – sort of.' Now, why had she said that? She should have told him that she was getting married soon, that she was deliriously happy and that Declan was the love of her life.

Of course he picked up on it instantly. 'Sort of?'

'We were supposed to get married next month,' she explained, 'but Declan had to go to Japan on business.'

'And you're pissed off at him,' he deduced, with a grin.

She pulled a face. 'You could say that.'

'So, what next?'

'We haven't set a new date, we'll probably wait until next summer.'

'Why?' He frowned when she hesitated. 'Sorry, none of my business.'

'Oh no, that's okay.' She smiled. 'You were always very direct, I'd forgotten that.'

He chuckled. 'I try to be more tactful these days, but I don't always succeed. So, why are you having second thoughts about marrying him?'

She threw back her head and laughed, drawing a curious look from her sister. 'You're right, you don't always succeed.'

'You're avoiding the question,' he observed.

'I decided to wait—'

'*You* decided, interesting.'

'Will you shut up and let me answer the question?'

'Ooh, touchy—' He grinned as she held up a hand as if to strike him. 'Okay, I'll shut up.'

'Good.' She shook her head, but she was glad that he was teasing her; it was just like old times and it made her feel more relaxed. 'Declan just got this new job with a Japanese company and they sent him to their head office for an induction course. He neglected to tell them that he was getting married though, for fear of losing the job.'

Luke nodded thoughtfully. 'And you think he should have asked them to postpone the course, that the worst that could happen would be they'd say no.'

'Well, exactly.' Molly was impressed that he understood. 'Now, if you can understand that, why couldn't he?'

'Because he's the one in the dilemma, not me.'

'Or he doesn't want to marry me.'

'Is he the kind of guy that says one thing when he means another?'

'No, he's a very honest person,' Molly said, indignant.

'And why would he not want to marry you?'

Molly shook her head. 'I don't know, I'm just not sure he ever wanted it as much as I did.'

'So you proposed to him.'

'No.' She hesitated. 'But I may have nudged him rather hard towards proposing to me.'

'Is this guy a wimp?' Luke asked.

'No!'

'Then he wouldn't have asked if it wasn't what he wanted. He probably would have taken a bit longer about it, that's all.'

She smiled. 'Have you been married long?'

'Eight years.'

She felt a bit thrown by that; it hadn't taken him very long to get over her. 'Eight! Wow, you were so young.'

'Yes.'

'Any photos?' Now, why did she ask that? The last image she needed in her head was Luke's gorgeous wife.

'No.' His answer was clipped and he looked across at his group as if deciding it was time to move on.

'If you need to get back to your party, go ahead. I realize you're working.'

Luke shrugged. 'They seem happy enough for the moment.'

The men were surrounded by women eyeing them up hopefully. 'I suppose they get this treatment wherever they go.'

'Pretty much,' he agreed. 'But then they're young professionals, mostly single and they're great athletes, so I suppose you could call them a good catch.'

Molly grinned. 'They look like kids to me; I must be getting old.'

'Not you. So, what brings you to Galway?'

'Laura won this holiday in a competition, but her husband couldn't get away so she dragged me along.'

He raised an eyebrow. 'So you've grown closer as you've gotten older.'

'Not really.'

He laughed. 'Tell me about Rory, how is he?'

Molly smiled. 'Good.'

'And still a student?'

'Yes, like I said, he went off to Australia for a year after he left school and stayed for five.'

Luke frowned. 'Why did he go?'

'He went with a group of guys from his class and then Rory and one other guy decided to stay a bit longer.'

'There was probably a girl involved,' Luke guessed.

Molly grinned. 'Possibly, but he's not very lucky in love; he seems to attract very strange women.'

'If his sense of humour is still as zany as I remember, I'm not surprised—' Luke broke off as one of his group fell off a stool amid much clapping and jeering. Luke sighed. 'Excuse me for a moment.'

Molly looked over at Laura, whose body language made it clear that Molly had better not join them. Feeling like a spare part, Molly picked up her bag and went in search of the ladies.

When she emerged, Luke was waiting for her. 'I'm sorry, Moll, I'm going to have to take Anton back to the hotel. I'll be back as quick as I can if you're willing to wait. Or we could have a night-cap at the hotel bar once I get him to bed.'

'I'd like that.' She frowned. 'But do you think that Laura will be okay with Gerard?'

'I'll go and have a word in his ear and make sure that he behaves himself and sees her back to the hotel safely.'

'Thank you, I'd appreciate that.' They made their way back towards the bar and said their goodbyes. Laura looked triumphant, but whether that was because she was being left alone with Gerard, or because Molly was leaving with Luke, it was hard to say.

They left, practically carrying Anton between them. Luckily, he was the scrum half and not that big or heavy.

'Apparently, he's not a big drinker, but when he's away with the team, he insists on matching the others, pint for pint, and nearly always keels over,' Luke explained.

'How will he play rugby tomorrow?'

'It's just training and once he eats a good breakfast and drinks a few pints of water, he'll be fine.'

When they got to the hotel, Molly went to her room to get her laptop. She paused to brush her hair and touch up her make-up and, after only a moment's hesitation, she brushed her teeth too. With a guilty sigh, she studied her image. What exactly did she think was about to happen? What did she want to happen? Luke was a married man and she was engaged. With a dismissive shake of her head, she picked up her belongings and went down to the bar.

Chapter Nineteen

Molly was sitting in the lounge and had just switched on her machine when her phone rang. She paled when she saw the display. 'Hi, Declan,' she said, wondering if she sounded as guilty as she felt and praying that Luke wouldn't choose this moment walk in.

'Hello, Moll, how's Limerick?'

'I'm not in Limerick now, we moved to Galway.'

'Galway? How come?'

'The last hotel wasn't up to Laura's standards, so they offered us this one instead.'

'And it's all free; your sister has a hard neck.'

She laughed. 'Tell me about it.'

'And is this hotel good enough for her?'

'It's lovely.'

'So what are you up to?'

'Drinking tea in the lounge and going through my emails.' It was the truth, but not the whole truth.

'You really know how to party!'

'How are you?'

'Great, I'm really enjoying the experience. Missing you, obviously,' he added hurriedly.

'You don't have to say that.'

'I know, but it's true. As Sting would say, *The Bed's Too Big Without You*.'

'Ah,' she smiled, 'you old romantic.'

'Don't you miss me?'

'Not your snoring, no,' Molly joked, unable to cope with this unusually tender Declan.

'Listen, Declan, Laura's coming,' Molly said as Luke walked in and spotted her. 'Talk to you in the morning, okay?'

'Okay then. Love you, Moll.'

'Me too,' she murmured and switched off her phone just as Luke reached the table.

He smiled at her. 'I hope you didn't hang up because of me.'

'Of course not,' she lied.

'More tea?' he asked.

She shook her head. 'I'll never sleep if I have any more caffeine.'

'Hot chocolate?' he suggested.

Molly smiled. 'Lovely.'

Luke turned to the waiter who'd appeared at his side and ordered hot chocolate for both of them. He sat down in the leather chair next to her. 'We're like a couple of old-age pensioners.'

'Not good for the image,' Molly agreed. He was so close. She'd expected him to take the seat opposite.

'Was that Declan?' he asked.

'Yes.' Molly pretended to busy herself with switching off her laptop.

'Did you tell him about me?'

'There wasn't time; he was getting ready for work.'

Luke put his hand over hers and waited for her to look up. 'But you wouldn't have told him anyway, would you, Molly?'

She looked into his eyes and then shook her head.

He squeezed her hand. 'I wouldn't tell Adriana either, she would jump to the wrong conclusions.'

'Which are?' Molly searched his face.

'She would assume that you were the real reason I came to Ireland.'

'But if that were true, you would have done it long before now.'

Their drinks arrived, and Molly leaned forward to stir hers and take a sip. 'Anyway, she's no reason to be jealous. We just bumped into each other and are catching up like any old friends would.' When he didn't reply, she raised her eyes to his and swallowed at the expression in his eyes.

'We are not "any old friends", Molly. What we had together, and then what we went through—' He shook his head as if trying to make sense of things. 'I know Mum and Dad thought that moving to France was for the best, but I hated leaving. I wouldn't have needed to see a counsellor if I'd just been able to talk to you.'

Molly was taken aback by his vehemence. 'Then why didn't you phone me?'

He sighed impatiently. 'I couldn't talk on the phone, Moll, not about that. I wanted to be with you, looking into your eyes, holding you.'

'I'm not sure I would have been much use to you, I was a complete mess myself.'

'We could have helped each other. I'll never forget your face as Dad drove away.'

Molly swallowed back her tears and tried to smile. 'But we got through it, didn't we? And look at you now, a successful, married man with the world at his feet.'

His lips twisted into a bitter smile. 'Is that what you see?'

'Isn't it true?'

'Sometimes, most of the time,' he admitted. 'And then there

are times when I just don't know what I'm doing or why I'm here.'

Molly sighed. 'I know.'

He looked straight at her. 'You feel that way too?'

'Not as much as I used to.'

'I can never forget her, I just can't forget what happened; it colours everything I do. When I joined the French rugby club and won a place on their first team, I was thrilled, but . . .'

'Guilty.'

'Yes! And it's the same on birthdays or at Christmas, and when I got married.' He sighed. 'I miss her so much.'

Molly looked worriedly at the anguish on his face. 'Perhaps you should see someone.'

'I don't need to talk to a stranger and I've had my fill of tablets.' He looked at her. 'But it's good to talk to someone who understands. It's good to talk to you, Molly.'

She nodded in understanding. 'Mum and Dad were great, and I knew I could talk to them, but I was afraid that, once I started, I wouldn't be able to stop. I was afraid that I would scare them if I was completely honest, and so I talked to my counsellor and, otherwise, let people believe that I was getting on with my life.'

'But you didn't really, did you?' Luke asked.

'No, I did, sort of.' She tried to find the words to explain. 'I think I was numb for quite a long time. Sometimes it seemed as if I was a bystander, looking on, or as if I was watching a movie. I thought it was incredible that no one could see how I really felt. I thought the pain must be written all over my face.'

'And when you don't talk about her,' Luke said, 'no one else does. And then you get annoyed with them, thinking they've forgotten her, and you resent them for getting on with life as if everything is back to normal.'

'As if it ever could be,' Molly agreed. 'I used to get so annoyed that no one would mention her name. It was as if she'd never existed.'

'*We* haven't mentioned her name,' he pointed out with a sad smile. He lifted his mug of chocolate and looked up. 'Sorry, Ruth.'

Molly raised her drink too. 'Sorry, Ruth.' She wiped her tears away, and then blew her nose. 'Did you tell your wife about what happened?'

'She knows Ruth died in a car accident, I didn't go into any real detail.' He looked at her. 'Your fiancé?'

She shook her head.

'I wouldn't have told Adriana if I could have gotten away with it,' he admitted, 'but Mum has the house like a shrine. Ruth's photos are everywhere.'

Molly shuddered. It must be like a mausoleum. She couldn't think of anything that less suited Ruth's effervescent, electric personality; she wouldn't have wanted it. 'Do you hate going into the house?'

'Detest it. And when I'm in Ireland, I can't go near *that* part of Dublin either.'

'No.' Molly agreed. She didn't think she'd ever be able to return to the scene of the accident.

'I don't even go to Blackrock if I can help it. I think of us walking home from school, or going to the library, or you and Ruth watching me training,' tears filled his eyes, 'and it's like someone's punched me in the stomach.'

Molly squeezed his hand. 'Have your parents ever come back?'

'Dad comes on business from time to time, but he stays in the city centre. Mum won't set foot in the country.'

Molly nodded. 'I can understand that. What about Sandra?'

'Sandra's life is in France and she has no interest in coming back here. She was only twelve when we left Ireland and she adapted very well.'

'But she must miss her big sister, they were close.'

He shrugged. 'She never talks about her.'

Molly frowned, but said nothing. He was upset enough

without her giving him more cause for concern, but she doubted very much that Sandra was fine. She would have gone through puberty with a grieving mother and no big sister to comfort her. There was a lump in her throat as she thought of Sandra's pain. Another casualty of that terrible time, and one she'd hardly given any thought to. Luke's reaction made it clear that the rest of the family hadn't realized it either, probably thinking she was too young to experience real grief, but she might have suffered even more than her brother and parents.

'Are you okay?'

She looked up to see Luke watching her and she nodded. 'Yes, just thinking, remembering.'

'I bet you're sorry you bumped into me now,' he said with a rueful expression. 'This kind of conversation is hardly conducive to a happy, relaxing break.'

If only he knew, Molly thought. 'Hey, I'm with Laura, it's hardly relaxing,' she joked.

He smiled. 'It's so good to see you again.'

'You too.'

'Molly?' He looked at her, his expression serious again. 'Do you think we'd still be together now if the accident hadn't happened?'

Molly was temporarily at a loss for words.

'I'm sorry. I'm making you uncomfortable.' He glanced at his watch and went to stand up. 'I suppose I should—'

Molly put a hand on his arm. 'Don't go.'

He sank back into the chair.

'I've been thinking quite a lot about that ever since I saw you at the airport,' she admitted.

He let out a sigh of relief and took her hand. 'I have too. Any time I was in Ireland, I found myself watching out for you, and then suddenly you were there. And I walked away.' He shook his head in disgust. 'I don't know why I did that. I really wanted to talk to you, but I suppose I panicked.'

'I missed you so much when you left,' she said softly.

'I missed you too; it was a double grief. I'd lost my twin and I'd lost the girl I loved.'

Molly stared at him. 'You never really lost me, Luke. And I'm here now. You can talk to me now.'

He looked around the room and then back at her. 'Let's go for a walk.'

She blinked. 'A walk? Now?'

'Sorry, is it too late? Are you tired? It's just, I want to make the most of the little bit of time we have left, and I've a feeling that a gang of Frenchmen and/or your sister will walk in at any moment and ruin everything.'

She nodded, realizing he was right, and that she was damned if she was going to let this opportunity pass. 'Let me put my laptop upstairs and get a jacket, I'll meet you in reception.'

Upstairs, she dragged a comb through her hair and grabbed her jacket. She was about to walk out the door when she realized that she should really leave Laura a message or she might be worried or, worse, think Molly was in bed with Luke. She'd probably think that anyway, maybe even expect it. After a moment's thought, Molly ruffled the covers on her bed and punched the pillows, then she scribbled a note on the hotel notepad.

Can't sleep, gone for some air. M

She took the stairs rather than the lift, in case she met Laura, although judging by the way she was cosying up to Gerard, Molly didn't expect her home any time soon. Luke was pacing the reception, waiting for her, and her heart skipped a beat as she registered exactly how handsome he was. She did still care; he could still make her pulse race. For an instant, before he saw her, she thought of going back upstairs and barricading herself in her room. Then he turned, saw her and his face lit up and she was lost.

*

Without discussing it, they turned away from the town and started to walk towards the sea. The clouds had cleared to reveal a milky moon that was mirrored in the still water.

'Are you warm enough?' Luke asked.

'I'm fine.'

He took her hand, then stopped to look down at her, doubt in his eyes. 'Is this okay?'

'Of course.'

He smiled, relieved. 'It's been a long time since we went for a walk together.'

She thought about it. 'The last one I remember was coming home from the rugby club after a match and you moaned all the way back because you'd hurt your ankle.'

'I never moaned,' he protested, 'although I'm making up for it now; I pick up injuries a lot easier than I did when I was young.'

'Oh please, we're not that old,' she groaned. 'So you do still play?'

'Only for fun, or at charity events, but I still coach from time to time. My latest class are under seven and a mad bunch.'

'Are you getting broody, Luke Fortune?' she teased.

'It wouldn't matter if I was. Adriana can't have children.'

'Oh. I'm sorry.' Molly wasn't overly maternal, but she assumed that she would have children at some stage. She couldn't imagine how she'd feel if she was told it wasn't possible.

'Sorry, that was a real conversation-stopper.'

'Maybe we should talk about something else.'

He chuckled softly. 'I think that's a very good idea. Tell me about your work instead.'

Molly briefly explained about *Teenage Kix* and Carl and Tess, and ended up telling him about the letter from Smithy.

'That's really heavy, Moll, how do you cope?'

'I suppose I feel that, in some small way, I'm helping. I felt I needed to do a job that would, in some way, make up for how I failed Ruth.'

He swung her, almost roughly, to face him. 'You did not fail Ruth, do you hear me?'

'But if it hadn't been for me—'

'I won't listen to this, Moll. How can you still blame yourself after all this time? It was not your fault.'

She shrugged. 'Anyway, when I do manage to help a teenager with a problem, it makes me feel that I'm making up for that night.'

'I'm glad you're doing this, but that's because I think you're a wonderful listener and you care so much about people; you always have.'

'Most of the time, I'm advising kids about acne, braces and how to kiss,' she admitted with a grin.

He laughed. 'All very important issues when you're a teenager. I remember how terrified I was, the first time I kissed a girl.'

She pretended shock. 'It wasn't me?'

He pulled a face. 'Sorry, no. I was only twelve, and there was this really bossy girl on our road that almost attacked me. Two of my friends were there so I had to go for it, or they'd never have let me live it down.'

'So *she* kissed you.'

'Yes.' He grinned. 'Once I got the hang of it, I think I did quite a good job. She seemed happy.'

'She probably hated every minute of it and only did it as a dare,' Molly retorted.

He stopped and turned her to face him. 'I don't remember you complaining.'

She looked into his eyes, then at his lips and gulped. 'We can't.'

'Why not?'

His eyes twinkled mischievously, but Molly wasn't laughing; this was dangerous. 'Because it won't stop at one.'

His expression changed, becoming sober, and he cupped her

face with his hands. 'It's so strange. I feel like we've never been apart and yet, at the same time, you're a stranger. I feel I want to get to know you all over again.'

'You're married.'

'I'm not happy, and neither is she. It was a mistake from day one. We live separate lives, Molly.' His voice was urgent and his eyes searched her face. 'And you're still single.'

Molly felt weak and nervous, scared but elated. This was what dreams were made of. Here was her beloved Luke, offering himself on a plate; it was too good to be true. It was that realization that made her turn away. 'We can't.'

Chapter Twenty

The ring of her mobile phone woke them, and as Laura groaned and burrowed under the covers, Molly made a grab for it and stumbled into the bathroom. 'Hello?'

'Did I wake you?' Ellen asked.

'Yeah, we had bit of a late night.'

'Sorry. I keep forgetting that other people have lives and sleep normal hours. Will I go away and you can phone me after you've had a shower and a cup of coffee?'

'Would you mind?' Molly asked.

'Course not. Have you lots of news for me?' Ellen sounded hopeful.

'Lots,' Molly assured her, grimacing at the memory. 'Call you back in a couple of hours.'

She sat down on the edge of the bath tub and rubbed her eyes. As she thought back over the events of last night, she was pleased that she'd stayed strong. If she'd ended up in bed with Luke, hugely attractive though the prospect was, it would have defeated the purpose of the trip. She'd wanted to see him again to examine her feelings for him and for Declan. Falling into bed with him would have proved nothing other than she was as weak as the next woman. Perhaps she would end up in Luke's bed one day, but not yet. She owed it to Declan – oh, shit, Declan!

She hadn't phoned him. Her alarm mustn't have gone off, or else she'd slept straight through – highly likely given it was after three when she finally rolled into bed. She quickly sent him a text – it would probably cost the earth – apologizing and promising him that she'd call later. Then she went back into the bedroom to wake her sister. 'Laura, come on, breakfast finishes in thirty minutes.'

Laura groaned and burrowed deeper. 'I don't think I can eat.'

'A few cups of coffee and you'll be fine.' Molly assured her and went to take her shower. The bonus about not drinking was never having a hangover, and if the smell in the room was anything to go by, Laura was in for a stinker.

Molly and Luke had been sitting primly opposite each other in reception when Laura and Gerard had stumbled through the door, arm in arm, at about two o'clock. Gerard had been all set to accompany Laura to her room, but Molly announced, with a steely look in her eye, that she was going up soon. Laura didn't seem that bothered and, with a knowing wink at her sister, had gone to bed alone.

Molly hoped Laura would be too delicate to launch into an inquisition. She wasn't ready to talk about Luke yet and planned to escape straight after breakfast and find somewhere quiet to call Ellen from.

It was easier than she'd expected. Laura was positively green and, once she'd nibbled on a slice of toast and sipped some weak tea, she retreated to her bed, pleading a migraine. 'You go and look at galleries and churches,' she waved Molly away. 'Come back after lunch and we'll go shopping.'

'Shopping?' Molly frowned.

'There are some fabulous boutiques in Galway and I intend to visit every one.'

'Perhaps you'd be better doing that alone—'

'Not a chance. While I'm trying on clothes, you can tell me all about Luke.' Laura managed a lewd wink. 'I want all the gory details.'

Once Laura was safely tucked up in bed, Molly took her laptop down to the deserted veranda bar. She chose a chair tucked to one side of the doorway so that anyone glancing in from reception wouldn't spot her. She was fairly sure that Luke would have already left for Dublin, but she wasn't taking any chances. They had said their goodbyes and Molly wanted a couple of days' grace before seeing him again. She also wanted Ellen's reaction to the events of the last twenty-four hours.

Ellen answered on the first ring, sounding slightly breathless. 'Oh hi, Molly.'

'Are you okay? What are you doing? You know you should be resting.'

'Don't nag, just tell me what you've been up to,' Ellen instructed.

And Molly did, stopping every so often while Ellen exclaimed or asked questions.

'I can't believe you didn't kiss him,' Ellen murmured finally.

That wasn't strictly true, but Molly figured some things should remain private.

'And you're going to see him on Saturday.'

'If he calls.'

'Don't you think he will?'

'No, I'm pretty sure he'll call. So what do you think, Ellen?'

'Ask me a tough one, why don't you?' Ellen complained. 'Is he still as gorgeous as you remember?'

'More so,' Molly confirmed. 'His hair is shorter and his

eyes . . .' she sighed. 'I'd forgotten how amazing they are, dark-blue, practically navy. He's broader than he was, but not fat at all, and his voice is richer, deeper.'

'He sounds lovely,' Ellen said dreamily. 'And do you think he still fancies you?'

Molly remembered the look in Luke's eyes when it was time to say goodnight. 'He seems to.'

'And do you believe him when he says that his marriage is in trouble, or could it be just a line to get you into bed?'

'Luke was always honest, to the point of being rude. I know it's been more than a decade, but he doesn't seem to have changed that much.'

'It's unlikely,' Ellen agreed. 'Then I suppose the question is, Moll, how did he make you feel?'

'I don't know. I'm not sure if I'm still in love with him, or we're just close because we lived through a terrible tragedy together. Or, as you thought, that he's just come back into my life at a time when I'm feeling rejected and uncertain. If I was counselling myself, I'd advise caution.'

'But would you take your own advice?'

Molly groaned. 'Oh, Ellen, I don't know.' A mother had come into the lounge with a young baby in her arms and a little girl trailing after her. She settled herself at the far end of the room to breastfeed, while the child ran from table to table collecting beer mats and singing softly to herself. Molly wished for a moment that she could change places with the little girl.

'Okay, let's think about this sensibly, Moll. You've behaved impeccably, and you've both talked openly and honestly. Also, you've got until Saturday to reflect on what you currently have with Declan and what you might have with Luke.'

'Oh, Ellen, I feel like a treacherous bitch,' Molly wailed, earning herself a curious glance from the little girl.

'Don't be silly, of course you're not. You're just at a crossroads of sorts.'

'I should never have done this. I'm playing with fire. Even if my relationship is on the rocks, he's married.'

'And a grown man who's capable of making his own decisions.'

Molly closed her eyes, feeling close to tears. 'I don't know what I'm doing. I don't know what I want.'

'Then it's better to think it through now, than marry Declan and regret it later,' Ellen said bluntly.

'Oh, Ellen,' Molly murmured. The little girl came closer and gave her a sweet smile before running back to her mother.

'There is one thing I want to say, although you may not thank me for it.'

Straightening in her chair, Molly forced herself to concentrate. 'Go on.'

'You have two dilemmas, not one.'

'I do?' Molly stared at her phone, aghast.

'You have to decide whether or not you want to finish with Declan and you have to decide whether you want to get back with Luke and – here's the hard bit – they should be completely independent decisions.'

Molly said nothing as she digested Ellen's words.

'Molly?'

'I'm here. You're saying that if I decide to leave Declan, it should be regardless of whether Luke is waiting in the wings?'

'That's what I'm saying. Sorry, sweetie.'

'No, you're right. I'm not sure that I can be that noble though.'

'You're the noblest woman I know.'

'Thanks, Ellen,' Molly whispered, feeling the tears edge closer.

'I'd better go,' Ellen said hurriedly. 'My bladder is demanding a loo break. Oh, and I haven't even given you your thought for the day!'

'I think I have more than enough to think about, don't you? Go. And thanks, Ellen. Thanks for giving it to me straight.'

'I wouldn't be much of a friend if I didn't.'

*

Laura fell asleep as soon as her head touched the pillow. She wasn't used to such late nights or so much alcohol, and she'd been shocked at the haggard image in the mirror as she'd brushed her teeth before going down to breakfast.

It was the phone chirruping loudly, announcing an incoming text, that bounced her back to consciousness only minutes later. Groaning, Laura put a hand out to grab the offending article and peered at the display, expecting it to be Ash complaining about her best jeans not being clean or Adam looking for something to eat. It would never occur to either of them to go to Robert about such things. But it wasn't either of her children and she felt sick as she read the text.

> Laura, it was wonderful to meet you last night. You are a beautiful woman. I hope we can meet again in Dublin. Gerard X

'Oh, no.' Laura was wide awake now and staring at the message in horror. She couldn't remember giving the man her phone number. What on earth had she been thinking of? What if he kept sending her messages? What if Robert checked her phone and saw one? She gulped, swallowing back the queasiness that was no longer solely a result of alcohol abuse. She went to delete the text and then stopped, realizing that she should respond first, warning him not to contact her again. She paused, frowning. What if that just annoyed him and he thought she was being a tease; it could turn him into a full-blown stalker. 'Think,' she muttered, forcing her tired brain into gear. Gerard had seemed like a decent enough guy and they had gotten on well. He was probably just hoping for one more night together before he went home to France. Then she would never see him again, he would forget her and it would all be fine. And it would be nice to see him again. She smiled, remembering his hands on her skin and his lips against hers; he was an expert kisser, living up to the French reputation. Molly thought that, aside from a kiss and cuddle, Laura had been a relatively good girl. What she didn't know, was that she and Gerard had left the pub almost immediately after her, slipped into the hotel through the spa entrance and made love three times in Gerard's room – three times! Laura's body positively tingled at the memory. Sex with Gerard had been nothing like it was with Robert. His body was brown and hard, whereas her husband was white and, though not fat, he was flabby through lack of exercise. Gerard had done things to her that she'd only ever read about in books; it had been a revelation, making her realize how inexperienced she was. Sex with Robert was pedestrian and predictable, although that was her fault as much as his. She had never been the adventurous sort, and was quite self-conscious when she was naked, which is why last night had been even more of a revelation. Before Gerard, she had kissed and cuddled a few men, but her clothes had stayed on; that's the way she preferred it. But Gerard had positively worshipped her body last night and caressed and kissed her in an almost reverential fashion. And she had enjoyed it, relished it, and hadn't felt the remotest bit guilty. She had been a good and faithful wife for fifteen years, and she'd figured it was about time she had some fun before she got old and wrinkly.

Robert didn't deserve her devotion. He did nothing to make her feel special. Was it any wonder she looked elsewhere to find some love and attention? Not that she loved Gerard, or he her, but there had been respect last night and, indeed, affection; surely she was entitled to both? She reached over to pick up the phone and dialled the salon to book some beauty treatments. The earliest appointment was in two hours' time, so she could have a nice, long soak first. As she waited for the bath to fill, she phoned home and was surprised when Robert answered. 'You're home again today?'

'Hello to you too,' Robert replied, sounding amused.

'Sorry, I just assumed you'd be at work. I was calling to check the twins were behaving themselves.'

'They're fine. Ash is just loading the washing machine and Adam is hoovering.'

Laura almost dropped the phone. 'How on earth did you manage to persuade them to do that?'

'I'm taking them sailing, so they're being very helpful all of a sudden,' he chuckled.

'Sailing? You haven't gone sailing in years.' It was one of the things that had irritated Laura. Robert had been a keen sailor when he was younger, but had given up due to the pressure of work. Laura had enjoyed the social life attached to the yacht club, and been disgusted that Robert didn't realize how important it was from both a business and social standpoint.

'I've decided it's time I took it up again,' he was saying now, 'and I think it would be good for the kids to get involved. Ash is surprisingly keen on the idea.'

She should have known Ash would have something to do with this. 'Well, I won't keep you,' she said coldly, 'have fun.'

'What about you, darling, are you enjoying yourself?'

Laura felt just a flicker of guilt at the warmth in his voice, but dismissed it. 'I'm having a great time.'

'Good, I'm glad. I thought we could go out for dinner on Saturday night, all four of us; what do you think?'

'I'm afraid I already promised Penny that I would go to a charity fashion show with her,' she said hurriedly.

'Okay, no problem. I'll take them for pizza and to a movie and maybe you and I could go out Sunday night instead.'

'Lovely. See you Saturday.'

'Bye, darling, love you.'

'Me too,' Laura said brightly and quickly rang off. Why did he have to go and say that, she thought crossly, sliding into the water. And what was all this Wonder Dad business? Robert rarely took the kids out and when he did, it was usually at her suggestion or he'd been pestered by his daughter. That was probably it. She hoped that Adam wasn't being neglected. Still, she could make it up to him on Sunday. She'd have to make sure she didn't drink too much on Saturday night, although she imagined Gerard had other things planned. She smiled in anticipation as she soaped her leg, admiring its smoothness. She was thrilled that she'd taken advantage of the spa and was now waxed, buffed and moisturized to within an inch of her life. Gerard certainly seemed to have appreciated the results. He wasn't an easy man to talk to; his accent was thick and Laura got bored trying to figure out what he was trying to say, but he must be nearly ten years younger than her, was easy on the eye, and his body language more than made up for his conversational inadequacies. It didn't really matter if the rest of her time in Galway was a bore; she had a wonderful night to look forward to. Perhaps she'd find something really sexy to wear here in Galway. She'd told Robert she was going to a fashion show, so he'd expect her to get dressed up.

She congratulated herself on coming up with such an excellent excuse on the spur of the moment and made a mental note to phone Penny when she got home. The last thing she needed was for her friend to phone looking for her when she was out with Gerard. She shivered at the thought and sank down further into the warm water. She was quite happy to enjoy brief flings, but she didn't want to upset the applecart of her marriage. Robert might be boring, but he gave her security and a comfortable home and she knew the value of that. She had no wish to become a divorcée. The woman always seemed to come off worst; less money, no man and full responsibility for the kids, while the ex-husband moved into a bachelor pad, changed his hairstyle and finally started to wear fashionable clothes. Then, of course, he'd find a younger, prettier woman and start a second family. Now there was something that would wipe the smile off Ashling Dillon's face. No, Laura thought, divorce was definitely not an option. She would content herself with an occasional fling, but she would be discreet. And she would also try to be warmer towards Robert. Perhaps she'd even let him make love to her on Sunday, she could always close her eyes and pretend it was Gerard. Laura sighed. She wasn't sure she had that good an imagination.

Molly hadn't been entirely honest with Ellen. She and Luke had kissed, although not until much later, after Laura had returned and Molly knew she wouldn't be in a position to drag him up to the room. Once every member of his group had been accounted for, Luke had led her back outside, taken her in his arms and kissed her so tenderly at first, and then hungrily and passionately; it had been wonderful and it had been very hard to break away and go back inside. But they had, ordered some more tea, and sat up for another hour talking. They had talked about the past, about their lives since they'd parted and, finally, about their partners. Molly had felt disloyal talking about Declan, but she was careful to paint a very positive picture of her fiancé. Luke had no such reservations. His marriage had been a mistake and he'd realized it almost as soon as the ring was on his finger.

'I was just looking for an escape,' he'd said. 'I thought marrying Adriana would free me from my past, but of course it couldn't. She knew my heart wasn't in it, she knew I wasn't really in love with her, but she was determined to make it work. Then she started talking about having a family. I was dead against that. Here I was, trying to work up the courage to leave her, and she was talking about babies. It was such a mess. I should have ended it right then, but I was a terrible coward. I just fobbed her off, said we were young, and that we should have some fun before starting a family.'

'Did she agree?' Molly had asked, riveted.

'To my face, yes, but she stopped taking the pill without telling me and just announced one night that she was pregnant. She was convinced that, once I got used to the idea, I'd be as happy as she was.'

'And were you?'

He'd given a sad shake of his head. 'I couldn't really associate her pregnancy with a real, live child, my child, and I was so angry. I just kept thinking of how she'd tricked me.' He'd rubbed wearily at his eyes at that point. 'She miscarried at seventeen weeks.'

'I'm so sorry.'

'I was sad for her, Molly, but I have to be honest, I felt relieved. A child would have tied me to her for life.'

Molly had felt slightly shocked at his admission, but at the same time appreciated his honesty. 'But you're still together.'

'Only because I'm afraid to leave. Adriana fell apart after she lost the baby. She's on anti-depressants now. I have to stay with her until I'm sure she can stand on her own two feet.'

He'd looked into Molly's eyes, his own full of pain and sorrow. 'What else can I do?'

It was a dreadful mess and Molly felt sorry for him and his wife. Adriana had been wrong to trick Luke but, if anything, that just made the tragedy sadder. Molly believed Luke when he said he didn't love Adriana, but that didn't mean he still loved *her*. It was a mirror image of her situation. Had she just happened along at a time when Luke's life was falling apart and he was desperate to be saved? Did he think that if he got Molly back, he would also get some part of his beloved twin back too?

Molly felt weary and sick at this new situation she'd found herself in. Yesterday it had been simply a matter of figuring out who she loved. But she hadn't factored in Luke's personal life, or expected him to be the confused and depressed man he quite obviously was.

And as Ellen had so rightly pointed out, Molly had to come to a decision about her future with Declan, regardless of Luke. But that was easier said than done. The prospect of being alone again was a scary one. At the same time, she knew that she couldn't marry Declan unless she was truly in love with him. She had been so sure that she would know what to do once she talked to Luke, but it wasn't that simple; nothing ever was.

Chapter Twenty-one

4.22 p.m., Friday, 7th August

Molly's eyelids drooped and she leaned heavily against a pillar, her sister's bag and jacket bunched in her arms as her sister tried on yet another outfit. Where did the woman get the energy? This was the third boutique Laura had dragged her into, and Molly's late night was beginning to catch up on her. She was going back to the hotel for a nap and as soon as Laura came out of the changing room, she'd tell her so. It would be a relief to get away from her sister's constant probing. Molly had tried to fob her off, saying that she and Luke had just chatted about old times, his wife, Declan, and their impending marriage. Laura hadn't swallowed any of it. Molly thought all her attention had been on Gerard, but it seemed she'd managed to keep an eye on her sister and come to her own conclusions.

'He couldn't take his eyes off you! And as for you, you positively lit up when you saw him,' she'd said excitedly.

Molly thought this was an exaggeration. She was sure she'd played it cool, despite the fact that her stomach had been doing somersaults and her heart was thumping in her chest. The one plus about shopping was that, for the moment, Laura was more interested in clothes than her sister's love life. But Molly knew that the grilling would resume once they were back on the street; another excellent reason to return to the hotel for a siesta.

'What do you think?' The curtain swished back and Laura stepped out, turning this way and that to examine her image in the mirrored wall.

Molly forced her eyes open and then blinked rapidly as her weary brain tried to compute her sister's appearance.

'What?' Laura demanded, looking defensive.

Molly searched for a diplomatic way of telling her sister that she looked like a slapper. 'It's different,' she offered. The dress was a low-cut, tight, silky number, and the part that covered her breasts was practically transparent.

'It's time for a change. Penny says I dress too old for my age.'

Molly secretly agreed with 'Penny', but this was definitely not a step in the right direction. 'Change is good,' she agreed, nodding, 'but this dress really doesn't suit you.'

Laura twisted and turned in front of the mirror. 'It would probably look better without a bra.'

Molly laughed. 'Without a bra, it'll look like a negligee, and one that may well give Robert a heart attack.'

'Then maybe I should buy it,' Laura muttered, retreating into the changing room.

Molly stared after her, wondering if Laura was messing around with other men because there was something more serious wrong with her marriage; maybe she and Robert were having problems. How sad it would be if they split up, for the twins, at least. Ash, especially, would be devastated if the dad she so obviously adored, left and she had to stay with Laura. Conflict was quite common between mothers and daughters during the teenage years and, while Molly had always been close to Belle, Laura and their mother had often sparked off each other. It was a normal part of growing up, of pushing boundaries, of family life. Even laid-back Rory had got moody and difficult when he started to sprout hair and notice girls.

The curtain was pushed back again and Laura emerged, grabbed her bag and jacket and made for the door. 'Let's find a pub, I need a drink.'

Molly hurried after her. 'I can't, I'm exhausted—'

'Me too. We'll find somewhere comfortable and you can tell me all about Luke.'

'There's not a lot to tell, and I really could do with forty winks.'

Laura stopped and fixed her with a hard stare. 'You always shut me out. You can't wait to tell Ellen every last detail, but you tell me nothing.'

'That's not true,' Molly protested.

'Yes it is, and you're just the same with Mum. Don't think I haven't noticed the way you shut up when I walk into the room. There was a time when you followed me around like a puppy and I was very good to you, Molly. I let you use my make-up, try on my shoes, and Robert and I took you to the zoo and the park—'

Molly stared at her. 'Is everything okay, Laura? You seem a bit stressed.'

'Shut up! Just shut up!' Laura looked like she might explode. 'I don't want bloody counselling, I want a drink.' Turning on her heel, she stormed off and Molly stood staring after her, unsure of whether she was expected to follow or not. She was tempted not to bother. It was typical of Laura to cast herself as the injured party. It never occurred to her to ask herself *why* Molly didn't confide in her. If Rory was here, he'd have let her have it, but Molly didn't have the energy. Turning on her heel, she went back to the hotel.

Laura sat at the bar of the pub they'd been to the night before, nursing her second gin and tonic. Drinking in the afternoon was turning into a bad habit, but could anyone blame her? She was treated abominably by her daughter, taken for granted by her husband and son, made fun of by her brother and barely tolerated by her mother and sister. Her dad was always nice and affectionate, but then Dad was like that with everyone, including other women, she thought darkly. Perhaps he was only nice to her because he was afraid of her spilling the beans. Not that she would. She'd only told Robert and Molly, although she had hinted at it to Rory one time when he was going on about what a great couple Belle and Oliver made. 'If only you knew,' she'd mumbled, but Rory had just looked at her in disgust and walked away. He was so naïve, even now at twenty-eight, and absolutely hopeless when it came to women; that Natalie was a ridiculous creature, definitely not the full shilling.

A man came to the bar and ordered a pint. Turning towards her, he smiled as he waited. 'Nice day.'

She gave a sullen shrug. 'Is it?'

'Ah, someone's not in good form. Need some cheering up?'

Laura shot him a speculative look from under her lashes. He was quite plain with slightly greasy skin, and he wasn't much taller than her, but he wore a beautifully tailored suit and exquisite shoes that screamed money. 'Shouldn't you be in an office somewhere?'

'No, I've just secured a rather impressive deal for my company,' he said proudly, 'so I've decided to take the rest of the afternoon off.'

She gave a grudging nod. 'That seems fair enough.'

He pulled a stool up and sat down. When the barman returned with his drink, he pointed at Laura's glass. 'Stick another one in there like a good man.'

'Thank you,' Laura said politely.

'Johnny Donohoe.' He held out his hand.

'Molly Jackson.' Laura put her hand into his slightly damp one.

'So what has you so miserable?' he asked.

'I've had a quarrel with my sister.'

He pulled a face. 'Families, who needs them, eh? Cut them loose, that's what I say.'

Laura raised an eyebrow at the fierce note in his voice. 'That's a bit drastic.'

'It's good economic sense. Mine never bothered with me until I started earning a few bob; then they all started to crawl out of the woodwork. Add to that, I have a grasping ex-wife and an ungrateful, useless lump of a son.' He shook his head in disgust.

'It seems to be the lot of a parent to be taken for granted, but I think I deserve some respect from my sister. I was so good to her when she was little, even though she could be a moody little madam and spoiled rotten.'

He raised an eyebrow. 'The youngest?'

Laura nodded.

'I knew it,' he crowed. 'It was the same for me. My brother and I were expected to earn any bit of pocket money we got, but the baby brother' – he snorted '– he never had to lift a finger. Would you believe, he's twenty-five, still living at home, and the mother is still waiting on him hand and foot.'

Laura gave a nervous jump as he thumped the bar. She looked around, realizing that, apart from two old dears in the corner drinking tea and the elderly barman, they were alone and, judging from Johnny's flushed face, he'd had a few drinks already. She'd leave straight after she finished her drink and, in the meantime, it might be an idea to calm him down. 'Let's talk about something more pleasant,' she suggested. 'Tell me about your deal.'

He shot her a suspicious look. 'You wouldn't be interested. I'm in the paint business and the only thing more boring than watching it dry is selling it.'

She laughed. 'Very droll. I do love a man with a sense of humour; my husband can be a terrible bore.'

'So you're up for a laugh,' he said, a speculative gleam in his eye.

'Life's too short, isn't it?' she parried as she stood up. 'Excuse me, I need to find the little girls' room.'

In the back hall, the barman was standing in a fire exit having a sneaky cigarette. 'You know,' he said, conversationally, 'if you follow that lane, it leads right back to the square.'

'Thanks,' she said with an embarrassed grin, and hurried past him. She didn't slow down until she was safely inside the shopping centre. Relieved but drained, she stumbled into the nearest coffee shop and ordered an espresso. As she sipped, she thought about how stupid she'd been. Talking to strange men when she was in safe surroundings was one thing, but if it hadn't been for an observant barman, she could have been in deep water back there. In future, she must be more careful. She gave an involuntary shudder as she remembered how she'd gone down an alleyway with that man in Limerick city – she couldn't even remember his name – and then gotten into a taxi with him. Well, she definitely wouldn't be doing that again. The flash of temper that she had just seen on Johnny Donohoe's florid face had been an eye-opener, and she was grateful that Molly hadn't been there to witness the scene. How pathetic had she become that she was allowing herself to be picked up by weirdos?

When she'd finished her coffee, Laura did what she usually did when she was feeling down: she went shopping. There were few moods, she found, that couldn't be lifted by buying some lingerie or a piece of jewellery.

By the time she returned to the hotel, Robert's card had been put to good use and Laura was feeling better. When she walked into the room Molly was sitting up in bed, wearing that dreary T-shirt that she used as a nightdress, and working on her laptop. 'Hi.'

Molly didn't look up. 'Hi.'

'Any news?'

'No.'

Laura flopped into a chair with a sigh. 'You're not sulking, are you?'

'No. Why would I be sulking?'

Laura scowled and stood up again. 'Oh, be like that; I'm going to have a bath.'

Molly sighed as the bathroom door closed behind her. Thank God they were going home in the morning, she couldn't stand many more of her sister's erratic moods.

Her mobile phone rang and she groped among the covers looking for it. But it had stopped by the time she'd found it. 'Shit,' she muttered and went into the missed calls log. Laura's phone started ringing the same moment she discovered the missed call had been from Rory. She jumped out of bed and pulled Laura's phone out of her bag; it was Rory.

'Rory?'

'Laura?'

'No, it's Molly, what's wrong?'

'It's Mum.' Rory's voice wavered. 'She's in hospital.'

It was less than two hundred kilometres to Dublin, but Molly felt it was the longest journey of her life. She divided her time between sending Rory messages and sitting on her hands.

'Anything from Rory?' Laura asked.

'No, and he hasn't got my last message; his phone must be switched off.'

'He'll be in casualty.' Laura shook her head and tutted. 'What on earth was she doing up a ladder?'

'It was only the small stepladder; she was probably cleaning windows or reaching for something.'

'Where was Dad? Why couldn't he do it for her?' Laura grumbled. 'Useless bloody men.'

'He was out. Look, Laura, accidents happen. Even if Dad had been there, it would never have occurred to Mum to ask him for help; why would it? She's well capable of doing things for herself.'

'Apparently not. Try Rory again.'

'There's no point. He promised to phone as soon as she was out of X-ray.'

'I hope he's telling us everything,' Laura said, shooting her a worried look.

'Why would he keep anything from us?' Although Molly knew the answer: they were far away and he would want them to get back to Dublin in one piece. It was unlikely he'd tell them if Belle had been seriously hurt, or . . .

'I'll never forgive him if she's dead and he's keeping it from us.'

'Don't be so bloody melodramatic,' Molly snapped. 'Anyway, what difference would it make?'

'If she was on her deathbed, Robert could have arranged a private plane or helicopter or something and we could have been with her in minutes,' Laura said stubbornly.

'For goodness sake, will you stop talking total rubbish and just drive?' Molly turned her face away, digging her fingers into the seat to stop herself reaching over and throttling her sister. It had occurred to her, of course it had, that Rory might be protecting them, but she'd dismissed the idea almost immediately. Rory had joked about Belle having one too many and falling over. He'd never have done that if he was hiding anything. Still, his voice was shaking and he was clearly worried about their mother. Belle was never sick, and if anything happened to her, Rory and Dad would be lost without her, well, they all would. She shook her head to banish her negative thoughts; she was as bad as Laura now, jumping to conclusions. Belle would be fine.

Molly pulled out her phone and checked the battery and the signal; both were fine, but there was still no message from Rory. She sighed heavily.

'Call him,' Laura urged. 'If he's in the hospital, the phone will be switched off so what harm can it do?'

Molly dialled and it went straight to the answering service. 'Satisfied?'

'There's no point in biting my head off,' Laura said, then the phone rang.

Molly grabbed it. 'Rory?'

'Hi, Moll.'

'How is she?'

'Just back from X-ray. She's broken her ankle.'

'Is she conscious?' Molly asked, alarmed.

'What is it, what's wrong?' Laura demanded.

Molly shushed her while she listened to Rory.

'No,' Rory was saying. 'Still, the doctor says that's to be expected.'

'But what does that mean? Is she brain-damaged? When will she wake up?'

Laura had pulled into the side of the road now and was staring at her with frightened eyes.

'They'll know more when she wakes up, Moll.'

If she wakes up, Molly couldn't help thinking. 'How's Dad?'

'I think he's in shock. He found her on the floor in the kitchen; he didn't know what had happened.'

'Get him a cup of tea and put plenty of sugar into it.'

'Natalie's gone to get one.'

'Natalie's there?' Molly said and Laura rolled her eyes.

'Yeah, we were in town together when Dad called. Where are you?'

'Where are we?' Molly asked Laura.

'Just coming into Kinnegad.'

Molly repeated this to Rory.

'That's good.' Rory sounded relieved. 'Sorry, I've got to go, Dad's calling me.'

'Will you phone me if there's any more news?'

'Of course.'

'Tell me!' Laura demanded as Molly put down her mobile.

'Her ankle is broken and she's unconscious.'

'Oh my God.' Laura crossed herself. 'Is she going to die?'

'Of course she isn't! Dad found her on the kitchen floor.'

'How long had she been lying there?'

Molly shook her head. 'I don't know, I didn't ask any of the details. Rory's a bit flustered.'

'And Natalie's at the hospital?'

'Yes.'

Laura sighed. 'I thought – I'd hoped she'd be long gone by now.'

'Don't start,' Molly said wearily. 'It's going to be a long night and we have to think about Mum and Dad, they come first.'

'All I said—'

'Just leave it, Laura.' Molly glared at her. 'Mum could be seriously ill, and there's not a damn thing we can do other than get back to Dublin as quickly as we can.'

Chapter Twenty-two

Belle's face was ashen against the pillow. Her right leg, now plastered, was suspended in some kind of contraption above the bed and her right cheek and jaw were bruised and swollen. She still hadn't woken up. Rory and Natalie had gone back to the house to pack a small bag for her and Laura had gone in search of a doctor to find out what was really going on. Molly sat holding her dad's hand and staring worriedly at her poor, unfortunate mother.

'She was just lying there when I came in,' Oliver was saying for the umpteenth time, grey under his tan, his eyes never leaving Belle's face.

Molly winced. 'Any idea how long she may have been there?'

'I'm not sure. When I left the house at nine this morning, she said that she was going to do some baking.'

'And what time did you get back?'

'Four o'clock,' he broke off on a strangled sob.

Molly clutched his hand tighter. 'It wasn't your fault, Dad, it was an accident.'

He shook her off and stood up. 'I should have been with her, not out with my hiking club.'

Molly looked at him, momentarily distracted. 'Hiking?'

'The salsa classes weren't working out and I need some kind of exercise.'

'Well, even if you had been there, it wouldn't have made a blind bit of difference. She'd have thrown you out of the kitchen, telling you not to be getting under her feet and she'd still have fallen.'

'Yes, but I would have heard her call out,' he pointed out, refusing to be comforted.

'Stop beating yourself up, Dad, it won't make any difference. You can stick to her like glue when you get her home, and wait on her hand and foot.'

This drew a small smile and he sat back down and patted her hand. 'You're a good girl.'

'Her ankle will heal quickly,' Molly assured him. 'Rory says it's a straightforward fracture.'

'Yes, but what about her poor head?' Oliver leaned over his wife to gently brush the hair back off her forehead.

Molly stood up. 'I think I'll go and get a drink. Can I get you something?'

He shook his head.

'Okay, won't be long.' As Molly walked down the corridor towards the lifts, Laura emerged from the nurses' station with a grim-faced doctor.

'Is everything all right?' Molly asked.

Laura turned to her, her expression furious. 'Who knows? Nobody is telling me anything.'

The doctor levelled Molly with a hostile gaze, obviously thinking that she was going to give him a hard time too. 'As I've already explained, Mrs Jackson is stable, her scan was clear and now all we can do is wait.'

'Thank you, doctor,' Molly smiled.

'Is that it?' Laura hissed as she fell into step with her sister.

'It's common for the body to close down while it heals itself, Laura.'

'But when will she wake up?'

Molly sighed. 'I don't know.'

'But there must be something they can do,' Laura insisted.

'All they can really do is monitor the situation. Mum's the one who's got the work to do, and while she sorts herself out we just have to wait.'

When they arrived back at the room with several bottles of water and juice, Oliver and Rory were talking quietly in a corner.

'The nurse has just been in. She said that Mum's doing very well, but it's unlikely she'll wake up before morning.'

'Where's Natalie?' Molly asked, perching on the arm of her brother's chair.

'I dropped her home; she was shattered.'

'She's been wonderful,' Oliver said, earning a grateful smile from his son.

'She's not the only one who's tired,' Molly said, looking at her dad's drained features.

'I'm exhausted.' Laura yawned. 'That was such a long drive.'

Molly and Rory exchanged amused looks. 'Dad,' she said. 'Why don't you go home and get some sleep? I'll stay with Mum.'

'Oh no, I couldn't leave her—'

'She's asleep, she doesn't need you now, but she will in the morning.'

'Do you think she'll be okay when she wakes up, Moll?' Oliver asked.

'Of course she will.'

'I'll stay with Molly, Dad. Laura can drop you home.'

'I'm not sure—' Laura started, frowning.

'It's an extra five minutes' drive, for God's sake,' Rory hissed at her. 'Or, if you prefer, you can stay here with Molly and I'll take him home.'

'No, it's fine,' Laura said hurriedly. 'Come on, Dad, let's go.'

Oliver went to the bed and dropped a gentle kiss on Belle's forehead. 'Promise you'll phone me if she wakes up?'

'Of course.' Molly hugged him tight. He looked so lost and exhausted, not at all his usual effervescent self. 'Goodnight, Dad.'

After he'd walked them out to the lift, Rory came back, plonked himself in a chair and stretched out his legs. 'So, what do you think?'

'I think she'll be okay; they'd have her in the ICU if they were really worried about her.'

Rory nodded towards the window of the office where a nurse was working. 'I thought this *was* ICU.'

Molly shook her head. 'It's a special care unit,' she explained. 'You're kept here if they need to keep an eye on you, but you're not considered to be in danger.'

'I suppose that's good,' Rory yawned. 'So, tell me, how was the trip?'

'We didn't kill each other.' Molly took a pillow from the end of the bed and settled herself in the other chair.

'How did you end up in Galway? Weren't you supposed to be going to Limerick?'

'Yeah, but Laura wasn't happy with the accommodation, so she got us transferred to their sister hotel in Galway.'

'Typical,' he shook his head. 'So, what did you do with yourselves all day?'

'I behaved like a tourist and Laura spent her time in the spa or shopping.' Molly cursed as her phone chirruped loudly and she rummaged furiously in her pocket for the offending article. By the time she found it, the caller had hung up. 'Declan.' Molly groaned. 'That's the third time I've missed him.' She quickly sent her fiancé a text, telling him she was back in Dublin in hospital with her mother, and that she'd call him tomorrow. Then, leaving her phone on the chair, she stood up.

'You should really turn it off.'

'I'll leave it on for a couple of minutes. I need the loo. Will you answer it if he calls back? If I take it with me and it rings when I'm passing the nurses' station, I'll be frogmarched out of here.'

'Fine, leave it. I suppose I can muffle it under a pillow.'

'Great,' she grinned, 'back in a mo.'

The hallways were deserted now, except for silent staff drifting around. In the loo she grimaced when she saw her reflection in the mirror above the washbasin. She should have brought her bag and tidied herself up, but as she was about to spend the night in a chair, there probably wasn't much point. She dragged her fingers through her thick bob, doused her face with water and soaped her hands thoroughly, mindful of the health warnings throughout the hospital – the last thing her mother needed right now was to contract a super-bug. Feeling refreshed, she retraced her steps and let herself back into Belle's room.

'You missed a text.' Looking perplexed, Rory handed over her mobile.

'Declan?' Molly sat back into her chair, wriggling to get comfortable. 'Is he pissed off with me? I don't know why, I told him what happened . . .' She trailed off as read the message.

Thinking about you. Luke

She groaned and looked up at her brother. 'It's not what you think.'

'I only know one guy named Luke.'

'I met him yesterday.' Lord, was it really only yesterday? It felt like weeks ago now.

'In Galway?' Rory shook his head in confusion. 'I didn't even know he was back in Ireland.'

'He isn't. He brings rugby groups to Ireland a few times a year.'

'And you ran into him? What an incredible coincidence.'

'It wasn't a coincidence,' she admitted, blushing. 'I went looking for him.'

He was still looking at her, completely baffled. 'What?'

'After I saw him at the airport, I couldn't stop thinking about him.'

'Yeah, I remember you looking him up on the Internet.'

'That's right. Then, when Declan decided to go to Japan, I thought it might be a good idea to check out how Luke was doing.'

'So he asked you to meet him in Limerick?'

'No, I checked on his website and saw that he was coming over this week, but he was flying into Shannon. Only it turned out that I'd gotten the dates wrong and he'd moved on to Galway, so Laura suggested we follow him.'

'Excuse me? Laura's in on this?'

'Yeah, she insisted on coming with me.'

'What about the competition?'

Molly frowned. 'What competition?'

'The free holiday?'

'Oh she made all of that up. She knew you'd all be suspicious of us going away together unless there was a good reason.'

'I had no idea you were so devious. So you met him?'

Molly nodded, flushing.

'And?' he prompted.

'We're meeting up again tomorrow night.'

'Oh, Molly, why?' Rory stared at her in dismay. 'What about Declan? I know he pissed you off, postponing the wedding like that, but he doesn't deserve this.'

'Deserve what?' she challenged. 'I haven't done anything wrong, Rory, and I'm not planning to. I just knew that day when I saw Luke in the airport, that I really wanted, really needed, to talk to Luke about what happened. Declan going to Japan just presented me with an opportunity to do that.'

Rory looked at her, his lovely blue eyes clouded with concern. 'And did you talk?'

'Yes, but we're not finished. There's so much to say.'

'Leave it, Moll. It's not going to help, not after all these years. It's a bad idea.'

'Why is it? What harm can it do? You always got on well with Luke,' she reminded him.

'I was a kid that adored rugby and he was my idol, but I remember how messed up you were after he left.'

'That was hardly his fault, and he was just as messed up as I was, probably more so. Don't you get it, Rory? No one can understand how I feel, the way he can, and it's the same for him.'

'I understand that, Moll, really I do, but then what? Will he go back to France? Will you go back to Declan? Will you carry on as if it never happened?'

'I suppose so,' Molly murmured. 'He's married.'

'Oh, Moll,' Rory massaged his stubbled chin.

'I'm not doing anything wrong, Rory. Quite the contrary, I'm making sure that I'm marrying the right man.'

'Hang on a second, I thought you said this was about Ruth?'

'It is, sort of, but it's about Declan too.' She leaned back in the chair, feeling tired and defeated. 'I'm not sure he really wants to marry me, and when I saw Luke in the airport, well, I realized that I still had feelings for him. So I decided to make sure that I was doing the right thing, that I was marrying the right man.'

'And if you decide that it's not Declan, are you planning to break up Luke's marriage?'

'I'm not planning anything, Rory,' she cried. 'If I decide not to marry Declan, it will be regardless of what happens with Luke, and I would never ask him to leave his wife.'

'He wouldn't send you a text like that if he didn't think there was some hope.'

'Okay, so we connected,' she admitted wearily. 'But it's much more complicated than that. I went looking for him in search of answers, and now he has questions of his own. I'll see him tomorrow night and then on Sunday he'll fly back to Bordeaux.'

'And you'll never see him again?' Rory asked.

She held his gaze. 'I can't answer that yet.'

'Oh, Moll, this is madness.'

'I know, Rory, but can you honestly blame me for wanting to be sure that I'm doing the right thing?'

'I don't blame you, I just don't want you to screw things up with Declan on some romantic whim. You two are great together, I've always envied you.'

Molly looked at him in surprise. 'You've got Natalie now.'

'Yeah, and I really like her,' he sighed, 'which is a sure indication that she's probably about to dump me.'

'She's not. Why would she? You're a nice guy, and you're not *that* ugly,' Molly teased.

'Why don't you like her?' he asked suddenly.

'I do,' she murmured, avoiding his eyes.

'You don't, and neither does Laura, although I don't care what she thinks.'

'I hardly know her, Rory.'

'But?' he pushed her.

'I just felt she was a little bit patronizing. The very first time she met us, she questioned our religious beliefs and morality.'

'She didn't mean to insult anyone, she just worries about people who have no faith; it really bothers her. I've never known anyone agonize so much over other people's souls.'

'Well, good for her, but it's a very private subject, and not one most people are comfortable discussing with a stranger.'

He nodded. 'I know she's a bit keen, but give her a chance, eh, Moll?'

She smiled at him. 'Sure. Sorry if I was hard on her. It can't have been easy meeting the whole gang of us in one go.'

Rory nodded, rolling his eyes. 'Yeah, that was probably a mistake, although she and Dad hit it off and I think Mum's mellowing.'

'Why don't we meet up some night in town?' Molly suggested. 'I'd like to get to know her better.'

He shot her a suspicious look. 'Are you just buttering me up so I won't give you a hard time about Luke?'

She sighed. 'No, I'm trying to make up for being a crap sister.'

He grinned as he settled back in the chair to sleep. 'Fair enough, but no double dates, at least, not until Declan gets back.'

'Agreed,' Molly said and closed her eyes.

Chapter Twenty-three

12.15 a.m., Saturday, 8th August

It was after midnight when Laura got home, and she'd expected the children to be asleep and Robert sprawled in front of a football match or a movie. But when she turned into her road, she could hear music and, as she drew closer, she realized that it was coming from her house. The lights were blazing from both floors and, not only were the gates open, but the front door too. 'Ash,' she muttered grimly. It would never occur to Adam to throw a party, but no doubt he had jumped on board once Ash had suggested it. But where the hell was Robert? How could he go out on a Friday night and leave two teenage kids alone to get up to God only knew what? She jumped out of the car and braced herself for what she might see. Adam in bed with a girl, Ash in the loo snorting coke or downing Es . . . She shivered, unable to decide which was worse. Inside, the hallway was crawling with teenagers; she didn't recognize anyone. She poked one boy in the chest and glared at him. 'Where are Adam and Ashling?'

He shrugged. 'Kitchen?'

Laura marched on, and flinging open the kitchen door, stopped in her tracks at the sight that greeted her.

'Laura!' Robert stood up from the table. 'What are you doing here? I wasn't expecting you back until tomorrow.'

'What's going on?' she hissed, her eyes travelling around the room. There were several people at the table and around the island, drinking wine and coffee, chatting happily and oblivious of her entrance.

Robert came over to kiss her. 'The kids were pestering me to have a party and I told them they were too young. Then I thought they could always have a small get-together and bring the parents along too. I think you know everyone.' He turned and raised his voice. 'Hey, guys, Laura's home!'

There was a chorus of hellos and a few waves.

Laura smiled through gritted teeth and managed a stiff wave. 'I don't know these people; we only ever say hello when we're dropping the kids off at school.'

'Well, I must say, they're a very nice bunch. I've quite enjoyed myself.'

Laura took in his flushed appearance. 'I can see that. How much have you had to drink?'

'Just a few beers.'

'And have you any idea where your children are and what they're up to? It doesn't look like there's much supervision going on.' Looking at the way a couple of the women were playing with their hair, and leaning forward to reveal cleavages, Laura thought that perhaps it was the adults who needed supervising.

'They're fine, don't worry. We take it in turns to patrol. Penny and Mark are on duty at the mo.'

'Penny and Mark?' Laura said faintly.

'Yes, their Neil and Ash seem to be great pals, did you realize?'

'No, but then Ash tells me nothing, does she?' She gave him a brittle smile. 'I'll go and say hi.' Laura went back into the hall and stuck her head into the front lounge. Mark, Penny's husband, was standing chatting to a few kids; he smiled when he saw her.

'Hello, Laura, how are you?'

'Great, thanks! Any idea where Penny is?'

'Upstairs, making sure that no one is making use of your accommodation,' he said with a wink.

'Oh, right.' She winked back and stepping around the bodies on the stairs, found Penny in her daughter's room. She was applying make-up to Ash's eyes while three other girls looked on, entranced.

Penny looked up and smiled. 'Laura, sweetie, how are you? I'm just teaching the girls how to create the smoky look.' She stepped back and appraised her work. 'There! Turn around and show your mum.'

Ashling spun around, smiling. 'Look at my eyes, Mum, aren't they amazing?'

Laura swallowed at her daughter's childish delight. 'You look stunning, sweetheart.'

'Why don't you try the same technique out on Katie while your Mum and I catch up?' Penny suggested.

They moved into the hall and Penny closed the door behind them, before turning amused eyes on Laura. 'So I believe we're off out tomorrow night.'

Laura looked at her aghast. 'Oh, Penny, I'm sorry. I never meant to put you on the spot. What did you say?'

'I said, "Yes, Robert, that's right" of course.'

'Thank you,' Laura said humbly.

'I've always been good at thinking on my feet; you have to be when you have secrets, don't you?'

Laura searched Penny's face. 'You?'

'I like to have a bit of time away from my family, like most mothers.' Penny gave an innocent shrug. 'It's perfectly natural, don't you think?'

Laura sighed with relief. 'Of course.'

'So who is he?' Penny's eyes twinkled. 'Anyone I know, or someone you met in the west?'

'Oh, it's nothing like that, Penny,' Laura assured her, looking around with nervous eyes.

There were kids everywhere, and she didn't want any of them going to Ash or Adam and telling tales.

Penny studied her friend with narrowed eyes. 'You haven't fallen for someone, have you? Not planning to dump dear old Rob—'

'Please shut up,' Laura hissed.

Penny raised her eyebrows. 'Only if you spill.'

'I will, just not here and not now.'

'We should go and get our nails done tomorrow; we want to look our best tomorrow night.' Penny winked. 'Have to make a special effort when you're surrounded by all those willowy models.'

Laura scowled. 'I won't be able to, my Mum's in hospital. She had a fall today, that's why I'm back early.'

'Oh, I'm sorry,' Penny said, not sounding it at all. 'So, when?'

'Let's meet up on Monday and then I'll be able to tell you how it went.'

'Excellent.' Penny rubbed her hands together. 'I'll look forward to that. You are a dark horse, Laura, I didn't know you had it in you.'

Laura fabricated a complicit smile. 'We'd better go back downstairs.'

'Absolutely, we don't want the boys wondering what we're gossiping about, eh?'

'I'll follow you down, I just want to find Adam.'

'Outside, playing football in the dark,' Penny laughed, over her shoulder.

'Thank God,' Laura mumbled, delighted that her son still preferred soccer to girls, although she knew it wouldn't be for much longer. She couldn't begin to imagine how she would feel when Adam started to date seriously. She currently had to compete with Ash for his affections; she wouldn't get a look in once he found a girlfriend. Feeling decidedly tired and a little sorry for herself, Laura followed Penny back down to the kitchen. She still couldn't believe that Robert had organized all of this; it was totally out of character.

As she walked into the room, he was standing by the island chatting to a small blonde who was laughing up into his face, her hand on his arm. Laura recognized her as the mother of one of Ash's wilder friends, a recent divorcée and someone who was obviously on the look-out for a new man. Smiling broadly, she crossed the room to her husband and put her arm through his. 'This was a great idea, darling, getting everyone together like this.'

'I can't take the credit, I'm afraid,' he admitted, 'Cheryl actually suggested it.'

'How very clever of you, Cheryl,' Laura purred. 'I'm so glad I came back a day early, I'd have hated to miss it.'

The other woman had the grace to blush. 'It was a general suggestion, really. Robert just decided that he'd be the first one to give it a go.'

Laura nodded and then frowned. 'And when was this?'

'Oh, we met up at the bowling alley yesterday,' Robert said, oblivious of the undercurrents. 'The place was packed and we hadn't booked a lane, so Cheryl suggested that we share one.'

Laura's smile was getting frostier by the second. 'That was kind.'

'Well, it was Lottie's idea; she adores Ash and wasn't interested in playing with just her brother once she saw her best friend was there.'

Ashling didn't exactly volunteer information these days, but Laura was pretty sure that she wouldn't describe Lottie as her best friend. More likely, the girls were being thrown together because mummy had her eye on Robert. Laura turned to her husband, effectively cutting off Cheryl. 'Darling, Mum has had an accident, that's why I came back early. She's in hospital.'

Robert's brow creased with worry. 'But that's terrible. How is she?'

'She broke her ankle and she's unconscious, although they don't seem worried about her. They did a brain scan and said it's clear, and that she'll wake up in her own time.'

'I'm so sorry, darling, what a shock. Why didn't Oliver or Rory call me?'

Out of the corner of her eye, Laura noticed Cheryl move away. Mission accomplished.

'Dad doesn't know whether he's coming or going, and Rory knew that you were home alone with the kids, so he didn't bother you.'

'Poor Belle. But what happened?'

'I'll fill you in later, when we have the place back to ourselves.' She sank into the nearest chair and covered a yawn.

'You look exhausted.' Robert tucked tendrils of hair behind her ear. 'It's almost one, and about time this lot went home. Why don't you have a glass of wine and I'll get rid of them?' He kissed her hair before turning to the other adults. 'Okay, people, time to gather up the little darlings and get them to bed, preferably their own!'

There was good-natured laughter as everyone drained glasses, exchanged hugs and kisses and went in search of their offspring. Laura watched in silent admiration as Robert moved among them, gently chivvying along the lingerers and accepting gratitude and good wishes with humility and ease. This was a side of Robert that she rarely saw; he usually left the organizing to her, saving his managerial skills for the office. The realization annoyed her. He'd soon realize how much she did for him if he left her for an air-head like Cheryl. Whereas before she'd felt guilty about her assignation with Gerard, now she decided her behaviour was not only understandable, but justifiable. If she didn't take matters into her own hands, she would sink into middle-aged suburbia before she hit forty without even noticing. But she had no intention of letting that happen, nor did she plan to end up alone and desperate like that ditzy blonde, Cheryl.

She looked up to see Penny at her side, a sly smile on her face. She sighed. The fact that Penny knew what she was up to made her feel very uneasy. A few glasses of wine on the next girly outing and the woman would be telling everyone that Laura had a lover. She would have to somehow convince Penny that it had all been a silly mistake and had come to nothing. She forced herself to hug the woman. 'Thanks for everything,' she murmured.

'Good luck tomorrow,' Penny whispered.

'Thanks. I'll call you on Monday.'

'Be sure you do.' Perhaps it was just tiredness that made Laura think it sounded like a threat.

Molly stretched, grimacing at the crick in her neck, and then, remembering where she was, turned quickly towards the bed. Belle's eyes remained closed but, thankfully, her breathing was silent and even. The nurse had been in several times through the night checking her eyes and pulse, and she seemed pleased with Belle's progress, though Molly and Rory didn't really understand why. She stood up and tiptoed to the door and, rubbing her eyes, she hurried downstairs and went outside into a rather damp and gloomy morning. Pulling out her mobile she sent a text.

CAN U TALK?

She leaned against the wall, combing her hair with her fingers as she waited for a reply. It felt greasy and tangled and she couldn't wait to have a shower. Rory had already left and once Oliver arrived, Molly could nip home and get cleaned up. She thought she should probably cancel her rendezvous with Luke, but it was too early to call; she'd contact him later. She was a bit upset that Belle hadn't woken yet, but the nurse assured her it was still early days.

The phone rang and she pulled it out and held it tight to her ear. 'Declan?'

'Hey, Moll, what's going on? I've been worried sick about you all day.'

'It's Mum, there's been an accident.' She quickly filled him in on the details.

'Sorry, Moll, I wish I was there for you.'

She felt a pang of guilt. 'Don't be silly, what difference would it make? How are things going with you?'

'Tough,' he admitted. 'There's so much to learn, but it is interesting and I think they're happy with me.'

'Why wouldn't they be, you're the best.'

'Thanks, Moll,' he said and then yawned loudly. 'Sorry.'

'Go to bed,' she advised. 'I'll text you when I have more news on Mum.'

'Make sure you do. I miss you, Moll.'

She closed her eyes tight, feeling consumed with guilt. 'Me too, but it won't be for much longer. Bye, Declan.'

'Bye, Moll. Love you.'

'Me too.' She went back inside, trying not to dwell on the fact that the words 'I love you too' had stuck in her throat. Guilt, she decided, only natural and nothing to worry about. She hurried back upstairs to the room and stopped dead when she saw that a nurse was helping her mother to sit up. 'Mum! How are you feeling?'

'Like a freight train's running through the middle of my head.' But Belle managed to give her a small smile.

The nurse smiled. 'She's going to be just fine.'

An overbearing doctor breezed in with a posse of students and the nurse shepherded Molly outside while they examined her mother.

'I'd like to talk to the doctor,' Molly said firmly.

'Of course, but he'll do his rounds first, and then come back and have a word later when the results of all the tests are in.'

Molly hurried back outside and phoned her dad, Rory and Laura, and then sent a text to Declan.

'I'm on my way,' Oliver said and hung up.

'Thank God,' Rory said and promised to drop by again later once he'd had some sleep. 'Go home, Moll,' he said.

'I will once Dad gets here,' she promised.

'Does she seem okay?' Laura asked sleepily after Robert had woken her and handed her the phone.

'She's complaining of a headache, but she seems okay. The doctor's with her now.'

Molly hurried back upstairs and after checking with the nurse, went back into her mother's room.

Belle opened her eyes. 'Hello, darling. Where's your father?'

'On his way.' She perched on the chair next to her mother and looked at her anxiously. 'Do you remember what happened, Mum?'

'Just that I was taking down a baking tray. I can't have set the ladder up properly, and it fell. I whacked my head on the edge of the worktop, and then I remember hitting the floor like a ton of bricks, but after that, nothing.'

'What did the doctor say?'

Belle smiled. 'He told me I was a very lucky woman; if I'd had the energy, I would have punched him.'

Molly laughed. Belle might be suffering physically, but her brain was obviously as sharp as ever.

'What do I look like?' Belle looked with dismay at her plastered foot and put up her hand to touch her injured face.

'Like you've been in a fight,' Molly admitted with a grin, 'but the bruises will fade and mercifully you didn't even need stitches.'

Belle grimaced. 'Yes, I know, I'm very lucky.'

Oliver arrived shortly after, and Molly left in order to give them some time alone and went in search of the doctor. At the nurses' station she was told that he would be down to see Oliver presently, and was warned that, though Belle was recovering well, she needed rest and visitors should be limited to two at a time at most.

'Sleep is what she really needs now,' the nurse told Molly.

Molly went down to the café, bought tea and a scone, and then came back up to her parents.

'You've just missed the doctor,' Oliver told her.

'Pretentious old fool,' Belle mumbled.

'He's very pleased with her progress and says she can come home in a couple of days.'

'So soon?' Molly was alarmed. Belle had only just woken up, was she really okay, or was this about cutbacks and hospital beds?

'He gave me a list of symptoms to watch out for,' Oliver held up a piece of paper, 'but says that once your mum's seen a physiotherapist and had a lesson on crutches, she can go.'

Molly could see that Oliver looked as uncertain as she felt. 'Well, we'll all help out, Dad. Don't worry. And I'm sure, Mum, you'll be happier at home.'

'I certainly will,' Belle said with feeling. 'I've always hated these places. Now, Molly, you must go home, you look exhausted.'

'The nurse did say that we should keep visiting to a minimum, that you needed plenty of rest.'

'I *am* tired.'

'Go on, darling,' Oliver stood up and hugged his daughter. 'You've done your bit. Go home and have a sleep.'

Molly kissed her mother and went out in search of a taxi; public transport was beyond her at this stage.

It seemed only minutes after she'd crawled into bed, that the phone rang. 'Go away,' she groaned and decided to ignore it. But then, what if it was Dad and there was something wrong with Mum? She launched herself across the bed and grabbed the phone. 'Hello?'

'Hi, it's me.'

'Laura? Is everything okay?'

'Not really.'

'What's happened; is it Mum?'

'No, of course not. I'm still in bed, I haven't seen Mum yet.'

Molly grimaced. 'I thought you'd be up at the hospital by now.'

'I do have a family to look after too, you know.'

'From bed?'

'Molly, I didn't phone for an argument. It's about tonight.'

'What about tonight?'

'You're seeing Luke, aren't you?'

'I haven't talked to him yet, but that's the plan, yes.'

'And I'm seeing Gerard.'

'Oh, Laura—'

'Don't.'

Molly sighed. 'Okay.'

'The point is, I think it would be best if we all go out together; it would look less suspicious if we ran into anyone.'

Molly sat up, rubbing her eyes. 'But it would defeat the purpose, Laura. I can't talk to Luke in front of you and Gerard.'

'Of course I'm not suggesting that; just that we go to the same venue. I thought the bar in the Shelbourne hotel would be a good, central location. Gerard and I could sit at the bar, you and Luke at a table, but if anyone saw us, we could meet up and be seen to leave together without the guys.'

That did make a lot of sense, Molly realized. She had been nervous of seeing Luke in Dublin, especially given that Declan was out of the country. 'Have you done this before?' she asked suspiciously.

Laura gave a short laugh. 'No, I'm just a better planner than you, remember? Will I pick you up?'

'Yes, I'll phone you with a time after I've talked to Luke.'

'And Robert thinks I'm going to a fashion show with Penny, so try and look presentable. If we are seen out together, I can always tell him that I invited you along to cheer you up.'

'This is getting so complicated,' Molly said, exhausted and shamed by the lies and deception.

'You just need to be careful, and then no one will be any the wiser. And remember, don't mention names when you're texting. I hope if Luke's number is in your phone, you've put him under a different name.'

'Of course,' Molly lied and as soon as she rang off, she went into her address book and altered Luke to Lucy. True, Declan wasn't around to pick up her phone and discover her secrets right now, but Rory had already found her out and she needed to learn to be more careful – or conniving – like her sister.

Chapter Twenty-four

7.15 p.m., Saturday, 8th August

On the taxi ride into town, Laura and Molly were silent, each lost in thought. Molly felt overdressed and very self-conscious, but Laura had explained that she was supposed to be attending a fashion show, and that it would look odd if her sister was in jeans. Molly could see the sense in this but, equally, didn't want Luke to think she'd dressed up for him. She'd compromised by wearing a purple shift minidress with a black jacket, opaque tights and platform sandals that added two inches to her height and gave her confidence. Laura looked very chic in a black dress that seemed demure until she let her wrap slip down, revealing a deep V at the back.

Luke had sounded pleased and relieved on the phone when she agreed to see him. Molly had thought she'd have to cancel on account of her mum, but Rory had called her at lunchtime to say Belle was doing well, but sleeping a lot and it would be better not to visit again until tomorrow. Laura had also dropped in to the hospital and phoned Molly straight afterwards.

'It looks like she'll be coming home on Monday. I was thinking that I could make up some casseroles, curries, things like that, and stock the freezer so Dad can concentrate on looking after her.'

'Good idea. I'll call out to the house tomorrow and change the sheets and make sure the place is tidy.'

'Great. After that, we'll just have to see how it goes. I hope Rory realizes he's going to have to help out more.'

'He will. We could put him on shopping duty. And I'll come over and do Mum's hair or help her shower, whenever she wants. Don't worry, Laura. Between us, we'll make sure that she's well looked after.'

'We're here,' Laura said, her voice shaking slightly as the taxi came to a stop outside the hotel.

Molly started out of her reverie and looked at her sister. 'I know why I'm here,' she said. 'Do you?'

Laura's expression hardened. 'I know I want a life.'

Molly shrugged. 'Fair enough, but have you thought through the consequences if Robert ever finds out what you are up to?'

'But he's not going to find out, is he?'

'Not from me.'

'Good.' Laura handed over the fare, stepped onto the pavement and led the way into the hotel.

Molly saw Luke as soon as she walked into the room. He and Gerard were at the bar, looking casually smart in jackets and open-necked shirts. She made to go over, but Laura put a hand on her arm.

'It would be better if we wandered around first and found someplace to sit. That way, if there's anyone here we know, we'll see them before they see us.'

Molly gave a brief nod and followed her sister; Laura really was way too good at this. They circled the room twice, as if looking for friends, before settling at a table almost behind the door. It was an excellent position to observe people coming and going, yet tucked away enough to allow some privacy. Molly sat facing the wall, while Laura took the seat opposite, where she could keep an eye on everything.

'This was a bad idea,' Molly murmured, suddenly nervous. 'We're obviously together, and it's going to look very odd if you end up up in one corner with Gerard, and I'm in another with Luke. We may as well have "guilty" tattooed across our foreheads.'

'Keep calm,' Laura told her. 'I'll wave at the guys to come over, as if I've just spotted them and then, as far as all of these strangers are concerned, we've just bumped into old friends. Then, after a while, we can split up. It will be fine. Ready?'

Molly swallowed hard and nodded. Laura watched the bar and after a moment, Luke looked around and she waved to him, smiling as if she'd only just noticed them. 'Have they seen you?'

'On their way over.' Laura settled back and smiled, letting her wrap slip slightly.

Molly groaned inwardly.

'Laura!' Gerard came over, stinking of cologne, Luke on his heels. Laura exchanged kisses with Gerard, while Luke and Molly stood smiling shyly at each other.

'You look lovely,' he said, giving her a chaste kiss on the cheek.

'I should be at a fashion show,' she explained, self-consciously, and then laughed when he frowned in confusion. 'Never mind.' She turned to say hello to Gerard and then watched while Laura and Luke hugged briefly. Gerard beckoned a waiter and ordered drinks, then turned back to the others. There was an awkward silence and Molly smiled at the Frenchman. 'Have you enjoyed your trip?'

The younger man's face lit up. 'I had a wonderful time,

although I do not think my rugby has improved.'

'That's because you drank too much of the black stuff.' Luke grinned.

'Pah! You are too pure with your water all the time, not even wine with your food.' Gerard splayed his hands and looked to Laura for support. 'Does this make sense?'

'To each his own,' Laura shrugged. 'So, Gerard, tell me more about what you do . . .'

Luke turned to Molly. 'How are you?' he asked quietly.

'I'm okay.'

'You look amazing.'

Molly shifted uncomfortably as he studied her, his eyes warm.

'Sorry. I don't mean to make you uncomfortable.'

'I feel ashamed just being here,' Molly blurted out.

'You shouldn't, you've been completely faithful to Declan, despite my efforts.'

'It wasn't easy,' she admitted. 'And I'm not sure what we're doing here tonight, or what we think it will achieve.'

'To learn more, to understand what happened, to talk about our lives.' He shrugged.

'It's dangerous,' she murmured.

'It's exciting,' he replied, eyes twinkling.

'Yes, but I'm not sure it's real.'

'What do you mean?' he asked.

Molly sighed. 'Perhaps the only reason we are attracted to each other is because of our history, or because we're both having relationship problems at the moment.'

'I don't agree. For me, it's simple. I think you were always the only one for me. I loved you then, and I still love you now.' He touched her hand. 'Maybe more so.'

She gasped at his directness, not knowing whether she should laugh or cry.

'Sorry.' His smile was sad. 'Too honest for you?'

'It's a shock to hear you say that. But if it's true, why didn't you ever come back for me?'

'It wasn't possible at first, and then—'

Laura and Gerard stood up. 'We'll be at the bar.' Her sister put a gentle hand on Molly's shoulder. 'Just call if you need me.'

Molly looked up in grateful surprise and nodded.

Luke watched them leave and then turned back to face her. 'I couldn't do it to my mother, Molly. She'd lost Ruth and, as far as she was concerned, you were the reason she died. My coming back to you would have seemed like the worst kind of betrayal.'

'She blamed me?' Molly looked at him in horror and put a hand out to grip the table as a wave of nausea engulfed her.

'She wasn't thinking straight, Moll. Her daughter was dead and she had to blame someone.'

Molly nodded in understanding and got to her feet.

Luke put a hand on her arm. 'Molly? Are you all right?'

She gave a strained smile. 'Sure, I just need to use the loo.'

She was standing trembling at a sink, wiping her mouth with a paper napkin, when Laura walked in.

'What is it? Are you sick?'

Molly nodded and shrugged. 'Must be nerves.'

'You're as white as a sheet.' Laura's eyes were sharp. 'What is it? Has he upset you? Do you want to go home?'

Molly took a shaky breath. 'Not yet. Anyway, if I do, I'll just hop in a taxi. There's no reason for you to cut your evening short.'

Laura raised an eyebrow. 'I thought you didn't approve.'

'It's your life,' Molly mumbled, tiredly.

'I'm not having much fun, to be honest,' Laura said, taking out her lipstick. 'He seemed a lot more attractive when I was drunk.'

She turned Molly gently towards her. 'Here, let me touch up your make-up.'

Molly allowed Laura to make her presentable and then pulled a comb through her hair.

Laura smiled at her in the mirror. 'Ready?'

'You go on ahead, I'll be out in a minute.'

When her sister had gone, Molly sat down on the chaise longue, rested her head against the wall and closed her eyes. She still felt slightly queasy as she remembered Luke's words. Mrs Fortune blamed her for Ruth's death. Why was Molly surprised? It was true. She blamed herself too, she always had. Ruth died, and she had walked away from the accident with hardly a scratch. Her scars were on the inside. She was sorry now that she'd seen Luke at the airport and regretted even more that she'd pursued him. It had been selfish and wrong, and she should never have come back into his life. She stood up and took a deep breath. It was time to go and end this, once and for all. Whatever happened with Declan, it was clear that Luke was not destined to be part of her future.

He jumped to his feet the instant he saw her, concern and regret in his eyes. 'I'm sorry, Molly, that was a stupid, thoughtless, cruel thing to say—'

She held up a hand to stop him as they sat down. 'But true. I suppose I always knew how she felt. Mum said she didn't want to see me simply because she was hurting too much and because I was a reminder of the accident, but I knew there was more to it than that.' She looked at Luke. 'Tell me, please?'

He said nothing for a moment, and then gave a reluctant nod. 'In the first few days after the accident, Mum was sedated most of the time. Any time they let the tablets wear off, she went into total meltdown. Then, after a couple of weeks, she calmed down.

But she was like an automaton, wandering around the house, talking to no one, barely eating. And then she started to ask questions; she wanted to know all about the accident, about Ruth's injuries, about what had actually killed her. She was distraught that she had been too upset to go into the morgue and view the body.' He shook his head, his eyes bright with tears. 'She even begged Dad to get them to exhume the body, just so she could see Ruth one more time.'

Tears rolled down Molly's face as he talked and she clutched his hand. He patted it absently.

'Then she started to talk about you, about how it was your fault, about how if it wasn't for you and your bloody car – her words not mine – Ruth would still be alive. She was furious that Ruth had been drinking and driving. She couldn't understand how you had let her get behind the wheel, especially as you were sober and supposed to be driving.' He looked at her. 'We tried to explain the circumstances so many times, but I suppose she just didn't want to know. I'm sorry.'

Molly dabbed at her eyes with a tissue and took a couple of deep breaths before replying, she couldn't fall apart in the middle of the Shelbourne bar. 'It's okay,' she reassured him. 'If it had been the other way round, I'm sure my mum would have reacted the same way.'

'So, after that, I was afraid to contact you, and I was even more terrified that you'd come to the house. I wanted to protect you from her anger. I talked to Dad, and I think he phoned Oliver.'

Molly nodded, remembering how hurt and confused she'd felt when her parents had sat her down and gently explained that it would be best if she didn't contact Luke for a while; that the family was going through a difficult time and should be left to deal with their grief as a family. 'And then you were gone.'

'I'm sorry, Moll, I should never have left you.'

'You had no choice. You were only eighteen, and it would have devastated your parents if you'd refused to go with them.'

'Sometimes it feels like I've spent all of my life worrying about their feelings, and forgetting my own,' Luke said, bitterly. 'I don't think I'd have married Adriana if it wasn't for the fact that I just wanted to escape them and that bloody house; I really would have been better off here.'

'If you'd stayed, we wouldn't have lasted a month,' Molly assured him. 'We'd have been racked with guilt and, every time we met, Ruth would have been there between us.'

'But she loved us both, she would have wanted us to be together,' he protested.

'I know, but we were too young, and hurting too much, to be of any use to each other. Your parents did what they thought was best.'

'They ran away.'

'Now you sound like a sulky little boy,' she teased, trying to lighten the mood. She hadn't expected him to be so full of hurt and anger. 'Who knows whether they were right or wrong, but if you'd stayed, you can't honestly believe that we'd have gone on as before, as if nothing had happened?'

He sighed. 'I suppose not.'

'Life is cruel, Luke, and it has been especially cruel to you. Don't let it destroy you. Ruth wouldn't want that.'

'But now, Moll, now we've been given a second chance. Don't you think we should grab it with both hands?' He searched her face. 'Let's do it, Molly. I love you and I think you still love me.'

She pulled her hand away and shook her head. 'This is madness, you're not thinking straight. We're just emotional—'

'That's crap,' he said angrily. 'I know my own mind.'

'And your mum?'

'I'm almost thirty, I think it's about time that I started living my life without worrying about her feelings. Anyway, she can't still blame you.'

'But what if she does?'

He shrugged. 'Then it will be her problem, not mine, not ours.'

'And your wife, Luke? You're married, remember?'

'I told you it was over, Molly.'

'I'm sorry, Luke,' she said, feeling immeasurably sad. 'I don't think I could be happy at everyone else's expense. I'm lucky. I have so much. My family are great and I'm engaged to a wonderful man. I shouldn't even be here with you. Ellen was right, the past should stay in the past.'

'Who's Ellen?' he asked.

'My best friend.'

'Doesn't sound like we'd get on,' he muttered.

She smiled. 'Actually, I'm sure you'd love her. I think I should go now.'

'But you can't,' he protested. 'There's so much more to talk about—'

She bent to pick up her bag. 'I thought so too, Luke, but there really isn't.'

'Please, Molly.' He took her hand again. 'I haven't felt this alive in such a long time. I love you, I want you. You've no idea how many times I've dreamed of making love to you.'

She closed her eyes. When he looked at her like that, it would be easy to give in.

'Come back to the hotel with me,' he murmured, leaning into her. 'Let me hold you.'

She was tempted. It would be so easy, no one need ever know. But then she thought of how she'd feel if she was lying in Luke's bed when Declan phoned, and she knew she couldn't go through with it. 'I'm sorry.'

'Okay then,' he relented, 'but I'll be in Dublin again next month; meet me then.'

'There's no point—'

'Please, Molly?' he begged. 'If you still feel the same way, then I promise I'll never contact you again.'

She nodded slowly and tried to smile. 'Okay, then.'

*

Once Molly assured her sister she was okay, Laura elected to stay on for a little while longer, saying it would look odd if she arrived home so early. There were no taxis and it had started to rain, so Luke drew Molly back into the shelter of the porch to wait. Molly knew he was going to kiss her and that she should-n't let him, but would it be so bad, just one last time . . .

'Oh, Molly.' He groaned and slid his arms under her jacket and pulled her close.

Molly closed her eyes and turned her face up for his kiss.

'Molly?'

She sprang away from Luke and looked past him, her eyes widening in horror. 'Gareth!'

'Hi.' He looked from her to Luke and waited. 'This is . . . a sur-prise.'

Molly recovered her composure and made the introductions. 'Gareth, this is Luke Fortune, an old friend of mine. Luke, this is Gareth, Declan's brother.'

She was very impressed when Luke smiled calmly and stretched out a hand. 'Pleased to meet you.'

Gareth looked taken aback, but shook Luke's hand.

'We just ran into each other,' Molly explained, 'after twelve years.'

'Really?'

'My family moved to France,' Luke explained. 'I'm just here on a short visit and I go home tomorrow.' He smiled at Molly. 'I can't believe what a stroke of luck it was bumping into you like this.'

A taxi pulled up and Molly looked from one man to the other. 'Well, I'll say goodbye.'

Luke bent and kissed her on the lips, a defiant look in his eye. 'Take care, Molly.'

'And you,' she said, flustered. 'Bye, Gareth.'

'Any chance of a lift?' her future brother-in-law asked.

'Oh, well, yes, of course.'

Gareth held the door for her and, after a last desperate look at Luke, Molly had no choice but to climb in.

'Goodbye, Luke. Have a safe journey home,' Gareth said.

'Thank you.' But Luke wasn't even looking at him. 'Goodbye, Molly.'

Molly fought back the tears. 'Goodbye, Luke. Take care.'

Gareth slammed the door, gave the driver directions, and then turned to look at her.

'Okay, Molly, want to tell me what that was all about?'

Chapter Twenty-five

11.25 a.m., Monday, 10th August

Molly turned into the cul-de-sac and freewheeled the last few feet to Laura's gate. She hadn't seen her sister since she walked out of the hotel on Saturday night. Belle had been kept in hospital until this morning and while Molly had spent Sunday tidying her parents' house, doing the laundry and changing the bedlinen, Laura had cooked up a storm in order to stock up their freezer. Rory had been dispatched with a list to do the shopping and everything was ready for Belle's return this morning.

Once her mother was sitting up in bed, tired but happy to be home, Molly had left and, on impulse, decided to come and see Laura and tell her about Gareth's unexpected appearance. Molly was glad that she'd been so busy over the last couple of days, it meant she didn't have too much time to dwell on Luke. But as she'd cycled towards Clontarf, Molly re-lived Saturday night, still able to picture Luke's anguished expression. After all these years he was still hurting so much from the loss of his twin and Molly guessed that he was right and that it was, in part, due to putting his mother's feelings before his own. It had taken Molly a long time and a lot of counselling to forgive herself for her part in what happened that night. But having listened to Luke talk, witnessed his pain and heard all about his poor mother, Molly felt her guilt re-surface. If Ruth hadn't been her usual brave, fearless self, she would never have climbed behind the wheel that night. If Molly had managed to pull herself together, she'd have been driving and Ruth might be still here now. 'What ifs' – a pointless exercise, and Molly forced the negative thoughts to the back of her mind as she cycled up Laura's drive and leaned her bike against the wall. She rang the doorbell before taking off her helmet and shaking out her hair. After a few moments, her niece answered with an uncertain smile. 'Hi, Molly.'

'Hi, Ash.'

'Mum's not here.'

'Oh?'

'She's gone into town.'

'Oh.' Molly sighed and dragged her sleeve across her flushed face.

'Want to come in? I could get you some water or a coffee or something.'

'Water would be nice.' Molly smiled gratefully at her niece, following her through to the kitchen. She perched on a stool and watched as Ash got a glass and crossed to the fridge to fill it with chilled water. She was a pretty girl on the verge of adulthood, Molly realized. The simple T-shirt and leggings emphasized her slim frame; budding breasts and the slight curve of the hips hinted at the emerging woman. 'Where's Adam?'

Ashling shrugged. 'I think he's gone over to a friend's house.'

'I thought you two went everywhere together.' She nodded her thanks as Ash handed her the glass.

'Not really, not any more. We're into different things.'

'What are you into?' Molly asked, slightly ashamed that she didn't know. She spent her life communicating with teenagers and yet she knew very little about what her own niece and nephew were up to these days. It had been different when they were small – she'd looked after them for Laura on a regular basis – but in recent years she usually only saw them at the

Sunday brunch. She'd have to make more of an effort to connect with them in future, she decided. She'd take them out somewhere before they went back to school in September, maybe make it a regular affair during school holidays. 'Well?' She gave her niece a smile of encouragement.

Ash looked back at her, slightly suspicious. 'Music, reading, writing—'

'Writing?' Molly's eyes widened.

'Just poems and short stories,' Ash mumbled, looking sorry she'd mentioned it.

'I'd love to read them,' Molly enthused.

Ash stood picking at her nails, her hair falling over her face. 'It's private. I don't show them to anyone.'

'Not even Adam?'

'No way!'

'Well, I think it's great. I used to keep a diary and I wrote everything in it. It was mostly boring stuff, but I felt better for doing it.'

Ash said nothing, just sneaked a look at her watch. Molly smiled and decided to take the hint. 'I'd better go. Thanks for the water.'

'I'll tell Mum you called in,' Ash quickly led her into the hall and opened the door.

'Great.' Molly was about to leave when her attention was caught by a copy of *Teenage Kix* on the hall table. 'Oh, you read it?'

'No way!' Ash retorted, then reddened. 'Sorry, it's just not my thing. It belongs to a friend, Lottie, she left it here the other day.'

'Of course.' Molly nodded, feeling a bit silly. 'Well, I'll get going then. Bye, Ash.'

When she reached the gate, she turned to wave, but Ash had already gone inside and the door was firmly closed. 'Bye, Auntie. Nice to see you, Auntie,' she muttered, jamming on her helmet and peddling away. With time to spare, she decided to pay Ellen a visit. She had phoned yesterday to fill her in on Saturday night, but it would be nice to have a proper chat and as Ellen's delivery date neared, she planned to pop in and see her on a more regular basis.

She got a much better reception in Marino and she smiled as she watched Ellen bustle around making tea and finding biscuits.

'What?' Ellen paused to look at her.

'Sorry?'

'You're grinning at me.'

'I'm just thinking that, in a few days' time, that bump is going to be in a cradle in the corner.'

'Can you believe it?' Ellen smiled. 'I just hope that I don't go into labour during the night. I don't want to wake up in the dark alone and in a pool of water. Mum offered to move in, but she'd drive me round the bend fussing. Anyway, I'm going to need her more when I come home from the hospital.' Ellen placed a mug in front of her and then poured some boiling water into another and sprinkled in some ginger.

'Why don't I move in?' Molly suggested. 'It would give you some peace of mind, and I'd be able to bring you straight to the hospital.'

Ellen's eyes widened. 'That would be wonderful, but are you sure?'

'Absolutely.' Molly nodded enthusiastically. 'And it'd certainly be more fun than sitting in the flat, worrying.'

'What, or who, are you worrying about?'

'Everything. Everyone.' Molly pulled a face. 'I went to Limerick looking for answers, but I seem to have ended up with more questions.'

'And got caught out by Gareth.'

Molly groaned. 'Don't remind me. I nearly died on the spot when I saw him. Of all the lousy luck.'

'Do you think he believed your story?' Ellen asked, taking a sip of her drink and wincing.

Molly thought about it. 'I'm not sure. He's very observant for a guy; the complete opposite of his brother. I'd have to snog someone starkers right under Declan's nose before he got suspicious.' Molly shook her head as Ellen laughed. 'I felt positively sick. Like I told you, I kept as close to the truth as possible—'

'You just didn't mention that you'd tracked Luke down and trailed around the country after him.'

Molly grinned. 'I haven't even admitted that to Luke.'

'Well, you wouldn't.'

'I told Gareth I was out with Laura, and just ran into Luke in the hotel. I admitted we were having a little cuddle for old times' sake and, of course, I made sure he knew that Luke lived in France and was married.'

'He won't tell Declan, will he?'

Molly thought about it and then shook her head. 'I don't think so. He's no angel himself, so he probably won't attach too much importance to it.'

'Then forget it, you've enough to think about. Like, whether or not to meet up with Luke when he comes back to Dublin.'

'I don't think I should. He seems very troubled, Ellen. I'm beginning to feel bad about this whole escapade; I didn't think it through. Anyway, Declan will probably be home by then, it would mean sneaking off behind his back.' She shivered. 'I'd be as bad as Laura.'

Ellen's eyes widened. 'Why, what's Laura been up to?'

Molly bit her lip. 'Oh, nothing, I shouldn't have mentioned it.'

'Ah, you can't stop now,' Ellen protested. 'Come on, Moll, you know I won't tell a soul.'

'Cross your heart?'

'My heart and everything else.' Ellen sat forward, rubbing her bump. 'Come on, spill.'

Molly shifted uncomfortably. She knew that Ellen was trustworthy, but it didn't feel right telling her Laura's business. 'She flirts,' she said finally.

Ellen stared at her. 'That's it?'

'She drinks a bit too much, and then starts flirting with strange men.' Molly rolled her eyes. 'Anyone and everyone.'

'Ah, sure, we all do that,' Ellen laughed. 'It's how you know you've still got it.'

Molly shrugged and smiled. 'I suppose you're right.'

Ellen's eyes narrowed. 'Come on, there's more to it than that.'

'She hit it off with one of the guys in Luke's group and arranged to meet him on Saturday night.'

Ellen still didn't seem bothered. 'And now he's gone back to France?'

Molly nodded.

'Well, then, there's no harm done.'

'But what if it was a friend of Robert's who'd seen us instead of Gareth? Her marriage could be down the tubes, simply because she's a bored housewife.'

'Maybe she wants to get caught,' Ellen said. 'Maybe she wants a divorce.'

'That's very Freudian,' Molly grinned. 'No, I don't think Laura is putting a whole lot of thought into what she's doing. I certainly don't believe she wants a divorce. She loves her life, her house, her status—'

'And Robert?' Ellen raised her eyebrows.

Molly sighed. 'I suppose. They're a bit of an odd couple, they don't seem to talk much or do things together.'

'They do say opposites attract.'

Molly nodded, although she didn't really think that Robert and Laura were opposites. She drank the last of her tea and stood up. 'Right, I'd better go home and pack.'

'You're sure?' Ellen braced herself on the table and got to her feet.

'I'm sure.' Molly hugged her friend, glad to be able to do

something useful. Ellen seemed to be finding these last few weeks very tough. 'I'll see you about six.'

Ellen crossed over to the small dresser and took a key from a glass sugar bowl. 'You'd better have this, and then you can come and go as you like.'

Molly quickly attached it to her key ring and picked up her helmet. 'I'll bring the car so that we don't have to worry about transport when the time comes.'

'We can easily call a taxi.'

'No, and it's probably safer here than outside an empty flat.'

Ellen hugged her again. 'Thanks, Moll, you're a star.'

Back in the flat, Molly was pulling out jeans and tops when the phone rang. She rushed to get it. 'Hello?'

'Hey, Moll.'

'Declan! What are you doing calling at this hour, shouldn't you be asleep?'

He groaned. 'I should, but I'm sick.'

She clutched the phone tighter against her ear. As usual, there was a damned echo making it difficult to hear. 'What's wrong, Declan?'

'I think it was something I ate, I've spent the last couple of hours in the loo.'

'Oh, poor you. Perhaps you should call a doctor?'

'By the time I'd explained what's wrong, and they did something about it, I'd probably be better or dead.'

She laughed. 'Oh, I wish I was there to look after you.'

'That would be nice.'

'Have you got anything you can take?'

'Not really.'

'Call reception, the hotel is sure to have a first-aid kit.'

'Yeah, I'll ask.'

'And then try to get some sleep,' she advised. 'But if you're no better in the morning, promise me you'll go to the doctor.'

'I promise. How are you doing? Any news?'

'I'm just packing, I'm moving in with Ellen until she has the baby. She's terrified of going into labour during the night all alone.'

'That's good of you.'

'Not really, I'm not exactly enjoying being on my own in this place.'

'It won't be for much longer, Moll. Before you know it – oh, no.'

'Declan?'

'Sorry, need the loo again, I'll call you later.'

'Bye, take—' But Declan was already gone. 'Care.' She smiled and put the phone down. The sound of his voice accentuated the silence of the flat and she was glad she was going to Ellen's. She switched on the radio and turned up the volume, dancing around the room and warbling along to Lady Gaga. After her bag was packed, she tidied the bedroom, and was cleaning the bath when the music was interrupted by an ad break. It was only then that she realized someone was leaning on the doorbell.

'Finally!' Laura stood tapping her foot impatiently. 'How is it that someone who lives in such a tiny flat never seems to hear the doorbell?'

Molly laughed. 'Sorry, I had the radio turned up.'

'Make me a coffee, would you?' Laura begged. 'I've had a hell of a morning.'

Obediently, Molly led the way into the kitchen and reached for the kettle while Laura dropped into a chair and eased off her sandals. 'I called home and Ash said you'd dropped in. Anything wrong?'

'No, I just wanted to talk to you about Saturday night.'

'Oh, Molly,' Laura groaned. 'I had a drink with Gerard and

went home, end of story. I've just spent the last couple of hours trying to get that through to Penny, but I just know she doesn't believe me either.'

'Penny?' Molly frowned.

'Oh really, Moll, don't you listen to a word I say? She's the woman I was supposed to be out with on Saturday night, remember?'

'Oh, yes,' Molly said, although she wasn't sure that she did.

'The woman makes me look like a positive nun, the stories she told me.' Laura shook her head. 'Anyway, because she played alibi, she now thinks we're best friends and confidantes.'

'She sounds awful.' Molly looked at her in horror.

'She is,' Laura said grimly, 'and when I had nothing much to tell her, she wasn't impressed.'

'Were you telling the truth?' Molly asked.

'Maybe, maybe not.' Laura smirked.

Molly stared at her. 'You didn't!'

'What if I did? Don't be so sanctimonious, Molly. Are you honestly telling me you and Luke didn't do some horizontal jogging in Galway? You must have been dying to see if he'd improved with age and experience.'

'Nothing happened in Galway; Luke and I have never . . .' Molly trailed off.

'Never what?' And then Laura's eyes widened in astonishment. 'Are you saying you've never had sex with Luke – ever?'

Molly gave a reluctant nod.

'I can't believe it. You were dating for two years!'

'He wanted to, but I was afraid.'

'Afraid?' Laura looked baffled, and then realization dawned on her. 'Oh my God, you were afraid of ending up like me.'

'No.'

'Yes! You were afraid of getting pregnant.'

Molly sighed. 'Well, you know how much I wanted to go to university. I decided I wasn't willing to risk it.'

'Who would have guessed that I actually managed to teach my clever sister something?' Laura said with a pained smile.

'Laura, please.' Molly could have cut her tongue out. However much Laura annoyed her, she wouldn't hurt her for the world.

'No, Molly, really, it's okay. I'm glad you didn't take the chance. I'm glad you learned from my mistake.'

'The twins were the result of your "so called" mistake, so it wasn't such a bad one in the scheme of things.'

'No.' Laura turned on a bright smile. 'Well, that puts a whole new light on your obsession with Luke. No wonder your relationship was so intense.'

Molly sighed. 'Sometimes I wish we had done it.'

'It certainly adds a touch of mystery to the man,' Laura agreed. 'And he has grown very handsome.'

'Hasn't he?'

'So what happened on Saturday?'

'I told him it was over.'

'Just like that? After all we went through?'

'Not just like that, no, but the more we talked, the more convinced I became that the real connection between us isn't love, but Ruth. Anyway, that's not the reason I wanted to talk to you. When we went outside, he kissed me goodbye and, just then,' Molly closed her eyes at the memory, 'Gareth appeared out of nowhere.'

'Declan's brother?' Laura's eyes were out on stalks now. 'Oh, Molly, that's terrible.'

'The stuff of nightmares,' Molly agreed. 'We shared a taxi home and I told him it was all completely innocent, that we'd been childhood sweethearts and just shared a kiss and a cuddle for old times' sake.'

'Did he swallow it?'

Molly sighed. 'I'm not sure. Wouldn't it be just typical, Laura, if he told Declan just after I'd decided to do the right thing?'

'Beg Gareth not to tell him,' Laura told her. 'Tell him it was just a laugh, tell him you were hurt because Declan waltzed off to Japan.'

'I did all that.'

'And he's a nice guy, an intelligent guy. He won't want to mess things up for you and Declan, will he?'

Molly sighed. 'Let's hope not.'

Chapter Twenty-six

Laura drove out of Molly's small, gloomy estate and turned right onto the seafront road for Blackrock. She'd felt tired and miserable when she woke up, and her day hadn't got any better since then. First, there had been a row with Ashling. Laura wasn't even sure what it was about, or why her daughter had lost her temper to such a degree. Laura had simply stuck her head round the door to see if her daughter needed anything in town. She was feeling guilty about going out yet again. Having arrived home late on Friday, she'd spent the weekend in the hospital, out with Gerard, and then cooking for her parents. To make it up to Ash, Laura had planned to treat her daughter to something pretty from Accessorize, but her daughter's irrational tirade had put paid to that. Ash had accused her mother of barging into her room without knocking, and that really annoyed Laura. She never barged anywhere, and she always knocked. Ash had simply been reading at her desk and too engrossed in what she was doing to hear her. Realizing that there was no point in trying to reason with her daughter in that mood, Laura had simply walked out and gone into Adam's room looking for sympathy. 'She just wants to be on her own all the time these days, Mum,' Adam had said, looking very sober. 'She shouts at me all the time too.'

'Well, thank goodness it's not just me!' Laura had laughed and given him a quick hug and a kiss – at least he still let her – and left.

She had met Penny in Starbucks on Grafton Street, although Laura preferred the more muted ambience of Bewley's. After exchanging air kisses and admiring each other's sandals, handbags and skin, Penny had launched straight into the subject at hand.

'So, tell me all about him. Where did you go?'

Laura had rehearsed her speech all the way into town. For Penny to swallow it, she needed to supply the woman with some details, although not enough for Penny to use them against her in the future. The thought of trusting her with even the sketchiest of information made her feel sick; Penny was not to be trusted. They had met when on a school fundraising committee and, within a couple of days of meeting, Penny was feeding Laura gossip about parents and teachers alike. It had been entertaining, but Laura didn't want to become the subject of school gate tittle-tattle. But Penny was no fool, and she'd have to come up with something convincing to fool her.

With a dramatic sigh, she'd clutched Penny's hand and launched into her script. 'I am so embarrassed, Penny, I've made such a fool of myself.'

'I'm sure you haven't.' Penny had almost licked her lips in anticipation.

'I'd had too much to drink, you know, the usual story.' Laura rolled her eyes and Penny nodded with a grin. 'I was on holiday, so I thought I'd have a couple of cocktails, and they went straight to my head. And then in walks this group of French rugby players.'

'Rugby players.' Penny's eyes lit up. 'Young?'

'Younger than me, that's for sure,' Laura laughed. 'But one

guy came over and started to chat me up. Well, I was flattered and drunk, and he had that wonderful accent.'

'Lovely.' Penny was captivated. 'So what happened?'

'Well, luckily I was with Molly, my sister, and she dragged me back to the hotel before I could make a complete fool of myself.'

Penny looked disappointed, and then suspicious. 'But you arranged to meet him again.'

'Yes, and I gave him my number, can you believe it?' Laura groaned. 'That's when I told Robert I was going to the fashion show with you. But all day Friday he was sending me texts and it really started to freak me out; there was no way I was going to meet him. But Molly, my sister, said that the only way that I was going to get through to him that I wasn't interested was if I met him. Thankfully, she came with me.'

Penny was looking sceptical. 'So what happened?'

Laura shook her head. 'I don't think I'll ever drink again. The guy was not only ugly, he was obnoxious too; talk about beer goggles. I told him my husband was very possessive and that if he found out that I'd even talked to another man, he'd kill us both. Then I made him delete my number from his phone, right there in front of me.'

'Good thinking!' Penny was obviously disappointed that the story wasn't as juicy as she'd hoped, though she seemed to approve of the way Laura had handled herself. Sadly, though, that wasn't the end of it. Thinking that she now had a new best friend, Penny had proceeded to divulge her own numerous indiscretions, and left Laura feeling positively virtuous by comparison.

Exhausted by Penny's confidences, Laura had finally escaped, pleading that she was on the way to visit her mother. She'd phoned home on the way back to the car and a frosty Ash had told her of Molly's visit, so she'd decided to drop in to see her sister en route, only to hear yet another secret. She still couldn't believe that Molly and Luke had never slept together. Laura had managed to keep Robert at bay for six months, but after that they were at it every chance they got. She'd felt so grown-up at the time. As a college student, she'd gloried in being free from the stifling rigours of school and, as a result, ended up pregnant with twins at just nineteen. Laura was determined that wouldn't happen to Ash. And if that meant her daughter hated her, well, that was all part of being a parent; one day her daughter would understand.

Her thoughts returned to Saturday night, and she shuddered when she thought of Gareth catching Molly kissing Luke. What if she'd been the one to bump into a friend of Robert's? How could she possibly have explained sitting at the bar with a man, his hand on her bare back, hers on his leg? And it hadn't stopped there. Though Gerard wasn't as handsome, debonair or sexy as she'd remembered, she had still gone back to his hotel with him. The sex had been good, that was something she had remembered correctly, but it didn't feel right. Somehow, being in Dublin, with Robert only three or four miles away, brought home the fact that she was committing adultery. Yes, she had flirted with other men before, but she hadn't taken it to the next step until she'd met Gerard. Why? Because he'd flattered her? Because he was there? Because sex with any man was preferable to sex with Robert? She sighed miserably. How, at the age of thirty-three, had she turned into such a pathetic, needy loser?

As Laura pulled up outside the family home in Blackrock, she wondered if it had been just Oliver who'd been tempted to stray, or if Belle had also hankered after some extra-marital activity. She dismissed the thought with a shake of her head; she really didn't want to go there.

It was her brother who answered the door, looking distinctly fed up. 'Hey.'

She frowned. Why did he insist on talking like an American? 'Hello. How are things?'

'Dad's burned lunch, Mum's lost her tablets and the electricity bill is enormous which, apparently, is all my fault.' He gave a resigned shrug. 'Apart from that, everything's fine.'

Laura followed Rory into the kitchen and grimaced when she saw Natalie at the sink, scrubbing the frying pan. 'Hi, Dad.' She bent to kiss her father's cheek.

He looked at her over his glasses and then back at the bills in his hands. 'Hello, darling. Can you believe this? The electricity bill is five hundred and thirty-five Euros; is yours ever that high?'

'No idea, Dad, Robert takes care of all that.'

'There's a surprise,' Rory muttered.

Laura glared at him. 'Not really, given that we are a one-income family.'

'Rory, stop baiting your sister. And you'd better put your efforts into thinking of ways to cut down on our expenses; you could start by switching off lights and not leaving your PC on all night.'

Laura shot her brother a triumphant smile before turning to greet his girlfriend. 'Hello, Natalie. Can I help?'

'No, nearly finished, thanks.' Natalie rubbed the pan more vigorously.

Laura wrinkled her nose. 'What was that?'

'Omelette.'

Laura looked at her father in surprise. 'What happened?'

Oliver sighed. 'I only took my eye off it for a moment. I was distracted by these,' he pointed ruefully at the bills in front of him.

'If you need money, Dad—'

'What? No, of course not, don't be silly. Don't mind me, I'm just a bit grumpy.'

Laura shrugged. 'I'll go up and see Mum.'

'Tell her I'll be up with a cup of coffee in a minute,' Natalie smiled.

Laura grimaced as she climbed the stairs. Belle had a husband

and three children to take care of her, she didn't need Natalie hanging around too. She opened the bedroom door gently, in case Belle was sleeping, but her mother was propped up, glasses on her nose, reading a book. 'Hi, Mum.'

Belle put down the book and smiled. 'Hello, darling.'

Laura hugged her, then went to sit on the stool by the dressing table. 'How are you?'

'Fine.'

'You don't look it,' Laura told her, concerned at her mother's pallor and the crease between her brows.

'You're wonderful for my ego,' Belle said drily.

'Oh, you know what I mean.'

'I'm tired, that's all. I found it very hard to sleep in the hospital. I'll be fine now that I'm back in my own comfortable bed.'

'Did they give you pills to help you sleep?'

'Yes, but I've no intention of taking them.'

'Mum—' Laura started, feeling irritated. Her mother had an unnatural abhorrence and fear of medication.

'Don't.' Belle held up a hand. 'I'll drink some warm milk and I shall sleep like a baby.'

'Natalie said she was getting you a coffee, but I'll tell her not to bother; that's the last thing you need. What is she doing here, anyway? You're hardly in form for visitors. Honestly, Rory doesn't have an ounce of sense.'

'Don't say anything, Laura. She's a nice girl and Rory really likes her.'

'She's an oddball, I don't know where he finds them.'

'Why don't you take the trouble to get to know her?' Belle said mildly.

'There's no point in getting to know her; she won't be around for long. Now, Mum, are you doing your exercises?'

'I've only just got home,' Belle protested, 'and the physio in the hospital made me go up and down the corridor three times before I left.'

'Still, it's important you keep moving, Mum. Don't get into the habit of staying in bed.'

Belle sighed. 'I won't, Laura. I'm not a complete idiot.'

There was a gentle tap on the door and Natalie edged in with a tray.

'She's not drinking coffee,' Laura said shortly. 'Mum is finding it hard to sleep, so caffeine is not a good idea.'

'Don't mind her, Natalie, you're very kind. I hope my husband and son aren't sitting back and letting you do all the work,' she added.

'I don't mind.' Natalie set the tray down on the bedside table and then helped Belle to re-arrange the pillows.

Laura watched, resenting the easy camaraderie between the two; how had that happened in such a short space of time? Natalie seemed to have her feet firmly under the table.

Once Belle was settled, Natalie turned to leave. 'Just call if you need anything else.'

'I'm here if there's anything she needs,' Laura retorted, earning a stern look from her mother.

'Why must you be so rude?' Belle said crossly, when the door had closed.

Laura shrugged. 'She's just annoying.'

Belle winced and shifted on her pillows.

Laura stood up. 'What's wrong?'

'Oh, this blasted foot; it's so hard to get comfortable and the plaster weighs a ton.'

'You need to prop it up.' Laura took some of her mother's decorative cushions from the window seat and built them up on the end of the bed before gently raising her mother's foot and settling it on top. 'There, how's that?'

Belle smiled. 'Better, thank you, darling. So, tell me about your holiday; we haven't had a chance to talk properly.'

Laura returned to her seat. 'It was fine. I had lots of beauty treatments and Molly went for lots of walks.'

Belle's brow knitted in concern. 'Is she okay, do you think?'

'I think she's having second thoughts about marrying Declan.'

'But that's terrible.' Belle looked at her in dismay.

'Why? Isn't it better than rushing into marriage and regretting it?' Laura looked at her watch and jumped to her feet. 'Oops, sorry, Mum, I've got to go. I promised the twins I'd take them out for pizza.' She went over to kiss her mother.

Belle grasped her arm and looked into her daughter's eyes. 'You know you can always talk to me about anything, don't you?'

Laura smiled. 'Everything's fine, Mum, other than that I'll have two very hungry kids if I don't get a move on.'

In the car home, Laura wondered how her mum would react if she told her what was really going on. How would she react when she learned that her elder daughter shrank from her husband, but was ready to sleep with total strangers? She wiped a tear from her eye and decided that, sometimes, honesty was definitely not the best policy.

Chapter Twenty-seven

11.20 p.m., Wednesday, 12th August

Molly put down her mobile with a smile, plumped up the pillows on Ellen's sofa bed and reached for her laptop. She'd just had a warm, loving chat with Declan – illness had softened him and made him homesick – and she had felt close to him in a way she hadn't since he'd announced the trip to Japan. Life might actually get back to normal. Luke was safely back in Bordeaux. Belle was home from the hospital. Laura was hopefully fast asleep next to her husband. And Ellen was tucked up in bed with a novel, a mug of warm milk and some chocolate biscuits. Feeling better than she had in days, Molly signed into the *Teenage Kix* website. Though it was late, she felt alert and ready to concentrate on someone else's problems for a change, and not before time. She had been relying heavily on Carl and Tess, and hoped fervently that her confidence in their ability was not misplaced. She started off with the milder topics to wean herself in gently. Skin problems, homework difficulties, kissing with braces; all the little worries that troubled teenagers on a daily basis. Laura could mock *Teenage Kix* all she wanted, but Molly knew the service would have been hugely appreciated when they were growing up. The Jackson children had been lucky and hadn't needed that kind of help; Belle had been able to talk to her children on any topic without embarrassment, and she'd always handled problems with sensitivity and good sense. But Molly knew that some of her friends had been less fortunate and had written to magazine agony aunts for help. It wasn't as successful then, though. Only a few letters were ever printed, and the magazines never replied. The Internet had changed all that and, despite Laura's scorn, Molly knew that they helped a lot of children. As she was about to go into the section that dealt with the more serious issues, a message flashed up to let her know that Tess was online. She quickly typed in a message.

Can't sleep?

Moments later, Tess replied.

No, too mad! Had a row with Ed.

Ed? Molly frowned. Oh, the new boyfriend. They were rowing already?

Want to talk about it?

No, that's OK, I'll get over it! Check out thread from 'GS'. Think it may be your little friend again.

Molly sighed. So much for a quiet night.

Thanks, Tess.

She quickly went to the relevant page. There were four entries. The first one was from GS, talking about a friend's depression and asking for advice. It was almost exactly like the original entry from Smithy, but if that was the case, she hadn't taken any of their advice, despite Molly's more detailed reply in the magazine. GS ended:

We always had this deal that we would never tell each other's secrets, but she doesn't trust me with hers any more. Does that mean I'm free to tell hers?

Molly sighed in frustration. If only she could sit down and talk to this child. Perhaps it was all fabricated. It wouldn't be the first time that a child faked a problem just to get attention. Yet she didn't get that feeling from Smithy/GS, and it would be unusual for a child like that to write in on someone else's behalf; they usually only wanted to talk about themselves. Molly read the various replies to GS's post. One was compassionate and caring, but the next was from Jay, who said that Smithy was full of BS, and it was girls like her that screwed up the message boards for everyone. Another post from Zizi commented on the fact that GS had been on the boards before about this and got plenty of good advice, why wasn't she taking any?

Molly chuckled. 'Just what I was wondering, Zizi.' And, not only was there the question about why GS/Smithy wasn't taking advice, she was back using a computer as well; what had changed? Molly yawned and closed down her laptop, deciding to sleep on it. Perhaps she should ask the twins' advice. She could take them out like she'd promised herself and get their opinion; maybe they could go swimming. Resolving to call Laura first thing, Molly turned out the light and snuggled down on Ellen's surprisingly comfortable sofa.

Laura sounded doubtful. 'Adam doesn't like swimming and Ash is very body-conscious these days.'

'Fine, I'll take them to the zoo,' Molly replied.

'The zoo? I'm not sure—'

'Laura, why don't you just get Adam or Ash, and I'll ask them myself?'

Laura sighed. 'I'll get Ash. Adam will go along with whatever she wants, but she'll say no to everything unless it's her idea.'

'Fine.'

'Hold on, she's probably still asleep.'

Molly waited as she heard Laura go upstairs. After a moment, Ash came on.

'Hi, Molly.'

'Hi, Ash, how are you?'

'Fine.'

'I was wondering if you and Adam fancied doing something today.'

'Er, like what?'

'I don't know, it's a lovely day, we could go to the zoo or the beach, or the water park.'

'I don't really like water,' Ash said quickly.

'I'll tell you what, why don't you and Adam have a think about it and I'll pick you up in a couple of hours.'

'Okay.'

'Great! Bye!' Molly hung up. Ash hadn't exactly sounded keen, but at least she'd agreed. Hopefully, Adam would be more enthusiastic, or it could prove a very long day. If they hadn't decided on what to do by the time she got there, she'd take them into Stephen's Green and they could sunbathe and chat and have a picnic and then, if they ran out of conversation, they could always go to the cinema, although given how rare it was to have such perfect weather, that would be a shame. Still, it was their day, and if they wanted to sit in the dark shovelling popcorn down their throats, so be it.

'What are you looking so pensive about?' Ellen asked, bending to put clothes in the washing machine.

'Here, let me do that,' Molly sprang to her feet.

'I'm not an invalid,' Ellen protested.

'Okay, just trying to help. Want some toast?'

'Lovely.'

Molly put the kettle on to boil and then cut the brown loaf and put four slices under the grill. 'I'm taking Ash and Adam out for the day.'

'That will be fun.' Ellen straightened and switched on the machine.

'I'm afraid it may be hard work,' Molly admitted. 'But I've decided that I need to be a better aunt. I spend my days giving advice to teenagers, but I hardly ever talk to the twins.'

'I promise you, they won't have noticed, and they definitely won't care. When you're that age, all you think about is what's happening in your own little world.'

'You'd think so.' Molly turned the bread and then made tea. 'But I have a case at the moment about a girl who is worried sick about her friend.'

'Lucky friend,' Ellen said, pulling out a chair and sitting down.

'Yes,' Molly agreed distractedly.

'What?' Ellen prompted.

'I don't know. There's something about it that's not quite right, but I can't put my finger on it. I thought I might ask the twins' advice.'

'Ah, so you're not really being a kind auntie, you have an ulterior motive,' Ellen teased.

'Cheek!' Molly grinned as she rescued the toast and poured herself some tea. 'Are you having some?'

'Yes, please.' Ellen reached for the jar of honey and spread it liberally on her toast.

'You seem well this morning,' Molly commented, noting Ellen's bright eyes and perky mood.

'I am. I had the best night's sleep that I've had in months, and the most wonderful dream about the baby.'

'Oh, tell me!'

'Well, I was asleep in the dream, and then I felt something pushing me and I sat up to see what it was, and there was Buster lying beside me, smiling!'

'Oh, that's lovely. Maybe it's a sign that your time is near.'

'Somehow I don't think it will be quite as easy as in my dream,' Ellen said ruefully.

'You never know, you hear of some births happening very quickly.'

'But most take days.'

Molly smiled. 'You'll be fine but, if it is tough, remember you'll have your beautiful baby at the end of it.'

'It probably won't be beautiful at first,' Ellen warned her. 'They're usually red, squalling and crumpled.'

'A baby made by you and Andrew couldn't be anything other than beautiful,' Molly assured her, then cursed silently as a shadow crossed Ellen's face. 'Sorry.'

Ellen shrugged and smiled. 'That's okay. I can't exactly pretend he had nothing to do with it and, whatever his faults, he *is* a hunk.'

Molly laughed. 'He is.'

Ellen chewed thoughtfully on her toast. 'Maybe I should call him.'

'I think you should wait,' Molly cautioned. 'You're going to have enough to deal with over the next few weeks, and you don't know how he'll react. And, once you've told him, you won't be able to exclude him from your life unless you move again.'

Ellen sighed. 'You're right.'

Molly watched her friend as she sipped her tea. It couldn't be easy for Ellen going into childbirth without the father; especially as Molly knew her friend still loved him. 'Would you like me to do a little detective work?'

'What do you mean?'

'Maybe I could see if I can find out how he's doing.'

As Molly suspected, Ellen's face lit up. 'Could you?'

'I can try,' Molly said with a shrug.

'But where will you start?' Ellen asked, sitting forward.

'Perhaps I could "bump into" his sister; Barbara, isn't it?'

Ellen nodded. 'Yes, she has that little accessories shop in town.'

'So it would be simple. I could just wander in.'

'But how will you ask her about Andrew?' Ellen frowned. 'She doesn't know you.'

'I'll tell her I'm your friend and you recommended her shop, simple.' Molly smiled, pleased with herself. Laura would be proud of her.

'But you mustn't tell her where I'm living or working.'

'Of course I won't!' Molly said.

'Sorry.' Ellen gave a nervous smile. 'So, when will you do it?'

Molly looked at her watch and stood up. 'Well, not today: the twins await me.'

'But soon?' Ellen urged.

For a moment, Molly wondered what she'd got herself into, but it was a bit late now, Ellen obviously loved the idea. 'I'll go this week,' she promised.

Chapter Twenty-eight

11.15 a.m., Thursday, 13th August

When Molly pulled up outside Laura's house, Adam was in the garden, kicking a football around without much enthusiasm. 'Hi, Adam,' she called as she jumped out of the car.

'Hey.' He offered her a shy smile.

'So, where are we off to?' she asked.

He shrugged. 'I don't mind.'

'Okay, let's go talk to your sister.'

Adam led the way down the side of the house and they went into the kitchen where they found Laura arranging roses.

Molly smiled. 'Good morning. Aren't they lovely?'

Laura nodded. 'They're from the tree Mum gave me, it's positively thriving.'

'Have you talked to her this morning?'

'Dad was just on. He says she's managing better on the crutches, although she's still nervous.'

'It's early days.'

'Yes. Adam, go and tell Ash Molly's here, please.'

Adam shuffled out of the room, leaving the sisters alone. 'Thanks for this, Moll, I'll be glad to get rid of them for a few hours,' Laura confided. 'They're not getting on at all these days; I don't know what's got into them.'

Molly grinned. 'I remember Mum used to say we were always difficult during the holidays because we had too much time on our hands.'

'It's true. I asked Robert to arrange some summer work for them in his office, but they're not taking anyone on this year.'

'Can't they mow lawns or wash cars or something?'

'Ash doesn't want to do anything. When she's not slinking off with her friends, she's on the phone or sending texts or holed up in her room. And Adam,' she sighed, 'seems lost without her.'

Molly frowned. 'Doesn't he have friends?'

'Lots, but no one he's really close to; it's the downside of being a twin—' She broke off as they heard the children coming downstairs.

Molly smiled as the two entered the kitchen. 'Hi Ash.'

'Hi.'

'So, where are we off to?'

She shrugged. 'I'm really not bothered.'

'Don't be so rude,' Laura said, brow wrinkled in annoyance. 'Molly has given up her day to take you out; you could show some gratitude.'

'It's fine, Laura. If you'd prefer it, guys, we could just have a wander round the shops and then take a picnic into Stephen's Green and feed the ducks.'

'Oh, not shopping,' Adam groaned.

'The zoo's fine, Molly, really,' Ash said. 'We can drop Adam off at the monkey cage; he'll feel right at home.'

'Yeah, well, we'll drop you off at the hippo enclosure; you're about the right size.'

Ash swatted her brother across the head, but she was smiling and Molly thought that perhaps it mightn't be a total disaster of a day after all.

'Feed them both to the lions if they give you any trouble,' Laura advised as she walked them to the door.

Adam swept her up in his arms in a hug. 'Ah, Mumsy, you know you'd miss us!'

'I'd be inconsolable,' Laura said dryly, and turned to kiss her daughter.

Ash brushed her cheek to her mother's and moved quickly away. Molly saw the hurt look in her sister's eyes.

Laura pressed fifty Euros into Adam's hand. 'Share that with your sister and don't forget to buy your auntie something.'

'Cool, thanks, Mum.'

'Okay, off you go,' she waved them towards the door. 'I'm going to have a lovely, peaceful day in the garden.'

'Enjoy.' Molly smiled.

'Bye, Moll, and thanks.'

Ash sprang to life and ran to the car. 'Bagsy front seat.'

'That's not fair!' Adam complained. 'My legs are much longer than yours.'

They both turned questioning eyes on Molly. 'Take turns.'

'I'm first,' Ash said with a triumphant look at her brother and, with a resigned shrug, he pulled the seat forward and climbed into the back.

'Seatbelts, please,' Molly said as she got into the car.

'I'm fine,' Ash said.

'Ash!' Adam muttered angrily.

'Sorry,' Ashling had the grace to flush and shot Molly a contrite smile as she hurriedly reached for her belt.

Molly's smile was strained. 'Right, let's go. Wave to your mum,' she said as she tooted the horn.

Adam yelled goodbye and waved wildly at his mother, while his sister raised a limp hand. Molly felt an uncharacteristic empathy for her sister. It couldn't be easy living with hormonal teenagers.

'Can I put on the radio?' Ashling asked.

'Sure,' Molly said and the twins began to argue about which station they should listen to and who was cool and who was crap.

'What music do you like?' she asked.

'Fat Boy Slim, Pearl Jam, Radiohead—'

'He has no taste,' Ash said with a roll of her eyes. 'I love Snow Patrol, the Blizzards and The Script is an amazing band.'

'I love them too,' Molly agreed, surprised she had something in common with someone half her age.

'You are so much cooler than my mum; all she listens to are boy bands and Celine Dion.'

'Everyone has different tastes,' Molly said, unwilling to join in ribbing Laura. 'Declan sometimes still listens to his old Duran Duran CDs.'

'Who are they?' Adam piped up from the backseat.

Molly shook her head, laughing. 'Never mind.'

'Dad loves jazz,' Ash said. 'Some of it's really good.'

'Yeah, I like it too,' Adam agreed.

Molly nodded. 'Jazz is good, but I'm afraid I don't have any.'

'It's okay, this station is cool,' Ash assured her.

'So, where to first?' Molly asked as they stood in front of the map. 'Penguins, lions, gorillas?'

'Lions,' Ash said.

'That's dumb. We should just work our way around from right or left. Let's start in the reptile house.'

'Urgh, it stinks.'

'Then stay outside,' Adam retorted and turned away.

Molly watched Ash bristle and quickly tucked her arm into her niece's and tugged her after her brother. 'Boys always love this kind of stuff, Declan's the same. I'll go in with him, although I'll probably have to keep my eyes shut; I'm terrified of spiders.'

'I don't mind them. I wonder, do they have any tarantulas,' Ash said and quickened her pace.

*

When they were halfway round, they stopped to buy chips and drinks and took them outside to sit on the grass.

'Why can't the weather always be like this?' Adam said, stretching out and turning his face up to the sun.

'It would be nice,' Molly smiled.

'I don't like it when it's too hot,' Ash said.

'That's 'cos you get freckles,' Adam said. 'Zillions of them.'

Ash hurled a chip at him. 'Shut up, granny.'

Molly raised an eyebrow. 'Granny?'

'He's the favourite?'

'Shut up, Ash,' Adam growled, scowling.

'The apple of Mum's eye?' Ash continued, ignoring him. 'Granny Smith!'

'Ah, I see,' Molly nodded and then stopped as the words sank in. Granny Smith. GS. Smithy. Oh, shit.

It took all of her concentration to behave normally, but as they chatted over lunch, Molly studied her nephew looking for signs of the stress that was so clear in his posts. Of course it might not be him, but it seemed an incredible coincidence. Who was this girl that he was worrying about and why couldn't he help her? As soon as Ash went off in search of a loo, Molly seized her chance.

'So, Smithy, or should I call you GS? Let's talk.'

'Sorry?' Adam dropped his head and busied himself gathering up their empty cartons.

'Don't pretend, Adam. I know now, so let me help. Together, we can help this girl. I can come with you and talk to her myself if you like.'

He raised pained eyes to hers and sighed. 'You don't have to go anywhere, she's right here.'

Molly's eyes widened and her heart missed a beat. 'Ashling?'

'I wanted to talk to you about her, but I couldn't risk it. Then I had the idea that I could contact you anonymously through *Teenage Kix*.' He pulled a face. 'So much for that.'

'I'd never have made the connection if Ash hadn't called you Granny,' Molly reassured him. 'But why haven't you taken my advice?'

'I've tried.' Adam looked around to make sure his sister was nowhere within earshot.

'I've asked her to talk to Gran, or to you, but she just tells me I don't have a clue what I'm talking about and that I should mind my own business.' He shook his head. 'We've always argued and bickered, but when it comes down to important things, we've always been able to talk to each other. Now she just clams up when I ask her what's wrong. I backed off, because she told me if I interfered, I would regret it.'

Molly reached out to squeeze his hand, moved by the sadness in his eyes. 'How come you stopped going online and wrote that letter?' she asked.

'Ash and I share the laptop. We're supposed to only use it downstairs, but Ash started sneaking it up to her room; I was afraid she'd read my posts.'

Molly nodded her understanding and patted his hand. 'Don't worry, Adam, everything's going to be okay now; I'll talk to her.'

'But you can't.' He looked at her, horrified. 'What if she runs away or, or, worse.'

'She won't,' Molly said firmly, holding his gaze. 'We'll talk to her together; it will be fine.'

He gulped. 'When?'

Molly shrugged. 'No time like the present.'

'She'll kill me,' he said, with conviction.

'She probably will be furious at first, but then she'll be relieved. Problems always seem huge when you're dealing with them alone. Once they're out in the open, things never seem quite so scary. So you haven't talked to anyone at all about this?'

Adam shook his head. 'No. Like I said, I was afraid of what she'd do. I try every so often to talk to her, but she just walks away or hides in her room. Today is the longest we've spent together in weeks and she seems almost normal.'

'She certainly isn't behaving as if she's depressed,' Molly agreed.

'I'm not imagining it,' he said fiercely.

'I believe you, Adam. You know Ash better than anyone, and if you think there's something wrong, I'm sure you're right.'

'She's coming,' he muttered, turning away slightly.

'Okay. Let me do the talking.' Molly looked up and smiled as her niece approached.

'The loos are disgusting, some kid's thrown up.' Ash shuddered and lowered herself down delicately beside her brother. 'So, where are we going next?'

'I thought we'd stay here for a while.' Molly smiled at her.

Ash frowned. 'But it's almost two and we've still loads left to see.'

'We have plenty of time, but first I want to talk to you.'

'What about?' Ash shot her brother a suspicious look, but he refused to meet her eyes.

'Adam's worried about you, Ash. He thinks you have something on your mind and he's noticed that you've changed a lot in recent months.' Molly watched her niece closely. There was no doubt that Ash was troubled and secretive, but she definitely didn't look dejected or depressed. She was too focused, too sharp, and there was nothing remotely lethargic about the girl, although there was definitely some anger.

'I told you to stay out of my business,' Ash growled at Adam.

'You would do the same if you were worried about him,' Molly said.

Ash shook her head, obviously frustrated. 'But there's nothing to worry about, I keep telling him that.'

'Then why don't you hang around with me any more?' Adam demanded. 'Why do you spend so much time in your room? Why are you always writing stuff that you won't let anyone read?'

Ash reddened. 'It's private.'

'And we don't want to invade your privacy, Ash,' Molly said

gently. 'But it's clear that you're worrying about something; perhaps we can help.'

'You can't.' Ash shook her head. 'You've got it completely wrong; I'm not the one with the problem.'

For a horrible moment, Molly wondered if Ash had found out about her mother's behaviour; it would certainly account for her hostility towards Laura. 'Who is?' she asked, although she wasn't sure that she wanted to hear the answer.

Ash sighed. 'It's Neil.'

Molly frowned. 'Neil?'

'He's a friend,' Ash told her.

'Since when?' Adam asked in disbelief. 'You always said that you thought he was a bit of a dork.'

'Yeah, well, we worked on a science project together last term and I realized he was okay really. And he's really brainy; he's in my maths class too, and he's always top of the class. And then he started to lose interest and, instead of being top of the class, suddenly he was getting Ds. He got cheeky too, the teachers have been giving out to him about his attitude.'

'They must have written to his parents,' Molly said.

Ash nodded. 'They did, and his folks sat down and had a talk with him and he told them he was feeling a bit down and that he wasn't sure if he wanted to go to school any more or even carry on living.'

'Jeez.' Adam shook his head.

'And then he was on a high for a while.'

Molly frowned. 'How do you mean?'

'Look, this is confidential, right?' Ash asked.

'Of course.'

'Neil says his parents have been having problems. His mother goes out a lot, and then there are rows about where she's been. He was convinced she was going to walk out on them, on him, and he got really upset, that's why his work started to suffer.'

'That makes sense, poor kid,' Molly said with a sigh.

'Yeah, only after his folks read him the riot act, he realized that if he continued to mess up at school and seem depressed, his Mum wouldn't leave.'

Adam blinked. 'So it's all an act?'

Ash shrugged. 'That's how it started but he seems pretty screwed up to me. He can't talk about anything else; he's obsessed with his mum and whenever she's out, he's a nervous wreck. And now he's started writing these weird stories about suicide and stuff and mailing them to me.'

Adam reddened. 'I saw one of them,' he admitted. 'I thought you'd written it.'

Ash glared at him. 'You shouldn't have been prying—'

'I was worried! And when I read that stuff—' Adam ran a hand through his hair.

'Sorry,' Ash relented, nudging him gently. 'I wanted to tell you, but Neil was completely paranoid. He said that if I told anyone the truth, then his mother would probably leave and he'd kill himself.'

'Oh, Ash, you poor thing.' Molly shook her head sadly. 'No wonder you've been distracted.'

Ash's eyes filled up. 'I just didn't know what to do, Molly, and the more it's gone on, the stranger Neil's been behaving. He may have started off pretending to be disturbed, but now I'm beginning to think he really is.'

Molly sighed. 'It's hardly surprising, given all he's going through. Putting on this act must be a huge strain too. I'm glad he has at least opened up to you.'

'But I haven't been able to help and I'm a bit fed up with it all. My friends are pissed off with me because I hardly see them and Adam and me are always rowing.'

'That's because you were being so secretive,' he told her again. 'We're cool now.'

She gave him a contrite little smile and then turned to Molly. 'Do you think there's anything we can do?'

'It's not an easy one,' Molly admitted. 'Maybe your mum could have a word with his mother—'

'No way!' Ash looked horrified.

'Okay, okay,' Molly soothed her. 'Let me have a think about it.'

'Promise you won't do anything without talking to me first?'

'I would never do that, Ash. And well done, you've been a very good friend to Neil.'

'I've never seen us as friends at all,' Ashling admitted.

'He was always a nerd,' Adam chipped in. 'But our mums are friends.'

'They're not friends,' Ash corrected, 'they've just been on school committees together. I don't think Mum really likes Penny that much.'

Molly smiled, impressed by her niece's keen observation. Thoughts of Laura, though, were enough to sober her mood. If Ash were to learn of her mother's recent behaviour, she would be disgusted. 'Let's go and see some more animals. I don't know about you, but I could do with some distraction.'

They trudged around the zoo and Molly was struck by how much more relaxed Adam and Ash were together now, falling around the place laughing at a pair of rather amorous baboons. It did Molly's heart good that they were best friends again. If only she could think of a way of helping the poor, unfortunate Neil. Molly wasn't quite sure how to handle this one. It would be best if Ash told Laura about the situation and Laura then tipped off Penny. Molly only wished she could trust her sister to handle it delicately. But of course she was jumping the gun. First, she needed to persuade Ash that it was the best solution.

*

'No way,' Ash said when Molly broached the subject on the way home in the car.

'But what choice do you have, Ash? You can't let things go on as they are. Neil needs help.'

'You could talk to him,' Adam suggested. He was in the front seat and in charge of the radio, but he'd turned the volume down and shifted in his seat so he could look at them both.

'It would be great, only that would mean I'd told someone, and he'd be furious,' Ash pointed out.

Adam shrugged. 'Like Molly says, you don't have many choices, and at least she's a professional.'

Molly pulled up at a red light and tapped the wheel thoughtfully. 'What if I just happened to bump into you when you were with him?'

'What do you mean?' Ash sat forward and leaned on Adam's seat.

'Perhaps if we pretended to meet by accident and you and I just got talking, perhaps we'd be able to draw him out.'

'That's it.' Ash bounced up and down excitedly. 'He loves attention and he'd be really impressed if you were to show some interest in him.'

'No one talks to him much,' Adam added, ''cos he's such a—'

'dork, yes, you said,' Molly nodded.

Adam grinned. 'Well, he is. There's something about him that makes you want to run away.'

'Well, thankfully, your sister didn't.'

'No, but I wanted to,' Ash admitted. 'That's horrible, isn't it?'

'No, it's honest,' Molly smiled, 'and it's even more to your credit, given that you've been such a good friend to him. But now I think it's time for you to be a little selfish.'

Ash looked relieved. 'So you'll talk to him?'

Molly nodded. 'You have a think about a way we could meet up without arousing his suspicions and I'll try and figure out how to subtly bring up the subject.'

Ashling smiled and, looking in the rear-view mirror, Molly felt guilty that she hadn't noticed how unhappy her niece had been, and Adam too. Even if she had missed it as an auntie – no surprise there – with her professional hat on, she should have realized that something wasn't quite right. She'd let them down, and she'd let her sister down.

'Do me a favour, guys,' she said quietly as they neared home. 'If anything is ever bothering you, talk to me. It doesn't matter whether it's about homework or drugs or sex or bullying or acne. It doesn't matter whether it's a problem, whether you need a sounding board or whether you just want to let off steam, promise you'll come to me.'

She stopped the car outside their house and looked at each of them in turn. 'Will you do that?'

Adam flushed but nodded and Ash put her arms around Molly's neck and gave her a hug. 'Promise.'

Chapter Twenty-nine

5.45 p.m., Thursday, 13th August

Laura had wanted to talk to her sister, but Molly left the car running and, making some garbled excuse, hurried off. The kids had raided the kitchen and were now sitting in front of yet another episode of *The Simpsons*. 'Good time?' she asked, perching on the arm of a chair.

'Yeah, cool,' Adam smiled, but didn't take his eyes off the screen.

'Except for the smell,' Ash added.

Laura laughed. 'Well, it is a zoo. Did you eat?'

'Just chips and ice-cream. What's for dinner?' Adam asked, despite the fact that he'd just guzzled down a cheese sandwich and two chocolate chip cookies.

'Lasagne.'

Ash wrinkled her nose. 'I'm not hungry.'

Laura frowned. 'I hope you're not on a silly diet.'

Ash looked genuinely puzzled. 'Why would I be?'

'No reason, you have a gorgeous figure, much better than mine when I was your age.'

Ash smiled, looked almost friendly. 'Dad said you were always worrying about your weight but he didn't know why; he thought you were gorgeous.'

'Oh, please,' Adam groaned. 'I'm going to be sick if you start all this lovey-dovey stuff.'

Laura laughed. 'It won't be long before you have a girlfriend of your own and then you'll be all lovey-dovey too.'

'Lottie fancies him.' Ash grinned. 'She only hangs around with me so she can see him.'

'She's a dork.' Adam blushed so hard his ears turned red.

'She must be if she likes you,' Ash teased and ducked as a cushion came flying at her head.

'And who fancies Ash?' Laura asked, enjoying this rare moment of being included.

'Julian.' Adam grinned triumphantly.

'Who's he?'

'A conceited, big-headed twat,' Ash laughed, hurling the cushion back at her brother. 'The only one he fancies is himself!'

'Well, you're a bit young for any of that yet.' Laura stood up. 'You need to concentrate on school for the next couple of years; romance can wait.'

Ash rolled her eyes. 'Oh, Mum, you could at least wait until the school holidays are over before you start nagging us about studying hard.'

'I'm not nagging, just reminding you that—' Laura broke off as her mobile started ringing and she hurried out into the hall to look for it.

'Saved by the bell,' Adam grinned.

'I heard that,' Laura called back, but she was smiling as she lifted the phone. 'Hello?'

'Laura?'

She froze. 'Speaking,' she said coolly and, hurrying into the kitchen, closed the door behind her.

'Laura? Can you hear me? It is I, Gerard.'

'Gerard, why on earth are you calling me? I told you to delete my number.'

'How could I do that after Saturday night?' he murmured. 'I cannot stop thinking about you, Laura.'

'You must,' she hissed, keeping her back pressed to the kitchen door so no one could walk in on her. 'I'm married, forget about me.'

'I can't.'

'Fine, but you simply mustn't call me any more; it's too dangerous. It was nice, Gerard,' she admitted, her voice softening at the memory, 'but it's over now.'

'But it doesn't have to be, Laura. What if I told you I'm coming to Dublin again next month?'

'What did you say?'

'It's true. I am coming over for a conference. I'll be in Dublin for four days.'

'Would you be coming to this conference if you hadn't met me?' Laura asked.

'Perhaps not,' he chuckled. 'So, what do you say? Will you meet me again?'

Laura thought of how nice it would be to sneak off and see him. To feel that surge of excitement, to feel sexy, to feel wanted.

'And it doesn't have to end there,' he was saying. 'You could come to France.'

'How could I possibly do that?'

'You're a beautiful, fashionable woman. Would it be so strange for you to come to Paris on a shopping trip?'

Paris! Laura closed her eyes at the thought. To be in that romantic city and with a lover . . .

'I'll call you when I know where I'm staying,' Gerard said. 'But please, in the meantime, Laura, call me if you feel like it. I love to hear your voice. And you have my email address—'

'I have to go now.'

'I will look forward to hearing from you. Goodbye, Laura. *À bientôt.*'

Laura put the phone down and sank into a chair. This was

madness, it was dangerous. What if Ash had answered her phone? Perhaps she should throw the phone away and pretend she'd lost it. Then she could have a new phone, a new number and Gerard wouldn't be able to contact her again. It would be the right thing to do. Laura fingered the offending object and then slipped it into the pocket of her jeans. Sadly, she wasn't sure she wanted to do the right thing.

Ellen wasn't in when Molly got home and she wondered for a moment if perhaps her friend had gone into labour. A note on the kitchen table, however, informed Molly that Ellen was out shopping with her mother and would be home, with dinner, at about 6.30 p.m. Molly was musing whether to have a shower, do some work or go for a bike ride, when her mobile chirruped. It was a text from Gareth suggesting they meet up for a drink in Sandymount. Molly was nervous at the thought of seeing him, but he would be suspicious if she said no. She sent him a text saying she'd see him in their local at eight. That would give her time to catch up on some work, have dinner with Ellen *and* cycle over to meet him.

Gareth was at the bar when she walked in, chatting to the girl behind the counter. She was smiling, flicking her hair in the way all girls seemed to when he showed them the slightest bit of attention. Molly marvelled that he was still single at thirty-one; she'd have thought he'd be beating them off with a stick. She'd known him five years now and couldn't remember any of his relationships lasting more than a few months.

She crossed the room silently and slipped on to the stool beside him. 'Stop monopolizing the staff, there's a guy down the end of the bar gasping for a pint.'

The barmaid whirled around and hurried off to serve the irate customer as Gareth hugged her. 'Hi, Molly. How are things?'

She smiled brightly. 'Fine. You?'

He shook his head. 'I was afraid of this.'

She gulped. 'What?'

'That it would be all awkward between us after the last night. I'm sorry. Moll, I was completely out of order.'

Wow. She hadn't been sure what to expect, but it certainly wasn't this. 'It was perfectly understandable. I was thinking about it. If Ellen saw Declan in a clinch with some woman, she probably would have punched him.'

He smiled. 'Well, he'd deserve it, but you don't.'

'I doubt your brother would agree.'

'Then he shouldn't have left you.' Gareth turned to catch the barmaid's eye. 'Drink?'

'Coffee, please,' Molly said faintly. Whatever she'd been expecting Gareth to say, it hadn't been this.

Gareth gave the order and turned back to face her, his expression serious. 'I know you would never cheat on Declan; I don't think he has a clue how lucky he is.'

Molly flushed at the admiration in his eyes. 'I'm no saint, Gareth.'

'You liked this guy, Luke, a lot, didn't you?'

Molly nodded, realizing honesty was, in this case, definitely the best policy. 'He was my first boyfriend and we were together for two years; we went through a lot together.'

'Why did you split up?'

Molly was about to give her usual reply, but something about the way Gareth was looking at her made her decide to tell him the truth. 'I was in a car accident with his twin sister; she died.'

Gareth reached for her hand. 'I'm so sorry. Were you hurt?'

Molly shook her head. 'Apart from some cuts and bruises, I walked away unharmed.'

'And I suppose you've been riddled with guilt about that all these years.'

Molly gave a sad shrug. 'You could say that.'

'Did you break up because of the crash?'

'No. Luke's mother was a mess and his dad decided to take a job in Bordeaux. They moved a few weeks later.'

He remained silent for a moment, stroking her hand in an absent fashion. 'Poor Molly.'

'It was a long time ago.' She tried to smile, but realized that she was closer to tears.

Gareth looked up into her eyes. 'Does Declan know?'

'I told him I lost my best friend in a crash. I didn't really go into detail.'

His eyes searched her face. 'Why not? Or, maybe the real question is, why have you told me?'

She sighed. 'I didn't tell him because, by the time we met, I'd just got back on track and I wanted to stay there. As for telling you, I suppose I wanted you to know he'd been a big part of my life and I don't make a habit of going around kissing other men.'

The barmaid set the coffee down on the bar in front of her and Molly pulled her hand away and took a sip. 'Urgh, this is too bitter for me.' She reached for a couple of sachets of sugar, slowly emptied them into her cup and stirred. She was conscious that Gareth was still watching her, but she didn't turn back to face him.

'What about Declan?'

She glanced at him. 'What do you mean?'

'Was he second best?'

'No, of course not.'

'Sorry.' He sighed and seemed to be searching for words. 'When Declan told me you didn't want to set a new date for the wedding, I thought that was it. I thought you were going to break up with him. Were you?'

Molly frowned as she tried to recall her feelings that night.

'I'm not sure. I don't think I knew what I wanted, but I thought I knew what he wanted.'

'Which was?'

'Not to be married,' she said simply. 'I felt I'd cornered him into proposing, and the first opportunity he had to opt out, he took it.'

'You make him sound spineless.'

'I don't mean to,' Molly said quickly, turning back to face him. 'I know he loves me, I'm just not convinced he wants to marry me.'

He looked at her. 'And if you're right?'

Molly shook her head. 'I don't know.'

Gareth took a sip of his pint. 'Do you miss him?'

'What is this, Gareth? Why the inquisition, has Declan put you up to this?'

Gareth shook his head. 'Sorry.'

Molly checked her watch. 'I should get back to Ellen.'

'She's staying with you?'

'No, I've moved in with her, I'm staying until she has the baby.'

'Are you on the bike?'

'Yes.'

'Then have another coffee and I'll drop you home.'

She opened her mouth to refuse, but something in his eyes stopped her. 'Okay, but no more coffee. I'll have a tomato juice.'

He smiled. 'And I'd better have the coffee.'

'I do miss him,' Molly murmured when they'd got their drinks. 'I hate that flat at the best of times, but when he isn't there, it's unbearable.'

'I can imagine.'

'Can you?' She shot him a curious smile. 'Have you ever lived with anyone?'

He shook his head, smiling. 'No woman would be able to put up with me.'

'I'd say there are plenty who'd risk it,' Molly teased. He'd dated so many girls over the years, and many of them had been crazy about him, but as soon as it looked like getting serious, Gareth finished it. A bit like she used to before Declan came along.

'What?' he asked when he saw her frowning.

'I just realized that I used to be like you before your brother came along. As soon as a guy got close, I ran.'

'Why?' he asked.

She stared into her tomato juice. 'I was afraid of being hurt.' She looked back at him. 'You?'

'Why settle for one, when you can have plenty?' he joked.

'Don't make out you're a hard-hearted bastard,' Molly said impatiently, 'I know you're not.'

'I'm not,' he admitted. 'I'd happily settle down with the right woman. Just like your friend Luke.'

'Luke's married, I told you that,' Molly reminded him.

'But it's not his wife he's in love with,' Gareth insisted. 'I saw the way he looked at you, Moll.'

'Does Declan look at me like that?'

Gareth seemed momentarily thrown by the question. 'Of course.'

Molly swallowed back her tears. 'You took just a second too long to answer that.'

They drove to Ellen's house in silence and when Gareth lifted her bike out of his boot and rested it against the wall, he took her hand. 'I didn't mean to upset you.'

'You haven't.'

'What about Luke?'

She didn't meet his eyes. 'What about him?'

'Will you see him again?'

'He's back in France, Gareth.'

He watched her steadily. 'You're avoiding the question.'

'I don't know,' she admitted and looked into his eyes. 'Are you going to tell Declan?'

Gareth thought for a moment and then shook his head.

She reached up to hug him. 'Thank you. You're a lovely man. And one day you'll meet the right woman.'

He released her and walked back to his car. 'What makes you think I haven't already?'

Chapter Thirty

Molly had a busy day ahead. Ash had sent her a message an hour ago, asking to meet in the coffee shop in the shopping mall across from the school at three-thirty. Her dad had called last night, asking her to come and see Belle because he was worried she might be a little depressed. Laura had phoned first thing, but Molly had let it go to voicemail; she was too distracted to deal with her sister today. And Ellen, poor Ellen, hyper about the fact that tomorrow was her due date, was pestering her about going to see Andrew's sister, which was why she was currently peddling up Baggot Street. But Molly was glad to have so much on her plate. It prevented her thinking about Gareth and his rather cryptic parting remark and wondering whether Declan did actually love her after all. Gareth's hesitation had brought to the surface all of her doubts.

Molly had once done a placement with a relationship counselling service, and she'd been amazed at the variety of things that held couples together, quite apart from love and children. For many, it was companionship and the fear of the unknown or the fear of not finding someone else to love them. It was why, one counsellor explained, many older people walked out on a marriage after years of apparent happiness. They were the lucky ones, the ones who caught a glimpse of what might be, of what a richer life they could have and they took it and didn't look back. Was she Declan's safety net? Had he stayed with her because it was easy? Had she become like a pair of old slippers and it was only when faced with the commitment of marriage that he'd started to have doubts? The thoughts went round and round her brain but she found herself no nearer to finding an answer.

She forced herself to concentrate on the task ahead. Ellen had insisted that Andrew's sister, Barbara, must not suspect that Molly had come in specifically to see her about Andrew so she decided that her best bet was to tell Barbara that she was looking for a bag to match her going-away outfit and Ellen had told her to try this shop.

She locked her bike to a lamppost near the small boutique and went in. Immediately, a girl emerged from the back of the shop and gave her a friendly smile. 'Hello, I'm just back here. Call if you need anything.'

'Barbara?' Molly smiled.

'Yes?'

'I thought it must be you, you're very like your brother.'

Barbara came forwards, pushing the flowing mane of dark curls back from her heart-shaped face. 'You know Andrew?'

'I did. I'm Molly, a friend of Ellen's.' She held out her hand.

'Oh, I see.' Barbara shook it but her smile falatered.

'I'm looking for a bag to match my going-away outfit and Ellen said I had to come and see you,' Molly looked around in admiration at the huge range of accessories of every colour, 'and I can see why.'

'Thank you.' Barbara searched Molly's face. 'How is Ellen?'

Molly had a mental image of her friend puffing her way up the stairs as she was leaving. 'She's fine. How's Andrew doing?'

'He doesn't say much, but he obviously misses her. He's working hard and trying to sort himself out.'

'So he's clean?' Molly asked.

Barbara nodded, crossing her fingers. 'Has been for a couple of months.'

'But that's wonderful news,' Molly said, delighted.

'He's working at an animal rescue centre,' Barbara added, wrinkling her nose, 'and stinks to high heaven most of the time, but he seems happy.'

Molly laughed. 'Of course, he was studying to be a vet, I'd forgotten.'

Barbara nodded sadly. 'And he would have been brilliant too.'

'If he gets his act together, perhaps he could go back to college.'

'Maybe.' With a bright smile, Barbara switched back into professional mode. 'So, what colour is your outfit?'

Molly opened her backpack and pulled out a tiny silk shrug wrapped in tissue paper and handed it over.

Barbara shook it out and held it up to examine it. 'Beautiful, and this shade of green will look wonderful with your eyes . . .'

Wrap and new bag safely tucked into her backpack, Molly cycled out to Blackrock to see her mother. Her father had asked her to drop in, but warned her not to mention that he'd called.

'Your mum's very prickly at the moment,' he'd said, 'and she'll murder me if you tell her I asked you to come over.'

He hadn't been able to talk for long, and it occurred to Molly that perhaps she should call her sister back before seeing Belle, in case Laura had any more news. She veered off the main road and headed for her flat – that way she could collect her post, check the answering machine, have a coffee and call Laura.

There was the usual pile of junk mail, fast food menus and bills. Molly put the post in her bag to look at later and chucked the rest in the bin. While she was waiting for the kettle to boil, she listened to the messages on her answering machine. The first was from the garage saying something about a service. Molly cursed under her breath. That was Declan's department; she had as little to do with the damn car as she could get away with. The second was from her dad, recorded yesterday before he'd called her on the mobile. He was obviously able to talk when he'd made this call as he'd rambled on for a couple of minutes sounding agitated and miserable. Molly was glad she was going straight over there. The last message wasn't actually a message, just a muttering and the sound of machinery in the background, then the phone went dead. It had been left late last night. Molly wondered if Declan had called here, forgetting that she was staying at Ellen's.

She quickly made her coffee and dialled her sister. 'Hey, Laura.'

'Molly? Thanks for ringing back. I have to see you.'

'What's wrong?'

'I can't talk on the phone, we need to meet.'

Molly closed her eyes. 'I really can't, Laura, I have a very busy day. I'm on my way now to see Mum.'

'And where are you going after that?' Laura demanded.

'Back to check on Ellen and do some work.'

'Okay then, I'll meet you at Mum's and then I'll give you a lift to Ellen's and we can talk on the way.'

Molly didn't get a chance to answer, as Laura had already hung up. With a resigned sigh, she took a sip of coffee, poured the rest down the sink and grabbed her bag and helmet. She'd better get a move on, or she wouldn't get an opportunity to talk to Belle alone.

As she cycled, Molly thought about the meeting with Ash later. She hated going behind Laura's back, but reasoned that, technically, this was nothing to do with Ash and so none of her sister's business. She still wasn't quite sure what she was going to say to Neil though. She had hoped to have an opportunity to talk to a colleague from her family counselling days and get her advice on the matter, but she was on holiday in Thailand so Molly was on her own. It was so important that she handled it carefully; it might be the only chance she'd have to help Neil. If she got it wrong, she could make things worse. It was an awesome responsibility, but she had to do it for the twins' sake. She sighed as she glanced at her watch, wondering how she was she going to fit everything into this increasingly crazy day.

Her thoughts turned to Laura, who'd sounded quite distracted on the phone. Was it man trouble, or had she finally realized what her son had noticed weeks ago: that something was troubling Ashling? Molly found it hard to feel sympathy for her sister after her day out with the twins. Laura was so wrapped up in herself that she hadn't a clue what her kids were going through. Ash and Adam were off school and hanging around the house most of the time – Laura had said as much – so how had she not seen that they were clearly troubled?

Molly peddled harder in an effort to dissipate her anger. She couldn't say anything to Laura, she'd promised and she had to keep that promise. God, life was complicated at the moment, but it was still easier to concentrate on problems other than her own.

When she let herself into the house, she found her father on his knees in front of the washing machine, muttering under his breath. 'Dad?'

He looked up, but couldn't even summon up a smile. 'Hello, darling, I don't suppose you know how to work this damn thing, do you?'

Molly crouched down beside him, twisted the dial and pressed start. 'I thought Rory was in charge of laundry.'

'He has a full day of lectures and left early.' Oliver straightened and yawned.

'Are you okay?' Molly asked. He looked washed-out and there was an uncharacteristic slump to his shoulders.

'I'm fine, just worried about your mum. She seems to be in a lot of pain and is very down.'

'It's early days, Dad.'

'I know, but the physio's given her exercises to do, but she just seems to want to stay in bed all the time.'

'Will I go up and have a chat?'

'Please. I'll bring you up a cuppa and then I'll go out and mow the lawn and give you girls a bit of space.'

Molly ran upstairs, knocked gently on the bedroom door and stuck her head in. 'Hello.'

Belle opened her eyes and smiled. 'Molly, this is a surprise.'

'I was checking on the flat so I thought I'd come on out to see you.'

'How's Ellen?' Belle asked, sitting up slowly.

Molly hurried to fix the pillows for her. 'Fed up.'

Belle chuckled. 'Poor girl. Still, not long now.'

'Tomorrow's her due date,' Molly confirmed, pulling up the bedside chair and sitting down. 'How are you getting on?'

'Not very well,' Belle admitted. 'This has been the longest week of my life. I'm so fed up being helpless. How am I going to survive six weeks like this?'

'But you won't be six weeks like this, Mum,' Molly reminded her gently. 'Once you've adjusted to the weight of the plaster and got used to the crutches, you'll be able to do what you please.'

'I'd like a bath and I can't do that. I'd like to go swimming and I can't do that either.'

Molly smiled. 'Okay, if you're going to concentrate on the negatives—'

Belle patted her hand. 'I know I'm being a terrible patient and

I have driven your poor father round the bend, it's just that I'm used to doing things for myself; I like to be independent.'

Molly raised an eyebrow. 'Then why are you in bed?'

'It takes too long to get up, dressed and downstairs, that's why,' Belle said crossly.

'Lord, you are feeling sorry for yourself, aren't you. You're only going to gain independence by getting up and about and finding new ways of doing things. Look on it as a challenge.'

'You supposed to be looking after me, not nagging me.'

'Make up your mind. A moment ago, you were complaining about being dependent . . .'

'I know.' Belle sighed. 'If you want the God's honest truth, I'm feeling old.'

Molly squeezed her hand. 'That's perfectly understandable, but it's only temporary.'

'I know I've been relatively lucky, but this whole business has just made me feel so vulnerable.'

'I know, Mum. As you said, you're normally a very active and independent woman. We all rely on you and now our positions are reversed. I don't think Dad's coping too well.'

'He isn't,' Belle agreed, 'not that he says anything. He's just taken to muttering to himself.'

Molly laughed. 'Now you know what he'll be like when he's a decrepit old man.'

'If he's going to be like that, I'll be long gone,' her mother chuckled.

Oliver arrived with two mugs of tea. 'Well, I'm glad to see someone can put a smile on her face,' he observed, handing his daughter one and putting the other down on the bedside table.

'Sorry, darling,' Belle looked at him with affection. 'Are you ready to trade me in for a younger, fitter model?'

He bent to drop a kiss on her hair. 'Never.'

Molly watched them, thinking that only a few days ago, she would have thought her parents one of the happiest couples in the world, but after what Laura had said, she found herself looking at her father with new eyes.

'I'm going out to mow the lawn,' he announced. 'Call me, Molly, when you're leaving.'

'I'll be here for a little while, I'm waiting for Laura.'

Belle looked at her in surprise. 'Laura's coming too?'

'Yes, I was talking to her earlier and she said she was dropping by.' She grinned at her dad. 'She's probaby dropping off another dozen casseroles.'

Oliver brightened. 'Oh, good, Rory's got through most of the first lot.'

Molly grinned. 'I'd have thought he'd be spending all of his time with Natalie.'

'We all are,' Belle said, 'she's practically living with us.'

'She believes family should stick together at times like this,' Oliver added. 'Lovely girl.'

'Don't you mind Natalie being around so much?' Molly asked after her father had left them. 'If you like, I'll have a word with Rory.'

'No, it's fine and chatting to her is probably the only thing that's keeping your father's spirits up.'

'Rory really seems to be in love this time, doesn't he?' Molly marvelled.

Belle smiled. 'Yes. I'm glad he's finally found someone. He's not strong like you and Laura.'

Molly looked at her in surprise. 'Do you think I'm a strong person?'

'I know you are. I've seen you go through things in your young life that would have floored someone twice your age.'

Molly shrugged. 'I suppose you just deal with things when you have to.'

'You certainly did.'

The front door banged and Molly heard Laura's heels click across the hall. 'Here comes sis.'

'Are you two getting on these days?' Belle asked.

'I haven't seen that much of her since we got back.'

'I'm sorry you cut your break short for me,' Belle apologized.

'It really wasn't a problem; I was ready to come home.'

Laura pushed the door open, a large bouquet of carnations in her arms. 'Morning, Mum.'

'Oh, Laura, they're beautiful, thank you.' Belle smiled affectionately as her elder daughter kissed her cheek.

'I'll put them in water after I've had a chance to catch my breath,' Laura said, perching on the side of the bed.

'I'll do it,' Molly offered, standing up. 'Shall I bring you back a cuppa?'

'Oh, yes, coffee, please.'

Molly left them to chat and took the flowers downstairs. As she arranged them, she watched her father through the kitchen window, pushing the old mower back and forward across the grass. Belle wasn't the only person who'd been knocked for six, nor was she the only one finding it hard to cope. Oliver wasn't used to being needed on this level. He was a free spirit who was out of the house more than he was in it. Molly wondered if he was suffering from cabin fever, or were both her parents finding spending so much time together a trial? She tried to imagine what it would be like spending all day, every day, with Declan. She thought it would be lovely, but knew that they would probably get on each other's nerves after a while. The way he was always drumming his fingers or clicking his nails off his teeth would drive her mad. Declan had a lot of nervous habits, now she came to think about it. Was he like that all the time or just when he was with her, she wondered, and then groaned at her own paranoia.

She caught a glimpse of the clock as she was adding sugar to

Laura's coffee and cursed. Her sister was going to have to knock this back; the day was marching on and there was still so much to do.

When she walked back into the bedroom, Belle was on the edge of the bed and she looked up at her daughter with a triumphant smile. 'We've decided to go for a walk.'

'We have time to take her round the block, don't we, Moll?' Laura asked.

Molly hesitated only a second before nodding enthusiastically. 'Of course we do.'

Chapter Thirty-one

Molly waved Laura off, parked her bike under Ellen's front window and let herself in. Though Molly had planned on dragging Laura away as soon as they'd gotten back from their walk, Oliver had prepared a celebratory lunch for them and, looking at the buoyant, if bushed Belle, Molly couldn't find it in her heart to leave. Then there followed the journey home with Laura, when Molly had to sit on her hands to stop herself taking a swipe at her self-absorbed sister. At first Molly couldn't understand why Laura was even telling her about Gerard, and then she realized that her sister wasn't looking for forgiveness, but rather trying to justify her actions. When Molly thought of the scenario Ash was currently immersed in, she had to really bite her lip. Instead, when Laura finally paused for breath, Molly told her a story about a divorcée she'd counselled a few years earlier.

'She and her husband were fighting all the time and she was in love with another man, but couldn't bring herself to leave, so instead had an affair. It was nearly three years before she was found out.'

'What happened?' Laura asked.

'Her husband threw her out, her kids wouldn't have anything more to do with her and her lover went back to his wife.'

'You're just making that up to scare me,' Laura accused, scowling.

'I'm not, Laura. I just want you to think very carefully about what you're doing. You don't love Gerard, and yet you're ready to lose everything for the sake of a meaningless fling. Is it really worth it?'

Laura hadn't been impressed with that, but Molly was too annoyed to hide her feelings; why was Laura taking such risks? Robert was a mild-mannered man, but Molly still couldn't see him forgiving adultery. And though soft-hearted Adam might come round and forgive his mother, Ash would be much harder to win back.

Molly hurried inside to explain to Ellen that she had to rush off out again, but was surprised to find the house quiet and apparently empty. She went in search of a note and found one propped up against the kettle.

> Gone to the salon – Ruby offered to do my hair to cheer me up and so I'll look gorgeous for the baby photos! See you later, E.

Molly sighed with relief. Ellen was relaxing with friends and being pampered. Now she needn't feel guilty about rushing off to see Ash. She quickly went upstairs, fetched a clean shirt out of the chest of drawers Ellen had given her in the baby's room – the tiny clothes only took up one drawer – and went into the bathroom to tidy herself. Ten minutes later, she was peddling towards the small café near the twins' school where the teenagers hung out. Thankfully, she didn't have to worry about bumping into Laura. After dropping her off, Laura had been going into the city centre to get her hair done; she wouldn't be back for hours.

Molly smiled as she chained up her bike outside the trendy little café. When she was Ash's age, she and her friends had met in the park, outside the shops or in each other's houses. They hadn't had the luxury of hanging out in places like this. It was a perfect spot for bored young people, Molly saw, as it had Internet access, a jukebox, a pool table at the back of the room and the menu was basic and priced to suit the clientele.

Molly had agreed with Ash that she would text her once she was inside, and after buying a Coke and spreading her books and notes out on a table by the window, she did this. She had told Ash yesterday that she must simply follow her lead and hopefully Neil would join in. Molly had decided to tell the teenagers that she was preparing for a counselling session that evening with young adults who self-harmed. Molly had considered saying it was for children of divorcées, but figured that might make Neil suspicious. Instead, she would concentrate on the reasons children cut themselves or pulled their hair out, and just hope that the boy was able to make the connection. A lot of it she would have to play by ear. Hopefully, starved of attention, Neil would be happy to talk, even if he didn't admit anything. At worst, it would give Ash something she could talk to him about later.

When the door swung open, Molly buried her head in a tattered textbook and waited. When she heard her niece's rather falsely bright greeting, she looked up and feigned surprise. 'Ash, hi!' The boy with her was tall, thin and colourless, his skin almost transparent and, though his eyes were curious, he hung back when Ash approached.

'What are you doing here?' Ash asked in the high-pitched voice.

Definitely not the next Keira Knightley, Molly decided. 'I have a meeting nearby and I'm just trying to prepare. I'm not getting very far though.' She gave an exaggerated sigh, hoping her acting skills were better than her niece's. 'Let me get you and your friend a drink.'

'Great. Two chocolate milkshakes, please.' Ash turned and gestured to the silent boy. 'This is Neil. Neil, this is Molly, my aunt.'

Molly stood up and smiled. 'Hello, Neil, nice to meet you.'

The boy gave a glimmer of a smile. 'Hi.'

Molly ordered at the counter and then turned back to Ash. 'So, what are you two up to?'

'Nothing much, just hanging out.'

Molly paid for the shakes and handed them over with a grin. 'I don't suppose you could spare me a few minutes, could you? You can still have the drinks, even if you say no!'

'Sure,' Ash laughed and pulled up a chair. 'You don't mind, do you, Neil?'

He shrugged and sat down. He was obviously uncomfortable, but in the face of Ash's strong personality, seemed content to go along with whatever she wanted.

'So, what's the problem? Molly's a psychologist,' Ash explained to Neil.

Molly watched the boy stiffen slightly, but she ignored it and, shaking her head, consulted her notes. 'I'm going to see a seventeen-year-old girl. I've never met her before. A few people have tried to help her, but with little success. I'm sort of the last resort.'

Ash leaned forward, folding her arms on the table. 'What's wrong with her?'

'She self-harms.'

This got Neil's attention and he too leaned forward. 'What does she do?'

Molly winced at the boy's eagerness. 'She pulls her hair out, scratches herself and sometimes cuts herself too.'

Ash's eyes widened in shock. 'Oh, that's so sad.'

'Where does she cut herself?' Neil asked.

'I'm not sure,' Molly told him, unwilling to put ideas into his head. 'Anyway, I'm more interested in why she does it.'

'Why *does* she do it?' Ash asked.

'That's the question. Her father died when she was little, her mother remarried five years ago, and now has three more children; two-year-old twin boys and a six-month-old baby girl.'

'Well, there you are then,' Ash said, 'it's obvious she's feeling left out. Her mother has a new family to fuss over and her husband is their father. She's the square peg in the round hole.'

Molly consulted her notes. 'I don't think so. She seems to love her brothers and sister, gets on well with her stepfather and is very close to her mother. I wonder if perhaps she's being bullied at school.'

'Why are you so sure it's not about her family?' Neil said sharply.

'Why would it be? She now has a ready-made, happy family.'

'Things aren't always what they seem,' Neil muttered.

'Neil's right. She might be a really good kid who's doing her best to be a good daughter and big sister, but watching her mother play with this baby girl . . .' Ash shook her head. 'I think I'd probably feel a bit jealous.'

Molly chewed on her pen, pretending to consider this for a moment, then she looked up at Ash. 'She hasn't said anything to her mother and hasn't complained about being left out.'

'Maybe she's afraid to.' Ash shot Neil a look. 'Maybe she doesn't want to risk upsetting her mum, the only person she's got left.'

Molly nodded thoughtfully. 'Well, if you're right, the solution is relatively simple.'

Neil looked at her in disgust. 'How can it be?'

'I need to persuade her to talk to her mother. Once it's out in the open, she'll realize that no matter how many babies her mother has, she won't stop loving her.'

'But what if her mum rejects her?' Ash asked, playing devil's advocate.

Molly shook her head. 'I can almost guarantee you that her mother is unaware her daughter feels this way and will be devastated to hear it. She's not intentionally excluding the girl, just doing what every mum does, giving her time to the most vulnerable

person in the family. She probably thinks her daughter understands that and, anyway, she's at an age where her mother is
probably trying to step back to allow her more privacy and independence.' She smiled at Ash. 'You're only fourteen, but you don't
want your mum in your face all of the time now, do you?'

'No way!' Ash agreed.

'But you don't want to be ignored or neglected either,' Neil
said, sullenly.

'No,' Molly agreed, afraid she was losing him. 'I think this
may simply be a communication problem. The mum is too
wrapped up in the small kids at the moment to notice her daughter's hurting. She's human, you know? I know you kids think
that adults always have the answers, but we have problems too.
The only way to resolve this situation is for the girl to tell her
mother exactly how she feels. In fact, that's usually the solution
in most cases. If people stopped brooding in silence and spoke
their minds, I'd be out of a job.'

'But how will you persuade her to do that?' Ash asked, with a
sidelong glance at Neil.

Molly sighed. 'It may take a few sessions. I have to try and make
her see that she is achieving nothing by harming herself. Whether
you're right about her feeling excluded, or I'm right and she's being
bullied, her only way forward is to confront her problems.'

'You make it all sound easy,' Neil said, with a shake of his head.

'I don't mean to.'

'For all you know, maybe her mum doesn't give a damn about
her.'

'From what I've read,' Molly said, tapping the notes in front of
her. 'I doubt it. But if you're right, she would still be in a better
position if she talked to her mother.'

'How do you figure that out?'

'Because, simply by saying it out loud, she will have got rid of
a weight off her shoulders.'

'And you think she'll stop self-harming?' Ash asked.

'That may take a while, but she'll have taken a step in the right direction.'

'I don't think we've helped you much,' Ash said. 'You seem to have got it all figured out.'

'Not true, I was convinced she was being bullied, but now I see you could be right. I hadn't considered it because, on paper, her home life seems perfect and her mother appears to be a lovely woman.'

Neil shrugged. 'But that's on paper. You don't actually know what she's really like.'

Molly sighed inwardly. This wasn't going as well as she'd hoped. Still, hopefully Ash would be able to get through to him after she was gone. 'You're right, Neil. But at least now I have some ideas of the questions I should be asking. Thank you both for your help.' Molly smiled at the two of them. 'I'd better get going or I'll be late.'

'Good luck,' Ash said, standing to hug her.

'Will you let us know how it goes?' Neil asked.

'Sure,' Molly said, gathering up her things. Maybe she'd got through to him after all. 'Thanks again, guys.'

It was almost six when she let herself back into Ellen's house and she found her friend cleaning out the kitchen cupboards. 'What on earth are you doing?'

'Just tidying up. Busy day?'

'Mad. How are you? I like your hair.'

Ellen grinned. 'Isn't it nice? And Ruby did my nails too.' She fluttered them under Molly's nose. 'It was lovely to be back, we had a great laugh.'

'I'm glad.' Molly said, starting to restock the pristine shelves. 'Tell you what, I'll treat you to a curry for dinner and see if we can shift Buster.'

Ellen closed her eyes, smiling. 'Oh, I'd love that. Let's go out. We could walk down to that new place on the seafront.'

'Are you sure you're up to it?' Molly asked, glancing at Ellen's swollen ankles.

'We can take our time and it would be nice to get some air.'

'Okay then. Why don't you have a cool shower and get ready? And I'll finish up here,' Molly offered.

'That would be nice. Isn't it just typical that our first decent summer in years happens when I'm heavy with child? I seem to sweat all day long.'

Molly laughed. 'You'll be glad of the good weather in a couple of weeks when you're trying to get dozens of babygros dry.'

Ellen looked wistfully out at the clothes line. 'I can hardly imagine it. Oh, Moll, what if I'm a rubbish mother?'

'You'll be the best,' Molly assured her.

'I'm afraid.'

'I'd be worried about you, if you weren't!'

'But what if I can't cope alone, Moll?'

'You're not alone—'

'No, I know I have you and Mum, but I mean about being a single parent. All the decisions will be mine alone; it's an overwhelming thought.'

'So don't think about it,' Molly told her. 'Take each day as it comes and you'll get there; you'll be fine.'

Ellen nodded and sniffed back her tears. 'Of course I will. Sorry, I'm just feeling a bit emotional today.'

'I wonder why?' Molly said dryly.

Ellen smiled tremulously. 'You didn't get a chance to go and see Barbara yet then?'

Molly clapped a hand to her forehead. 'Oh, Ellen, I did! I'm so sorry, I completely forgot. It's been a mad day.'

'Never mind that, just tell me.' Ellen sank into a chair and looked at her expectantly.

Molly closed the cupboard door and came to sit opposite her.

'It's all good news, Ellen.' She smiled. 'Andrew is working in an animal rescue centre.'

Ellen's eyes softened. 'That's good, he'll be happy there.'

'And, he's clean, at least it appears that way,' Molly added hurriedly, aware how clever addicts could be when it came to hiding their habit from those closest to them.

'Did Barbara ask about me?'

'Yes. And I told her you were fine and left it at that.'

Ellen nodded and stood up. 'Thanks, Molly.'

'Doesn't it help, knowing he's okay?' Molly asked, frowning.

'Yes, of course.' Ellen sighed. 'I just wish he was here.'

'Maybe he will be, sooner than you think.'

'Even if we've no future together, Moll, I'd love him to be a real father to this little one.'

'And in time, he might.'

Ellen nodded. 'Don't worry, I'm not going to call him and beg him to come home and play happy families. I didn't go through all this just to give up now.'

Molly stood up and put her arms round her friend. 'You've been very brave.'

'I didn't have much choice,' Ellen pointed out.

'Barbara said he misses you,' Molly blurted out. Maybe it wasn't a good idea to pass this nugget on, but Molly felt Ellen needed a lift.

'I miss him too,' Ellen said with a sad smile and went upstairs.

Chapter Thirty-two

3 p.m., Saturday, 15th August

Laura stood at the kitchen window watching the twins sprawled on the lawn, deep in conversation. They had been very close these last couple of days and tended to stop talking when she walked into the room. It was making her nervous. Still, they couldn't have overheard her talking to Gerard and she'd been careful to delete his messages from her phone. If she needed to contact him again, she would email him. She was the only one who used the battered old PC that sat in a corner of the study; Robert used a company laptop. In fact, she thought, her pulse quickening, maybe she'd slip in and send Gerard a message right now, it was as good a time as any. Robert had gone off on some golf outing and wouldn't be home until late, and the children were unlikely to seek out her company. Ash went out of her way to avoid her and Adam, though as affectionate as ever, only ever came looking for her when he was hungry.

Feeling decidedly sorry for herself Laura went into the study and switched on the PC. As it took forever to warm up, she went back out to the kitchen to make a coffee. When she was finally settled in front of the screen, a mug at her elbow, she mulled over what to say. Should she play it cool or live dangerously and tell him how much she wanted to see him? Tell him she was living for his next visit – truer than she could believe – or would it be better to pretend to be in two minds about the rendezvous? She was amazed though, at how cool she actually was. She didn't feel nervous or guilty. She felt no shame or disloyalty. As a wife, in principle, she knew what she was doing was wrong, but when it came to Robert, she found she felt very little any more. It was sad. She had thought she would always love him and would always be happy together, but life wasn't like that. She knew many of the women she met at the school were unhappy, despite their large houses and larger bank accounts. She wasn't so different.

She signed into her email and typed in Gerard's address. She'd memorized it, terrified of having anything on paper or on her phone. Perhaps she was being over-cautious, but better that than careless. She was trying to decide exactly what to write when the phone rang. Muttering under her breath, she flicked off the screen and hurried out to answer it, praying it wasn't Penny.

'Hello, darling, hope I'm not interrupting you.'

'Dad, hi. No, I'm just pottering around tidying up. How's Mum?'

'She's so much better, Laura. Taking her out for that walk yesterday did her the power of good, it's really perked her up. So much so, that she wants everyone to come to brunch tomorrow.'

'Great,' Laura said, relieved, 'but don't let her do too much too soon, Dad.'

'Ah, yes. Well, that's why I'm calling. I was wondering if you could pop over a little earlier than usual and help me with the cooking.'

'Of course. Is the girlfriend going to be there?'

'Natalie? Oh, I should think so, she's always here.'

'Don't you think it's time Rory moved out, Dad? You have enough on your plate without having to entertain her too.'

'Oh I don't mind, and she's good company for your mother.'

'Natalie?' Laura's eyebrows arched in disbelief.

'You need to get to know her better,' her father said, sounding slightly reproving. 'She's very nice and a great influence on your brother.'

'That's as maybe, but it's a bit much her and Rory shacking up with you and Mum.'

Oliver burst out laughing. 'Shacking up? You must be joking, your brother's lucky to get a kiss.'

'You mean they're not—'

'Natalie doesn't just talk about her religious beliefs, Laura, she lives them.'

'Wow!' Laura mumbled, lost for words. It was one thing Molly saying she and Luke had never made love, but for a couple of nearly thirty in this day and age – weird.

'Got to go, darling,' her father was saying, 'see you tomorrow.'

As Laura put down the phone and crossed back through the kitchen, she glanced out the window and saw that the twins had gone. She quickened her step, but was relieved to see the study was empty. She went back out into the hall. 'Adam? Ash? Where are you?'

'In here,' Adam's voice came from the sitting room.

Laura popped her head round the door to see the brother and sister bent over a computer games console. 'What are you up to?' she asked.

'Soccer and I'm winning hands down.'

'Don't count your chickens,' his sister warned.

'I'll leave you to it,' Laura smiled and, going back to the study, she closed the door and sat back down in front of the PC. After several unproductive minutes, she sent a simple, straightforward and honest message.

Hi, Gerard. It was nice to hear your voice again, although it was a bit of a shock. I think it might be better if we stick to email from now on.

She hesitated about how best to sign off; she wasn't going to write 'love' and 'best wishes' seemed a little formal given their intimate relationship. Finally, she just wrote 'Laura' and pressed send before she lost her nerve. Switching off the screen again, she stood up and went back out to the kitchen. Just in time to hear the doorbell; it was all go today. It would be one of the kids' friends, she reasoned, and left them to answer it. It was cloudier than yesterday, but still warm and she thought maybe she'd weed the flower beds. If her hands were covered in muck, it would stop her coming in and out like a lovesick teenager, checking for Gerard's reply.

'Cooee,' the door opened and Penny walked in on a wave of perfume. 'The kids said it was okay to come through.'

Laura saw Ash hovering behind Penny and smiled politely. 'Of course, Penny, come in. Would you like a coffee?'

'A glass of cold wine would be nicer. I have so much to tell you.'

'Sure. Did you want something, Ash?' Laura added, as her daughter continued to stand in the doorway.

Ash's eyes went from Penny to her mother and back again. 'No, nothing,' she mumbled and disappeared.

'Teenagers.' Penny rolled her eyes and sat down. 'What can you do with them? Still, your two aren't so bad. My Neil wanders round looking like the grim reaper these days.'

Laura had to laugh, it was an incredibly accurate description of the morose boy. She took down two glasses and poured the wine.

'Thank goodness he spends so much time with Ash, if he didn't have her, he'd have no one.'

Laura looked at her in surprise as she handed her a glass. 'I didn't know they spent time together.'

Penny nodded. 'She must be very patient, because he has hardly a word to say for himself. I don't know who he takes after, Laura, I really don't. Mark and I have always been outgoing.'

'They're all the same, Penny. They talk to each other, just not us.'

'I suppose you're right. Anyway, wait till I tell you where I went the other night—'

Laura heard the click of the sitting-room door and realized that her daughter must have been listening in on their conversation, yet another reason not to confide in Penny. As the woman went into embarrassing detail about her latest conquest, Laura tuned out, wondering why her daughter was eavesdropping. Perhaps Penny was the attraction. Had Ash overheard any of their previous conversations and the salacious minutiae of Penny's love life? Laura felt sick at the thought. 'It's probably better not to discuss this now,' she cut in on Penny now, nodding towards the door.

'You're probably right,' Penny agreed, 'although Neil doesn't seem to care what I do most of the time.'

'Ashling's the same,' Laura admitted. 'Sometimes I think she hates me.'

Penny looked amused. 'Of course she hates you; she's your daughter. Are you telling me you got on well with your mother when you were fourteen?'

Laura chuckled. 'No, she drove me mad. And all my friends thought she was cool, which made me even madder. But she *was* cool, she still is. I don't know why I didn't realize it then.'

'Because you were engrossed in your own world, where the leading lady's name was Laura.'

'True.' Laura poured Penny more wine. For all her shocking ways, the woman was good company.

'We should go out,' Penny announced. 'A girly night would be fun.'

'I didn't think you'd be interested in going out with other girls,' Laura teased.

'Of course I am, men are only good for one thing! If you want to have a lark, you need a girlfriend. What about it?'

Laura laughed. 'Why not?'

'You're going out with Penny?' Ashling looked at her, clearly taken aback.

Laura looked up from where she was dicing meat for dinner. 'Yes, why? Is that a problem?'

Ashling and Adam exchanged worried looks.

'What is wrong with you two?'

'She's not exactly your type, Mum,' her son said. 'She's a bit of a slapper.'

'Adam!' Laura looked at him, shocked. 'What a thing to say.'

'But he's right,' Ash mumbled. 'Neil says she's always out clubbing.'

'Yes, well,' Laura concentrated on her chopping, 'we're not going clubbing, just out for a meal and a chat.'

'Neil says that's what she always says and then she rolls in drunk at all hours,' Ash blurted out.

Laura put down the knife and eyeballed her daughter. 'And how often do I roll in drunk?'

'Never,' Adam said loyally.

'Exactly. Now, I'm going out with Penny, not turning into her. Anyway, I'm sure Neil is exaggerating.'

'He's not exaggerating.'

Laura sighed and picked up the knife. 'Sometimes, Ash, I think your whole reason for being is to disagree with me.'

'Sometimes I think your whole reason for being is to make me miserable,' Ash retorted.

Laura looked at her, horrified. 'Ashling Dillon, how dare you talk to me like that?'

Ash shrugged and turned to leave.

'Don't you dare walk away from me,' Laura warned her. 'Get back here and apologize this instant.'

Ash turned around, but remained stubbornly mute.

'Ash,' Adam gave her a sharp nudge.

'Sorry.'

Laura met her daughter's defiant eyes and swallowed back the hurt. 'You look it. Get out of my sight.'

Ash ran from the room and Adam came over and put an arm round his mother. 'She doesn't mean it.'

Laura smiled and nodded, not trusting herself to speak.

'I'll go and talk to her.' He pecked her cheek and followed his sister upstairs.

Laura abandoned dinner, cleaned her hands and, wiping her eyes, went into the study. There was a message waiting for her and she hit the enter key gratefully.

My dear Laura, you have made my day with your message. I am
looking forward to my visit, although it seems so far away. If
only you could meet me in Paris. One night, Laura, will you? G

Laura stared at the screen. She couldn't possibly go. It was out of the question. And then she thought of a number of women she knew who often went on shopping trips to Madrid and Rome, Barcelona and Paris, even New York; why shouldn't she? But, she realized, she couldn't go alone, no one did that. She could pretend to be going with a group but, no, that was too risky. There was only one person she could take, only one person who wouldn't judge her, only one person who would think it was a great idea. The only problem would be explaining it to her family.

'Mum?'

She whirled around to see Ash in the doorway. 'What is it?' she said curtly, fumbling behind her for the switch.

'I'm sorry,' Ash mumbled, hanging her head.

Laura raised an eyebrow. 'Are you, or did Adam just persuade you to say so?'

Ash said nothing.

Laura sighed. 'Okay, apology accepted, just don't think you'll be going out tonight.'

Ashling's head sprang up. 'But I promised Neil—'

'Then you can un-promise him.'

'Please, Mum—'

'That's enough, Ash, you're grounded.'

'Fine.' Ash flounced off, leaving Laura feeling drained. So much for the apology.

Chapter Thirty-three

10.45 a.m., Sunday, 16th August

Molly shot a sidelong glance at Ellen. Her due date had come and gone, and she hadn't had as much as a twinge. The girl was putting on a brave face, but she was on edge and ready to fly off the handle at the slightest provocation. Molly was keeping her head down and trying to help by putting on the washing, hoovering, and making her friend some ginger tea and a banana sandwich – her latest passion.

'Stop fussing,' Ellen growled.

'Sorry.'

'And stop apologizing.'

'Sor—' Molly grinned. 'Why don't you come to brunch with me? My folks would be delighted to see you.'

Ellen shook her head. 'Thanks, Moll, but I'm not feeling very sociable.'

'That's okay, but if you won't come with me, let me drop you over to your Mum's.'

'No thanks, she fusses more than you do. I'll be fine here.'

Molly looked at her doubtfully. 'Then at least go back to bed for a couple of hours – you were up half the night.'

'It's hard to get comfortable, and I'm too wound up to sleep.'

'If Laura was here, she'd be saying you'd better sleep now because you won't have that luxury once the baby comes.'

Ellen gave a wry grin. 'There you go, another reason not to go to the brunch.'

Molly sighed. 'Will I stay?'

'No!' Ellen waved her away with her hands. 'Go and leave me to feel miserable in peace.'

'Call me if you get the slightest pain,' Molly ordered.

'I will, I promise.'

When she was alone, Ellen went up to her bedroom, lowered herself onto the bed and pulled her photograph album from the bedside press. It was full of snaps from her childhood and the early years of her career, with lots of shots of her and her friends with weird hairstyles in strange colours; they always made Ellen smile. She turned the pages until she found what she was looking for. There weren't that many photos of Andrew, despite the fact they'd been together for years. It was because Andrew fancied himself as a photographer and was usually on the other side of the lens. The first was one taken at a Christmas party. Her arms were slung rather drunkenly around his neck and he was laughing straight into the camera. Most of the other shots had been taken on her phone. Ellen had deleted them all, but not before she'd downloaded them to her PC and printed them off. She had broken up with Andrew, having decided her child must come first, but she hadn't stopped loving him. She rummaged for a tissue as a tear plopped on to the page. Damn, she was just so emotional these days. It was Molly's visit to Barbara that had started her off this week. It was great to know that Andrew was okay, wonderful to hear he was working, but at the same time it made her long for the feel of his arms around her. She ached to have him hold her, to touch and marvel at her bump, to squeeze her hand as she went through labour and to tell her he loved her as he held their newborn child in his arms.

The urge to pick up the phone and call him was intense and she had to sit on her hands to stop herself. She had been strong for so long, she couldn't fall at the last fence. Ellen released her hands and spread them across her bump, smiling through her tears as she got a hefty kick. 'It's all for you, buster,' she murmured. 'I hope you appreciate that. And maybe, just maybe, you'll get to meet your daddy sooner than we thought.' She winced as she felt a twinge in her lower back and stretched out on the bed, tucking a pillow under her bump. Perhaps a nap wasn't such a bad idea after all.

As Molly cycled along the seafront in the misty rain, she was thinking about Declan. He had called first thing, sounding rather agitated and proceeded to quiz her about what she'd been up to lately. It had been strange given that they talked most days and she gave him a running commentary on Ellen and her mum, she'd even told him about Ashling's troubled friend. When she'd reminded him of this, though, he'd been dismissive and irritable.

'Sorry I've nothing more exciting to tell you. Will I make something up?' she'd joked.

He'd been silent for a moment and then, 'Seen Gareth lately?'

'Eh? Yeah, we met up during the week.'

'You never mentioned that.'

'I forgot,' Molly lied.

'So?' he asked.

'So?'

'Why did you meet up?' He sounded annoyed.

'He wanted to make sure I was remaining faithful.'

'And are you?'

'I haven't had the opportunity not to,' she snapped, beginning to wonder why she'd held back with Luke if she was going to be under suspicion anyway. 'What is this, Declan?' And then she knew. 'You knew I'd met Gareth; you've talked to him, haven't you?'

'Yes,' he admitted.

'So why didn't you just say so? Were you trying to trip me up, trying to catch me out in a lie?'

'No, he just sounded a bit concerned about you and he got me thinking. It's hard, Moll, being all the way over here—'

'I didn't make you go,' Molly heard herself saying, 'or perhaps I did.'

He gave a tired sigh. 'Now, what does that mean?'

She hesitated, thought about holding her tongue, but maybe it was time for some honesty. 'I don't think you want to marry me, Declan. To be honest, I think that you were delighted when Enco asked you to go to Japan, it was the excuse you'd been looking for.'

'That's ridiculous!'

'Is it?' she challenged. 'I don't think so. If you think about it—'

'Hang on a sec, Molly.'

'Pardon?' She could hear him putting his hand over the phone and talking to someone else and then he was back.

'Molly, I have to go.'

'Why, what's wrong?'

'I'll talk to you tomorrow, bye.'

And he hung up, leaving her sitting there, and wondering what the hell was the point.

It had been very strange, she thought now as she peddled up towards the Merrion Gates. Perhaps he'd just made an excuse to get off the phone so as not to deal with her accusation, but there had definitely been someone in the background and it had sounded like a girl. She had this image of a sloe-eyed beauty with porcelain skin, complete with kimono and fan. In fact, uncannily like the doll that sat on her mother's dressing table. She grinned at her own silliness. It was probably just someone in work asking him a question. Although, when he'd called, it would have been about seven o'clock in the evening his time, and it was Saturday so he couldn't have been in work. She remembered that he had told her that one of his colleagues had invited him to his home a few times, so that must have been where he was calling from. Had this colleague a pretty, kimono-clad sister, she wondered? Still, at least he'd called. He'd hardly have done that if he was in the middle of chatting up some girl. It must have been room service, or a waitress in the hotel restaurant, that was it. But why had he hung up?

'You look as if you have the weight of the world on your shoulders,' her father remarked, as she took off her helmet and fluffed up her hair.

'No, I'm fine, just a bit worried about Ellen. I hate leaving her on her own, but she wouldn't come with me.'

'She's a sensible girl, I'm sure she'll be fine.'

'I know.' She reached up to kiss his cheek. 'How's Mum?'

He smiled happily. 'Sitting in the kitchen, giving orders.'

'Who's here?' Molly asked; she hadn't noticed any cars as she came in.

'Laura and Rory and Natalie too, only she's just been sent out for more bread.'

'I could have picked that up on the way.'

Oliver shrugged. 'It's okay, she didn't mind. She's a very obliging girl; your mother and I would be lost without her.'

He led the way into the kitchen. 'Molly's here,' he announced.

'Hi.' She bent to kiss her mother, who was looking pretty in a pink top and white palazzo pants that almost completely concealed her plaster. 'What great trousers! Good thinking, Mum.'

'It was Natalie's brainwave. She was in town yesterday and saw them. She thought they'd be perfect for me. She got me a pair in black as well.'

'Wasn't that kind of her?' Laura drawled, rolling her eyes at Molly, before turning the sausages.

'Don't start, you two,' Belle warned mildly.

'Don't start what?' Rory walked in, a duster and polish in his hand.

'Nothing.' Molly stared at him. 'What on earth are you doing with those?'

'Don't ask,' he muttered, then flashed his mother a bright smile. 'Anything else you want me to do, Mother dear?'

Belle smiled. 'No, darling, you can sit down now.'

'I think I'll go and meet Natalie.'

'You do have it bad, don't you?' Laura said, adding bacon to the pan.

Rory pulled a face at her and then slipped out of the kitchen.

'Is this as serious as it looks?' Molly asked, sitting down at the table.

'It seems to be,' Belle said. 'I've never seen Rory so content.'

'He's working hard too,' Oliver added, breaking eggs into a bowl. 'Natalie is a great influence on him.'

'That's something, I suppose,' Laura said grudgingly.

'I'm glad,' Molly said.

'How's Ellen?' Belle asked.

'Miserable. I asked her to come with me, but she's beyond socializing.'

'It's a stressful time,' Laura pointed out, 'and when you're that big, all anyone talks to you about is the baby and when it's due and what your birth plan is.' She shook her head at the memory. 'It's such a lot of pressure at a time when you really don't need it.'

Oliver frowned as he poured the egg mixture into the pan. 'What's a birth plan?'

Belle laughed. 'Nothing you need to know about, trust me. So, is she spending the day on her own?'

'She certainly is not. I'm going straight back after we've eaten.'

Laura shot her sister a scornful look. 'She's not a child. She can pick up a phone if she needs help.'

'I know, but she's very nervous, and a bit scared about going through this without Andrew.'

'Better than going through it *with* Andrew,' Laura retorted. 'Getting rid of him was the most sensible thing she's ever done.'

'She knows that, but it doesn't stop her loving him,' Molly pointed out.

'I still can't believe Andrew was a drug addict. He seemed such a nice boy and so much fun.'

'Didn't you wonder why he was such fun, Mum?'

Oliver looked up from his eggs. 'It's easy for you to be superior, Molly. I've never met anyone on drugs before.' He frowned. 'At least, not that I know of. If you don't know what signs to look for, you accept people at face value.'

'You're right, I'm sorry,' Molly offered her father a penitent look. 'And, to be fair, Andrew hid his habit better than most.'

'How is he now?' her father asked.

'Doing well, apparently, and working.'

Laura flashed her a look of alarm. 'Don't tell me that Ellen is back in touch with him?'

'No, of course not.' Molly was regretting that she'd opened her mouth. 'I bumped into Andrew's sister recently and she was filling me in.'

'So, if he's better, why don't they get back together?' Belle asked.

Molly shook her head. 'It's not that simple, Mum. He may be off drugs at the moment, but that doesn't mean he won't have a relapse. I think he'd have to be clean for a long time before Ellen could trust him again, especially around her baby.'

'Their baby,' Laura corrected her. 'And what about his rights?'

'The child's or Andrew's?' Molly asked, refusing to rise to the bait.

'Both,' her sister shrugged.

'The child will have plenty of time to get to know Andrew, if and when it wants to. As for Andrew, perhaps having a child will be the incentive he needs to help him stay clean.'

'Except he doesn't know about it,' Laura pointed out.

'Don't you think that Ellen and the baby's safety should be the first priority?'

'Absolutely,' Belle nodded vehemently. 'Ellen's done exactly the right thing.'

'Don't you agree, Laura?' Oliver was frowning at her.

'Perhaps.' Laura wiped her hands and picked up her mobile. 'Excuse me, I'll just go and phone Robert and see what time he'll be here.'

'Why on earth does she do that?' Molly fumed as soon as the door closed behind her.

'She's in one of her moods,' Oliver sighed. 'She's been taking pot shots at everyone since she got here.'

'That's why Natalie offered to go to the shops,' Belle explained. 'I think she's terrified of your sister.'

'Who isn't?' Molly replied.

'I'm worried about her. She hasn't been herself lately. Perhaps she's had a row with Robert.' Belle shot her other daughter a hopeful look. 'Why don't you have a word with her?'

Molly blinked. 'Me?'

'Stay out of it,' Oliver advised. 'If she wants to talk, she knows where we are.'

*

They were sitting round the table, but the conversation wasn't flowing as easily as it usually did. 'So, Dad, did you go to Mass today?' Molly asked, more to fill the silence than anything else.

He shook his head smiling. 'I'm staying close to home for the moment, in case your mother needs me.'

'Pity you didn't do that the day of her accident.'

'Laura!' Belle and Rory said at the same time, while Natalie looked on, her eyes sad and reproachful.

Molly shook her head, wondering why her sister was being deliberately provocative.

'Any particular reason you're being so offensive?' Oliver asked conversationally.

Laura flushed slightly. 'Sorry. Everyone's very sensitive.'

'Whereas you're your usual annoying self,' Rory retorted.

Belle shot his girlfriend an apologetic smile. 'Forgive my family, Natalie, I don't know what's gotten into them.'

'She's the one causing trouble,' Rory said, pointing at his elder sister.

Oliver sighed. 'Don't be so juvenile, Rory, you're as bad as each other.'

'Charming.' Laura pushed away her plate and stood up.

'Please sit down, Laura,' Belle said tiredly.

'I'm not hungry. I'm going for a walk.'

'Oh, come on, Laura,' Molly said, catching her sister's hand.

Laura shook it off. 'Finish your meal. Sorry for upsetting you all.'

'But what about Robert and the children?' Belle asked.

'I won't be long, Mum,' Laura promised, and was gone.

There was a pregnant pause, and then Rory turned to his girl-friend. 'You don't have to be mad to live here, but it helps.'

'I'm sorry, my dear,' Oliver added, 'it's hard to believe some-times, that my children are adults.'

'Hey, leave me out of this,' Molly protested.

'You have your moments too,' Oliver smiled.

'Is your family quite as mad as ours?' Belle asked Natalie.

'My family just don't talk at all,' she said honestly. 'I much prefer what you have, it's healthier.'

Molly looked at Rory, but he just shook his head.

'Any more food?' he asked his dad.

Oliver hopped to his feet. 'There's some scrambled eggs left.'

'Pile it on.' Rory handed over his plate.

'Glutton,' Molly grinned and turned to put more bread in the toaster for him.

Chapter Thirty-four

'Are you sure you won't come with us?' Robert asked, his voice cool.

'No, you know I hate those crash-bang movies.' Laura summoned up a smile for her family, and tousled Adam's hair. 'You go and stuff yourselves with popcorn and I'll curl up in front of the telly.' She watched them leave, Ashling hopping into the front seat, obviously delighted that her mother had stayed behind. Laura waved goodbye and then went out to the kitchen, took a bottle of wine from the fridge and poured herself a large glass. She should call her parents, but she wasn't up to an inquisition tonight; she'd call in the morning.

It had been a bit juvenile stomping out of their kitchen like that yesterday, but Laura didn't care. She'd had enough of her smug, self-righteous family that morning. She'd had enough of everybody. Her daughter, who barely talked to her, had added insult to injury by getting close to Molly. Robert was making noises about mounting bills and the need for her to curb her excessive spending – excessive! He should live with Penny for a week and then he'd realize what extravagance was. But she couldn't sell a trip to Paris to him when he was in this mood and it was unlikely he'd believe her if she said she'd won another competition.

So, with her mood already dark enough, watching her dad fussing around Belle like the world's greatest husband, had been just too much to take. Sometimes she felt an urge to tell Belle the truth about her husband, and yesterday had been one of those times. Still, at least her father's adultery – okay, she didn't know for sure he was adulterous – made her feel a bit more normal. It was easier than watching her brother behave like a love-sick puppy and Molly moon around about which of the two attractive men pursuing her she loved most. Everything about her family today seemed to highlight the lack of love in her life.

The passion she'd shared with Gerard was like nothing she'd ever experienced before. She found herself thinking about him a lot, especially in bed at night. And then, last night, Robert had appeared and slipped into bed beside her, a hopeful smile on his face. Right there and then, Laura knew that he'd agree to her flying to the Maldives for a month if she allowed him to make love to her, but she still couldn't bring herself to do it.

'For God's sake, Laura, it's been months,' he'd said angrily, swinging his legs out of bed and pulling on a robe. 'What's going on? Are you sick?' And then he'd turned to face her. 'Is there someone else?'

'Of course not,' she'd said immediately. 'I'm sorry, Robert, I'm just not in the mood.'

'You never are,' he'd muttered and left. When she woke in the early hours of the morning, she was still alone. It was the first time in their married life that he'd slept in the spare room.

Laura knew she should apologize to Robert and offer some excuse, tell him she hadn't been feeling well or something. He was a good man, and he'd done little to deserve her scorn, and a lot to deserve her gratitude and loyalty. But she couldn't look him in the eye and tell him everything was fine, she wasn't that good an actress; she wasn't Penny. And so instead, they weren't talking except through the children. Adam hadn't seemed to notice but Ashling was agog with curiosity and watching them like a hawk. She was also cuddling up to her dad and chatting away to him at any and every opportunity, and being more annoying than usual. It had been a relief when she'd suggested a movie and Robert had jumped at the idea. Ever the gentleman, he had invited Laura along, but hadn't seemed surprised or bothered when she'd refused.

As soon as they were gone, she picked up the phone. 'Hi, Penny, it's me.'

'Oh, hello, Laura. You're not cancelling Friday, I hope.'

'No, but I have the house to myself tonight and I wondered if you'd like to come over.'

'Love to. Give me thirty minutes. Shall I stop off and get some wine?'

'No, just bring yourself.'

Penny giggled. 'Boozing on a Monday, how wicked! See you soon.'

Laura hung up and quickly tidied the place, feeling brighter at the thought of some stimulating company. She had been very hard on Penny in the past, writing her off as an oversexed lush. But since she'd got to know her a bit better, and since Gerard had come along, Laura was better able to understand the woman's behaviour. She was a smart, vivacious character, and it took a lot to hold her interest; she wasn't really cut out to be a wife or mother. Robert didn't know how lucky he was; Laura felt she was much easier to please. A few hours' shopping a week and a visit to the beauty salon were enough to keep her happy. And though initially it had been hard, she'd thrown herself wholeheartedly into motherhood. In fact, she missed those days when the twins had pestered her to join in their games. She remembered how Ash used to love to play with her mother's hair, her small mouth twisted in concentration as she combed and plaited, rolled and twisted. They had been so much closer then, and Laura had assumed it would always be that way. But she realized now that she was the last person Ash would turn to if she had a problem, and that hurt.

Laura shook her head at her silliness. She shouldn't take it so personally. Ash was a teenager like any other, but her children's growing independence made her feel superfluous and old. She needed something or someone else in her life. She needed something or someone to satisfy her. If she had, she was convinced she could be the wife and mother that Robert wanted her to be. And if she was discreet, then no one would get hurt. The trick was to use Penny as her alibi, without the other woman knowing all the details. Though Laura liked her more now than she previously had, she knew she could never trust her to keep her mouth shut. Perhaps if she became Penny's confidante and best friend she would be too nervous to tell tales on Laura. Laura took out a box of chocolate truffles she'd been saving, and popped a second bottle of wine in the fridge. Robert and the twins would be gone for hours; that should be plenty of time for her and Penny.

Penny was on her third glass, her cheeks were flushed and her eyes bright, but whether that was as a result of alcohol or excitement, Laura wasn't sure. She had been careful to sip her wine, determined to keep a clear head, had kept Penny's glass topped up and encouraged the woman to talk. 'I don't know how you do it,' she said now, shaking her head in wonder. 'I would never have the courage to approach a man. The only reason I had that –' she hesitated delicately – 'brief encounter in Galway, was because he came onto me and I'd had too much to drink.'

'You're lucky to have met a Frenchman,' Penny said with an envious sigh. 'I've ended up with some boorish idiots. There's nothing more depressing than seeing them again when you're sober and you think, How did I end up with someone like that?' She waved her glass precariously. 'The evil drink has a lot to answer for. Still,' she gave a throaty laugh, 'it also oils the wheels and gets you in the mood. I'd never be able to have sex with Mark without a few gin and tonics inside me.'

Laura looked at her in surprise. Penny's husband was no Pierce Brosnan or Brad Pitt, but he wasn't exactly ugly. 'I always thought you two were quite active in that area.'

'Oh, you're so proper, Laura,' Penny gave a hoot of laughter. 'And yes, we are reasonably "active", but don't you find it all a bit boring at times? The reason so many people are unfaithful is down to the thrill of the chase. I know I can have Mark anytime and so,' she shrugged, 'I'm not really that interested. Show me a man that I can't have, however, now that's a different story.'

Laura digested this and nodded slowly. 'I see your point. Gerard made me feel special.

'Exactly.' Penny nodded vehemently. 'Husbands don't notice when you get your hair done or wear a new dress, and so you stop bothering. Before you know it, you're going to the supermarket in a tracksuit without make-up.' She shook her head gravely. 'It's a slippery slope, Laura. Mark should be grateful to my other "friends".' She made quote marks in the air. 'It's thanks to them that I can put up with him and, thanks to them, that I look after my body.'

'And you do look great,' Laura agreed. 'Your figure is amazing, and most twenty-year-olds would kill for your skin.'

Penny said, quite seriously, 'I gave up smoking, I stopped using sun beds – I don't want to end up at sixty with skin like leather. I should cut down on the drink too but, lord, you have to have something, don't you?'

'You wear lovely clothes too,' Laura sighed enviously. 'I passed up on a chance to go to Paris on a shopping trip because Robert's been complaining I spend too much money.' She slipped in the lie and hoped Penny would pick up on it. 'I was so disappointed, and annoyed, to be honest. I spend very little on clothes, and I've never gone on a girls' shopping trip before.'

'You and I could always go somewhere together,' Penny suggested.

Laura looked at her in delight, and sent up a prayer of thanks. 'Oh, Penny, do you think we could?'

'I don't see why not.'

'But what about Robert? He'd still be moaning about me wasting money.'

'Oh, we can easily figure that out, there are always lots of cheap offers on air fares these days. And I can hold on to any clothes you buy and you can sneak them into your wardrobe a few days later when he's not around.'

'God, you're devious,' Laura said, laughing.

Penny gave a drunken shrug. 'Comes naturally! Now, what about our night out? Where shall we go?'

'I don't mind where we go, but no chatting up men, okay?'

Penny's eyes widened innocently. 'Of course not, Laura, you can trust me.'

Yes, Laura thought, I think perhaps I can.

Chapter Thirty-five

When the text message came through, Ellen was sitting in the garden, pretending to read a magazine while Molly sat at the kitchen table working.

> I'm in Dublin airport for the next couple of hours, will you meet me? Luke

Molly stared at it, then looked at her watch. It would take her thirty or forty minutes to get to the airport so, if she wanted to see him, she'd have to move quickly. She went out to Ellen. 'Did you say your Mum's coming over?'

Ellen nodded absently. 'Yeah, she said she'd bring lunch.'

'Great, I just need to pop out for a bit.'

'Yeah?' Ellen eyed her curiously.

'I need to see Tess about a case. Can I get you anything before I go out?'

'I'm fine.'

'A cardigan?' Molly shivered. There was a definitely a hint of autumn in the air and Ellen had been out here for ages.

'No, I'm roasting,' Ellen assured her.

Molly studied her through narrowed eyes. 'You do look a bit

flushed.' She put a hand to Ellen's forehead. 'You're not coming down with something, are you?'

'I'm fine,' Ellen insisted. 'Now go.'

'Right. I won't be long. Do you want me to pick up anything while I'm out?'

Ellen shook her head. 'You know what Mum's like, she'll bring enough to feed an army for a week.'

Molly laughed. 'Okay, see you later.'

When she was in the car, she sent Luke a message.

See you in abt 30 mins.

As she set out, willing herself to drive a little faster than she normally would, she wondered what Luke was doing in Dublin and why he needed to see her so urgently. She had mixed feelings about seeing him again, but why was he back so soon? Something must have happened with his wife, she surmised. Either he'd realized he really did love her after all, or else he was definitely going to leave her. Strangely, both explanations made Molly feel sick. She instinctively felt jealous of Adriana, but didn't want to be responsible for either her or Declan's unhappiness. She must try to be strong and send Luke away. They had no future anyway; his mother wouldn't allow it, and who could blame her?

The traffic approaching the airport was as chaotic as usual, and then she had to circle the car park a few times before she found a spot. Luke had sent another text saying he would be at the meeting point in the arrivals hall and, once she'd locked the door, she sprinted through cars and between pedestrians laden with baggage, realizing as she went that she hadn't even thought to comb her hair. She was pulling her fingers through it self-consciously, as she walked into Arrivals, when she saw him wave frantically at her, a broad smile on his face.

'Hello, Molly.' He bent to kiss her cheek, then stood back and gave her a tender smile.

'Hi.' She looked up at him shyly thinking how handsome he was.

'Thank you for coming. I'm sorry for the short notice, but I'm on a flight to Shannon in a couple of hours.'

Molly frowned as she followed him to a table in the coffee area. 'I don't understand.'

'I'm taking a group to Limerick for three days. They flew directly to Shannon, but I came via Dublin because I wanted to see you.'

'Is there something wrong?' she asked, perching on the edge of a stool.

He shook his head. 'I've just been thinking about you constantly. I wanted to be sure that I hadn't made it all up in my head, and to make sure that I hadn't imagined your feelings.'

Molly looked into his handsome face with a sad smile. 'You have a bad memory. I told you, regardless of feelings, we have no future.'

'But you agreed to see me again and,' he took her hand, 'you're here now. That must count for something.'

'I haven't changed my mind, Luke. I don't want to hurt Declan, Adriana or your mother, for that matter.'

'Yet you're ready to hurt us,' he countered.

'This is pointless.' Molly looked at her watch.

'Don't go,' he said immediately, standing up. 'I'll get us some coffee.'

'Luke—'

'Please, Molly. Let me get some coffee. Let's talk, just for a few more minutes.' He looked into her eyes. 'Don't I at least deserve that?'

'Okay, Luke.' She sighed as she watched him join the queue at the counter. As usual, several women followed him with their eyes. She looked at him, seeing what they saw: a tall, confident man with a gorgeous smile and glorious blue eyes. Like them, she was able to appreciate his good looks. And then she realized that she was looking at him in a dispassionate, objective way. 'I'm not in love with him,' she murmured to herself and smiled with relief.

'Molly!'

She looked up and was stunned and horrified to see Declan waving enthusiastically at her, a wide grin on his face. 'Oh my God,' she muttered, standing up with a hesitant smile as he pushed his trolley through the crowds towards her. She looked around for Luke and saw that he was in the process of being served.

'You got my message!' Declan cried as he neared her and then, pushing aside his trolley, gathered her into his arms. 'We were just boarding in Heathrow when I sent it, but I wasn't sure it had worked. Oh, Molly, it's so great to see you.'

As he hugged her tightly to him, Molly watched Luke turn around with the coffees in his hand. He stopped in his tracks as he took in the situation. Some of the people around them were also looking on with amused curiosity. 'Let's get out of here,' she murmured into Declan's neck and, slipping her hand into his, tugged him towards the exit.

'Why are you here?' Molly broke in. Declan, uncharacteristically, hadn't stopped talking since he'd arrived. She put her ticket into the machine and, when the barrier rose, pulled carefully out into the road.

'Gareth called me again.'

Molly turned startled eyes on him. 'What?'

'Look out!' he yelled, and she braked hard as a man pushed a trolley straight out in front of her.

'Jesus,' she breathed and sat for a moment.

'Will I drive?'

'You've been travelling for two days,' she reminded him. 'You were saying?'

'Gareth called. I don't know what you two were talking about when you went out last week, but he seems to think you're on the verge of dumping me.'

'I never said that,' she protested.

'Well, maybe not, but he said that I should get my ass back here.'

She risked a quick sideways glance. 'What about your job?'

'I told my boss all about you, and he said that they were very pleased with my progress and that I could come home for a week to sort things out.'

'Sort things out? We're not talking about a dodgy boiler or an old car.'

'You know what I mean,' he said, clearly irritated. 'My God, Molly, I've just travelled halfway around the world to be with you, you could try sounding a little more . . .'

'What?' she prompted, raising an eyebrow. 'Grateful?'

'No, of course not. Why are you being like this?'

She sighed and patted his thigh. 'Sorry, but this is all so unexpected.'

'I understand.' He yawned widely.

'I'll drop you at the flat, you can have a sleep and we can talk properly later.'

'Where are you going?' he asked, sounding both annoyed and disappointed.

'I'm staying with Ellen, remember?'

'Oh, right. But now that I'm back—'

'Now that you're back, nothing!' She shook her head in disbelief. 'She's four days past her due date, Declan. I can't leave her on her own now.'

'No, of course not,' he agreed immediately. 'I tell you what, once I've had a snooze and a shower, I'll come over and take you both out to dinner.'

Molly shot him a grateful smile. 'Okay, thanks, that would be nice.'

'And when Ellen's tucked up in bed for the night, you can tell me why my brother was so worried about you.'

'You should ask Gareth that,' she replied, keeping her eyes on the road.

'I intend to,' he assured her.

They travelled in silence for a while, and then Declan asked, 'How's your Mum doing?'

'She's much better,' Molly said, relieved to change the subject. 'She can handle the crutches like a pro now.'

'And your dad and Rory, are they coping?'

She smiled. 'Just about. Laura's filled the freezer twice already, so at least they don't have to cook.'

'Any chance of her filling ours?' he asked hopefully.

Molly laughed. 'None. Anyway, if you're going to be hanging around doing nothing for a week, you'll have plenty of time to cook.'

He put a hand on her leg. 'I was hoping to spend my time in a more creative manner.'

'I don't have the week off,' she reminded him, 'and you're forgetting Ellen.'

His face fell. 'You don't have to be with her every minute of every day, surely?'

'I'll be there whenever she wants me to be,' Molly said stubbornly, at the same time wondering why she was being so difficult. Declan had come home because he was afraid of losing her; he didn't deserve this. 'You can come over every night and visit and we can go to the pub and talk,' she relented.

'And have a cuddle in the car?' he added with a wicked grin.

Molly shook her head, smiling. 'What are you like?'

*

After Molly left Declan, she drove around the corner, parked and sent Gareth a message.

Declan here. You have some explaining to do. Call me. M

After she'd sent it, she took a deep breath and called Luke. There was no answer, and it went to his voicemail. She thought about hanging up, but she had no idea when she might get an opportunity to talk to him again so, after the beep, she left a message, her voice shaking. 'Luke, it's me, Molly. I'm so sorry for walking out like that. I didn't know what else to do. Declan appeared out of nowhere. He thought I'd come to the airport to collect him. Text me and let me know when we can talk. I'm really sorry, Luke.'

She was nearing Marino when her phone rang and she grabbed it.

'Molly, it's Gareth.'

'Hang on, I'm in the car, let me pull in.' Molly saw a filling station up ahead and, indicating, she pulled in, parked and turned off the engine. 'Gareth?'

'Yeah, I'm still here.'

'What's going on?' she asked without preamble. 'I just picked Declan up at the airport and he says it's because you told him he should come home.'

'Yeah, I did.'

'But you said you weren't going to say anything!'

'I said I wouldn't tell him about Luke,' he corrected her calmly, 'and I didn't. But I felt he deserved an opportunity to come home and fight for you.'

'Fight for me? Gareth, this isn't the Middle Ages! I do have a mind of my own.'

'I just don't think he realized how upset you were about him leaving, and I thought he should,' Gareth defended himself. 'Aren't you impressed that he just hopped on a plane and came home to you?'

Molly said nothing for a moment. 'Well, he's here now and it's between us what happens next so, please, stay out of it, okay?'

'Okay,' Gareth agreed.

'Fine. Thank you. Goodbye,' Molly said and, with a weary sigh, started the engine again and drove on to Ellen's house.

Chapter Thirty-six

2.30 p.m., Tuesday, 18th August

'You just missed Mum,' Ellen said prone on the sofa, the remote control on her bump. 'We left you some quiche in the fridge.'

'Thanks, I'm not hungry.' Molly lifted Ellen's feet, sat down and rested them gently on her lap. 'I'm not sure I want to eat ever again.'

'What's up? Is it Luke?'

Molly nodded. 'And Declan.'

'What? Oh, my God, does Declan know?'

'No.'

'Come on, spit it out,' Ellen said impatiently.

'Well, I didn't actually go to a meeting,' she admitted, shooting her friend a guilty look. 'I went to the airport to see Luke.'

'You didn't!' Ellen's eyes widened in astonishment. 'So is this it? Are you two getting back together? Are you leaving Declan?'

'Slow down,' Molly protested, putting up a hand to ward off the questions. 'Luke rang me. He's on his way to Limerick, but came via Dublin because he wanted to see me. We didn't get a chance to talk properly because, while he was getting us coffee . . .'

'Yes?' Ellen prompted.

Molly met her eyes. 'Declan walked into the arrivals hall.'

'No!' Despite her bulk, Ellen bounced up and the remote fell to the floor. 'Declan's here?'

Molly nodded. 'I just dropped him off at the flat.'

Ellen shook her head in confusion. 'I don't understand.'

'I'm not sure I do myself.'

'Why on earth did you arrange to meet Luke at the airport when you knew Declan was flying in?' Ellen looked at her as if she was mad.

'I didn't *know* Declan was flying in! Apparently, Gareth rang him and told him that he should come home or he might lose me.'

'Wow. And he walked in on you and Luke together?'

'Thankfully, no. Like I said, Luke had gone to get coffees. It seems Declan sent me a message from Heathrow asking me to meet him—' She pulled out her phone and frowned at it. 'I never did get that message. Anyway, he just assumed that I was there to meet him.'

'And Luke?'

Molly groaned and shook her head. 'I grabbed Declan and got him out of there before he came back.'

'Poor Luke.'

'I thought you were on Declan's side.'

'I am,' Ellen said, 'but you've got to feel sorry for the guy. Did you call him?'

'I tried to, but his phone's switched off; he must be in the air. I left him a message.'

Ellen watched her closely. 'Saying?'

'Just that I was sorry and that I'd talk to him later.'

'So what will you say?'

'God knows,' Molly said miserably.

Ellen was thoughtful for a moment and then smiled. 'You chose Declan.'

'What?'

'On the spur of the moment, without time to think about it, you instinctively chose Declan.'

'He's my fiancé, of course I chose him.' Molly shrugged. 'He doesn't know anything about Luke, and I had to keep it that way.'

'But if you were planning to leave him, it wouldn't matter,' Ellen pointed out, her smile growing smugger by the second.

'Perhaps you're right,' Molly allowed, 'except I'd made my decision before Declan arrived.'

'And?' Ellen's eyes searched her face for the answer.

'There's no future for me and Luke.'

'Really?' Ellen looked relieved but confused.

Molly nodded. 'I was watching other women eyeing him up—'

'He's really that gorgeous?'

Molly chuckled. 'He really is.'

Ellen sighed. 'I can't believe you don't have a photo you can show me. How is that possible after dating him for so long?'

Molly looked away. 'There are probably some buried in a case somewhere in Dad's attic.'

'Have a look the next time you're over,' Ellen told her. 'Now, where were we?'

'I was just saying about the way women look at him. It was the same when we were dating.'

'Didn't that bother you?' Ellen asked curiously.

'No, Luke never noticed and he never flirted, despite plenty of opportunity.'

'Is there a bright-yellow circle around this guy's head?'

Molly laughed at Ellen's dubious expression. 'It's just the way he was, still is. Anyway, when girls looked at him, I just felt lucky and proud. But at the airport, I realized that I didn't feel proud or jealous or lucky; I didn't really feel anything except a great affection for a guy that used to be my best friend.'

'Oh, stop,' Ellen flapped her hands, 'you're going to make me cry. Though, to be fair, it doesn't take much at the moment. A sick lamb on *Emmerdale* and I'm in floods. So, Laura was right: meeting him has helped. Now you can marry Declan and live happily ever after.' She paused as Molly's smile died. 'What?'

'I know I've no future with Luke,' Molly agreed, 'but I'm not sure I have one with Declan either.'

'Oh, Moll.' Ellen swung her feet down and shuffled over to put her arms around her friend.

'It's okay, I'm fine,' Molly said, though she was close to tears.

Ellen sat back and brushed the hair out of Molly's eyes with gentle fingers. 'Is it just because he went to Japan?' she asked, offering Molly a tissue.

Molly took the tissue and twisted it between her fingers. 'That and something Gareth said.'

Ellen frowned. 'Gareth?'

'When we were talking the other night, he was asking about Luke again,' she explained. 'I told him he was barking up the wrong tree, making a fuss over nothing, but he said Luke loved me, that he could tell from the way he looked at me.'

'I really wish I'd met this guy,' Ellen grumbled. 'Go on.'

'Well, then I asked Gareth if Declan looked at me in the same way.' Molly sniffed and put a hand up to her mouth. 'But he couldn't answer, he was stumped.'

'Oh, don't read anything into that,' Ellen protested, 'you just caught him on the hop. Declan adores you.'

Molly looked at her with solemn eyes. 'Don't say that to make me feel better, Ellen. I was honest with you about Andrew, you have to be too.'

Ellen stared at her. 'Molly, really, of course he cares—'

Molly held her gaze. 'Please, Ellen?'

Her friend fell back against the sofa with a sigh. 'Okay, then.

I think he cares for you a great deal, probably more than he's ever cared for anyone before—'

Molly felt her stomach lurch. 'But?'

Ellen shifted around, looking uneasy. 'Well, he's not the most demonstrative guy. You're so giving and open, whereas he's quite controlled and unemotional.'

'He's a very private person,' Molly said, defensively. 'We can't all be chatterboxes.'

Ellen nodded quickly. 'Of course, you're right.'

'Don't placate me, Ellen.'

'I can't win, can I?' Ellen groaned.

Molly patted her hand. 'Sorry. I know Declan has been a bit off in recent months, but he's been working hard, worrying constantly, and trying to hide it, although he does confide in Gareth.'

'They're close?'

Molly nodded. 'Very. And Gareth can get through to him and make him see the lighter side.'

Ellen frowned. 'Can't you do that?'

'Sometimes, but not always. It's a drawback of my job. When I show any interest in Declan's problems, he complains I'm treating him like a patient.'

'I suppose that's natural.'

'Yeah, Laura's the same.' Molly grinned. 'It doesn't seem to bother you, though.'

'No, analyse away; I need all the help I can get,' Ellen laughed.

Molly laughed too. 'You're the sanest, most level-headed person I know.'

Ellen stretched back out on the sofa and looked at her. 'So, what will you do now?'

Molly sighed. 'Talk to him, I suppose. Declan's come all this way, so the least I can do is hear what he has to say. By the way, he wants to take us out for dinner.'

'Us? No way.' Ellen shook her head. 'You don't want me there.'

'Oh, please, Ellen, you have to come,' Molly begged her. 'I'm not ready for a heavy conversation yet. Anyway, if you come, you can observe us and give me your feedback.'

Ellen raised an eyebrow. 'What am I, one of your trainee counsellors?'

'It will be a good distraction from the other things on your mind,' Molly said with a meaningful look at Ellen's bump.

Ellen gave a weary sigh. 'I suppose it will. Okay, then, I'll come.'

'Excellent!' Molly beamed.

'But if you start getting all lovey-dovey, I'm out of there,' she warned.

Molly's lips twitched. 'No worries on that score, Declan's not the demonstrative type, remember?'

Declan had slept fitfully for almost three hours and, though exhausted, he knew there was no hope of getting back to sleep. He reached for the phone and called his brother, but just got his answering service. On impulse, he decided to go and visit Oliver and Belle; he hadn't seen them, after all, since the accident. Showered and dressed in fresh jeans and shirt, Declan took the train to Blackrock, stopping off to pick up a paperback and tired-looking carnations, but they were pink, and Belle loved pink.

It was Rory who opened the door, breaking into a smile when he saw his brother-in-law-to-be. 'Declan, how are ye?'

'Hi, Rory.'

'I thought you were gone for another few weeks.' Rory frowned. 'Wasn't that what all the fuss was about?'

'I'm only here for a few days, time off for good behaviour. I thought I'd visit the patient.'

'She's off out walking with Laura,' Rory said over his shoulder, leading the way towards the kitchen. 'Look who's here.'

Oliver, who was cleaning down the worktops, looked up and smiled when he saw Declan. 'Well, hello there.' He cleaned his hands and came to shake Declan's. 'This is a surprise.'

'I just got a few days off,' Declan said hastily.

'Excellent, I'm sure Molly is delighted.'

'I'm not so sure. She's so busy between work and Ellen, I'll be lucky to see her.'

'Ah, yes, she moved in with Ellen, I'd forgotten.' Oliver grinned. 'So you might have time to go for a pint one night?'

'I think that's a definite possibility,' Declan laughed.

'Coffee?' Rory held up the pot.

'Please. So, how is Belle?'

'Thriving,' Oliver said happily, sitting down at the table with Declan and accepting another coffee from his son. 'It took her a while to get used to the crutches, but now she's flying around.'

'I suppose she's banned from using ladders now.' Declan smiled.

Oliver raised his eyebrows. 'No one bans my wife from doing anything and, be warned, her daughters take after her.'

'I figured that out years ago,' Declan told him with a rueful smile. 'I keep my head down and do as I'm told.'

'Oh no, they don't like that either,' Oliver said. 'You have to be a man, just not too much of a man.'

'Shut up, Dad, or you'll put Declan off completely,' Rory laughed.

The phone rang in the hall and Oliver excused himself. 'That will be Larry. We're setting up a book club, Belle's getting involved too.'

'They've finally found something they can do together, that's nice.'

'It won't last a month,' Rory joked. 'They won't even be able to agree on *what* to read, never mind the book itself.'

Declan chuckled. 'So, how are things going with Natalie?'

'Good. In fact, very good.' Rory grinned. 'I may even take a leaf out of your book.'

'What, take four years to decide to marry?' Declan joked.

'Pop the question,' Rory said, turning bright red.

Declan almost choked on his coffee. 'Seriously?'

Rory shrugged. 'Thinking about it.'

Declan stared at him, searching for the right words. What would Molly say? 'It's a bit quick, mate. Don't rush into anything, you hardly know her.'

'I know her, Declan. She's a great girl.'

'Good, I'm happy for you but, like I said, there's no rush.'

'Well, I wasn't planning to do it today; I'll give it a few months.' Rory grinned at Declan's gobsmacked expression. 'Shouldn't you be selling this to me, Dec? Hope you're not having second thoughts?'

'Course not.' Declan scowled. 'I'd hardly be back in Dublin if I was.'

'Oh?'

Declan sighed. There was no harm in confiding in Rory, he was a good guy and knew how to keep his mouth shut. 'Gareth phoned me and said that he was worried about Molly.'

Immediately, Rory's face creased in concern. 'Why? What's wrong with her?'

'Nothing. Just, Gareth thought she might be having second thoughts about getting married.'

'Nah, I'm sure it's nothing. Don't get me wrong, mate, she was seriously pissed off at you going to Japan, but she's okay about that now. Mum's accident shook us all up, to be honest. When something like that happens, it kind of forces you to get your priorities in order.'

Declan nodded solemnly. 'True.'

'Still, you're here now, so you may as well make the most of it. Make a fuss of her, take her out and grovel.' Rory grinned. 'That usually works for Dad.'

Declan was sitting, reading a newspaper, at the kitchen table when Molly let herself into the flat a few hours later.

'Hi, Moll.' He stood up immediately and came to kiss her.

Molly smiled and moved out of his arms. 'Did you get any sleep?'

'A couple of hours. Then I went over to see your folks.'

She looked at him in surprise. 'That was nice of you.'

He shrugged. 'Nothing else to do, so I thought I'd say hello. You know they're setting up a book club? They've decided it's time they did something together.'

'It will never last,' Molly chuckled.

'They were already rowing about it when I left. Belle wanted to read *Ulysses*, and your dad was opting for the latest Dan Brown; they're a mad pair.' He grinned. 'I thought your mum looked well.'

Molly smiled. 'Yeah, she's doing great now.'

'She was out walking with Laura when I arrived; they'd been round the block twice.'

'Brilliant. So you were talking to Laura?'

'I kissed her,' he bragged, making her laugh. 'But I was only talking to her for a moment, she had to rush off.'

'Have you talked to Gareth?' she asked, not looking at him.

'No, but I left a message.' He nodded towards a vase of wilting carnations in the window. 'I got you those.'

She stared at them. 'Oh, right, thanks, that was nice of you.'

'So, any news? How was your day?'

'Okay.' How long exactly was he going to keep this up for, she wondered? Normally he'd barely look up when she walked in, rarely bought her flowers, and certainly didn't ask how her day had gone in that strange, falsely happy tone.

'Want a cuppa?'

'Declan, stop.' She sighed. 'You don't have to do this. Just relax, okay?'

He shrugged. 'Okay. Will we go for a walk along the seafront?'

She shook her head. 'Sorry, I'm tired and I'd love a long, hot soak.'

'No chance of that,' he joked.

She smiled and stood up. 'I'll settle for a short, tepid dip.'

He caught her hand as she passed, and pulled her to him. 'Want me to rub your back?'

'Declan, don't.' She pushed him away irritably.

'Oh, come on,' he said, a flicker of impatience in his eyes, 'I haven't seen you in nearly a month.'

'And whose fault is that?' she snapped before going into the bathroom and shutting the door firmly behind her. She was wrong, she knew; she should go straight back out and apologize, but she couldn't. He was behaving as if they should just take up where they left off. As if he was some kind of hero for having finally told his employer the truth. As if she should be grateful to him for coming home. She turned on the hot tap and sat on the loo as she waited for the bath to fill.

Life was strange. If Declan had walked into the arrivals hall just five minutes later, he'd have seen her with Luke. Maybe she shouldn't have dragged him away. Perhaps she should have allowed the two men to meet. Maybe it was the kick up the ass Declan needed. But then, that wouldn't have been fair on Luke. She reached over to dip a finger in the water and cursed when she found it was cold. Damn boiler. Now what? Did she stay in here like an idiot for thirty minutes or go back outside and face the music? As she was mulling over her limited options, there was a terse rap on the door and Declan walked in. 'You have a call,' he muttered and, shoving her mobile into her hand, walked out of the room and out of the flat.

Chapter Thirty-seven

7.45 p.m., Tuesday, 18th August

At first, Molly was riddled with guilt and shame, but now she was annoyed. Declan had not only walked out without his mobile, he'd taken the car, despite knowing that she needed it while she was staying with Ellen. 'Inconsiderate, selfish bastard,' she muttered as she cycled to Ellen's house. It was just ridiculous, storming out like that because a man had phoned her. Because, once Molly had got over her guilt and thought about it, she realized that Declan had no reason to think that she was up to anything. Talking to Luke had confirmed this. He apologized for phoning, but he'd been worried about her and had been careful enough to ask to speak to Miss Jackson when Declan answered.

'The only problem with that, is that you came up as Lucy on my phone,' Molly had explained.

'I'm sorry, Molly, I wasn't trying to cause trouble.'

'I know that,' she'd reassured him.

'Are you going to tell him about me?'

'I suppose I should. His brother has already met you, so it's probably only a matter of time before your name crops up. And now, after today . . .' she trailed off.

He was silent for a moment, and when he spoke, he sounded

hoarse. 'Will I see you next month, Molly? I could take some holidays, extend my stay—'

Molly had closed her eyes at the desperation in his voice. 'No, Luke, I'm sorry. There's no point.'

'He doesn't love you the way I do,' he said, sounding angry.

'You may be right.'

'But you don't love me the way you love him, do you?'

Tears had spilled onto her cheeks and she shook her head, even though he couldn't see her. 'I'm sorry, Luke.'

Ellen opened the door as soon as she stopped outside the house and held out her arms to welcome her friend. 'Hasn't he been in touch?' Molly had phoned to explain the situation and to apologize for being late.

Molly shook her head as she hopped off her bike. 'Stupid eejit. I finally gave in and called him, but he'd left his mobile in the bedroom.'

Ellen drew her inside and shut the door. 'He's probably with Gareth.'

Molly nodded. 'I'd like to be a fly on the wall for that conversation.'

'Are you worried?' Ellen asked sympathetically.

'No, I'm annoyed. He walked out of the house because a man phoned me. He didn't even give me a chance to explain.'

'What would you have said if he did?'

Molly sighed. 'I have absolutely no idea.'

'And you must remember that he got a call from his brother telling him to come home or he might lose you.'

'He still should have waited and talked to me,' Molly insisted. 'Oh, to hell with him. Come on, let's go and get some dinner.'

'We could stay in and order a pizza, if you'd prefer?' Ellen offered.

'No, let's go get you something really spicy and see if we can't shift this child of yours.'

They were sitting, munching their way through a basket of poppadoms, when Declan pressed his face against the window and mouthed 'Sorry'.

Ellen giggled. 'I think maybe he realizes he over-reacted.'

Molly suppressed a grin and studied her boyfriend, enjoying the fact that he was attracting a lot of attention, which was probably making him feel very uncomfortable.

He gestured to himself and then pointed at the empty chair at the table. Then he pointed at the poppadoms, licked his lips, patted his tummy, and then assumed the begging position of a dog.

There was a bubble of laughter in the restaurant. 'Oh, go on, love, let him come in,' one man called from a nearby table.

Molly looked back at Declan, rolled her eyes and waved for him to join them.

As he walked in, there was a short round of applause and he gave a small, embarrassed bow before sitting down. 'Thanks, Moll.'

'You're only here because you said you were buying dinner,' she told him.

He grinned from her to Ellen. 'My pleasure.'

They studied the menu and, after giving their order, Declan looked across at Ellen. 'Molly's been telling me that you're fed up waiting for Buster to arrive.'

She nodded. 'I think he's decided to stay in there; he's probably put up wallpaper and curtains and everything at this stage.'

Molly's eyes widened. 'You said he!'

Declan frowned. 'I thought you didn't know what it was?'

'I don't, but I have a feeling it's a boy,' Ellen admitted. 'It's probably something to do with the phenomenal kicks in the ribs I get.'

He laughed and then looked across at Molly. 'Sorry for running out on you, Moll.'

Molly shrugged, but said nothing.

'It's just that it said Lucy on your phone, but when I answered and it was a guy, well, it seemed a bit odd.'

'Then you should have talked to me,' Molly said quietly, 'not just marched out.'

'I should have. So?'

'Sorry?'

He held her gaze. 'I'm asking you about him now: who is he?'

'Ellen doesn't need to witness a row, Declan, she came here to eat.'

'It's not a row,' Declan said smoothly, watching Molly. 'We're just clearing up a misunderstanding, aren't we? You don't mind, Ellen, do you?'

'Actually, I need to use the bathroom,' Ellen said, struggling to her feet and leaving them to it.

Declan kept his eyes on Molly and waited.

'You're making her uncomfortable,' Molly said, fidgeting with her cutlery as she tried to decide what to do.

'Not as uncomfortable as I'm obviously making you.'

She met his eyes and gave a reluctant nod. 'The man who phoned today is called Luke Fortune. He was my first boyfriend. We bumped into each other recently.' Well, he didn't need to know *all* the details. 'He asked me to meet up with him again.'

'Why?' he asked, looking grim.

She took a deep breath. 'We went through a lot together and then broke up rather abruptly and he had lots of questions. I did too,' she added.

He took a long drink from his pint of lager before speaking again. 'So you went out with him.'

She nodded. 'Don't worry, we just talked and I won't be seeing him again. Anyway, he's married and he lives in France.'

'So why did he phone today?'

'Because he says his marriage is over and he thinks he never stopped loving me.'

Looking slightly shell-shocked, Declan mulled this over for a minute and then looked into her eyes. 'So what happens now?'

She shrugged. 'Nothing. I told him I wasn't in love with him and I didn't really think he was in love with me either. His marriage is in trouble and he's looking for a way out and, when he met me again, he thought he'd found it.'

'It is very romantic,' Ellen murmured as she returned to the table, then held up her hands as Declan shot her an incredulous look. 'Sorry!'

Two waiters arrived and started to set plates of food down in front of them. When they left, there was an awkward pause, and then Declan sat back in his chair and looked at Molly with accusing eyes. 'You told him about me postponing the wedding and going to Japan, didn't you? You led him to believe that it was over between us.'

'Of course she didn't,' Ellen said, jumping to Molly's defence.

'So you're in on all this?' Declan shook his head in disgust.

'I'm her best friend, why shouldn't she tell me?' Ellen challenged him.

He shrugged. 'True. I'm only her fiancé, why tell me? We've talked every day on the phone and you never mentioned this guy. Why? Were you weighing up your options, trying to decide who was the best bet?'

'Now you're just being ridiculous,' Molly said through gritted teeth.

'Well I'm sorry for getting upset about you chatting up an ex.'

'I told him I wasn't in love with him, haven't you heard anything I've said?' Molly's eyes narrowed. 'Or are you deliberately trying to pick a fight so you can rush back to Japan with a clear conscience?'

'Oh for God's sake, you're impossible.' He stood up, threw down a wad of cash and bent to give Ellen a brief kiss. 'I'm sorry, Ellen, but if I stay, I may say something I might regret.' And with that, he strode out of the restaurant, leaving the two women looking after him with their mouths open.

Laura put down the phone, shaking her head. Molly's love life got more complicated every day. Just when it seemed that she'd got Luke Fortune out of her system, Declan turned up and ruined everything. A couple of weeks ago, she was envying her sister being torn between two men, now she might end up with no one. Life was odd.

She went into the sitting room and curled up next to her son. She was rather glad that Robert was at the golf club and Ash had gone over to Neil's; it had been a long time since she'd had an evening alone with Adam. *The Shawshank Redemption* was on TV again, a movie they both loved, she had made popcorn and poured herself a large glass of wine. The two of them sat in companionable silence and lost themselves in the story. During an interval, Laura checked her watch and frowned. Ash really shouldn't be out so late. 'How come Neil and Ash are so close these days?' she asked Adam. She didn't like the thought of Ash being around Penny much, and that boy was definitely a bit odd.

'No idea.' Adam stood up and went to the door.

'Where are you off to?'

'Just the loo, Ma. That okay?'

She frowned. More like, he didn't want to talk. Was Ash really at Neil's, or was she just using him as a cover while she went on a date or to a club, or basically got up to no good?' Worried now, Laura went in search of her mobile and sent Penny a text.

Hi Penny, just checking; is Ash at ur house?

It was a few minutes before a reply came back, by which time Adam had returned with a pint-glass of milk and a fistload of chocolate biscuits.

When her phone beeped, Adam nudged her and grinned. 'Who's texting you at this hour of the night, the boyfriend?'

'Don't be silly,' Laura rolled her eyes, but her stomach knotted in guilt as she read the text.

Yep, they r in living room listening to depressing music. I'll give them an hour and Mark will drop her home

thanks

Relieved, Laura reached over to snatch one of Adam's biscuits.

'So, are you going to talk to your mum?' Ashling asked, after what seemed like an hour of silence.

Neil looked at her, frowning in annoyance. 'No point.'

'But after what Molly said—'

He gave a humourless smile. 'Ah, yes, your counsellor aunt that we just happened to bump into.'

Ash ducked her head so her hair covered her blush; she wasn't going to admit it had been a set-up, no way. 'What she was saying about that poor girl, didn't that make you think? I know your situations aren't remotely alike, but the fact is, talking is the only way to sort this, Neil.'

'If I talk to Mum, it will give her the licence she wants to walk away.'

'But that makes no sense,' Ash said, wanting to shake him. 'If she wanted to leave, she'd have done it by now.'

'She stays because she's worried about me,' he insisted.

'She doesn't seem that worried to me,' Ash retorted, thinking that it was time for the gloves to come off. 'Your mum doesn't even know there's a problem, don't you get that? She thinks you're being a typical teenager and your moods and bad grades are just down to hormones.'

Neil stared at her, looking like he might cry.

'Talk to her or your dad,' Ash begged. 'Please, Neil? You have to do something.'

He sat in silence for a moment and then nodded. 'You're right, I have to do something.'

Chapter Thirty-eight

5.45 p.m., Friday, 21st August

Molly threw herself into her work and tried not to think about Declan. When she wasn't working, she pampered Ellen, and when she wasn't doing that, she helped with the housework and the shopping and, when she wasn't doing that, she spent time with her mum. Despite Ellen's entreaties and Gareth's intervention, she refused to meet her fiancé. She wasn't too sure why she was being so stubborn, perhaps subconsciously she just didn't want to get married, but she was miserable and couldn't get him out of her head. Her mood wasn't helped by yet another emotional phone call from Luke. 'I'm sorry, Molly, but I just wanted to tell you that I've told Adriana I want a divorce.'

'Oh, Luke, I'm sorry.'

'That wasn't quite the reaction I was hoping for,' he joked, but there was a catch in his voice. 'So it doesn't make a difference?'

'No, Luke, it doesn't make a difference. I hope you didn't do it because of me.'

'No, I just finally got the courage to do it because of you.'

'You'll find someone, Luke,' she'd said, 'but please, in the meantime, get some help.' He had promised he would, wished her well, and rang off. It was sad, so very sad, but Molly couldn't be the one to get him through this.

She was now working at Ellen's kitchen table, conscious of her friend stomping around the room, muttering and sighing. Molly carried on regardless. She exchanged emails with both Tess and Carl, answered some posts, and was now writing her monthly report to the editor. But having been ignored for nearly an hour, Ellen finally lost patience. 'You can't let him go back to Japan like this,' she exclaimed. 'How many times have you told me that the whole foundation of psychology comes down to persuading people to talk about their problems and yet, instead of talking, you're behaving like a sulky toddler.'

Molly glanced up from her laptop and smiled. 'Hey, don't hold back.'

Ellen flopped into a chair with a sigh of frustration. 'I'm sorry, but it's just so ridiculous.'

Molly closed her machine and nodded. 'Yeah, I know. I'm going to call him and arrange to meet up.'

Ellen shot her a guilty look. 'You don't have to, he's on his way over here.'

Molly opened her mouth to protest, then shrugged. 'Fair enough.'

'You're not cross with me?'

'No. You're the one who should be cross, you've had to put up with the sulky toddler all week.'

'I didn't mean that,' Ellen said, her eyes full of remorse. 'I just hate to see you so unhappy and for no reason.'

'No reason?' Molly protested.

'I mean, nothing that can't be sorted out,' Ellen added hurriedly.

'Now, why don't you go and freshen up and put on something nice? He'll be here soon.'

Molly obediently went upstairs to get ready. She put on her denim dress and was standing at the mirror brushing her hair – it needed a cut, her brown fringe dipped down in front of her eyes – when she heard the doorbell. She took her time over her make-up, putting off the moment when she would have to face Declan. At the end of this conversation, she would either be getting married or starting a new life on her own; it was a scary thought.

When she finally went downstairs, it was to find him stretched out in one of Ellen's garden chairs, chatting easily.

He looked up and smiled with affection when she came out to join them. 'Hello, Moll, you look nice.'

'Thanks.'

He turned back to Ellen. 'So, are you going to join us tonight?'

She shook her head emphatically. 'Not a chance. Auntie Ellen has done her best, now it's up to you.'

They went to the cheap and slightly dilapidated Chinese restaurant round the corner; Molly was adamant that she didn't want to be too far from Ellen. 'She's been uncomfortable all day; it won't be long now,' she said, and checking that she had a signal, set her mobile phone on the table between them.

'Shouldn't they be taking her in and doing something at this stage?' Declan asked.

Molly smiled. His comprehension of the intricacies of childbirth was even sketchier than hers. 'She was examined on Wednesday and they said that if she hasn't gone into labour by next Wednesday, they'll take her in and induce her.' He nodded, although she was pretty sure he didn't know what that actually involved, and probably didn't want to.

As they ate, he made small talk. Molly listened, nodded, answered his questions and then finally put down her chopsticks with an impatient sigh. 'You didn't come here to talk about Ellen or my mum, or whether the car needs to go in for a service,' she protested.

'No,' he agreed, 'but I'm almost afraid to ask the questions I want answers to.'

Her eyes widened in surprise. She didn't think anything or anyone scared Declan, certainly not her. 'I'll tell you whatever you want to know,' she said simply.

'Then tell me about you and Luke, tell me about what it was like when you were dating.'

Molly frowned. 'But why? We were just schoolkids. It was all over by my eighteenth birthday.' Her voice caught and she reached for her water glass.

He watched her steadily. 'Humour me.'

She thought for a moment and then nodded slowly. 'Do you remember me telling you about a girl called Ruth?'

He frowned. 'That was your friend who died.'

She nodded. 'That's right. What I didn't tell you was that I dated her twin brother.'

'Luke?'

'Yes. I fancied him, but I didn't think he felt the same. I thought he was just nice to me because I was Ruth's best friend; the three of us went everywhere together.' She sighed and pushed the dregs of her green tea away. 'Let's get out of here and go for a walk.'

While Declan paid the bill, Molly stepped outside and phoned Ellen to check on her.

'I was just going to call you,' her friend said, sounding breathless and excited. 'I think it's started, Molly.'

'We'll be with you in two minutes,' Molly promised and

turned as Declan joined her. 'I'm afraid the rest of the story will have to wait, Ellen's in labour.'

Declan drove, while Molly sat with Ellen in the back, clutching her hand. Ellen had insisted they spread plastic sacks over the seat and floor.

'My waters might break and destroy your car,' she explained.

'Don't worry about stuff like that,' Declan said kindly, 'you're about to have a baby!'

'I'm so excited and completely terrified too, of course.'

Molly smiled. 'You'll be fine. Are you sure you don't want me to phone your mum?'

'No, let's get into the hospital first. If they think I'm about to pop, I'll call her then, but there's no point in dragging her in if we're just going to be hanging around all night. Besides, she'll drive me mad, fussing.'

Declan smiled at her in the rear-view. 'We'll stay with you and fuss over you instead.'

'Ah, thanks.' Ellen's smile turned into a grimace as she was gripped by another contraction.

'Hold on to me and breathe, you'll be fine,' Molly said calmly.

When the contraction was over, Ellen smiled at her friend. 'You're good at this.'

'This bit is easy, although I probably should have worn padded clothing,' Molly grinned, massaging the place where Ellen's nails had dug in.

'Sorry.'

'Any time,' Molly assured her.

'Nearly there,' Declan called back to them. 'I'll just take a short cut through this estate—'

'No speed ramps,' Ellen warned him, 'or you may find your-self delivering a baby.'

'Oh, right.' Declan nodded nervously. 'I'll stick to the main roads so.'

Ellen managed to wink at Molly. 'I think that's probably a good idea.'

Chapter Thirty-nine

8.20 p.m., Friday, 21st August

'You're doing well, Ellen, but you're only one centimetre dilated, so I'm afraid you've a long way to go yet.' The midwife smiled cheerfully as she tucked the sheet back into place.

Ellen looked at her in dismay. 'So it could be hours?'

'I'm afraid so, my love. Your best bet is to walk – around the corridors, up and down stairs, walk, walk, walk, it's always the best way to shift Baby.'

Immediately, Ellen flung back the covers and looked at Molly. 'Let's walk.'

Declan hopped to his feet when they came out of the ward. 'Well?'

'She has to walk,' Molly told him. 'We're going to go for a wander around the hospital. You may as well go home.'

'No way.' He looked from Molly to Ellen in dismay. 'Unless you want me to—'

'You're welcome to stay,' Ellen assured him, 'but it's not going to be much fun.'

He shrugged, and dug his hands into his pockets. 'I don't mind. It's just, it's my last night and—'

'Oh, God, I'm sorry, of course! You two go, I'll be fine.'

'Don't be ridiculous, I'm not leaving you,' Molly protested, glaring at Declan.

'But, Molly—'

'I am not leaving you.'

'Of course we're not going to leave you,' Declan echoed.

'Now, are you hungry?' Molly asked. 'Shall we go to the shop first?'

'No. I shouldn't eat in case anything goes wrong and I need a section.'

'You won't, will you?' Declan looked worried.

'No idea. Childbirth is unpredictable; apparently you have to be prepared for anything. Now, no more talking about all that, it just makes me nervous. If you're going to stay, you have to distract me. Tell me about dinner.'

'I had chicken chop suey and Declan had the duck in—'

'Not the food.' Ellen rolled her eyes. 'Tell me if you two are any closer to resolving your differences.'

'We were in the middle of things when I phoned,' Molly admitted.

'Sorry, guys. I've really messed up your evening, haven't I?' Ellen gave them a sheepish grin. 'If you want, you can continue where you left off and I'll be the ref.' Ellen's smile faltered when Molly said nothing. 'Hey, I'm just kidding, it's none of my business.'

Molly immediately put an arm around Ellen's shoulders. 'Of course it is, you're my friend.'

'And mine.' Declan smiled.

'So,' Molly started. 'I was telling Declan about how Luke and I got together in the first place, through Ruth.'

'Oh, right.'

Molly took Ellen's arm and nodded for Declan to take her other one. 'Not long after we started dating, Dad and Mum started teaching me and Ruth to drive.'

'What's this got to do with Luke?' Declan asked.

'Will you just let me tell the story, please?' Molly shook her head. 'Luke didn't have time for driving; he was on the school's rugby team and spent nearly all his spare time training.'

'Rugby, eh?' Declan muttered.

Molly smiled at his petulant expression. 'Dad said that, if I wanted, I could start saving and that, when I was eighteen, he would match what I'd saved and I could buy a small car.'

Declan looked impressed. 'I think I got a CD player for my eighteenth.'

'It was just a banger,' Molly reassured him. 'Dad had a friend in the business, and he got me a real bargain.' She paused for a moment as she remembered how happy she'd been then. She had a wonderful friend, boyfriend, her own car, and she would be starting university in a couple of months; life was perfect.

'Go on,' Ellen prompted. They'd reached the end of the corridor and started down the stairs.

'We picked it up a few weeks before my birthday. I was so excited the day that Dad took me to collect it. I couldn't wait to stick my L-plates on and get driving.'

Declan shot her a curious look over Ellen's head. 'That doesn't sound like you at all, you hate driving.'

'I was pretty good at it then, believe it or not. But Mum and Dad were very patient teachers. They took me out again and again before letting me loose on my own.'

'But as a learner, you're not allowed to drive alone, are you?' Ellen frowned.

'You were in those days,' Molly told her. 'But, like I said, Mum and Dad were quite strict about when and where I could drive.'

'Was Ruth jealous?' Ellen asked.

'No,' Molly shook her head, 'she wasn't interested in owning a car; she wanted to travel. She really only did the lessons because she was bored when I was off driving and Luke was training.' She paused as they came to the end of another corridor and they decided which way to go. 'Then, one evening shortly before my birthday, Ruth phoned to say that she'd been given two free tickets for a concert outside Dublin. We would have had to take two buses to get to the venue and probably wouldn't have made it on time, so I wanted to take the car. Dad wasn't keen, he even offered to drive us there. Of course, I lost my temper and accused him of not trusting me,' she shook her head, 'all the usual teenage nonsense. Anyway, Mum persuaded him to let me drive.' Molly swallowed. 'She said I was a good driver, that I was very sensible and I'd be fine, so he agreed.'

'What happened?' Declan asked, obviously realizing that she was building up to something.

Molly clung to Ellen's arm, forgetting that she was supposed to be the one supplying the support. 'We got there okay and left the car in a car park a few streets away. When we went inside, Ruth stopped off at the bar while I went to find our seats—' She stopped when she saw Declan's eyes widen. 'No, of course I wasn't drinking alcohol! I stuck to water the whole night.'

'Go on,' Ellen encouraged her.

'The seats weren't that great. I could hardly see the band, and there was a rowdy bunch of lads behind us, but the music was good and we were having fun. Of course, as the night went on, the lads drank more, and got progressively louder. Ruth was losing her temper and, the more she had to drink, the braver she got. She started giving them dirty looks and telling them to shut up.'

'Weren't there any bouncers at this gig?' Declan asked.

'Yes, but we were in the cheap seats at the top of the stadium, and the place was jam-packed; even if the bouncers had realized there was a problem, they wouldn't have been able to get near us, certainly not in time to help. Then one of the lads started making all these lewd comments, saying what he'd like to do to her if he got her alone. Ruth just turned around and said very loudly that she doubted he'd know what to do, or have the equipment to do it.'

Declan laughed. 'She sounds like a laugh, but she was mad to take them on; a gang of lads like that, they could have done anything.'

Molly flinched. 'She was quite tipsy, and past caring, but I wasn't happy, so I grabbed our stuff and dragged her out of there. We stood and watched the rest of the show in the aisle near the exit, so we could leave straight away if they came after us. When the concert ended, I wanted to get out quickly before the crowds, but Ruth needed the loo. There was a huge queue, naturally, and I said that I'd wait for her outside.'

Ellen doubled over with a moan.

'Ellen, are you okay?' Declan looked in alarm at Molly. 'Should we go back to the ward?'

'The contractions are still too far apart,' Ellen said through gritted teeth. 'I've got a while to go yet. Let's find somewhere to sit. I need a break from all this walking.'

Immediately, Declan put an arm around her to support her, and Molly led the way to a seat at the end of the corridor.

Ellen did her deep breathing as she'd been instructed, and then gave Molly the nod to continue. 'You were waiting for Ruth to come out of the loo—'

Molly sat down beside Ellen and stared into space, remembering. 'I didn't want to wait at the door, I was afraid of meeting those lads. So instead, I walked down to a fire exit further along; that way I'd be able to see Ruth come out, but keep out of sight.'

Ellen nodded. 'Good thinking.'

Molly shook her head. 'I was too late. One of them had already come out and was obviously waiting for us. He came up behind me and, before I could say a word, he had a hand over my mouth and was dragging me back into the doorway. I struggled, but though he wasn't that big, he was strong and,' she stumbled over her words, 'he had a knife.' Ellen silently took her hand and Molly looked up to see Declan watching her, fury and helplessness in his eyes. 'He held it to my throat and somehow, with the other hand, he managed to get his fly open, and then he was pulling down my pants,' she continued, hearing the quiver in her voice.

'Oh, Moll.' Ellen stared at her, tears streaming down her face.

Molly barely heard her. She was back in the moment now, could see him, could practically smell the tobacco and alcohol fumes on his breath. 'It was weird, he didn't seem to be aware of me, really. He was completely focused on satisfying himself. I remember wondering if it would be better to let him rape me or struggle and risk dying.'

'Jesus!' Declan breathed.

'And then Ruth was there. She jumped on him and started clawing at his eyes with her nails – she had really long nails.' Molly smiled slightly at the memory of her friend fighting like a tiger. 'He dropped the knife as he tried to pull her fingers away, and then he pushed her off him. She grabbed my hand and we ran all the way back to the car.'

Declan put his arms round her.

'What a terrible story, you poor thing,' Ellen said, rubbing her back.

Molly summoned up a smile. 'Aren't I supposed to be doing that to you?'

'Forget about me for the moment.'

Molly had to take a deep breath before continuing. 'When we got to the car park, I was shaking so much that I couldn't get the ticket out of my pocket, never mind put it into the machine. Ruth did it, and then practically carried me to the car. But when we got there, I was still shaking.'

'As we were standing there, me trying to get the key in the lock, we heard footsteps. Ruth just shoved me into the back seat and got behind the wheel.'

'Drunk?' Ellen's eyes widened in alarm.

'Believe me, she'd sobered up a lot by then, and I suppose she figured it was a lesser evil than the two of us being raped, murdered or both,' Molly defended her friend. 'But it was the first time for her to drive my car and she wasn't familiar with it. I was trying to tell her what to do, but I could hardly talk. We were both hysterical and crying. She got the car started, but it cut out a couple of times. She finally got it going, hit the accelerator and drove towards the ramp. I fell back in the seat so I didn't see exactly what happened, but the next thing I knew, there was a bang and I flew forward into the back of her seat and lost consciousness.' Tears were rolling down Molly's cheeks now and she was hiccuping and sobbing. Declan held her hands as she talked and Ellen just kept rubbing her back. 'When I came to, they were loading me into an ambulance. I asked where Ruth was and they said she'd already been taken to the hospital. They gave me something to calm me down and I slept. When I woke again, I was on a trolley in A & E and Mum was sitting beside me crying. She was the one who told me that Ruth had died.'

As Declan pulled her against his chest and held her, Ellen moaned and slid to her knees.

'Oh my God!' Molly pushed Declan aside and put an arm around her friend.

'I think it may be time to go back to the ward,' Ellen panted.

While Declan helped Ellen to her feet and half-carried her down the corridor, Molly dashed her tears away, blew her nose and phoned Ellen's mother. Then she hurried after them. When she got to the ward, Declan was pacing outside.

'They're examining her,' he explained, before folding her into his arms. 'Are you okay?'

'I've been better.'

'Did you ever find out what happened?' he asked after a while.

Molly stood back and leaned against the wall. 'Yes. Ruth had gone down the entrance, rather than the exit ramp, and hit a car coming in the other direction.'

'Shit.'

'It wasn't that bad, we weren't travelling particularly fast, there was very little damage to the cars. Apart from a bump on my head and a cut on my shin, I was fine, and the people in the other car weren't injured at all. But Ruth . . .' Molly shook her head. 'They said she was just unlucky. She wasn't wearing her seatbelt, and the force of the crash propelled her forward and back, causing a bleed in the brain. They worked on her for hours, but it was no good.'

'Why have you never told me about this before, Moll?' Declan asked, looking hurt and confused.

She put a hand up to his face. 'It wasn't just you, Declan, I haven't talked about it in detail to anyone except the counsellor I saw after it first happened. It was all so painful, and by the time my life got back to some kind of normality, I just kind of filed it away.'

'And Luke?'

She shook her head. 'I hardly saw him after that day and, when I did, we were both too stunned and upset to really talk. Then, the next thing I knew, he was moving to France; he was gone within weeks.'

The cheerful nurse emerged from the ward and smiled at them. 'You can come in now, if you want.'

Molly hugged Declan tightly before hurrying after her.

Ellen was now propped up in bed, a gas and air mouthpiece in her hand. She gave Molly a tired smile, 'I've still a couple of centimetres to go, apparently.'

'Your mum will be here any minute,' Molly comforted her.

'Are you okay?'

'Don't worry about me.'

'Are you?' Ellen demanded.

Molly nodded. 'I'm fine.'

'You and Declan should head off now—'

'I am not leaving until your mother gets here,' Molly said

firmly, then looked around guiltily as her phone rang. 'Damn, I forgot to switch it off after calling your mum.' She sighed and hurriedly put it to her ear. 'Hello?'

'Molly?'

'Yes?'

'It's Adam. Thank God I got you, I didn't know who else to call.'

'What is it, Adam, what's wrong?'

'Neil's missing and Ash has gone to look for him.'

'What? Are you at home, Adam? Where are your mum and dad?'

'Mum's gone out and Dad's down the country.'

'Did you call them?'

'Are you mad? Ash would kill me. Should I go after her?'

'No! Stay right there, Adam, I'll call you back.'

'What is it, what's wrong?' Ellen asked as Molly switched off her phone.

'That was Adam. Ash has gone missing.'

'Then go.'

Molly dithered. 'I can't leave you.'

'You can, the twins need you now.'

'Hang on.' Molly rushed out to Declan and filled him in on the situation. 'Will you stay with Ellen until her mother gets here?'

'Why don't I go and look for Ash? You're in no condition—'

'I'm fine, and there isn't time for me to explain everything to you. Please, Declan, don't argue. Just stay with Ellen?'

Declan sighed. 'Of course.'

'Thank you,' she said and led him into the ward.

'Will I do until the cavalry get here?' he joked.

'You'll do just fine,' Ellen assured him.

Molly hugged her. 'Good luck.'

Ellen grinned. 'Thanks.'

'Are you sure you're okay to drive?' Declan looked at Molly in concern.

'Of course. Phone me as soon as there's any news.'

'You too,' Declan told her. 'My phone's off, but I'll keep checking my messages.'

'Great. Take care of her for me, won't you?'

'I promise. Be careful.'

Chapter Forty

Adam came out to meet her as soon as she pulled up, his face pinched and drawn. 'Thanks for coming, Molly. I was going to call Granddad—'

'I'm glad you phoned me, Adam. Now, let's go inside and sit down and you can tell me everything.'

'Aren't we going to look for her?' he asked, his eyes large with concern.

'First we need to try and figure out where she might be. Now, do you know exactly where your mum and dad are?'

'Dad's at a meeting down the country. He's driving back tonight, but I'm not sure when he'll get here. Mum's gone out with Penny.'

Molly frowned. 'Did you call her?'

'No!' He shook his head vehemently.

'Okay, calm down. Tell me what happened with Neil.'

'I'm not sure. Ash saw him the other day, and she was telling him he should talk to his mum or dad; she really thought that she'd got through to him. And then, this afternoon, he sent her a message saying that he'd had enough, that he wasn't going to sit around worrying about things any more, he was going to do something.' He sighed, tears in his eyes. 'She was scared he was going to top himself, well, we both were. I said we should tell Mum, but Ash was afraid to. She tried to call you, but your phone was off.'

'I've been in the hospital with Ellen,' Molly explained.

'Well, then she decided to go over to Neil's house, but she phoned to say that he wasn't in and she was going to look for him.'

'But how did she know for sure he wasn't there?' Molly protested. 'He could have been in the loo or the shower or had headphones on—' She didn't add the other possibility, but it hung between them in the silence.

'I said that,' Adam said finally, 'but Ash insisted he wasn't there. I told her she should come home, but she said she had an idea where he might have gone and she was going to find him. Then she hung up on me.'

'Have you tried calling her since?'

'About ten times, but she's not answering.' His eyes searched her face. 'What do you think we should do?'

'Don't worry, Adam, we'll find her,' Molly said, hoping she sounded more optimistic than she felt. She thought that there was a good chance that, if Neil had gone out, he'd have gone in search of his mother. 'Where does your mum usually go when she meets her friends?'

He shrugged. 'Dunno.'

Molly sighed. This was hopeless. She forced herself to concentrate and tried to look at this from Laura's point of view. If she was simply meeting Penny for an innocent chat, then she would probably have stayed local. But if she was up to her old tricks, then she would go further afield. Perhaps Penny had regular haunts and Neil knew them and had told Ash— 'Hang on a sec.' Molly muttered and went out to the door, Adam hot on her heels. 'Your mum's car is gone.'

'Yes, she always takes the car unless she's planning to have a drink.'

Molly closed her eyes and sent up a silent prayer of thanks. There was no way Laura would go out looking for action without some Dutch courage. And, if she was driving, then it was more likely they hadn't gone far. She smiled confidently at Adam. 'Okay, let's go.'

'Where are we going?' he asked.

'To find your sister, of course. Grab your keys and your phone. Oh, and write a note saying you're with me, just in case Ash or your dad comes back.'

While Adam hurried off to do her bidding, Molly went out to the car and phoned her sister. 'Laura, don't say anything, just listen.'

Laura was sorry she'd come out tonight. It had been okay to start with; they'd had a nice meal in the restaurant and discussed the proposed trip to Paris. But Penny had polished off a bottle of wine over dinner and then persuaded Laura to come into the bar for a nightcap; that was at least an hour ago now. Laura had suggested they go home a couple of times now, but Penny was chatting rather loudly to two English salesmen and she didn't look likely to move anytime soon. Laura could have understood it if the men were attractive, but they were quite ordinary guys with little to say for themselves. She thought of her own behaviour in Limerick and Galway and wondered, had she looked as pathetic as Penny did right now? Neither man seemed remotely interested in her, and yet Penny was leaning into them, giving them ample eyefuls of her cleavage and using double entendres that would make a sailor blush. How could the woman make such a fool of herself?

When her phone rang, Laura happily excused herself and went into reception to take the call. 'Hi, Molly, what's up?'

Her eyes grew round with horror as her sister talked and, at the end of it, Laura hurried back into the bar and took Penny by the arm. 'Sorry, gentlemen, I'm afraid we must go.'

Penny shot her a furious look. 'Don't be silly, Laura, it's early.'

'We must call it a night anyway,' one of the men assured her and drained his glass, 'early start.'

'What are you playing at, Laura?' Penny demanded as the men left.

'I'll explain everything later, but right now we've got to get you cleaned up.'

'I beg your pardon?'

But Laura ignored her, ordered a pot of coffee and steered Penny towards the ladies.

By the time Neil and Ash walked in, the two women were sitting at a table, sipping coffee and chatting quietly.

Penny looked up at her son in surprise. 'Neil, what on earth are you doing here?'

Laura feigned surprise too. 'Ashling, is there something wrong?'

'I thought—' Neil started, his eyes flitting around the room and then back to his mother. 'I thought you were seeing someone.'

Penny's laugh sounded slightly forced, but Laura thought Neil was probably too distracted to notice.

'You were right, I was seeing Laura. Is everything okay, darling?'

His eyes filled with tears and he just stood looking down at his trainers.

'Neil needs to talk to you,' Ashling blurted out.

'Well, we were just getting ready to leave,' Laura said calmly.

'You go on, Laura,' Penny said, her eyes on her son. 'Neil and I will get a taxi.'

'Okay then.' Laura kissed Penny's cheek and stood up. 'Come along, Ashling, let's go.'

*

'It's Ash,' Adam told Molly as he put the phone to his ear. 'Where are you?' he asked as Molly carefully pulled into the side of the road and waited. He listened for a moment. 'Is Mum furious with you? Okay. See you at home.'

'Well?'

Adam nodded. 'She found Neil. You were right. He was out looking for his mum.'

'And he found her?'

Adam nodded. 'Yes, she was with Mum in the Clontarf Castle hotel.'

'And is everything okay?'

'I'm not sure, but Mum and Ash are on their way home.'

'That sounds good to me.' Molly smiled at him. 'Shall we?' He nodded, looking relieved and Molly turned the car.

Ellen took another whiff of gas and air and gave Declan a woozy smile, 'I'm so glad you and Molly have sorted things out, I always knew she didn't really love Luke.'

Declan smiled.

'Although, when she went rushing off round the country after him like that, I suppose I did have my doubts— Mum!'

Stunned, Declan backed away from the bed as Ellen's mother bustled in.

'I'll leave you to it,' he said quietly.

Ellen held out her arms to him. 'Thanks, Declan, you've been wonderful.'

He bent to hug her. 'My pleasure. Good luck, Ellen.'

Instead of turning left towards home, Laura turned right and pulled into a car park on the seafront.

'What are we doing here?' Ash shot her a nervous look.

'I think we need to talk, don't you?' Laura turned to face her daughter. She felt sick with nerves and relief, and she couldn't believe what a close shave that had been; thank God Molly had called. And even with her sister's caution ringing in her ears, 'you mustn't let her know I broke her confidence', Laura knew it was time for a mother–daughter chat.

'You mean, you'll talk, and I'll have to listen.' Ash's mouth settled into a stubborn line.

Laura gave her daughter a tired smile. 'Ashling Dillon, must you always be so cheeky?'

'Well, it's true,' Ash insisted, angry tears in her eyes. 'The only time you talk to me is to give out. I've been going through a really tough time and you haven't even noticed.'

Laura was stunned for a moment. Was it true? She did seem to spend a lot of time arguing with her daughter, but only because Ash was lazy and cheeky and never seemed to do as she was told. She took a deep breath, realizing that they would have to find some common ground if they were going to get past this. 'What happened today, Ash? Why did you and Neil come to the hotel?'

'Neil sent me a text saying that he'd had enough.'

Laura frowned in confusion. 'Enough of what?'

Ash looked at her from under her lashes. 'Not *of* what, of *who*: his mother.'

Laura swallowed. 'Go on,' she croaked.

'She's always going out clubbing and coming home drunk. He was convinced that she was seeing other men and that she was planning to leave him and his dad, and he didn't want that to happen. He discovered that if he was sick or in trouble, she stayed home more, so he started acting up all the time, hoping it would make her stay.'

'My God, why didn't you tell me?' Laura said, horrified.

Ash's eyes filled up. 'He swore me to secrecy, said that he'd run away if I told anyone. He's been so weird even Molly couldn't get through to him.'

'Molly?' Laura looked at her in confusion.

Ash reddened. 'Adam was worried about me,' she explained. 'He thought I was the one in trouble. He wrote to *Teenage Kix* for advice.'

'What?' Laura couldn't believe her ears. It was one thing for Ashling not to confide in her, but Adam too?

'He knew something was wrong with me and he was worried,' Ash said pointedly. 'Anyway, Molly figured out the letters were from him and the two of them confronted me. That's when I told her about Neil.'

'Will you tell me?' Laura said softly. She had got only the sketchiest of details from Molly in the hurried phone call and she realized it was important that she listen to her daughter's side of the story.

As Ash explained how Neil had been falling to pieces over the last few months, how Molly had made the connection between the letters from Smithy and Adam, and how the three of them had then come up with a plan to help Neil, Laura was filled with mixed emotions. She felt gutted that neither of the twins had felt they could turn to her. She was also shocked by the lengths Neil had gone to, purely to get Penny's attention. And grateful and relieved that the twins didn't know what *she'd* been up to recently. She also felt extraordinarily proud of both of them. Proud of Ash for trying to help Neil, even though they weren't that close after all, and proud of Adam for looking out for his sister. Laura wasn't sure she or Robert had anything to do with it, but they somehow seemed to have raised two decent and responsible children.

'So you went over to talk to Neil,' Laura prompted when Ash had reached the point where Neil had sent her that last text.

Ash nodded. 'I knew exactly what he was going to do. He'd

talked about following his mother before when she went out, so I thought that's what he must be planning to do tonight.'

'But you knew that Penny was only meeting me,' she said, keeping her voice light.

Ash nodded excitedly. 'Exactly! I thought, finally, this was an opportunity to show him that his suspicions were wrong.'

'Clever girl,' Laura murmured, feeling sicker by the second.

'But there was no answer at his house and his neighbour said I'd just missed him, so I went straight to the hotel.' Ash sighed. 'I found him crouched outside the hotel in the car park, terrified to go in because he wasn't sure what he'd find, so I dragged him inside.'

She sighed. 'I just hope that he's finally talking to his mum.'

'I'm sure he is.' Laura stroked her daughter's silky curls. 'Want me to call Penny tomorrow and make sure he's told her everything?'

'I suppose.' Ash looked at her with troubled eyes. 'But what do we do if he hasn't?'

'I don't think Penny will let him out of that hotel tonight without getting some answers. But, I tell you what, how about I talk to Molly before I call Penny and see what she advises?'

Ash nodded and smiled. 'Yes please, Mum.'

Laura pulled her distraught daughter into her arms and kissed her. 'I'm very proud of you, Ash. You did the right thing.'

'Thanks.' Ash drew back after a moment. 'Do you think Penny is planning to leave, Mum?'

'No, darling, I don't. Penny just enjoys being the centre of attention and when men are nice to her, it makes her feel good, attractive.'

Ash wrinkled her nose in disgust. 'But she must be at least thirty-five, and she's married!'

Laura smiled. 'We all need to feel special sometimes, no matter what age we are.'

'I never really liked Neil's mum,' Ash confided, 'but he loves her so much. He'd be devastated if she left.'

'And if it was me, you'd be packing my bags and throwing a party,' Laura joked.

But Ash didn't smile, just looked at her with solemn, tearful eyes. 'No, I wouldn't, Mum, I'd hate it. I know we fight lots, but you know that I love you, don't you?'

Laura hugged her daughter. 'And I love you, Ash, and I promise you, here and now, that I'm not going anywhere.'

When they got home, Robert's car was there. Ash looked at her mother. 'What do we tell Dad?'

'What do you want to tell him?' Laura asked.

Ash yawned. 'Nothing tonight, Mum. I'm really tired.'

'Okay then, why don't you go straight up to bed and I'll just tell him that Neil got a bit upset over something and that you were looking after him?'

'Great. Thanks, Mum.'

The front door opened as Laura stepped out of the car and Robert stood there, Adam shifting from foot to foot in the background. 'Everything okay?' Robert asked.

'Everything's fine,' Laura smiled. 'Now, you two, bed. It's late.'

Both children came to hug and kiss her before saying goodnight to their father and going upstairs without protest. Laura went into the sitting room, flopped down on the sofa and kicked off her shoes.

'Are they really my children?' Robert asked, following her and going to stand in front of the fireplace.

Laura smiled. 'We had a minor crisis with Penny and Laura's lad, Neil. I think they're just relieved that I didn't blame them. In fact, I must say, I was really quite proud of them tonight.'

Robert smiled. 'They're good kids, you've done a great job with them. I should say that more often.'

Laura looked up at him in surprise. 'Don't be silly—'

'No, Laura, I've been taking you for granted and I'm sorry. It was only when you went away and I was alone with them all day that I realized they could be so difficult. And then, the day we were bowling with Ash's friend and her mother –' he shook his head – 'I couldn't believe how little control Cheryl had over Lottie. The lack of respect that child showed her mother was unbelievable.'

Laura couldn't help smiling; it was nice to know that Cheryl's flirting had been in vain. 'Some of the other mothers think that I'm too strict, but I don't want the twins making the mistakes we did, Robert.'

'I agree. Don't get me wrong,' he added hurriedly, 'I have no regrets, but I want them to enjoy the remainder of their childhood and see a bit of the world before they settle down. Oh,' he fumbled in his pocket and pulled out a box, 'I almost forgot. For you.'

Laura blinked as she took the box. 'What's this?'

'My meeting was near the Newbridge factory so I slipped in and got you this; I know you love their jewellery.'

Laura opened the box, too stunned to reply. In it was nestled a delicate silver watch with a baby-pink leather strap. 'Oh, Robert, it's lovely!'

He beamed. 'Really, you like it?'

'I love it, thank you.'

'It wasn't that expensive, but I just thought you might like it.'

She stood up and gave him a quick hug. 'And I do.'

He touched her cheek tenderly. 'Why don't you go to bed, you look tired. I'll bring you a nightcap?'

'That sounds wonderful. And I am tired.'

'Have a lie-in tomorrow,' Robert suggested. 'I'm taking the

twins sailing again. In fact, why don't you meet us at the yacht club for lunch afterwards?'

Laura smiled. 'I'd like that.'

After Molly had dropped Adam home, she headed straight back to the hospital. She had only gotten one message from Declan, saying that Ellen's mother had arrived and he had left them to it. She'd tried calling to tell him she'd found Ash, but there was no answer. But then, he was probably out cold, given that he was flying back to Japan in the morning. She would just drop in to see Ellen and, hopefully, her baby and then hurry home to him.

It was ridiculously late when she presented herself at the labour ward but, unlike the rest of the hospital, it was busy and noisy and no one questioned her presence. As she made her way along the corridor, she looked up to see Ellen's parents walking towards her.

'Molly!' Ellen's mother gave her a warm hug. 'Thank you so much for looking after my little girl, and your fiancé too. What a lovely man.'

'Oh, you're welcome,' Molly smiled. 'So?'

'It's a fine, bonny little girl.' Ellen's usually grim father was beaming, tears in his eyes.

'With golden-blonde curls and the most perfect little nails,' Mrs Brennan said proudly.

'They're taking her up to a ward, but if you hurry, you should catch her.'

'Great, thanks and congratulations,' Molly waved to them and hurried on. She quietly opened the door of Ellen's room and paused to take in the scene before her eyes. The harsh main lights had been turned off and only the light above the bed remained, casting a glow over her friend, who was rocking a bundle in her arms and humming softly.

'Can I come in?' Molly whispered.

Ellen looked up and smiled. 'Of course.'

Molly moved over to the bed and bent to kiss her friend's cheek and the baby's downy head. 'Oh, wow, she's beautiful.'

'How did you know it was a girl?' Ellen frowned.

'I just met your folks. Your dad's going to need surgery to get that smile off his face.'

Ellen giggled. 'I know, he's over the moon.'

'Why wouldn't he be?' Molly looked down in wonder at the sleeping baby.

'Would you like to hold her?'

'Yes, please. Oh, hang on, let me wash my hands, I've been all over the place tonight.'

'Oh, sorry, I completely forgot to ask, did you find Ash?'

'Yes, she'd gone to help a friend, but now she's safe and well and at home with her mother.'

'Thank goodness for that,' Ellen said, and when Molly sat down in the chair next to the bed, she put her baby into Molly's arms.

Molly gasped in amazement. 'She's as light as a feather.'

'She's nearly eight pounds, but I know what you mean, she does seem tiny. I'm terrified I'll break her.'

'You'll be fine, and you're going to be fighting off volunteers wanting to babysit this little treasure. How was the labour at the end?' Molly asked.

Ellen pulled a face. 'Hell, but Mum was brilliant, and once they put the baby in my arms, I forgot all about the pain.'

Molly touched the baby's pink cheek and marvelled at her tiny golden lashes. 'She is adorable.'

'About earlier, Molly,' Ellen sighed. 'About Ruth, I'm so

sorry. I had no idea you'd been through so much, so many things make sense now.'

'Like what?' Molly asked curiously.

'Well, for one thing, why you never drink. Why you never let guys get too close.'

Molly sighed. 'I was always fine at the start of a date, but as soon as they started touching me, I'd remember that night and I wouldn't be able to go any further.'

'And your job . . .'

Molly frowned. 'I don't understand.'

'Laura's always going on about you not achieving your full potential. Is that because you felt guilty about living when Ruth died?'

Molly shook her head. 'No, you're wrong there. After the accident, I fell apart and Mum and Dad arranged for me to have counselling. Without that, I'm not sure I'd ever have recovered, to be honest. I had never considered psychology as a career, but suddenly it made perfect sense. I wanted to help people, just the way that counsellor helped me. Laura's always thought that I just gave up on my ambitions, that I let my grief ruin my life. She was sympathetic at the start, of course she was, but as time went on, it seemed to really frustrate and irritate her.' Molly gave a rueful smile. 'It still does. But she's wrong. I didn't give up on my career, I just changed direction. I found my true vocation because of Ruth.'

'I'm glad. And you're sure you're okay now?'

'Honestly, I am. Especially now that I've talked to Declan; it's like a weight has been lifted.'

'Wonderful.' Ellen smiled happily. 'Now, I have just two more questions for you, and they both concern this little angel.'

'Will I babysit? Absolutely. Will I still love you when you're covered in baby puke? Yes again.'

Ellen laughed. 'Okay, four questions.'

'Go on.'

'Will you be godmother?'

'Oh, Ellen, I'd be honoured.' Molly brushed her lips against the baby's silken head. 'I promise to be the best godmother in the world.'

'And the second question.' Ellen looked at her. 'What do you think of Ruth as a name?'

Molly felt tears bubble up inside, but she swallowed them and shook her head. 'I don't think so, Ellen. Ruth was my friend and I will never forget her, but this little one is going to be her own person and she deserves a name that belongs to her and her alone.' She shot Ellen a warning look. 'But it better not be Buster.'

Chapter Forty-one

8.15 a.m., Saturday, 22nd August

Molly opened her eyes and rolled over, enjoying the feeling of being in her own bed again. With a languorous smile, she shuffled over to cuddle Declan, but realized that he wasn't there. Sleepily, she headed into the sitting room to find him packing his shaving gear into a toilet bag. 'Hi. What time is it?'

'After eight.'

She opened her eyes, wide. 'Oh my God, why didn't you call me? What time do you have to be at the airport?'

'Nine. It's okay, I've called for a taxi.'

She shook her head in confusion. 'Why did you do that?'

He shrugged and said nothing.

She sat down on the arm of the sofa and studied him, realizing that he hadn't looked at her once since she'd entered the room. It was obvious too from his rapid, clipped movements and the set of his chin, that he was angry. 'Ellen had a baby girl,' she said.

There was a glimmer of a smile. 'Great. Are they both okay?'

'Wonderful.'

He nodded and went into the bedroom. Molly followed. 'She wanted to call the baby Ruth, but I didn't think it was a good idea.'

'Right.'

Molly sighed. 'What's wrong, Declan? I thought we were okay.'

'Did you?' he said, his voice like ice.

'Oh, can you please stop this and just tell me what the hell I'm supposed to have done?' she cried.

'Fine, I'll tell you.' He flung down the T-shirts he was holding and faced her. 'I'm angry because you've been treating me like shit because I postponed the wedding and went to Japan, and then I find out that, as soon as I was out of the way, you were chasing your ex-boyfriend around Ireland.'

Molly stared at him. 'Who told you?'

'Ellen, but she didn't mean to, I think she was a bit high on the gas and air.'

Molly collapsed on the bed. 'I'm sorry. I didn't tell you because it wasn't important.'

'It wasn't important?' he yelled. 'At the first sign of trouble between us, you go in search of your childhood sweetheart and you say that it's not important?'

'What I meant was—'

'And then you try to get me on side by telling me this sad story about his sister dying.' He stopped, shaking his head in disbelief. 'I can't believe that you could be so devious.'

Molly stared at him in horror. 'But, Declan, it wasn't like that at all, honestly.'

'Honestly?' He shot her a look of pure disgust. 'That's a word you really aren't entitled to use.'

A horn sounded outside and Declan picked up the T-shirts and, going back into the sitting room, shoved them into his bag. 'That will be my taxi.'

'Send it away,' Molly begged him. 'You can't go until I've explained.'

'Until you've concocted another pack of lies, you mean.' He zipped up the bag and sat down to put on his trainers.

'I didn't concoct any lies,' she protested. 'I just didn't tell you the full truth because I didn't want to complicate things.'

He stood up, shaking his head in exasperation. 'I really can't listen to any more of this crap,' he said and, picking up his bag and jacket, walked to the door.

'Please, Declan, let's talk about this,' she cried, panicking when she realized that he really did intend to leave.

He paused and looked back at her. 'You're big on talking, aren't you, Moll? Well, I came halfway around the world to talk to you, and all I got is lies and more lies. I'm done talking.' And with that, he walked out of the flat, jumped into the taxi and was gone.

She was lying on the bed, sobbing her heart out, when the door-bell rang. He's come back, she thought and, running to the door, flung it open, only to find her sister standing there.

'Morning!' Laura beamed. 'Sorry, I know it's early, but I just had to talk to you about last night. And you must tell me all about the baby, I can't wait to see her! Thanks for the text—' Laura stopped, noticing for the first time the state her sister was in. 'Moll, you look dreadful, what's wrong?'

Molly slumped against the counter. 'Declan's gone.'

'Oh, right. I'd forgotten he was going back today. Cheer up, he'll be back before you know it.'

Molly shook her head. 'He's not coming back. He found out about us going to Limerick to find Luke.'

Laura's eyes widened. 'What? But how?'

'Ellen let it slip. I told him all about Ruth last night, about the accident, about everything.' She sighed. 'But I left out the bit about me tracking Luke down. I pretended that we'd just bumped into each other. And now that he's found me out in a lie, he doesn't want anything more to do with me.'

'Oh, Moll.' Laura shot her a sympathetic look.

Molly blew her nose. 'I know it's my own fault, I brought it all on myself.'

'And are you really sure you're not in love with Luke?'

'Positive.' Molly sighed. 'I thought I might be until that night in the Shelbourne. But as we talked about the accident, I realized that it was probably Ruth I'd really been chasing after, not her brother.'

'I hope you're not going to start brooding about all that again, Moll, you've done enough of that over the years.'

Molly looked at her in surprise. 'I didn't realize you'd noticed.'

Laura shrugged awkwardly. 'Yes, well, you had your counsellor and Mum and Dad to talk to, you didn't need me sticking my oar in too. But I'm not completely stupid, I saw what you went through and of course I worried; you're my little sister.'

'Thanks.' Molly gave her a tearful smile.

Laura clapped her hands. 'Okay, come on, get dressed and put on some lippy.'

'What? Why?' Molly blew her nose with some kitchen paper.

Laura gave an impatient sigh. 'Because we're going after Declan, of course!'

'Stop that,' Laura snapped, as Molly sat in the passenger seat drumming anxious fingers on the leather armrest. 'You're a worse fidget than Adam.'

'I can't help it.' Molly glanced at her watch. 'What if we don't make it?'

'We'll make it,' Laura said, increasing the pressure on the accelerator pedal.

'Tell me about last night,' Molly suggested. 'I need the distraction.'

'Oh, Moll, if you hadn't phoned, it could have been a disaster.

Penny was pissed and chatting up these guys. Her mascara was smudged, her hair was a mess and she looked like a very sad drunk. If Neil had seen her—' Laura shivered. 'Anyway, I dragged her off to the ladies, cleaned her up, and told her that the kids were about to walk in on us and, between the shock and some strong coffee, she was quite presentable by the time they arrived.'

'So what happened then? What did Neil say?'

'Nothing, really. The poor kid just stood there, crying. I grabbed Ash, and we left them to it.'

'How is Ash?'

'She's okay but oh, Moll, you should have heard her, she was so scathing about Penny. Can you imagine how she'd have reacted if she'd ever seen me with Gerard?'

'Does this mean you're going to stop chatting up strange men in bars?' Molly teased.

'I'm going to try,' Laura said seriously. 'I was up at the crack of dawn this morning, deleting Gerard's texts and emails—'

'Emails!'

Laura sighed. 'I know it was stupid. I got carried away. But it's over now, and I certainly won't be going to Paris.'

'Paris!'

'Must you repeat everything I say, Moll? Gerard asked me to go over, so I was going to pretend Penny and I were going on a shopping trip.'

'Penny!'

Laura looked at her with raised eyebrows.

'Well, I'm sorry,' Molly shook her head in desperation, 'but how could you take that woman into your confidence?'

'I'm not completely stupid. Of course I didn't tell Penny that I was planning to meet Gerard when we were over there. Anyway, like I said, it's off. I'm not going to lose the twins over a man.'

Molly looked at her. 'And Robert?'

'He's not a bad man,' Laura admitted. 'I suppose we've just

got into a rut, I'm probably as much to blame for that as he is.' She shot Molly a sidelong glance. 'I was thinking perhaps we should go for counselling.'

'That's a great idea, Laura,' Molly said, delighted. 'You should also try to spend more time together without the children.' Molly nudged her. 'You could always go to Paris with him instead. I'd mind the twins.'

Laura smirked. 'Thanks for the offer, I'll get back to you on it.'

'What about Penny and Neil?' Molly asked as Laura turned into the airport grounds.

'What indeed? That's why I came over this morning. Ash was worried about how we should handle things from here on. Do we follow up on last night or mind our own business and pretend it never happened?'

'Well, what was Penny's reaction when you told her about Neil?'

'She was completely stunned, she had no idea he was feeling that way.'

'Then I think you and Ash should keep in touch with both of them separately over the next couple of weeks and compare notes, then we can take it from there.'

'Okay.' Laura squeezed her sister's hand. 'Thanks, by the way, for looking out for the twins. I appreciate it.'

Molly flushed. 'No problem. They probably would have figured it all out by themselves in the end anyway. They're great kids, Laura.'

'Yeah, they are.' Laura swung the car into the airport, then pulled up on a double yellow line right in front of the entrance. 'Right, go get him. I'll drive round and you can phone me when you're ready to go.'

Molly leaned over to kiss Laura's cheek. 'Thanks, you're the best.'

*

As she sprinted through Arrivals and up the escalator to Departures, it occurred to Molly that this whole drama had started and would now finish in the airport. But, unlike Laura, she wasn't convinced that she could say anything to change Declan's mind. He was a straight-talking, honest man and he'd find it very hard to forgive her deceit. And, she realized, as she weaved between people and luggage and buggies, Ellen had been right. She had said that Molly would have to treat Luke and Declan as two completely unrelated problems and they were. Luke was gone. She didn't love him. But she might have lost Declan, the man she did love, so, so much.

Molly decided against going to the check-in desk, she was too late for that. In fact, knowing Declan, he had probably already gone through. The best she could hope for was that he'd been delayed in the queues at security. The crowds got denser as she neared the gate and she looked about her, suddenly realizing how completely hopeless this was. And then the crowds parted slightly and she caught a glimpse of him handing over his boarding pass and passport to a security man.

'Wait!' she roared, pushing her way through. 'Declan, please, wait!'

Everyone turned to stare at her, including the security man.

'Please, Declan,' she called again, stepping over a trolley.

'I think you're wanted, lad,' the security man said, nodding towards Molly.

'I'm going to miss my flight,' Declan muttered.

The man checked the boarding pass and looked at his watch. 'You're good for twenty minutes.'

Molly came to a standstill in front of him, slightly breathless. 'Please? This won't take long.'

Declan looked at her with sad eyes. 'Why are you doing this, Moll?'

She felt the tears prick her eyes. 'I can't let you go without telling you everything.'

He sighed and, with a curt nod, led her away from the queue to a relatively quiet corner.

Molly stood in front of him and though she felt ashamed of herself and slightly scared in the face of his obvious hostility, she forced herself to maintain eye contact as she talked.

'The day I dropped you here to go to the Enco interview was the first time that I saw Luke.' His eyes widened in surprise, but she just kept going.

She told him everything. She told him how she had thought about Luke, remembered the good times, looked him up online – he flinched at that. How when he'd decided to go to Japan she had been shattered, and had started to wonder if she was with the wrong man. She told him how she'd confided in Ellen and Laura. And then she told him of the moment in the Shelbourne hotel, when she'd realized that her infatuation with Luke was actually her grasping the opportunity to talk about Ruth. She saw the look of disbelief on Declan's face and watched him check his watch. She forced herself to keep going, even though she knew it was probably futile. She finished her story by telling him the real reason she'd been at the airport last Tuesday. She told him how, seconds before he'd walked in, she'd watched Luke and realized that she felt nothing for him other than warm affection.

'Luke isn't in love with me either,' she told Declan, 'only he hasn't realized it yet. He's still grieving for his sister; he rushed into marriage in order to escape his mother and her obsession with Ruth and so that's falling apart too. When he saw me, he saw someone who knew Ruth, who loved Ruth, who could understand all he'd been through and he latched on to that. I told him that night in the Shelbourne that it was a mistake, but he begged me to meet him again the next time he came to Dublin. I wouldn't agree, but I didn't say no either,' she admitted. 'I know you will probably doubt my motives, Declan, but I just felt guilty that, having been the one to get in touch, I was now turning my back on him.' She took a deep breath. 'The next time I heard from him was the morning you came home; he phoned saying he was at the airport and would I come to meet him.'

Declan frowned. 'But you came to pick me up.'

'No.' Molly shook her head sadly. 'I never got your message. I was there to meet Luke. He had just gone to get us coffee when you walked through the arrivals gate. I nearly died when I saw you. In that instant, I realized that I might lose you and I was devastated. So I turned my back on Luke and walked out of there with you.'

She stopped for a moment but he said nothing, just continued to stare at her, his expression blank.

'As soon as I dropped you at the flat, I tried to contact him to explain, but he was on a flight to Shannon so I left a message. He called back later,' she sighed, 'and you answered. I told him that I was sorry, but I wasn't in love with him and I didn't want to see him again.'

'Was that it?' he asked, eyes narrowed.

She shook her head, beginning to wonder if honesty really was the best policy. 'No, he phoned me one more time. I told him that I loved you and I asked him not to call again and he hasn't.' She sighed, feeling exhausted. 'I think that's everything. Other than to say that, in the unlikely event that you can forgive me, I don't think we should get married.'

'What?' Declan looked up as there was an announcement that his flight was now boarding. 'What did you say?'

She sighed. 'You wanted honesty and I'm trying to be as honest as I can. The reason I was really upset about you going to Japan was because I felt you were using it as an excuse not to marry me. But I don't care about that any more. I've finally realized that I don't need to have a ring on my finger; all I want is you.'

'That's bullshit,' he said irritably, glancing at his watch again. Her heart sank. She nodded, tried for a smile, but couldn't quite manage it. 'It's not, but, well, thanks for listening,' she said and turned away.

'Wait.'

She turned back, hardly able to see him as her eyes filled with tears.

He reached out, gripped her shoulders and shook his head in frustration. 'It's bullshit that I didn't want to marry you.' His expression softened and he sighed. 'It was never about you. I just didn't want to marry anyone, ever. Not because I didn't love you, Moll, but because I saw what a lousy job my parents made of it and I swore I would never get myself into the same situation.'

There was another call for Declan's flight and he started to draw her back towards the queue.

Molly wiped her eyes with the heel of her hand. 'But we're not your parents,' she protested.

'I know, Moll, but you've no idea what it was like living at home with them fighting all the time. Gareth and I hated it; we sometimes talked about running away. And then Mum left and Dad went into this depression and seemed to forget we even existed. Then we realized that there was something worse than living with parents who argued all the time; it was living without them.'

Molly's tears fell unheeded now and she put her hands up to cup his face. 'We're not your parents, Declan,' she repeated. 'We've been together all these years and we've been happy, haven't we?'

He nodded silently, covering her hands with his.

'Do you honestly think that a piece of paper is going to change that?'

'Probably not,' he admitted with the glimmer of a smile.

'Anyway, it doesn't matter—' She broke off as the security man called for him to hurry up or he'd miss his flight.

'I'm sorry,' Declan kissed her tenderly. 'I have to go.'

She nodded, gulping back her tears and trying to smile.

He pulled her close and kissed her. 'I love you, Moll, don't doubt that.'

'I love you too.'

'I'll call you from Heathrow,' he said, backing away from her.

She nodded. 'Please.'

He turned and pushed his way through the queue and the security man hurried him through, giving him a paternal pat on the back.

Molly pressed forward to catch a last sight of him, but he'd already been swallowed up by the crowd. And though she craned her neck to see him, it was useless. And then she heard his voice.

'Molly? Molly, can you hear me?'

'Yes?' she yelled back, using the barrier to raise herself up an extra, precious inch.

'Will you marry me?' he yelled.

'What?' she called back, thinking she must be hearing things.

The security man rolled his eyes. 'He says, will ye marry him?' he relayed back to her.

'Yes! Yes, Declan, of course I will!' she called back as loud as she could, and then she saw him wave his hand and whoop loudly. 'Yes,' she called again and then started to laugh as the people around her began to clap and cheer.

'Finally!' Laura nodded her approval as she pulled on to the motorway and headed back towards the city. 'We'll go straight over to Mum and get cracking on the arrangements. I don't suppose you had a chance to discuss a date? Never mind, ask him when he calls. Now, we need to get Rory to go with Dad and get fitted for a suit, you couldn't trust him to do it alone. I suppose he'll insist on Natalie coming to the wedding.' She sighed. 'That girl will probably try and take over the whole thing. You mark my words, she'll be telling you what hymns and readings to choose and making you go to confession every week before the big day . . .'

Molly tuned out and gazed down at the engagement ring on her finger. The next few weeks would be hectic, and Laura would quite probably drive her mad in the run up to the wedding. In fact, Rory would probably take a bet that they'd be at each other's throats again before the end of the week.

Molly smiled. It would be good to get back to normal.

Acknowledgements

As always I owe a debt of gratitude to Suzanne, Libby and all of the team at Simon & Schuster UK for their enthusiasm and support.

Thanks also to my lovely agent and friend Sheila Crowley and the team behind her at Curtis Brown.

I am hugely grateful to the Caddle men, who remain tolerant, patient and kind despite my increasingly erratic and distracted moods!

And to my mother, my eternal thanks; you are a daily inspiration.